F
muc

Return to
RIBBLESTROP

Also by Andy Mulligan

RIBBLESTROP
TRASH

Return to RIBBLESTROP

Andy Mulligan

SIMON AND SCHUSTER

First published in Great Britain in 2011 by Simon
and Schuster UK Ltd, a CBS company.

Text copyright © 2011 Andy Mulligan
Map copyright © 2009 Andrea Kearney

Simon & Schuster UK Ltd
1st Floor, 222 Gray's Inn Road
London WC1X 8HB

A CIP catalogue record for this book is available from the British Library.

ISBN: 978-1-47112-154-8

1 3 5 7 9 10 8 6 4 2

Printed and bound by CPI Group (UK) Ltd, Croydon, CR0 4YY

www.simonandschuster.co.uk
www.andymulliganbooks.com

For 11AC

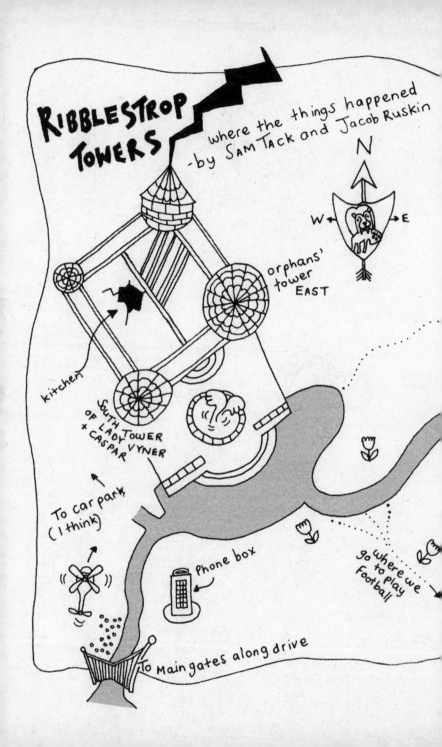

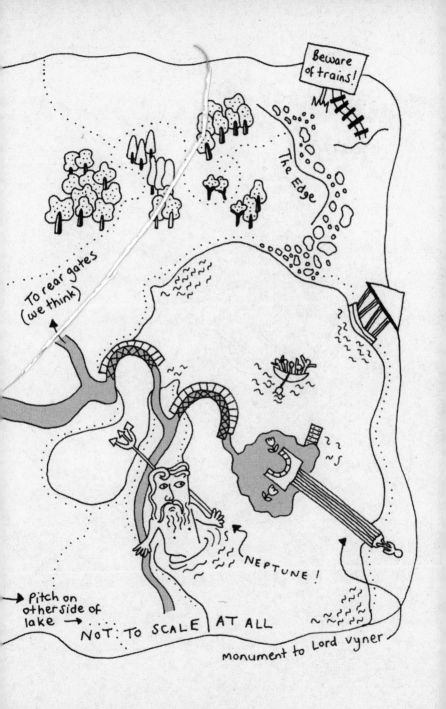

Beware of trains!

The Edge

To rear gates (we think)

NEPTUNE!

Pitch on other side of lake

NOT TO SCALE AT ALL

monument to Lord Vyner

Chapter One

Rules about hitch-hiking, when you're a child: rule number one – don't hitch-hike; rule number two – don't hitch-hike on your own; rules three, four etc – if you *have* to hitch-hike alone, tell people where you're going, start early, take a phone, keep the door unlocked, and don't ever ever *ever* find yourself penniless, on the side of a deserted road, in some wilderness you've never been before, without a map, just as it's getting dark.

Millie had broken all the rules.

She was on her way to school. She'd spent her train fare on unbeatable bargains in a duty-free shop, and now she was stuck. Her plane had got in early, but getting out of Heathrow had taken hours; she'd finally been picked up by a milk lorry which took her close to Stonehenge. She'd had no lunch, so she smoked several cigarettes. Light-headed, she got into the car of a farmer with an accent so thick she could barely understand him. He had a sheepdog on the back seat and, in a short while, they were off the road bumping over farm tracks. They had to pull over once for a convoy of army tanks, and there was the distant sound of gunfire left and right. The farmer chuckled while his dog yapped, and after some time they came to a little bus stop and Millie clambered out with relief. The farmer drove off into a field, leaving her to study a weathered timetable. It was the sort of stop that might see one bus a week.

Amazingly, however, a bus did struggle into view within ten minutes. No passengers, just a toothless driver who accepted a box of cigarettes instead of Millie's fare, nodding and grinning. This got her to a main road and she stood on the kerb wondering which way was west. It was very cold and the streetlamps were coming on; there was sleet in a spiteful wind. Millie was now frightened.

'You bring this on yourself,' she said, aloud.

She thought of her friend Sanchez back on the ranch in Colombia. He would shake his head and say, 'Millie, you're crazy.'

'This *is* crazy,' said Millie.

She had slept rough once before, after someone's party, and it had been a night of shivering in a shed. She dreaded the thought of sitting through a long, freezing night – she wondered if she would survive it. She drew her gold-striped blazer tighter around her. It was good quality wool, at least, so there was some warmth to it. Her hands, however, were freezing: particularly the left thumb, which was extended hopefully at the speeding traffic.

Darkness fell.

Millie was virtually invisible until a vehicle's headlights hit her, and no driver was going to see her in time to stop. The sleet became rain and her blazer soaked it up. It ran down her legs into her shoes and Millie began to realise just how vulnerable she was. She decided to walk on, but just as she did so, a white van shot past, buffeting her in its slip-stream. It braked hard, hooting and squealing, and somehow veered left into the lay-by. It hooted again, long and hard, and Millie ran through mud to the passenger door. Peering

2

in, she could see it was crowded with young men; she could hear thumping music and laughter, and she caught a whiff of beer.

A window came down halfway.

'Where you goin'?' said a boy. It was a builders' van, and the men were in paint-spattered overalls.

'Ribblestrop,' said Millie. 'It's the other side of Taunton, but if you're—'

'Ribblestrop? Hey!'

'She's goin' to Ribblestrop!'

'That's where we're goin', my beauty!' The van revved loudly. 'An' we'll get there before you! Yahhhhh!'

The driver accelerated fast into the rain and the passengers' laughter spun away down the road.

Millie swore quietly. She was trembling now and she started to walk, just to keep warm. The mud turned into soaking grass and her shoes were soon saturated. It was hard to keep upright. She decided she must find a village. Someone would take pity on her, as they did in those sentimental films where a waif gets taken in by some kindly childless couple, to be given soup by the fire. A large lorry thundered by and Millie nearly fell in its slipstream.

The rain turned into a pelting downpour.

'Oh, why do you take unnecessary risks?' shouted Millie at herself. 'Why put yourself through this, if – in the end – you're just a scared little, weak little, stupid, useless little girl who's afraid of the dark?'

She came round a bend. There was a stationary car ahead, with two wheels up on the verge. Millie hadn't seen it stop, but it couldn't have been there long. The traffic was braking to get round it – a car hooted angrily; it was a bad place to stop, especially in this rain.

Millie ran towards it. As she ran, the car shunted forward – it was trying to get off the road completely, up onto the

3

grass. It was a small family car, and she could make out a driver and a passenger. She got to the passenger's window, and stared in, trying to look lost and forlorn. The occupants didn't notice her; they were deep in conversation.

Millie tapped on the glass. Still they didn't look up – they were engrossed in a map and appeared to be arguing.

She tapped again, louder, and frightened eyes turned to meet Millie's. The glass came down a few centimetres.

'I'm sorry to bother you,' said Millie. 'I'm stuck – I need help.'

'Pardon me?'

It was the passenger who spoke. He had a soft, Irish brogue.

'I said, I'm stuck,' replied Millie. 'I missed my bus. Could you give me a lift to the next town?'

'Open the window!' said the driver. His voice was louder than the passenger's. It was broad Irish again, but fierce and bad-tempered. 'Get the blessed thing down, Doonan, and ask him the way!' He was leaning across his passenger, peering up at her. Millie saw that he wore a dog-collar. She closed her eyes briefly and rejoiced.

'We're trying to get to Taunton,' called the driver. 'We missed our road and Doonan's led us way off the beaten track. We're both new to this, and –'

'I think we left the A30 by mistake,' said Doonan. 'There were some roadworks –'

'I know the way to Taunton!' lied Millie. 'Could you give me a lift?'

'Oh no, we don't pick up hitch-hikers,' said the driver. 'There's no reason for hitch-hiking, not with all the trains and buses. If you give a lift to one hiker, then suddenly it's everyone and his mother saving their bus-fares and taking advantage.'

'I'm so cold,' said Millie. 'The bus didn't come and I'm stranded.'

A car behind hooted loudly.

4

'Oh, for the love of God, Doonan, we're still in the way!'

'We *could* take her to the next town, Father,' said Doonan. 'It's a wild night for a young girl to be out on her own.'

The driver leaned forward as far as he could and stared harder at Millie. He had a lobster-red face under a bald, flaking cranium. The nose was big and hooked, and the eyebrows were thick white, over tiny black eyes. A huge truck revved behind them and sounded its horn, long and ferocious. The noise was like a gale and the car rocked from side to side.

'Very well, get in,' said the driver. 'Hurry, now!'

Both men struggled to open the back door. There were suitcases over the seat, but Millie was inside in seconds, shoving her own bag in hard. 'We'll get you to the next town, but I'm not sure . . . Oh, look at this mad fool, Doonan! Alright, alright!'

The truck behind was still blaring its horn. It had levered itself out into the oncoming traffic, which had come to a halt, and was inching past.

'Put your flashers on, Father,' said Doonan.

'Doonan, if I knew where the blasted things were, I'd have put them on long ago. Is the child in?'

'Yes!' shouted Millie.

'So steamed up I can't see . . . where's the damned indicator? Oh!'

The windscreen wipers had been chugging away evenly, now they doubled their speed. The car shunted forward once more, bounced down from the kerb, and stalled. There was a new flurry of furious horns and someone was yelling.

'Do you think this is the right direction?' said Doonan. He had to twist himself round in his seatbelt, and Millie saw that he was young and friendly, with a spray of pimples.

His eyes blinked under pale lashes and he seemed to be panting.

'Damn and blast!' cursed the driver. 'If we can't get this louse of a car started, we're in trouble! Say your prayers, both of you.'

'You know, you really shouldn't be hitch-hiking,' said Doonan. 'You meet strange people, and—'

'Damn and blast, she's dead as a door-nail!' The driver turned the ignition again and the car coughed hysterically.

'Hold your foot flat down, Father,' said Doonan. 'I think she's—'

'I'm doing exactly that! Start, damn you!'

The engine roared into life, for a racing-car start. There was a furious knocking under the floor, so Doonan had to shout to be heard. 'You say you're going to school? It seems a bit late to be starting off—'

'Boarding school,' said Millie. She raised her voice over the screams of second gear. 'It's the other side of Taunton and I'm supposed to be there by six. It's called Ribblestrop Towers.'

A startled look came into the young man's eyes. He clutched the headrest and stared harder. 'You didn't say *Ribblestrop Towers*, did you?'

'Yes. You've probably heard of it because of what went on last term. It was in the papers, and a TV station came down—'

'Not Ribblestrop Towers, surely! The house owned by Lady Vyner?'

Millie was nodding.

'Father, listen to this!'

'I can barely see the road, Doonan – we're steaming up. Nor can I find . . . third blasted gear . . .'

'But listen, Father, listen to this! This child is on her way to Ribblestrop Towers! Now is that not the Lord's doing?'

He looked back at Millie and laughed. 'We're going there ourselves! This is Father O'Hanrahan, the new chaplain. And I'm Brother Doonan, I'm just a trainee. We're on our way to that very place!'

The car picked up speed, swerving madly as the driver wiped a vision hole through the mist on the windscreen. Oncoming lights were also swerving and hooting and it occurred to Millie that she'd exchanged rain and discomfort for danger of a more lethal kind.

'This is remarkable,' prattled Doonan. 'You see, Father O'Hanrahan wrote to the headmaster offering to help out with the chapel. He'd heard about the monks, you see.' He laughed. 'I might be your teacher! I'm trying to get a little work-experience – I failed my exams so the college had to let me go.'

Millie raised her eyebrows and tried to smile.

'Oh, but what a fantastic coincidence!' laughed the boy. 'Maybe it's my map-reading skills after all!'

'It's the guidance of God, Doonan,' said Father O'Hanrahan, heavily. 'Ask her if she's met the Brethren. They've had that vow of silence for some time, but she might have *seen* them round the grounds.'

'I hear they're a very devout order –' said Doonan.

'Do you know the little chapel?' interrupted the driver. He turned round in his seat and peered at Millie. 'What's your name, child?'

'Millie,' said Millie.

'There's a little chapel, Millie, with a crypt. Have you been down to it?'

'No.'

'Can you *get* down? I heard it had been bricked up, so I was saying to Doonan that our first job is to get all that sorted.'

'I don't know.'

'Have you spoken to the Brethren? They're still there, aren't they?'

'Yes, but you hardly—'

'There's a walking ghost too, so we heard,' said Brother Doonan. His eyes grew round with excitement. Millie guessed his age as about seventeen.

'Yes,' she said. 'The ghost of Lord Vyner, but you don't actually *see* him—'

'That's what we heard!' cried the driver. 'That's the very one: a soul in pain, carrying secrets and sins, slipping around the place. I'll be putting that fellow to rest – that's one of my first duties.'

'Father O'Hanrahan is an *exorcist*,' said Doonan. 'Do you know what that is?'

'I saw the movie,' said Millie.

'It's a gift that the Lord put in my hands,' said Father O'Hanrahan. 'I don't keep count of the demons I've dealt with and I take no credit. If I can wrestle a soul from Satan, then it's to the glory of God. And this Lord Vyner character, well! A violent past, as I understand it. It's not surprising he can get no rest. That's what I told your headmaster: you can't run a school with a walking ghost! The school needs a chaplain it can trust.'

The car picked up speed and Father O'Hanrahan laughed. 'Oh yes – the Lord is certainly with us today!' he cried. 'Goodness knows what would have become of this girl if we hadn't been passing. What's her name again?'

'Millie,' said Millie.

'Well, Minnie. I hope we can rely on your total and unconditional help after this. That chapel needs to be looked after, and we're going to need all the hands we can get. Is it true that some of the children are heathen?'

'Father, I don't think they allow that word any more—'

'I'm asking the *child*, Doonan – don't tell me what I can

8

and can't say! Is there a living faith, Minnie? Will I get resistance or cooperation?'

'There's no faith at all that I'm aware of,' said Millie. 'The only time anyone prays is before a football match, and that's because we're desperate.'

'Well,' said Father O'Hanrahan. 'If that's the case, I think we should say a prayer right here and now, and start as we mean to go on. And you, Miss Minnie: you should open up your proud heart and find it in your proud self to thank God for this deliverance – or you'd still be on that road, prey to any passing madman.'

'What do you think, Millie?' said Doonan. 'Do you have a favourite prayer?'

'I don't believe in God,' said Millie. 'I'm an atheist.'

Doonan stared.'

'*What* did she say?' said Father O'Hanrahan.

'She said she doesn't believe, Father.'

'Then our work has surely started. Will you take the wheel a moment, Doonan? I'm going to say a few words and make this fool mindful of her salvation.'

Chapter Two

The rain was beating harder than ever. Doonan put a hand on the steering wheel, and peered through the misted windscreen.

'I can't really *see*, Father, to be honest.'

'If the child herself won't show gratitude,' said Father O'Hanrahan, 'we'll show it for her.' He clasped his hands over his chest and changed his register. He spoke softly and earnestly, as if to a friend. 'Look down on us, oh Lord. We thank you, here and now, for this encouraging sign. We thank you, God, for keeping us safe.'

'Amen,' said Brother Doonan.

The car was veering right; Doonan eased it left.

'We all need help, and most of us are humble enough to ask for it. We ask you now to open the eyes of the blind, and as we seek to work with your brethren, may we bring the chapel back to glory and reinstate what is lost.'

'Amen to that.'

'We know there will be obstacles and hazards, like the stubborn child behind me.'

It occurred to Millie that both men had their eyes closed. She couldn't be sure, but a kind of rapture had descended. She could also see what looked like a build-up of traffic ahead and the red lights of an intersection.

'We're going too fast,' she said softly.

'Do you think so?' said Doonan. 'Well, the Holy Spirit can be a frightening thing, but you have to trust—'

'Seriously,' said Millie. 'We're going too fast.'

'It was like that for me,' said Doonan. 'I was just your age, and one day I found myself speeding towards the presence of God, and—'

Millie was fired by instinct. She jumped forward and grabbed the wheel.

The two men jerked their eyes open and saw the danger at once. For a second or two, they fought, with flapping hands. Father O'Hanrahan stamped on the brake just as Doonan screamed.

Time slows down when you crash.

The slow-motion cuts in and you get to see every amazing detail. From Millie's point of view, there was a great comet-shower of red lights hurtling towards them. The soundtrack was an agonising howl of brakes and horns. Brake lights, traffic lights, and the long, pink strip of a petrol garage: the colours ran together in the rain, and as she twisted the wheel, she got the vehicle clear of the stationary cars. They fishtailed wildly as the wheels locked, and Father O'Hanrahan snatched them away from an oncoming truck. Thus they skimmed into the centre of the junction: the great box of the A312 and A303 interchange, beside the Family Roadgrill and Travellers' Sleepeasy. Millie's car floated through at twenty miles per hour; a family saloon emerging from the garage crawled into her path at less than five.

They smashed together in a shower of glass.

Mercifully, everyone was belted in, so the worst injuries were three whiplashed necks and a nosebleed. It could have been so much worse, and the police said that many times over the next few hours.

Who was driving the family saloon? A cautious driver by the name of Donald Tack. His wife, Edith, was next to him, and in the back, amongst comics, games, and sweet-wrappers, sat Sam Tack, Jacob Ruskin, and a newcomer to the school: nine-year-old Oli, brother to Jacob. Their car was spun three hundred and sixty degrees, and two of the windows burst over them, but it was actually no worse than one of those fairground rides you pay several pounds for. Oli had the nosebleed, but that was shock, not impact. He was reading his advanced guide to radio technology and was mortified to get blood on it. But he didn't cry. Nobody did.

The children were herded into the Family Roadgrill by teams of helpful garage staff. Millie's vehicle was crunched up against a lamp-post, but the back door opened easily enough. She was pulled out, and was able to stand shakily in the fuel and water that poured out of the broken car. The adults stayed where they were.

'Millie!' said Ruskin.

The two children looked at each other, thunderstruck. There was Ruskin, short and wide, built like a balloon. He snatched off his glasses to clear them of raindrops, grinning happily. 'Unbelievable!' he said.

He started to laugh. Sam was more worried about his parents, but a forceful waitress led him and the others firmly to a table.

'Of all the incredible coincidences, what are you doing here, Millie? How was Canada?'

Millie was trembling with shock. 'I didn't go to Canada,' she said.

'Yes you did – you went with Sanchez. You patched things up at the end of term, and everyone said you were going to Canada!'

'Sanchez lives in *Colombia*.'

'Did you go?'

'Yes. Ruskin, what are *you* doing here? Were you in that car?'

'Yes! Sam's dad was driving. We're on our way to Ribblestrop, same as you.'

He sat down at the table and Millie joined him.

'We were delayed,' continued Ruskin. 'Ironic really. Sam forgot his cap, so we had to drive over to his house and no one could find it. When we did find it, we were running late, so my father got a bit cross and we decided to go in Sam's car instead, and have tea on the road. In fact, this is our table – I bet there's a cup left in that pot.'

'You and Sam spent Christmas together?' said Millie. 'That must have been . . . mesmerising. Could I have a hot chocolate?' she said to the waitress.

'We actually live quite close to each other,' said Ruskin. 'So we've been taking it in turns to have sleepovers. The fun we've had, honestly! We've got some super stories. Sam's dad had a fall and had to go into hospital. That meant we had the house almost to ourselves – and the things we got up to!'

'Could I have another glass of water?' said a quiet voice, nervously.

Millie looked again at the third member of Ruskin's party. Ribblestrop uniform, same as the rest. But this child was smaller, thinner, and altogether weirder. He had a tuft of pale hair on the top of his head and slightly protruding teeth. His eyes were huge and his little pink hands clung to the table top. He had the look of a foetus, born very prematurely and dressed up in clothes that would never fit. His grey shirt collar didn't touch his neck, and he didn't appear to have any shoulders.

'Who's the alien?' said Millie.

'Pardon?'

13

'You've brought a pet. What's its name?'

Ruskin closed his eyes. 'This is my little brother, Millie. His name's Oli.'

'No way,' said Millie. 'It must have been a Christmas present.'

'Actually, Millie, you're wrong and you're rude,' said Ruskin. 'And I had forgotten how hurtful you can be. Oli's nine and he's got a GCSE in maths already, so don't insult him.'

'Mmm, hello,' said Oli, breathlessly.

'Wow,' said Millie. 'I love the voice.'

'I've told Oli all about you, Millie,' said Ruskin. 'I don't think I mentioned your insensitive side, though. We may not look the same, but we're alike in many ways, or that's what our parents say. So if you think you're going to pick on Oli, you'll be dealing with me and Sam first.'

'Oh no,' said Sam.

The others looked up. Sam hadn't joined them at the table. He was at the window, nose against the glass. The first blue light had appeared, closely followed by another. There were distant sirens too. Floodlights were going up on stands, reflecting broken glass: a couple of men from the garage were directing traffic, and both crashed vehicles were still full of grown-ups. Sam watched as the first couple of stretchers emerged from an ambulance.

Ruskin got up and went to his friend. 'Don't worry, Sam, they always use stretchers these days. I think it's for training – it doesn't mean anyone's badly hurt.'

'Dad has only just got well,' said Sam. 'They've just taken the cast off!'

'Psst,' said Millie. Oli snapped his eyes up to hers; they had been wandering crazily over to the windows, then to his hands. 'Oli Ruskin.'

'Hello,' said Oli.

14

'Did your brother tell you about the new system we have this term?'

Oli's eyes fluttered. 'Mmm,' he said. 'He told me some stuff.'

'It's a bit like the old days, at all those posh public schools. New boys are assigned to the more senior pupils, like me and Sanchez. They have to run errands. Shoe-cleaning, toast-making, that kind of thing.'

Oli groped for a word.

'How old are you again?' said Millie.

'Nine,' said Oli. 'And a half.'

'Look. I don't want you getting bullied. If you play your cards right, I'll see you get put with me.'

Oli's eyes filled with tears, but whether they were from fear or gratitude wasn't clear.

'Why are you coming to Ribblestrop?' said Millie. 'Didn't your brother warn you what happens?'

'Mmm, well. I was . . . Mmm.'

Millie tried to put on a kinder face. She sat a little lower in her chair and tried to meet the boy's troubled eyes.

'You see, my primary school was a bit useless,' said Oli. 'I was really just repeating work, treading water really, which was hardly challenging. So they put me up to the next class but it wasn't any better – it had rather a *worksheet* methodology and I wanted something more project-orientated, something more stretching. I did a trial day at the big school, you know – the local boys' comprehensive. I—'

'Didn't you like it?'

'Mmm, all the boys. They were really quite rough and they were just doing things I'd done at home. I had a tutor, you see.'

'Did they beat you up?'

'I was only there for a morning. They said they would, though.'

15

'I don't think they'd have appreciated you. I think it was a wise call, coming here. I'll make sure nobody touches you, Oli. But you will have to do a few jobs – is that OK?'

Oli licked his lips nervously. His Adam's apple bobbed and he looked around him, as if to check nobody could hear. He leaned forward in his seat. 'You seem very decent,' he said. 'Do you have any, mmm . . . hobbies?'

'Hobbies?' said Millie. 'What, like stamp-collecting?'

Oli was nodding.

'No,' said Millie.

'I do.'

'I bet you do.'

'We've got a really good hobby. Sam's into it as well, so's my brother. If you like . . .' Again he looked around nervously and pulled a booklet out of a pocket. 'For a job, I mean . . . I'll show you how to make one of these. I've got loads of spares.'

'What is it?'

Oli pushed the booklet across the table and Millie glanced quickly down tiny columns of small print, taking in complex-looking cross-section diagrams. Oli's face had changed; it was now eager. He stood up and leaned forward, his nose close to the page. He was breathing quickly. 'Four-wheel-drives, radio-controlled. That's just the chassis, showing how to mount the clutch. Sam's got a Land Rover. I've got an earth-mover, more of a drill really. It's the sort of thing you use to make underground railways; it drills the soil and clears it. If you like, I could make you the submarine.'

'Could you do me a favour, Oli?'

The child nodded.

'While I'm reading this, could you get me a saucer I can use as an ashtray?' Millie had produced a cigarette. She was searching for her lighter. Oli gazed up at her, his tongue just visible between his lips.

'Your first errand,' said Millie. 'Go and get a saucer, and see what's happened to my hot chocolate.'

'OK.'

'In fact, Oli?'

The boy turned, hands up at his chest.

'Get the menu, will you? I want proper food.'

Oli trotted off. Outside a fire-engine manoeuvred past Father O'Hanrahan's car and got the foam hoses ready. It said something for Oli's new sense of responsibility that he didn't drift off to watch. He did everything Millie had asked, making sure she had salt and pepper cellars, a napkin, and even a towel for her dripping hair. Then he sat next to her and explained exactly how her submarine would work.

Millie discovered that she was getting quite interested. She put down her fork and took the boy's small, frail ear between her fingers.

Oli stopped talking and stared with big fascinated eyes.

'You're actually quite cute,' she said. 'I think we're going to be friends.'

The blood rushed to Oli's face and in three seconds he was scarlet.

Chapter Three

Back at Ribblestrop Towers, it was still Christmas.

Father Christmas himself was sitting on a desk. Opposite him stood a large snowman and on the sofa, looking anxiously through thick glasses, sat an elderly fairy. The school hadn't had a Christmas party at the end of the winter term; it hadn't seemed appropriate as the police were still in the grounds recovering the body-parts of the deputy headmistress. The headmaster, Captain Routon and Professor Worthington had therefore been keen to start the new term in celebration and style – hence the fancy dress.

Downstairs, the orphans were waiting, dressed as elves. The feast was laid, and there were gifts, jellies, and crackers plus an enormous gingerbread model of the school. There was to be a disco and finally a film.

The headmaster put the telephone back into its cradle.

'Bad news,' he said.

'What's happened?' said the captain.

'There's been a car accident and they're all stuck in Somerset. They won't be down till tomorrow.'

'Anybody hurt, Giles?' said the fairy.

'No, thankfully – everyone's fine. I didn't quite

understand the details; there was a lot of background noise. But it would seem that the Tack parents are in Casualty, just being checked over. They're with those two ... religious people.'

'What about the children?'

'They seem to be right as rain. They've been installed in one of those Sleepeasys for the night, and they're hoping we can send a vehicle tomorrow morning.'

'Easy enough, sir. I can take the van.'

'It's not really roadworthy, is it, Routon?'

'There's a few jobs left to do, but it gets from A to B. I'll leave first thing.'

'We'd better tell everyone downstairs. Drat it, I had so hoped to get off to a good start. The orphans were disappointed enough about Sanchez's late arrival ...'

'We can have the party tomorrow, Giles – it's hardly the end of the world.'

'Jellies won't keep, sir.'

'We'll eat the jellies and show the film. Poor kids! They'll be going out of their minds with boredom waiting at a motorway service station. You know, I had a feeling something was wrong.'

'Go!' shrieked Oli. 'Straight!'

'I can't control it!'

'Pull the throttle and get the drill *down* ... you've missed it!'

Oli Ruskin had climbed up onto the television, which was bolted to a high bracket in the corner of the Special Deluxe Supersize Family Room. From there he could supervise operations. The room was ideal: minimal furniture, all easy to move, and a smooth industrial carpet.

Millie sat on its far corner; she had the radio console in her hands and was doing her best to control the digger-vehicle. It had a mind of its own, but she was learning, and laughing with excitement.

'Reverse!' yelled Oli. 'Go left, go left!'

'I can't find reverse!'

There were three radio-controlled vehicles in operation, each one about fifty centimetres long. Ruskin Senior had a truck; Sam had a Land Rover. Ruskin Junior had a strange armadillo-like vehicle, with twelve small wheels and a sharp, rotating snout. The task was to get each vehicle through the obstacle course that they'd built from the Sleepeasy furniture. Oli had devised a series of penalties and rewards, and was in charge of the clock. The obstacles were mattresses, blankets, and a telephone cable stretched between bed-legs. It was the telephone wire that Millie was finding tricky; she had to find a point at which the snout of her drill could get under it. She was losing valuable seconds and Sam's time had been good.

The windows were all open, but the room still stank of engine oil and smoke. Ruskin Senior was in charge of refuelling, for the little motors ran down ridiculously quickly. Larger fuel tanks were on order, but Oli was worried they'd need complicated pumps.

'Rotate it!' cried Oli. 'Rotate it!'

'Damn,' said Millie. She rammed the toy forward and this time got the drill-head spinning. It severed the telephone cord and took a chunk out of a chair leg.

'Good!' shouted Ruskin.

'Yes, but she loses five for cutting,' said Oli. He scribbled a mark on the wall beside him.

Millie pressed the steering lever and, amazingly, the vehicle obeyed her and started up the mattress-mountain. Its wheels caught on the sheet and soon it was up to the apex – it nearly toppled over but righted itself – and started down the steepest part of the slope. They'd propped two

mattresses together over a low armchair, and it was a difficult thing to negotiate. All the toys had four-wheel drives
and magi-grip tyres; Oli had put a little extra weight on the
chassis of his vehicle, to keep the centre of gravity low.
Despite Millie's clumsy control, she was making good time
now.

'Oh, keep it steady . . .' shouted Oli. He was living every
half-metre of progress, his hands twitching at imaginary
controls. The engine noise was unbearable: high-pitched
and wasp-like. It sawed at the ear relentlessly, the clutch of
the little vehicle burning as it teetered down the slope.
There were pizza cartons scattered round the room. The
boys had torn up the polystyrene bases, and Sam had used
the pieces to lay out a curving road as part of the floor-
level steering test. Millie approached it now, in full
control.

'Slow down,' whispered Oli. 'Try and get the nose *up*.'

Ruskin walked along with the little car, intent on its
progress. His own vehicle had taken eleven minutes to
complete the course; Millie was on a very promising eight
so far. She turned into the first straight and missed the curve.
Reverse, try again. She oversteered. Black smoke was leaking from the engine and she couldn't work out how to close
off the drill. This was a problem as the razor-sharp edge was
cutting into the carpet, sending wool-threads spinning – the
friction was counting against her.

Nobody heard the hammering on the door.

Millie was stuck and the seconds were ticking by. Oli
and Sam were cheering. The finishing post was a pillowcase dangling over a coffee table, and it was going to be
very close. The drill was devouring the carpet, the nylon
threads melting and smouldering. Millie tried to reverse
again.

'Go!' shrieked Oli. 'You can cut through it!'

Ruskin was jumping up and down: 'She's stuck, she's stuck!' But Millie found reverse and somehow disentangled the drill. She went for the home stretch fast, missing the pillow and curving wildly. This time the drill slammed into the skirting-board, and the boys cheered louder, knowing she was losing more points. Sam leaped onto the mattresses, did a backward flip from the table; he punched the air, confident that he had the best time. He bounced to his feet and ran to Oli: the child was doing complicated sums on the wall, subtracting and adding points.

'Sixty-two!' he cried.

'Never!'

'Sixty-two, so Jake's seventy-nine points and you're eighty-one.'

'Yes! I'll go again,' said Sam.

'Hang on, I haven't even been!' said Oli. 'Millie just had my go. I haven't been!' He went to rescue his toy, which had split the wood and was now drilling through breeze-block. He was about to shut down the motor, when the bedroom door was thrown open and a man in pyjamas stood there, gaping. By his side stood the Sleepeasy receptionist.

'What the hell . . .' said the man. Millie and the boys stared at him.

The receptionist was a lady of middle-age: smart, stout, and carefully permed. She held a pass-key in her hand and her mouth was a little black hole of disbelief. She'd been on duty when the road accident had happened. She had been calm and efficient, and dealt with the worried Mrs Tack, agreeing to keep an eye on things. Sam in particular had reminded her of her own little boy, ten years ago. She'd meant to pop up and put an ear to the door earlier on, but there'd been a booking mix-up and some builders had arrived unexpectedly, needing accommodation. Then a big, foreign man had insisted on paying cash with a kilo of coins. The credit-card machine had gone down immediately after that, which led to the computer freezing. It was another guest who'd alerted her to the indescribable noises coming from the family room. Her eyes took in the smoke, the debris, the upside-down, flung-about furniture: her mouth opened wider as it hunted for an appropriate word. She looked at the children themselves. They had looked so smart, trooping in after the ambulances and fire-engines had departed. Now they stood there, tie-less and blazer-less – the sweet one had dirt over his face and his shirt had been used as a cleaning rag, the tails covered in what looked like oil . . .

The man in pyjamas said, 'I've never seen anything like this.'

'Were we keeping you awake?' shouted Ruskin, over the noise of Oli's digger. 'That was the last race. I'm ever so sorry.'

'Was not!' said Oli.

'Oli, you gave your go to Millie!'

'I didn't!'

The receptionist clutched the door frame. She was making small sounds, rather like a puppy. Just as she thought she had the right phrase, she noticed a new detail of the devastation. At last the fuel ran out and the engine stopped.

'We'll tidy up,' said Sam. 'It looks worse than it is, but honestly, we've been doing this at home all over Christmas.'

'We always clear up,' cried Ruskin. 'I say, are you alright?'

The receptionist was hyperventilating. She had seen the black gash in the peacock-blue carpet. Now she saw black smoke rising from the skirting-board.

'You need to sit down,' said Millie.

The receptionist looked up and noticed that the room's smoke alarm had been disabled: the wires hung out and the battery was gone. It was just as well, because acrid smoke hung under the ceiling – there was a breeze from outside and a wisp was blown into the corridor. The man in pyjamas was picking his way over the debris, his hands on his head. Unseen, the smoke continued to billow through the open doorway.

The receptionist's head started to jerk. She stepped into the room and found that her shoulders were locked up around her ears. Her fingers were splayed out in front of her chest as well, as if for protection. She looked up at Oli, sitting high on the TV, and his bug-eyes stared into hers. 'Can you help me down?' he said.

At that moment, the smoke alarm in the corridor decided it had had enough. There were various types of smoke all mixed together in a rich cocktail: now was the time to warn the world. An ear-splitting shriek blared from every speaker and then it settled into stabbing squeals that split the ear. Within five seconds doors were opening, and the noise jerked the receptionist back into action. At least this was a situation she'd been trained to deal with – there were routines for fire alarms.

'Outside,' she said. 'Quickly!'

'Why?' said Ruskin.

'Fire alarm. Car park. Everyone!'

'There's no fire,' said Millie. 'It's engine smoke – you can see it.'

In fact, there *was* a fire, though it was fairly small at present. The skirting-board had been so scorched by Millie's drilling that flames were appearing. The wallpaper above was vinyl and it was beginning to melt. A sheet on a nearby chair was getting warmer and would burst into flames very soon.

'Car park!' said the receptionist. 'Come on, quickly! Car park! Fire!' She had to shout over the din. The corridor behind her was now full of people, peering at the children.

'Get outside!' said the man. 'Do as you're bloody told, all of you! Outside!'

The children grabbed their blazers and meekly left the room. They joined a line of hurrying people, all shrugging themselves into coats.

'Sam,' shouted Oli. He was being hustled away by the receptionist, but Sam was still kicking on his shoes. 'Don't leave the toys! Get the toys! Wait,' he said.

But his voice wasn't strong enough and he was lost in a river of foul-tempered adults.

Oli Ruskin was just nine-and-a-half years old and had built all three radio-controlled vehicles with his own hands. His brother and Sam had helped, but he'd seen the project through from inception, so he felt the pure love of owner-ship. He'd washed cars, cleaned windows, and walked dogs to raise the money. He had a paper-round every morning, with a bag so huge and heavy he could barely lift it. The thought of his precious models being in an unlocked room made him breathless with panic, but what could he do? He was being herded along the corridor.

'Jake,' he said to his brother.

Ruskin didn't hear. He was saying something to Millie and the alarms had now switched to an urgent, angry throb that was guaranteed to make you panic. More and more people were emerging, and when they reached the recep-tion area, it was packed. People were doubling back to get warm clothes, parents were calling after children, and another receptionist had appeared and was screaming, 'It's not a practice!' over and over again.

Oli closed his eyes in despair. He slowed his pace, letting people overtake him. The woman who'd pushed him had gone. The angry man was running ahead. Oli took his chance and doubled back.

The fire doors had all swung shut and the emergency lights had come on bright and blue. Oli hurried left and scampered back towards his room. Was it right or left, though? He'd forgotten the number and all the doors looked the same. He stood in the corridor, peering this way and that, thinking only of his toys.

It was five minutes later that Millie noticed he was gone.

'Where's Oli?' she said.

Sam and Ruskin were arguing about scores and didn't hear her. One of the receptionists had found a loudhailer and was explaining her legal duties according to the health-and-safety executive. There was a cold wind blowing and it swept across the car park in gusts.

Millie's eyes jumped from group to group. A cluster of men squatted together, drinking from beer cans. A young couple were locked in an embrace, kissing. A toddler seemed to be imitating the fire alarm and its parents were trying to silence it. She walked briskly back to the reception area. If Oli had stayed inside – or gone back to the room to rescue something – could he find his way out? She imagined him frightened and alone, and quickened her step.

Once inside, she was faced by the same four corridors that had confused Oli.

She thought hard, but couldn't remember which one led to their room. She couldn't even remember the room number – Mrs Tack had done the business. She chose a corridor at random and pushed through the first fire-door. As it closed behind her, she started to jog. She needed to be fast if she had four corridors to search. She was about to call the boy's name, when she heard the most dreadful sound. It stopped her in mid-step and her body went ice-cold. The noise was close and the corridor gave it a terrible echo.

It was the roar of something wild. And there was the stink of animal.

Chapter Four

'Help . . .' said a voice.

Millie felt her heart lurch and she was drenched with sweat. She was looking at Oli. He was in the elbow of the corridor, just ahead of her, his back pressed against the wall. He was looking straight ahead, at something dreadfully, dangerously black. It was a cat and it was huge. As the fire-door clicked shut behind her, the beast spun round in panic – then it jerked itself backwards, ready to spring. Shoulders, paws, and a gigantic head; its mouth was slavering, lips pulled back to reveal a shark's mouth full of monstrous teeth. She couldn't move, she was held by the flashing eyes. The jaws were opening, it was ready to spring.

'Millie, don't move! Don't move!'

As Oli spoke, the cat spun again, unsure who to confront. Millie realised it was as terrified as she was. She tried to scream, but she simply didn't have the air to do it. She would die in silence, because the beast was turning once more, as if it had made up its mind. It was growling – a long, low, quavering groan as it went down low on its haunches. Its head was on one side, touching the floor, a demented look in its eyes. The claws were getting longer, sharp as meat-hooks.

'Oy!' said a voice.

Millie felt a hand on her shoulder. Strong fingers gripped her. They eased her back, slowly. She'd heard nobody, but then she'd been transfixed, waiting to die. The voice came again and she noticed a thick accent. The hand was drawing her back.

'Slowly, huh? Ver', ver' slow . . .'

She tried to speak but, like the receptionist, her jaws had been locked by the shock.

The voice whispered in her ear, 'Stay behin' me, alright? You OK now . . .'

Then, presumably to the cat, the voice hissed, '*You stay there and don' you even move!*'

Millie was drawn backwards. She smelled the sweat of the man, and now she saw him: he was short and powerful.

'Stay righ' behind me,' he whispered.

To Oli, he said, 'Keep still!'

The man wore pyjama bottoms and a vest. He had coarse black hair and huge shoulders: he was half animal himself, with dark skin covered in tattoos. He took a step towards the cat: it snarled, less confidently.

'Please help,' said Oli.

'Shh!'

The man dropped to his knees. He put his hand on the animal's snout, gently, and massaged its head. The cat relaxed slowly out of its awful attack-stance, but opened its mouth yet wider. The snarl turned into a yawn and the beast flopped onto its side.

The man rubbed the cat hard, between the ears, hard enough to hurt. Then he took it by the chin with his other hand and knelt over it. 'Five minutes,' he said, gently. 'I go for jus' five minutes!'

The cat lifted a foreleg and pawed him gently; Millie saw that the man's right arm was covered in scars.

Oli was still against the wall, peering down, his hands over his mouth.

'Five minutes,' said the man again. 'I jus' go to the truck for a little check, and – man-oh-man, end of the world! She *so* scared. Very scared, aren't you, baby? Huh? *What's going on*? is that what you thinking, eh?' He was crooning, as if to a baby in a pram, and all the time stroking the huge head.

He looked round at Millie. 'You don't say anything, OK?' he said. 'I am so sorry, but you get her so scared. We better go.' He looked back at Oli. 'This is big trouble – I am so sorry, I don' know why I come in here.'

He pulled the animal's head right round and the cat got to its feet and allowed itself to be led. As the animal faced him, Oli went into spasms, his hands shaking; a high-pitched cry wavered out of him.

'Is OK, OK!' said the man. 'She was thinking you danger-ous, but she knows now. Is OK, keep still! Give me your hand.'

Oli tried to snatch his arm out of the way, but the man caught it by the blazer sleeve. He took the child's wrist and led the palm over the cat's head. Slowly, carefully, he brought it round to the muzzle.

'OK, you see? Now she knows . . . Now she know there's no problem. Follow me.'

'I want my brother,' said Oli.

'One minute, jus' come with me one minute. Both of you.'

'Come where?' said Millie. She barely recognised her own voice. 'I think we should leave.'

'One minute.'

The man led his cat along the corridor. It had a heavy, powerful walk, and from behind Millie could see that its belly was huge and heavy.

Five doors down, they came to one that was open: a

section round the handle had been broken and was jagged shards of wood.

'Oh, *Violetta*!' groaned the man. 'You gonna get me in such trouble: we gotta go, right now . . .'

The cat's mood had changed. It was surly and bored, and it ambled into the room, clambering straight up onto the bed. The stink of wild animal was heavier than ever. Millie and Oli watched transfixed as the cat turned and turned, the bed-frame groaning under the weight. The sheets were torn and filthy. The cat settled; it dropped into comfortable repose and yawned again, as if to show off those magnificent fangs.

'What is it?' said Millie.

'Is a panther. Is a black panther.'

'I thought,' said Oli, 'I thought . . . that . . . it was going to eat me.'

'She don' want to eat no one; she's got other things on her mind. She gonna sling the babes any day now, I think tonight maybe. Thass why I put her in my room.'

'Oh . . . she's pregnant!' said Oli.

'Course she's pregnant – look at her! She got five or six babes there. Boy-oh-boy, she get scared so easy, man. You knock on the door, or what?'

'No,' said Oli. 'I was looking for my room. I was walking past and I heard the noise, and I thought someone was . . . possibly interfering with my things . . . And then suddenly . . .' The child's voice was wobbling. 'I was trapped!'

'Is OK,' said the man. 'You did good – you a very brave boy.'

'I thought I ought to stay calm, but she looked at me . . . She didn't seem to like me very much.'

The man was packing his things. 'Well, you mustn't take that personal! She jus' got a lot on her mind. They go crazy with the babes; all the animals do.' He had a small holdall

31

on a chair and was stuffing bits and pieces into it. The panther was starting to purr with a deep, recharging sort of sound.

Oli moved a trembling hand towards its ribs.

'Yeah, you can touch her. No problem, now she knows you.'

'You could have been killed, Oli,' said Millie. 'What the hell were you doing, wandering off by yourself?'

Oli said, 'I was looking for our models!'

'Where's your parents?' said the man. 'This is going to be big problem for me, you start telling everyone. Jeez, every little simple thing in this country go *so* wrong.'

'Where are you from?' said Millie.

'São Paulo. You know São Paulo? Big city in Brazil.'

'I know the airport,' said Millie. 'It's where I bought these.' She produced a crumpled cigarette packet. 'What are you? A circus?'

'No. Just a big mess is what I am – my name's Flavio.'

'Flav –?'

'It's Portuguese.'

'Why are you keeping a panther in your room? Shouldn't he be in a cage?'

'It's not a boy, OK? She's a girl: Violetta. Look at her, man – how can you say she's a boy? And she *was* in a cage, she's always in a cage. I take her to my room because any time now, she's gonna sling the babes. The truck's freezing. No one's sleeping out there, not with the heating like it is – truck's a whole pile a . . . rubbish, that's another story. So, yeah, I took a chance. Sometimes you gotta take chances. You gotta cigarette in there? Then we gotta go.'

She passed one to him. 'We've nearly been killed, haven't we?'

'No way. There's a-no way she kills you. She would a-messed you up pretty bad, maybe you don't do no more

32

walking. They don't know *strength,* thass the problem. I mean, the little boy – one bite and he's in a-two pieces, yeah? She's so hungry as well.'

He went into the bathroom and started gathering up his things. 'We run outta food, is a big problem. We run outta *everything.* They catch me here ... they see that ...' He nodded at the splintered door. Then he lowered his voice. 'I got no licences, no insure, nothing.'

As he said it, there was a knock and the smashed door swung open. The panther growled and there stood an impatient-looking Ruskin.

'Oliver!' he cried, seeing his brother. 'Where on earth have you been? You won't believe the problems you've caused ...'

He saw the panther. The problems died on his lips.

'Oh boy!' said Flavio, in despair. 'How many of you are there? Come in slow! Talk soft, alright?'

Jacob Ruskin was laden with bags and boxes. He'd managed to gather up the models and was now standing transfixed. 'That is the most beautiful cat I've ever seen!' he said. 'Oh my word, look at that! How old is she? Look at her coat!'

'Seven years, but she's in great condition, yeah? Considering.'

'Jake!' said Oli. 'I nearly got eaten – so did Millie!'

'Oh, she's pregnant, isn't she?' He put his boxes down and walked forward carefully. The fire alarms had been turned off and in the distance you could hear the sirens of emergency vehicles. 'She must be due any time!' said Ruskin. 'What a beauty!'

The panther purred, as a surprisingly fearless Ruskin moved in close and gently stroked her belly. Violetta's snake-eyes opened, glowing.

'We had a cat like this, didn't we, Oli? She had six kittens.'

'Where's Sam?' said Millie.

'Mm? Oh . . . Yes! That's why I'm here.' The sirens were getting louder. 'We've got a problem, Millie. Our room's on fire and I've lost Sam.'

Millie looked up. 'You've lost Sam?'

'We split up to look for you and now . . .'

Blue lights were flashing on the wall and there was the familiar sound of revving engines. Millie put her hands over her temples, remembering in an instant how one wrong turn seemed always to lead to another, until total chaos descended. Her time with Sanchez in Colombia had been so simple and calm. How was it that complications kicked in whenever she came near Ribblestrop?

'First you crash into our car,' she cried. 'Then your brother nearly gets me killed! Now you lose Sam, the most helpless kid in our school!'

'Now hang on!' said Ruskin, angrily. 'Sam went to look at the lorry! How was I to know —'

'We gotta go,' said Flavio. He drew the curtain fully back and got one leg over the windowsill.

'Why did Sam go and look at a lorry?' said Millie.

'We thought Oli might be there. Oli loves big vehicles and we noticed this one earlier on —'

'What lorry are you talking about?' said Flavio. He was half in, half out of the window, cigarette between his lips. Violetta watched him.

'Hmm? It's the big one, parked out the back. It's got a Scammel Coupler, which is the coupling device he wants to build —'

'That's my truck,' said Flavio, quietly.

'Is it?' said Ruskin. 'It's parked in a corner, kind of away from everything else.'

'Listen,' said Flavio. 'It's parked there so no one goes near it!' There was a note of panic in his voice. 'Whass your little friend gonna do? Man, I knew I shouldna come in here! We better go look!'

Flavio leaped out into the car park. Millie was at the window too and could see the truck, picked out in its parking lights. Beyond it, there was a confusion of blue lights and firemen. Then they all heard a sudden, furious snarl; the panther on the bed jolted awake and answered with a ferocious roar. Oli leaped backwards, slamming himself into a wall, and the picture that hung beside him dropped to the floor, glass shattering. The panther was on her feet and Millie screamed.

Flavio looked wild-eyed. 'Come on,' he said. 'Come this way – follow me! We better move!'

They piled out of the window and ran. The panther followed immediately, brisk as a guard-dog. In moments they were by the iced-up truck and the roaring was now constant. There were the sounds of rattling chains and a violent noise that sounded like splashing. The truck was rocking backwards and forwards, wood creaking. Flavio dipped under the trailer to the other side; the children did the same. It was too dark to see clearly, but what looked like a tarpaulin lay torn from its hooks, tangled over the truck's wheels. Revealed was a cage and the bars looked distorted. The stink of animal was stronger than ever, a real farmyard smell of dung and animal breath.

'Sam?' shouted Ruskin. 'Sam!' He peered into the cage.

'Stay away, stay under the truck!' said Flavio. He sounded terrified. He leaped up at his cab, fumbling with keys. He yanked the door open and reappeared with a huge flashlight. 'Sam?' he shouted. 'Oh my – this is bad . . . This is not what I need . . .'

He shone the light into the cage and there was a flurry of angry beasts, caught in the beam, backing away from it. Their eyes were on fire, glinting diamonds. They bared their teeth: there was a flurry of movement and the crashing of chains, and the children saw the dangerous fire of tiger-stripes. One of the beasts swung round and cuffed at the light with a paw. Through a partition was something humped and black. Beyond that, small creatures scuttled in straw and set up a desperate squeaking. Over it all, though, was the terrible sound of metal clanking and grinding over wood.

'Oh man,' said Flavio.

'What?' said Millie. 'What's happened?'

'She's gone. I knew I should of put her on the chain, but . . . This is bad!'

'Who's gone?' said Ruskin. 'At least Sam isn't in the cage, at least he's got more sense than that.'

'Sushamila. She's the only one was loose. Damn it, man: I told him, *it's cheap rubbish, man, it's a-falling to pieces*; he says, *fix it up*, we fix it up. Oh boy . . . She so hungry, you see. I ran outta food yesterday. They ver' hungry.'

'Oli, what have you got?' said Ruskin.

Oli had found something in the grass close by. He held it up to the torchlight. It was a black-and-gold cap, wet and misshapen. It had a chewed look about it.

'Lord,' said Ruskin. 'This could be serious.'

'Hey, hang on,' said Flavio. 'Don' jump to any conclusions; thass jus' somebody's old baseball cap, man, you don't know—'

Millie said, 'Was Sam wearing his cap for the fire-drill?'

Both boys nodded.

'You know Sam,' said Ruskin, softly. 'He was proud of his cap.'

'Put your stuff in the cab,' said Flavio.

'Why?'

'We gotta move. Is not as bad as you think. I know what to do.'

'What about Sam?' said Millie. 'What's happened to Sam?'

'I find him, don't panic! He'll be OK; she won't hurt him!'

36

They were by a small, scrappy area of wasteground. A little copse had survived the concrete development, along with a few square metres of bramble, which led down to the dual carriageway. This separated the Sleepeasy from a housing estate. Flavio stepped into the long grass and swung the torch left and right; then he gave out several piercing whistles. He was answered by a single gust of wind and a snarl from Violetta, who had climbed up into the cab and was watching.

'OK. You, Millie . . . You come with me.'

He looked at Ruskin and Oli. 'You drive a truck?'

Ruskin blinked several times. 'I've driven a van,' he said.

'You can work a gearbox, yes? Go slow, OK? Stay in a low gear, no problem. You see the garage? Go past, you come to a roundabout. Second left, half a mile. There's a little lay-by, got a little snack bar.'

He shoved a huge bunch of keys into Ruskin's hands. 'After the snack bar – all the space you need, OK? You park up there and we get your friend. I meet you in five minutes. Come.'

The boys stood motionless. Flavio stepped briskly onto a narrow path and whistled again. He peered into the undergrowth.

'Do what he says,' said Millie.

She ran past Flavio and waited for the torch beam to pick its way through the trees. 'Sam?' she called.

The path brought them steeply down to a subway under the road. Flavio broke into a run and they both descended, through the tunnel and up the other side. There was a shoe on the tarmac. A little black school shoe.

'Sam!' yelled Millie.

'Sam!' shouted Flavio and he whistled again: a long, plaintive whistle. Then silence, but for someone revving an engine. 'Wait,' he said. 'Just listen.'

He swung the torch slowly, left and right. The winter grass was high; the trees threw shadows and it was hard to make out anything at all. Black shapes, patches of bramble. They stood quietly, letting the torch illuminate swathes of empty wasteland. In the distance there was the hideous sound of gears mashing and more sirens wailing.

'Poor kid,' said Millie, softly.

'Jus' keep still,' said Flavio. 'I know Sushamila. You smell something?'

He moved the torch slower, picking through the undergrowth. Tree trunks, the tangled nettles and thorns. Then, unmistakable, because they were luminous and still, sudden in the grass: a pair of eyes, unblinking.

Millie stepped behind Flavio and he went down low on his haunches. It was a cat, for sure. It was low in the grass. Flavio kept the beam full on its face and was still as a rock. A minute passed – maybe he was letting the beast get used to his presence. Then – so slowly – he took a pace towards it. The fur was bleached out in the torchlight, but along the contours of powerful shoulders, you could see the brown of a lioness. As Millie and Flavio stared, the lioness drew her lips carefully back and snarled. Her rear end rose up and she seemed to slither away from the beam. Dipping her head, she picked something out of the grass and dragged it. She was nursing a kill.

'Sushamila!' whispered Flavio urgently. 'Give that up!'

Whatever the beast had was heavy and she didn't want to give it up. She lifted whatever she'd caught and moved backwards again.

Flavio moved forward, Millie behind him still. She saw the second shoe under her feet, and she knew for sure then that she was watching her dear friend Sam being dragged through brambles.

'Sushamila!' said Flavio. His voice took on an angry tone.

'You give him up now! Whatever you got, you give it up! Give!'

The lioness backed a little further off, transfixed by the light. This time she didn't drag her kill; she looked at Flavio and twitched, angrily.

Flavio approached cautiously. 'You stay back,' he said to Millie. But she had no intention of staying back: she stuck to Flavio closely, and so – after some time – they came to the little bundle in the grass. She knelt by the body and the lioness stared, the huge head on one side, the eyes mad and glassy.

Sam was in a foetal position, knees tucked up under his chin. He was soaking wet – the back of his blazer was thick with saliva.

Expertly, Flavio felt for a pulse in the neck. 'He's alive,' he whispered.

At first, they couldn't unfold the boy. His breaths were coming in high-pitched pants. After a few minutes of gentle massage and comforting words, he relaxed a little: enough to put his head up and gasp for oxygen.

Millie admitted later that what she dreaded was the sudden gush of blood: the sudden revelation that the child's torso had been clawed right open and he'd been holding in his guts all this time.

In fact, as they lifted him and he let his knees down, they could see that he was unscathed. No limbs hanging by a thread; not even a bite mark. He was bruised, yes: after all, he'd been carried between powerful gums. He'd also been licked by a tongue that on its own weighed nearly four kilos and was rough as granite. His eyebrows were gone, but his flesh had not been torn.

Sushamila, it turned out, was the oldest animal in Flavio's ex-circus and was senile. She had lost her teeth and claws years before and was nearly blind. She had smelled Sam wandering around outside and in some jungle-fantasy of her own had mistaken the boy for one of her many cubs from years ago. She made assumptions: her child was wandering defenceless in the cold. The old maternal instincts stirred. She'd done what any good mother would do: she took the struggling, helpless thing to shelter and gave it a good wash. Then she kept it safe and warm. Apart from the bruising, Sam's worst injuries were nettle stings.

Chapter Five

Oli had worked out the gears of Flavio's truck and his brother knew how to use the clutch. As the vehicle shifted forward, they steered together.

They rolled onto the roundabout very slowly. A flurry of cars swerved and braked; Ruskin ploughed on, shaking them from him. Only Oli noticed – in the wing mirror – the second trailer obliterate a bollard.

'First left?' said Ruskin.

'Second right,' said Oli.

'Right the way round? Back where we've come from?' Ruskin turned the wheel harder and removed a whole flower-bed of shrubs from the roundabout's edge.

'We're oversteering,' said Oli. 'Try and keep her further out.'

'You're right. You forget just how long you are, and – she's a heavy old thing, isn't she? Ooh!'

'You've hit the kerb.'

'Power steering is a marvellous thing,' said Ruskin. 'But so hard to judge. I'm going to have to go round again, aren't I?'

'Well, we just passed the turning – I saw the little van. And there's a police car behind us, Jake.'

As Oli spoke, the sirens wailed, and in the mirrors the boys saw not one, but three police cars, and another fire-truck. Racing down the dual carriageway towards them was an ambulance.

'That fire's taken hold,' said Ruskin. 'If that woman had used a bit of common sense . . .'

'Careful, they're overtaking. Slow down.'

'That's not clever, on a roundabout. There they go . . .'

Ruskin had slowed to crawling-pace and the emergency vehicles – thinking he was trying to let them past – sped either side and away to what was indeed a considerable fire. A mushroom of black smoke was spreading slowly in the darkness and there was a whole orchestra of sirens. The boys inched round to the exit Flavio had described and Ruskin managed to ease them into it.

'We're a long way from school,' said Oli, noticing the sign. 'Indicator, Jake! You know what Mum says when Dad forgets.'

'Sorry. Now, I've got to get this thing into the lay-by – that's going to need skill. I hope the animals are OK.'

'You're on the grass.'

'There seems to be way too much play in the steering wheel – I'm wondering . . . oops. I'm just wondering—'

'Careful!'

'. . . if this thing's been properly serviced. Have I hit something?'

'That was the burger-van.'

Joe's burger-van catered for those who couldn't face or couldn't afford the Family Roadgrill. Even in the winter it had a few plastic tables and chairs out on the grass, and from six in the morning till eight in the evening it did a good, friendly, value-for-money trade. Joe had been a trucker himself, so loved to see the lorries roll in. He always felt a little sad locking up and cycling home to his bungalow on the estate nearby. His wife used to pull his leg by suggesting he slept in the van if he still loved the road that much.

How lucky he didn't.

42

The corner of Flavio's trailer ripped into the little thing like a can-opener, stripping out the front and concertinaing it onto the road. Ruskin wrestled the cab to the right and got round it: the second trailer gave it another hard cuff as he came in to park and spread boxes of burgers all over the grass. The animals were manic now, but in the satisfying exhalation of his air-brakes, Ruskin didn't hear them. Hand-brake on: engine off. A safe arrival.

The boys jumped down and there, clambering up the bank, were Flavio, Millie, Sam – and Sushamila, led by a black-and-gold tie.

The walk had revived Sam, though he was a little unsteady. Without eyebrows, he had a surprised look, which seemed appropriate. Oli and Ruskin embraced him like a soldier back from the war, and they sat on the kerb as the boy did his best to describe the sensations of being carried in the mouth of a beast four times your size. Flavio put Sushamila in the trailer and did a quick repair of the damaged floor. Ruskin returned Sam's cap and Sam smartened himself up as best he could.

'What now?' said Millie.

'Back to where we stayed,' said Sam. 'We're meeting Captain Routon there. The headmaster said to expect him early.'

Millie looked at the lights and the smoke.

'I think we should probably avoid that place,' she said. 'Do you realise, Oli, you've caused a major incident on your first day? In fact, you've caused a major disaster.'

'I'm gonna go,' said Flavio. 'There's a lorry park a couple of miles from here. We make a call from there, OK?'

Millie said, 'Did you say you were out of food for the animals?'

'I got no money at all. Every last bit I gave that woman for the room.'

'Give me a hand, Oli. I can see a solution.'

*   *   *

Twenty minutes later, they were ready to roll. Oli wrote the note and stuck it, with a piece of Millie's gum, onto the burger-van's smashed up wall. The animals were well-fed, and calm.

Sir,

We are taking the precaution of not leaving our name and address, because we have done a number of illegal things and are hoping not to be caught. But we do not want you to think too badly of us.

Your excellent burgers have not gone to waste. They have fed hungry animals and hungry people. We hope you will be relieved to know that the wrecking of your van was a pure accident, and not an act of mindless vandalism by kids. We can only afford fifty pounds, which is a fair bit of the pocket-money we are carrying. One of us says you are probably insured, so might even make a bit, which we certainly hope.

We are really sorry for the inconvenience we have caused and if we come by this way again we will definitely eat here – if your business survives, that is. We much prefer it to the Family Roadgrill, which is way too expensive for what you get. A hot chocolate, for example, is now an unbelievable price, and I bet yours is better. Crazy!

Sorry not to sign this note with our names, but that would obviously make catching us rather easy.

TTFN and good luck.

The original note appears as an Appendix in the Somerset Police File, which was copied to D.C.C. Cuthbertson of the Devon and Cornwall Police. The offences Jacob Ruskin refers to were ultimately taken into consideration in the final police prosecution.

Chapter Six

The next morning saw a further series of connections as different journeys inched forward. Breakfasts were going on all over the world: a complex network of cookers, cups, dishes, knives, and forks. For example, in the crypt under Ribblestrop Towers, six elderly monks were eating porridge from wooden bowls. Over their heads, thirty-seven thousand feet up on a British Airways' 747, a slim, blond boy called Miles, in a grey shirt and a black-and-gold tie, drank fresh juice, while the chef prepared his omelette. His mother was still sleeping in the seat next to his. She would want only rosehip tea when she awoke.

Captain Routon was already on the road, speeding up the motorway having breakfasted on a Mars bar. Brother Doonan and Father O'Hanrahan were dozing fitfully in a hospital waiting room. The restaurant wouldn't open till nine-thirty due to staff-shortages, and the coffee-machine accepted money but refused to give drinks. Lady Vyner – the proud and insomniac owner of Ribblestrop Towers – ate Marmite on toast, with a glass of early-morning rum. Little Lord Caspar, grandson and heir to the estate, had a chocolate pancake. The orphans were finishing yet more jellies from the cancelled party, whilst Tomaz was in his glorious home under the ground opening a can of pineapple chunks.

In Colombia, Andreas Sanchez was fast asleep because it was half-past one in the morning, but a servant was preparing fresh bread for the household and the nightingales sang to the fireflies.

In the school's west tower, as the sun rose over frosty lawns, the headmaster had Ryvita with Professor Worthington – she brought jam and he brought marmalade.

It was going to be a very special day.

Sam, Ruskin, Oli, and Millie helped Flavio feed the animals, distributing the last burgers as fairly as they could. They had phoned the school and Captain Routon had details of their location. It was just a question of waiting for him, so they were happy to explore the truck. There were two tigers, who seemed to get hungrier however many boxes they dispatched. Sushamila the lioness nibbled more gently, content to let Sam feed her. She gazed at him with loving, short-sighted eyes. Flavio unlocked a partition, took down various shutters, and then – to everyone's amazement – produced a small camel, which he led down onto the tarmac. The camel looked utterly miserable and lapped at a puddle. It had thick brown hair, which rippled in the freezing wind. The children realised there were hidden chambers.

'Flavio, there's a fish-tank!' said Millie. 'What are you doing with a fish-tank?'

'You wanna go careful, man. That's the python.'

'Wow, you've got a python?' said Ruskin. 'I've always wanted a snake.'

'It's not in the tank,' said Millie. 'One dead mouse, that's all I can see.'

'Oh boy,' said Flavio, wearily. He pulled out his flashlight and played it from the tank to the floor. Sure enough, a large hole had been chewed in one corner, between the iron bars. 'She did this last week,' said Flavio. 'She gets cold, I guess – so she goes down to the engine. Then she gets hot, then she gets cold . . . Crazy. Come with me.'

He jumped down and crouched by a wheel. Sure enough, when he pointed the torch beam, they could see silver-grey skin. It was wrapped tight around the truck's undercarriage and the head appeared to be jammed up in the gearbox.

'Is it hungry?' said Sam. 'Shall I put some burger on its back?'

'She's not hungry. She's greedy as a pig. Got a dog on Sunday she's still digesting.'

The children stared.

'You gave her a *dog*?' said Millie.

Flavio shook his head.

'No. We parked up in this nice quiet street – no problem, we're minding our own business. Then this old lady comes by, walking this yappy little thing, and I'm just chatting away, being friendly . . . Next thing I knew, the dog's under the truck doing its business, then . . . Pythons move quick when they want to.'

'You seem to have a lot of bad luck,' said Ruskin.

'Ha!' snorted Flavio. 'Everywhere I go, is a problem. I think this is the end of the road, though – I don't think we can go much further.'

It had started to snow.

'Shall we get the camel back in?' said Oli.

'No, he loves it. It's a change from a desert, I guess. Let's get in the cab. When's this man coming to fetch you?'

'Depends what time he left,' said Millie. She pushed Violetta and managed to force her off the front seats. 'Flavio . . . why are you driving round England with a truck full of animals? It doesn't seem a very normal thing to be doing. I asked you last night, are you some kind of circus?"

'Some kind of nothing,' said Flavio.

'Another thing,' said Sam. 'What you were doing at that hotel place?'

Flavio sat back in his seat and pulled a face. 'It's a long story,' he said.

'*Are* you a zoo?' said Sam.

'Are you meeting someone?' said Oli.

'No.'

'Are you part of a . . . fun-fair?' said Ruskin.

'Hang on,' said Millie. 'Why don't we let him tell us?'

'I will,' said Flavio. 'I'll tell you everything – this is just a big load of trouble and it's gonna put me in jail. I got all this lot cut-price, friend of a friend. Just a big problem rip-off, is what it is. It was a zoo, then it was going to be a safari park . . .'

'So you're an animal trainer?' said Ruskin.

'I'm nothing, no. No education, no qualifications – nothing. I was at school for two years, OK? Two years, I just about read an' write. All they do at school is beat me up. I got out at eight years old, became an acrobat.'

Millie laughed. 'You ran away from school? To be an acrobat?'

Flavio laughed as well. 'Yeah. I ran away – best thing I ever did. This was a *favela* in São Paulo, OK? Little stinking place, seven brothers, three sisters. Anything, man, just to get out! I met these guys doing street work and I was small, so I do the trapeze, high-wire, pyramid stuff. They fire me out a gun, set me on fire up a rope –'

'Out of a gun?' said Sam. 'Like a cannonball?'

'Yeah, like a cannonball. They make a gun out of a sewer pipe, put some dynamite in a hole. I'm just a little kid, got a hard head. They shoot me out over the crowd, sometimes into a net, sometimes into the lake. That age, you just keep bouncing, yeah? We go all over Brazil, make a bit, lose a bit. I do motorbike stuff . . . fire. I been on fire so many times I don't feel nothing! We go up to Rio, Brasilia – it's a life, OK? Then I get to fourteen, some of us make a little show on our own, they bring us to Spain. There, we make proper money. For the first time.'

'Wow,' said Ruskin. 'You were really a circus boy?'

'Circus boy, stuntman for a little bit . . .'

'Stunts!' cried Sam. 'Like in the films? Can you do stunts?'

'I did a few movies, then I have a big bust-up with the boss over money – always money. I was dumb, I met some bad people, did a bank-job, and – they still looking for me in Spain, but I got out of there. We held up this bank, me and two guys. Some policeman starts shooting, everyone running. So I cross to Morocco, do some circus work. Then twenty-three, twenty-four: you get a bit old. You put on a bit of weight . . .' He slapped his belly. 'I can still do it, but . . . things are getting slow. Between you an' me, the last few years, I had a few little bad accidents, OK? I'm doin' a show in London. This is a few years ago, alright? There's a little gang of us, go from Marrakech to England. We do this jump – I gotta do a jump over some people . . . big mess. I don' make the jump.'

'I'm lost,' said Millie. 'You had to jump over some people? Is this on a motorbike?'

'No way, I can't afford a bike any more! This is a new show; we do it in shopping malls.' He closed his eyes. 'This is bad, OK? We're outside some big store. We get the people out of the crowd, all stand in a line. Long line, ten, fifteen, twenty people. All the mums and dads, little kids – my friend, the boss, saying, "Now, ladies and gentlemen! Presenting . . . Flavio Guamala! He's gonna fly! He's the birdman, yeah? Two somersaults, all the way from South

America!" I take a run, the drum goes – all that rubbish. Little trampoline, and I go up and turn over two times, OK? Why are you laughing?'

The boys were giggling. Millie was smiling broadly.

'Go on!' said Sam. 'It sounds amazing!'

'It was amazing when I get it right. I'm supposed to land in front o' the lass person on the line. Big, amazing thing, everyone cheering. This time, I don' know – maybe the trampoline was bad, I don' know . . .'

'Oh no,' said Oli. He had stopped laughing. 'You landed *on* someone?'

'Wow . . .'

'She go down hard, man.'

'A woman?' said Sam.

'She was the last in the line. She's OK; she's in a wheel-chair now. She's gonna be fine, is her back a little busted.'

Millie was open-mouthed. 'Flavio . . . you must be jinxed. You have the worst luck I've ever heard of, apart from Sam.'

'Yeah, well. I said it was bad.' He nodded sadly. 'That's when I say, no more jumping, you're no little boy no more. Is getting dangerous and the police say how come I got no papers, no insure. So I move, get outta there, go up north, to the seaside. End up in this big house with a zoo, and the guy says we need someone to look after the cats. I did cat stuff in Brazil, so I took it on . . . and that's how I come to meet all this lot.'

'But why is the zoo in your lorry?' said Ruskin, after a pause. 'You said there was a big house?'

'The zoo closed,' said Flavio. 'The house got sold, every-thing was sold. I tell you, the owner! Man, he's just drinking hard, all the animals are dying. The place is closing, nobody coming. Winter: no tourists. Then we get inspected and it's the same old thing, "Where's the papers, where's your insurance? Cruelty to animals!" Everyone's leaving and me? I'm waiting to be paid. I got no money, nowhere to go. Story of my life, man! I say to the boss, "Where's my money?" He says, "There is no money, everything's broke." He says, "Take the animals. Take the truck – it's no good, but it's somewhere to sleep." '

'This is very sad,' said Ruskin.

'We put the animals in the truck, 'cause we got to leave – the council is closing us down, we got the Animal Rights people all over us. I wake up – the boss has gone. I got a truck of animals and just a little, tiny bit of cash.'

'What did you do?'

'I didn't know what to do! There was a brown bear. He got flu – died about two weeks ago. I had a seal. Got out of the tank, found him dead in a puddle. I got a scorpion – he hasn't moved for three days, I think maybe he's dead as well.' He sighed. 'Yes, so . . . Today. I was meeting a man, we were gonna make a film maybe, maybe not. He says he needs animals, maybe . . . he's waiting for some money. But I phone last night, just before I met you. He's doing six weeks in Paris. Gone. You know how much money I got?' Flavio smiled bitterly and opened a thin wallet. A ten-pound note sat all on its own. 'Enough for nothing.' He leaned up to the back of the cab, where the panther was snoring gently. He patted her belly. 'She's ready to drop, and I don't know what to do. I was going to buy half a bottle of whisky and find a police station. Oh man . . . look at this weather.'

The snow had turned to a horizontal blizzard. The children would have been excited had it not been for Flavio's tragic story. Snowflakes came down thick and hard, and within a minute the windscreen was white. They were sealed in.

'But how will the animals survive the winter?' said Ruskin. 'They need sunshine.'

'They need meat,' said Millie.

'They need exercise,' said Sam. 'You see them on wildlife programmes: they're always running around hunting each other.'

'They're dying, man,' said Flavio. 'Had two parrots last week, happy and talking away. They in the back, got some kind of mange. Only that blasted camel likes the cold.'

'Maybe you could drive to Africa,' said Ruskin.

'Maybe you should come to Ribblestrop,' said Millie.

'You know, the RSPCA might help,' said Ruskin. 'Oli and I found an injured frog once, outside our shed. Do you remember, Oli?'

'She'd been half eaten by a cat,' said Oli. 'She only had one leg, so she was hopping in circles.'

'We got a matchbox and put her inside with a bit of blotting paper. Then we took her to an RSPCA charity shop. The lady who ran it was very pleased and told us we'd done just the right thing. I could telephone my father and get her number.'

'Why don't you bring them all to Ribblestrop?' said Millie. 'We could look after them there and do projects on them. It's supposed to be natural history this term. I bet the headmaster would love it.'

There was a silence.

'Did you say *bring them to Ribblestrop*?' said Sam.

Millie's words hung, suspended in the air. The three boys stared at the white windscreen as if they hadn't quite understood.

'Ribblestrop's a school?' said Flavio.

'Kind of,' said Ruskin. 'It's trying to be.'

'You know,' said Oli, quietly. 'If you brought them to Ribblestrop, we could make cages and exercise areas. We could put heaters into their stalls. We could get hay and bits of tree – you know, for the parrots. They'd be safe.'

'Somewhere for Violetta to have her babies,' said Millie. 'She'd be safe.'

'Hey!' said Sam. 'Professor Worthington said she was going to teach reproduction. We could study Violetta!'

'We'd have panther-pups!' cried Ruskin. 'We could train them! We could tame them and teach them tricks . . . We could—'

'A circus!' whispered Oli. His lips had gone dry – his voice was small. He started to nod, then he started to rock. 'This is the best idea ever!' he hissed.

Sam was standing up. 'The orphans!' he shouted. 'I bet the orphans could do circus stuff! They're amazing at everything – you should have seen them last term. And they can build and do stunts. We could have our own Ribblestrop circus!'

'Hang on—' shouted Flavio.

But Oli had found his voice again and was babbling loudly, shaking Sam, who had gripped Millie's arm.

Millie was grinning wildly, as Ruskin cried, 'A safari park! There's so much space! The barns and the woods. We could be a zoo in the daytime and in the evening we'd learn tricks!'

In the whooping and cheering, as ideas bubbled and burst, the hammering on the lorry-cab door went unnoticed. It was only when the cab started to rock that Violetta sensed an intruder and roared over the top of the din, silencing everyone. The hammering continued.

'Oh man,' said Flavio, softly. 'I bet it's the police.'

'Start the engine!' cried Oli. 'Let's just go! Drive to Ribblestrop!'

Flavio gritted his teeth and swung the door open. Everyone peered out, and in the whirl of snowflakes a large bear-like figure swayed in and out of their vision. The blizzard had worsened.

'Looking for some children . . .' came a voice. Then it disappeared again. Two hands appeared and managed to grasp the lorry's mudguard, and the figure hauled itself closer. Under a shawl that was laden with snow, an anxious red face was visible. The eyes focused and moved quickly from Sam to Millie to Oli to Ruskin – the eyes took in the panther and the driver and narrowed with astonishment. Then the face broke into a smile of sheer delight and relief, and whatever he said was drowned in a renewed frenzy of cheering.

It was Captain Routon.

Chapter Seven

Millie had two bottles of very fine duty-free champagne in her bag, and had planned a serious midnight feast with the orphans. However, it was clear that this was the moment for a celebration.

Captain Routon was hauled into the cab. The stories were told, back and forth – everything explained. Captain Routon moved from horror to laughter, from amazement to joy, as the children relived their experiences. Flavio went through his history again and they started the second bottle.

'It's the best idea I've heard in a very long time,' declared the captain. 'How much fuel have you got, sir?'

'Next to nothing,' said Flavio.

The captain was pulling out his wallet. 'So lucky our paths crossed, I would say. I was only talking to the head-master the other day and he was saying how we needed some kind of project. Some kind of . . . *focus* for the term.' He took a five-pound note and laid it on the dashboard. 'He will be delighted! So will the orphans! Now – can you follow me? Might be best if the children stay here where it's warm. Where it's . . . warm.'

He faltered suddenly. 'Oh no,' he said. 'I've forgotten . . . The van.'

The children stared at him. He seemed anxious.

'What have you forgotten?' said Sam. 'What's the problem?'

'How long have I been sitting here?' he said.

'About an hour,' said Ruskin.

It was true. There had been so much to explain and plan that the time had shot past.

'I've left those priests in the van. They'll be frozen stiff – there's no heater! I said I'd only be a minute. Oh my word, they'll be blocks of ice!'

Captain Routon leaped out of the cab and the children followed him. The blizzard had eased, but visibility was still very poor. There was no sign of another vehicle.

'Where did you park?' shouted Millie.

'I don't know,' said the captain. He had lost his sense of direction. Then, as they listened to the wind, they heard a forlorn hooting. It might have been the cry of a lonely seabird echoing over an Arctic wasteland. It came again, seemingly more distant than before, and the children set out towards it. At last, out of the swirling white, a grey igloo came into view.

Sam found a handle and managed to get the door ajar. The rest of the party were soon helping, prising it open on its frozen hinges. The interior light came on and revealed two figures. One was moving; the other seemed unnaturally still. Millie recognised them both at once, of course. The old priest was seated, his face a rigid mask of suffering. His skin was deathly pale. The younger man – Brother Doonan – was kneeling on the seat next to him, rubbing the man's hands, in a desperate attempt to keep his circulation going.

'Oh my word,' he said. 'An answer to my prayers!'

'It's over, Doonan!' said the old man, faintly.

'It's not, Father! Help is here – we've been found! I knew we'd be heard!'

'I'm so sorry,' cried Captain Routon. 'I forgot all about you! Wait, I've got rum somewhere . . .'

'Oh, I don't think that's wise,' said Doonan. 'Father O'Hanrahan never drinks—'

'Nonsense, it will pull him round. I cannot begin to apologise, gentlemen.' He heaved himself into the driver's seat and rummaged in the glove compartment. Seconds later, he was administering the spirit to Father O'Hanrahan. 'Boys. Millie. Go back to the truck and tell Flavio to put his lights on. I'll come and find you in a moment . . .'

He started the engine. The windscreen wipers dislodged two great shovelfuls of snow onto the ground. In a short while, the truck came into view, its headlamps carving out tunnels of whirling snowflakes. The lights flashed and it slid behind them. Captain Routon hunted for first gear.

'Maybe we should look for that Travellers' Sleepeasy,' said Doonan. 'Try to get warm, perhaps . . .'

'We'll make it, sir!' cried Routon.

'I'm just thinking, it might be wise to hole up against the weather.'

'We must press on. We've got to get those animals to safety and there's a party tonight.'

'Animals?'

The school van nosed its way forward.

It's one tail-light was just visible to Flavio and he crept up as close as he dared. A smile had spread across his face and it was the first time he had smiled in several months. He nursed the truck forward, out of the lorry park and onto the road. There was scarcely another vehicle to be seen.

The motorway was almost impassable and several pile-ups kept all the police cars in the region busy. This was lucky, as Flavio's truck had been described by a number of witnesses. Had it been spotted and stopped, the driver would undoubtedly have been arrested and – with his chain of convictions – deported. If that had happened, the Ribblestrop circus would never have existed.

Instead, the two vehicles crawled slowly west together and the children taught Flavio the school song.

Chapter Eight

Back at Ribblestrop, Lady Vyner heard the arrival from the south tower. She sat in her broken sofa and as the truck arrived, she put her head in her hands. Her grandson was working quietly at the corner table. They looked at each other as the engines revved and tyres mashed the gravel. The horn sounded long and hard, and they winced. Minutes later, the air was ripped to pieces by volleys of fireworks, the detonations ricocheting round the grounds.

The old lady pressed her fingers in her ears, but still the school song rose upwards, shouted on and on to the accompaniment of sticks hammering dustbin lids.

'They're doing a procession,' said Caspar, peering out of the window. 'Such a load of babies.'

Lady Vyner started to moan.

'He's still dressed as Father Christmas. The orphans are dancing – they're still in those stupid elf-suits.'

'Shut up, Caspar!'

'Oh – they're going back inside.'

Moments later, the tower started to vibrate to the low thud of disco music. This lasted for two hours and then there was a precious silence. The old lady hobbled to the kitchen to make cocoa and the Christmas carols began.

'Not again,' she hissed. 'Not again . . .'

The children and their teachers were at last enjoying the party they had longed for.They sat in the hall under a roof they'd built with their own hands. A million fairy lights were strewn from the rafters and a nine-metre Christmas tree twinkled, laden with candles. Father Christmas had wept, openly, as he welcomed everyone home. Professor Worthington had waved her fairy wand and made wishes for every child, and the gifts had been distributed, rewrapped for the fun of it and distributed again. Just before midnight, Tomaz – who had made a brick oven in the giant fireplace – produced the biggest goose anyone had ever seen, sizzling amongst roasted vegetables. Now the children sat back, wrapped in duvets, surrounded by the debris of their celebrations. Nobody could dance another step. Nobody could take another mouthful, solid or liquid. Brother Doonan had been welcomed and a frost-bitten Father O'Hanrahan had been wheeled in briefly. Flavio had been introduced, but had left immediately to sort out the animals. There was only one thing left and an expectant hush had descended.

'Well, boys,' said the headmaster. He pulled off his beard and hat, and stood before his school. His eyes were shining. 'Boys and Millie. What adventures we have had together . . . And here we again, facing new ones. Who knows what is about to happen this term . . .'

'Sanchez, sir?' said a young orphan.

The headmaster raised a hand. 'There were times last term when I said, "That's enough, Headmaster! The Ribblestrop dream has died!" But it was you who relit the candle and took the candle to the torch. It was you who showed me that a true Ribblestropian never gives up, and never says, *enough* – indeed, that could be a second motto, couldn't it? *Never enough!* We are ready, aren't we?'

'Yes, sir!' shouted everyone.

'I am so glad. You will be aware, of course, that we have been fortunate in acquiring a zoo within the last few hours. Our thanks must go to Sam, Oli, Millie, and Ruskin for that sensational piece of foresight. I am awarding each of them a house point, which is just one of the new initiatives this term. House points will be awarded for acts of care, courtesy and courage. Indeed, *any* act that develops Ribblestrop as a community will be eligible for a house point, for a community cannot—'

'Time for the film, sir?' said Captain Routon, quietly.

'Yes! I just want to add, before the excitement of the video . . . that we will be holding Speech Day in a tent, at the end of this term. I have had a very quick consultation with my colleagues here and we feel that the term should climax in a circus.'

There were immediate gasps.

'A circus in which you will be the performers, of course. So I will be inviting all of your parents . . . I know that some of you don't *have* parents, but that should not prevent you taking part and . . . receiving your prizes.'

The orphans looked confused.

Professor Worthington touched the headmaster's arm. 'Time for the film, Giles.'

'Yes. So I want you to think about that and ask yourselves, "What can I do for Speech Day?" Now I am going to hand over to our newly appointed Head Boy—'

There was another, louder gasp of excitement.

'No, no – not in the flesh. As I explained, Sanchez is in South America—'

The excitement broke into disappointment.

'I told you that! He has been delayed by family business –

quiet, please. However, his friend Millie Roads – who travelled with him intrepidly through the mountains of Colombia – has brought a videotape, on which I believe he has recorded some wise words. Is that right, Millie?'

'Yes, sir.'

Millie had sent her luggage ahead from the airport, but the one item she had not let out of her sight was the Sanchez video. She had helped him make it. She had been sworn to secrecy and not mentioned it to anyone except the head-master. She produced it now, wrapped in tinsel and foil.

'And Millie,' said the headmaster. 'I wonder if now is the time to announce to the school that just as we have a Head Boy, we also have a Head Girl.'

Millie blinked. 'What?'

'Yes, we've done a lot of planning over the holidays, and as a staff, we went into this very carefully. You are Ribblestrop's Head Girl.'

Sam started to clap and very soon the applause was deafening.

'But I'm the *only* girl,' said Millie.

'We think that you and Sanchez will provide the neces-sary leadership. We could think of no better role models.' He stood to shake her hand and pressed a small enamel badge into her hand.

'What am I supposed to do?' said Millie. 'I'm not sure about this –'

'All ready to go,' said Captain Routon, taking the parcel gently from her.

'Let's not waste time!' cried the headmaster. 'Sanchez cannot be with us for a little while yet. He is visiting his mother, who died recently, due to . . . circumstances beyond her control. However, I think you will agree when you see his message, that we have a very special term ahead of us. Thank you, Captain!'

Captain Routon pressed the switches and the lights dimmed.

The children huddled forward as a great white beam flashed upon the wall. A complicated set of lenses and bulbs meant that the image was projected huge, and the children were bolt upright, peering hopefully as white dissolved into a million specks of black and grey. Suddenly, it was blue. And then, as if he was there in the room by magic, a face three metres high flickered into life. Andreas Emilio Sanchez was smiling at his friends, and the children burst as one into yet another volley of unstoppable cheering. The camera was close up and their friend looked radiant and healthy. Clear skin, shining eyes, oiled hair.

He started to speak, but of course the words were lost amongst the howling of the waving children. Routon had to pause the movie and shout for quiet.

'Hi,' said Sanchez, at last. He was a softly-spoken boy and there was now a hush as the congregation listened. 'I'm really sorry I'm late back, guys. I'm looking forward to seeing you again, obviously. Hi, Millie! Hi, Sam, Ruskin – hope your brother's with you – and hi, Tomaz, and hi, Asilah, Israel, Sanjay, Anjoli, Henry, Podma, Eric . . .'

He went through all the names.

Captain Routon stopped the projector again, because some of the younger orphans were up against the screen, running their hands over Sanchez's chin.

Millie's eyes were moist and she looked from her friend to the little badge in her hand and back again, deeply confused. When the film started again, the camera pulled back – and again, a hush fell. Sanchez was normally seen in his school clothes, like everyone else. It was a shock to see that he was wearing something very different, and as the children took in what his costume was, several mouths fell open.

The room was silent.

Sanchez was wearing football kit. He wore a striped football shirt and the stripes were black and gold. The shorts were black with a golden bar down each thigh. The socks were black with three golden bands. He even had black-and-gold wristbands. He shone like a young golden god.

'Millie and I designed this kit,' said Sanchez. 'She promised she wouldn't tell, so I hope she didn't – well, I know she wouldn't, because one thing I know is Millie doesn't break a promise. So . . . I hope you like it. My father made a load of them, so . . .' Sanchez looked off-camera and laughed at something. 'We're going to have a proper strip now, all of us. All different sizes, no problem, and the boots and the footballs . . . everything we need. It's all in a box and I'm bringing it with me. In time for our first game!'

The audience was in pain. To keep silent after announcements like these was physical torture, and there was groaning. Sam was on his feet.

'More important than that . . . I need to introduce you to a friend of mine.'

The shot changed to a panorama of a warm, sandy beach. The camera wobbled and then it zoomed in on Sanchez again. He was still in his football kit, limping towards the camera with a football under his arm.

'There're a lot of kids in Colombia who don't have much,' he said. 'You know what I mean – don't have *anything*, is what I mean. Street kids and that – so if you're a girl or a boy, all you dream about is making it big. Football is a big business out here. Everyone knows the story: if you get seen – if you get selected – you can be the richest boy in Colombia.' The camera was closing in on Sanchez's face. 'There're boys on this beach, which is where I live, who play football with me. They're the best footballers I ever saw. And there's one guy . . .'

The screen went black.

Many of the children were standing now, with clenched

64

fists. They knew by instinct that something even more special was about to happen. Sam was rigid.

The screen lit up again, muddy yellow this time. It was hard to work out what you were supposed to focus on: it looked like the sand. The camera moved and a bent Coke can came into view. The camera drew back and there was a small, brown foot. A girl's voice – Millie's voice – said, quietly, 'OK, dimwit, go.'

The foot got under the can and with a flick of the toes rolled it up to shin height. With the instep, the can was passed up onto the knee, where it bounced three times. The camera drew back further, and Sam saw a long-haired boy of eight or nine years. He was wearing tatty shorts and nothing else. He was concentrating only on the can: it went from knee to knee, to foot to head to shoulder to knee. The kid spun round and caught it with his heel, knocked it up to his shoulder again, fed it back to the head and knocked it higher and higher, jumping now to get the can two, then three metres, up off his head. He brought it down to his knee, raised it up and suddenly – just as you'd got used to the momentum – he flung himself on the ground, slashing in an overhead kick. The can came at you like a missile, your hands flew to your face. It struck the camera lens and the film jarred for a moment. Then it was back on the boy's feet and this time he was dribbling a football. Sam wiped his eyes quickly: this was ball-control as he'd dreamed of it.

The boy's feet leaped and hopped, blurred in the air, and the football zig-zagged as if it was alive. Alive, but on a wire, it scribbled in the air, those feet conducting it upwards and sideways. It was gone; it was there; it was still; it was snatched away in a blur of brown legs. Sanchez was trying to tackle the boy, but stood no chance. There was laughter, there was wrestling, but still the magic feet kept the ball and kept it moving.

'No . . .' breathed Sam. He had to close his eyes: the light was too bright. He was in the lion's mouth again.

Sanchez returned and by this time the whole audience was pressing close to the screen in stunned silence. Sanchez was sitting on a wall and the footballing boy was sitting next to him. Both wore the bright, wasp colours of the new Ribblestrop kit. The little footballer looked self-conscious, smiling at his toes, peeping at the camera.

'This is Imagio,' said Sanchez, putting his arm round the boy.

Imagio grinned and said, 'Hul-lo,' shyly.

'And this is the surprise. I hope it's OK if I say it? My father phoned our headmaster a little time ago, OK? He asked if Imagio could come to the school, 'cause he doesn't go to school out here.'

'Yes,' whispered the children.

'And we were told, *yes*. So . . . we got Imagio a blazer. And he's been having English lessons and he's really good – aren't you?'

Imagio had covered his face with his hands.

'So we want you guys to be good and train hard. I mean, we are the best school, so that's not a problem. But we are going to have the best football team as well in the whole country!'

The children couldn't contain themselves any more: Anjoli was yelling and jumping up and down; Israel was simply screaming, 'Yes! Yes!' over and over again.

As if he knew, Sanchez spoke up. His voice was loud, his gaze firm: 'A few days, OK? I know we got a lot on, with nature study and stuff. But, Captain – you keep two places for us, yes? This term is gonna be . . .' The noise was deafening. 'The best!' were his final words, but nobody heard them. Imagio waved self-consciously and then, as if he could stand the formality no longer, he put a hand over his friend's mouth and threw himself backwards off the wall. Sanchez disappeared in a flurry of legs.

The movie finished.

'By remarkable coincidence,' said the headmaster, once he'd got silence, 'the High School coach telephoned me this afternoon.' He unfolded a paper carefully and cleared his throat. 'First game of the season. Tuesday, three weeks hence, at eleven o'clock in the morning. Here at Ribblestrop.'

'Quiet . . .' said Routon.

'We have a lot to do this term! Boys! Listen! Stay where you are!'

There was no stopping them, though. Every child moved as one and the headmaster found that he was no longer standing on the podium. He was in a forest of hands, and those hands were lifting him higher and carrying him. The school song rose again, the voices soaring. No choir could have matched that passion. It was a wonder the roof stayed on. There were harmonies. There were soaring descants. Every voice was trumpeting:

> 'Ribblestrop, Ribblestrop, precious unto me;
> This is what I dream about and where . . .
> I want . . .
> To be . . .'

The new term had started.

Chapter Nine

Ribblestrop's Inspector of Police, Percy Cuthbertson, had recently been promoted. According to the official report, he had shown *exceptional courage in an undercover situation*. He had saved the day and been sung as a hero. A number of important people – for reasons far too complicated to go into here – had worked together to protect him from the suggestion that he was, in fact, corrupt, dangerous, and motivated only by personal greed. He was now the county's Deputy Chief Constable. He had been given a new uniform, with bright buttons and extra-large epaulettes, and he had a fine office on the ninth floor of city headquarters. He had his own coffee machine, his own sofa, and mint-edition copies of *Policeman's Weekly*. He had a personal assistant in a sub-office outside who didn't mind calling him Deputy Chief Constable every time she spoke.

When you consider these triumphs, you might assume that D.C.C. Cuthbertson's interest in Ribblestrop Towers would now be at an end. You might have thought that it would hold only painful and embarrassing memories, and that he'd avoid the place.

You'd have been wrong.

D.C.C. Cuthbertson had, for a long time, known things

about the school that he hoped would make him wealthy. He'd been researching its secrets for more than a year, noting the rumours and filing reports. If Ribblestrop Towers was the honey-pot, then D.C.C. Cuthbertson was the desperate, dangerous wasp that would never stop circling it. Soon, he hoped to make another move.

It was unfortunate that the officer had so little to do, and that his new title was simply a way of keeping him idle. He had time to imagine all kinds of revenge for the humiliations he'd received, and he would sometimes sit at his desk smiling at the wall for ten or twelve minutes at a time. He'd refused to give up his old office at Ribblestrop Police Station, insisting that one day he might need it again. As he was the only one with keys, there wasn't much his underlings could do.

On this particular Thursday morning, he was in private conference. He sat with his elbows on the desk, and in front of him, just as hunched – nursing chapped, swollen hands – sat an elderly man disguised as a priest: Father O'Hanrahan. The two men had known each other for many years – policeman and convict.

'It doesn't surprise me,' growled Cuthbertson.

'Then it might have been nice to receive warning,' said the man opposite.

'What I mean is, *nothing* surprises me. I'm not saying I predicted exactly what they'd do to you. There is nothing about that school or the fool who runs it that could ever surprise me again. I learned the hard—'

'I have also learned the hard way!' said Father O'Hanrahan.

Cuthbertson smiled. 'My wife put her finger on it,' he said. 'She said, "You underestimated them, Percy," and she was right. But I tell you something else: they had luck on their side and that's going to turn. You know about this?' He waved some documents. 'Came in yesterday – a full report from Taunton. Black-and-gold blazers in a Travellers' Sleepeasy – before the night's out, the place is on fire. An articulated lorry carving up the traffic, smashing up a road-side cafeteria – and what's at the wheel? A black-and-gold blazer. Vandalism, intimidation, and carnage. I tell you what: they're on borrowed time.'

'Why aren't you arresting them, then? They're living it up at school thinking they've got away with it!'

'Ah, but it's not my patch. All that happened in Somerset.' Cuthbertson leaned further forward and lowered his voice. 'But it's all going into that safe,' he whispered. 'Every shred of evidence I get, I put it in the file. I lock it up at night and I tell you something – that headmaster's got a shock coming. Every crime, every mistake, every accident he has . . . When I get him, it won't be for a traffic violation. It will be for the whole catalogue! That school will close and he'll do ten to fifteen years. I know prison officers and that man will suffer.'

'I can't believe the school is still open. From what I've seen in the last few days, all they do is have parties.'

'You'll see a lot more yet.'

'You could close it today, man! There's no discipline, no care. I don't believe they're even qualified to teach! And the zoo animals!'

'Give them the rope – they'll hang themselves.'

'But if you closed them down *now*, it would make the job so much easier! We could get people in, turn the place upside down—'

'Oh no, no! Listen. If that school closes, you won't have any business on the premises, will you? The only reason you're in there is because you have a job to do. No school, no chaplain. If the old woman died, it would be a different story, but—'

'Why?'

'When she dies, all the leases automatically come to an

70

end – everything would close down and then it would be easy. We'd get the Brethren out and we could take our time . . .' He paused. 'In any case, they've got an H.O. And you can't touch someone with a government H.O. I've been told that, in no uncertain terms.'

'An H.O. is what? A health order?'

'Hands Off. It's an official *leave-them-alone-at-all-costs, we-don't-want-any-more-bad-publicity*. They could turn cannibal and eat each other and we'd have to stand back – especially me. That's why we go gently and that's why you're so important. How's the boy?'

Father O'Hanrahan looked blank.

'Whatsisname, the youngster you brought over? Is he going to help us?'

'Doonan? He's an idiot.'

'Then what did you bring him for? I told you –'

'They wanted a younger chaplain! It was all a big compromise. Doonan had just failed his exams, the college didn't want him –'

'So how's he doing?'

'He's loving it. He's been there a week and thinks it's wonderful!'

The policeman struggled to stay calm. 'So it's just the two of us, is it? Have you told him anything?'

'He knows nothing. So yes: it's just the two of us.'

'Have you spoken to the Brethren?'

'Not yet.'

Father O'Hanrahan squirmed with embarrassment and the blood rose in his face.

The two men stared at each other and dislike crackled between them.

'The Brethren,' said Father O'Hanrahan, 'are on a vow of silence. Which doesn't end till July. The timing could not be worse.'

'You mean they won't speak a word? Not even to you?'

'No.'

'What about pencil and paper?'

'A vow of silence is a devout act in which you commit to prayer and meditation. It is undertaken precisely to avoid communication on . . . external matters. To make things worse, they are very hard to track down – they run like rabbits.'

'But your disguise! I thought you'd be on the same side!'

'They see me as an outsider! I visited the chapel on the first morning – despite my . . . injuries! I was *not* made welcome. The crypt has been bricked up, so there's no way down. The monks are protective and I'm not even sure they believe my credentials. They closed the door in my face!' The old man looked around and lowered his voice. 'They see themselves as *guardians*, I think. They've been tracking this thing for years. They obviously believe they're close, or why would they stay there?'

'They're close all right.'

'What about Lady Vyner – surely she knows about it?'

'No. They hardly spoke to each other. She thinks everything was sold – which is what everyone thought.'

'Well, getting anything up is going to be nigh-on impossible. The kids are everywhere – you turn a corner and they're poking around. And your people didn't help, blocking up every staircase.'

'They weren't my people. And there must be many ways down still!'

'Have you not seen the old air vent, under the monument? Twenty tonnes of rock and a thousand gallons of concrete! That's a fairly successful way of blocking up a tunnel!'

Again, the two men looked at each other in silence, the D.C.C. chewing his lip. At length, the policeman rose, and fished a key out of his pocket. It was on a chain, stitched into his tunic. He moved to the safe, fiddled a moment, and swung the door back. Papers, box-files, envelopes – something wrapped in brown paper. And, on the middle shelf, in total contrast, a bottle of red wine.

Father O'Hanrahan looked at it.

'I said I had some news,' said the policeman. 'I'd better let you have it.'

'Is it good news?'

'It's very, very interesting. Are you still a drinking man, Father?' The policeman smiled grimly. 'I remember you enjoying the old communion booze after hours.'

'I am strictly teetotal. And you do not need to call me *Father* – I was a priest for a very short time.'

'I still think the title suits you and the disguise is perfect. I was hoping you'd taste this rather special bottle for me and give me your educated opinion as an ex-alcoholic.'

Cuthbertson took a glass from a shelf. The cork had been loosened, so he flicked it out and poured himself a small measure. Then he set both bottle and glass on his desk, before O'Hanrahan. 'Clos de Beze, nineteen hundred and four – produce of Burgundy. In nineteen hundred and four the vineyard reached its peak, I believe. That year, they made less than a thousand barrels, and half the bottles were laid down. For thirty-eight years. Are you following me, Father? You look confused.'

'I was a spirits man, I know nothing about fine wines.'

'If a winemaker knows he's on to something special, the bottles are *laid down*. Put in the cellar, untouched, and left to mature. The wine gets better and the value rises. It's like an investment: once the wine peaks, you bring it up and sell it. Now this particular wine was saved from destruction by a friend of ours . . . the ever-successful Cyril Vyner. He stole it from the vineyards as the German army moved up through France. It's been in his cellars ever since.'

Cuthbertson stopped and lifted the glass. He took it to the window and held it up to the light: the soft liquor glowed, ruby red. 'I don't drink the stuff, either,' he said. 'I wouldn't know a Burgundy from my own backside. But I have to say . . .' He sipped. 'This is good stuff. Even I'd go to church if they were serving this. No, listen, Father – I'm getting to the point, but you need a bit of back-story. This wine would sell for close on a thousand pounds, just this one bottle. There are people out there who'd pay that kind of money.'

He sipped again and smiled. 'And there's a shopkeeper in the Ribblestrop off-licence with a constant supply. Had a bottle a week for the last five months. Where do you think he's getting it from?'

'From the school,' said Father O'Hanrahan. 'From the cellars underground.'

'You'll make a detective yet.'

'He's found a way in. What else has he found?'

'Ah, you're right about the first part – but he's not been down himself. Somebody else is going down for him. Somebody has accessed the Vyner wine cellars, and that somebody has been bringing this stuff up, bottle by bottle.'

'Who?'

'Can't you guess?'

'One of the children?' cried the priest. 'One of the teachers? If they've found the wine, God knows what else they've found! We should be moving! Will you not just tell me what you know and get it over with?'

'I'll tell you everything, Father – don't get excited.'

'But what if they've found . . . what we're looking for?'

'Wait! Shh!'

The priest had turned the colour of the wine. He was licking his lips and it was only with enormous self-control that he stayed in his seat. From outside the window rose the sound of traffic and, in the distance, the laughter of children. He forced himself to relax.

'This off-licence chap got into a few problems,' said Cuthbertson. He looked out of the window, distracted by the excited chatter from below. 'He's been caught selling liquor to kids – easy to do, they all look eighteen. But he's about to lose his shop, because the magistrate says it's happened once too often. So. He comes to me: can I pull any strings? And he tells me . . .'

The policeman faltered. Something in the street had caught his eye.

'What?' said the priest.

'He tells me . . . I don't believe it. About a little boy with long hair . . . This is incredible.'

'What's the matter, man?'

'Talk of the devil and the devil shall appear. I'm looking at him – he's on the pavement, over the road. A boy called Tomaz.'

Father O'Hanrahan struggled to his feet and moved next to Cuthbertson. Drawing the curtains back further, they peered down onto the narrow high street of Ribblestrop Town – a high street that hadn't been widened or bypassed, so that trucks still shouldered their way through, forcing the pedestrians to walk in strict single file. There, on the opposite side of the road, was a column of black-and-gold blazers, with a cheerful youth in the lead.

'It's Doonan!' hissed the old man. 'He's brought them into town. I told you he was enjoying himself and he's brought the little monsters into town!'

Chapter Ten

Sure enough, Brother Doonan was leading, the children behind him trying to hold his hands whilst imitating his walk. Captain Routon brought up the rear, steadying a giant of a boy who seemed nervous to be in the open air. This was Henry, who'd arrived that very morning, crammed into the same uniform as everyone else, but looking like he should be working in a quarry or a wrestling ring. They moved purposefully along and their birdsong chatter floated up loud and clear.

'I'll be damned,' whispered Cuthbertson. 'They usually stay in school – this is the first time they've been allowed out!'

'They're not safe to be in a public place. Especially with Doonan in charge!'

'I don't like it. Look, though! I can show you Tomaz. Halfway down, maybe a bit more. There's a boy with long hair, tied back.'

'That's a girl.'

'Behind the girl! Ooh, I could tell you a few things about her! Look at her.'

'I met her first of all. Minnie Roads.'

'Her name is *Millie* and I came so close. If I have another chance, she'll be dead meat, you understand me?' His voice had fallen to a low, menacing rumble. He was holding the curtain, mashing it with his fingers.

Father O'Hanrahan looked at him nervously. 'She seemed disrespectful to me. She—'

'I nearly drowned her. I just pray we'll meet again. Dammit, she's seen me – step back! This is bad . . .'

The two men drew the curtains across, as swiftly as they could. They put their eyes to the narrow slit that remained. 'We don't want her seeing us together, that would be fatal. But look – can you see behind her?' He found himself whispering. 'Behind the one who's just fallen over – the one with the snowball.'

'Got him. He's been cooking my breakfast. I thought he was a servant.'

'He's not a servant. That boy's called Tomaz and I believe—'

'Tomaz? One of the foreigners?'

'He was the first orphan they brought over. He ran away, and for a number of weeks everyone thought he'd gone back to wherever he'd come from. What he'd done, I reckon, was moved down to the tunnels. He's the one who found the underground bunker, so I believe he's found the wine cellar.'

'He's no more than ten years old!'

'He's older than he looks. The shopkeeper says he's a smooth little operator. That child has been sneaking up after dark with a bottle of fancy wine each week. He's been exchanging it for cash and bits and pieces . . . The wine-merchant thinks he was building a den. Said he even tried to follow him home once, but that the lad was too quick. Then a few months ago, it all stopped.'

'Why?'

'I don't know.'

'Then all we have to do is talk to him. Bring him in for questioning!'

The children were turning right and Tomaz was about to disappear.

The priest grabbed Cuthbertson's arm. 'Go and get him!' he cried. 'You're a policeman, you can do what you want! He's been dealing in *stolen goods*, you could arrest him!'

'And do what?'

'Put him in that chair! Beat it out of him!'

As he spoke, there was a terrific thump on the window and the sound of a whip cracking across the glass. Cuthbertson jerked back, the curtain ripped from its rail. Father O'Hanrahan yelped with shock and stumbled over his chair. A large, icy snowball was sliding to the sill. Water droplets oozed between the broken glass, which had a crescent-shaped crack from top to bottom. Both men gaped.

Half crouched on the opposite pavement, forming another snowball, was the familiar form of Millie Roads. Beside her, Anjoli was punching the air and dancing.

The second snowball came with a handful of small stones and spread watery muck all over the policeman's desk. He dragged the remaining curtain closed, gasping in fury. Both men stood, helplessly, waiting for the next assault.

A minute passed and it didn't come.

'I told you,' whispered Cuthbertson. His voice was shaking. 'I told you, five minutes ago: there's an H.O. and my feet would not touch the ground! I survived the last . . . *fiasco* by the skin of my teeth, I am not taking any risks! They can do what they please!'

'But if a boy's found a way into the stores . . .' hissed O'Hanrahan. 'If he's got his hands on —'

'Nothing else has come up! I've spoken to every shopkeeper in the town. This is not an emergency yet. We still have time.'

He turned away from the window and moved to the other side of the office. He was trembling.

Father O'Hanrahan leaned against the desk, his head and shoulders sagging.

'I don't think the boy knows what he's sitting on,' said Cuthbertson. He drank the rest of the wine and poured another large glass. 'He probably hasn't found the full set of chambers – I'd been looking for months and that's when I had full access to the tunnels. But if we could find how he gets down, I'm sure we'd be close.'

'A secret way . . .' said the priest.

'It might be a little hole up in the woods. A little foxhole, that only a child could use. If we could find that, then we'd be making progress. This is your job, O'Hanrahan!'

'How? They all stick together, that's one thing I've observed. And they don't like talking to me!'

'Then you have to get close to them. That's why you're here.'

The two men stared at each other.

'Worm your way into their confidence. Be nice to them.'

Father O'Hanrahan closed his eyes. 'Look,' he said. 'I'd better be honest. I've never been good with children and this lot are impossible. I can pretend to be a chaplain, but to spend time with the little swine, listening to their disrespectful blather!'

'There's so much at stake, man! It's what you came to do!'

'I don't have the patience and they don't like me!'

'*Learn* patience! *Make* them like you!' Cuthbertson was pleading and his fists were clenched. 'Try and befriend them,' he said softly. 'Especially Tomaz . . .'

The priest stood in silence, chewing his lip. 'They need a . . . housemaster,' he said, weakly. 'The headmaster was saying the other day how he wanted someone to live in with the foreign boys. They have a disgusting dormitory and he wants someone to sort it out.' He paused again. 'What if I told him I'd do it?'

'He'd be delighted, wouldn't he?'

'The thought of sharing a room with that lot, though!' The old man shuddered.

'Think what's at stake,' said Cuthbertson. 'If we pull this one off, we'll never have to work again. We'll be out of here forever.'

'I'll do it. I'll talk to the Tomaz boy – leave it with me.'

Chapter Eleven

What were the children doing walking along Ribblestrop High Street?

A week had passed – and a week at Ribblestrop was like several months in most schools. *No time to sleep!* had been on the school-motto shortlist, and though it had been rejected, it contained an undeniable truth . . . there was never enough time.

Flavio had parked his truck by the crumbling outbuildings round the back of the school. A term of nature study was to be adapted to a term of zoology and circus skills, so most of the timetable was abandoned in favour of construction work and football practice. The warmest barn had been given to Violetta and the lorry-cab had been parked close to it, so Flavio could be next to her. The camel was given a small, roofless paddock as he seemed to enjoy the snow. Interestingly, the school donkeys had found him and now spent a lot of their time in the same paddock, nuzzling. The python had been coaxed back to his aquarium, which moved to the orphans' dormitory in the east tower, along with the possibly-dead scorpion and the parrots. The parrots were not as ill as they had been pretending to be and soon perked up when Podma made a batch of rum truffles. This left the

81

big cats and a crocodile, and Flavio kept them in the trailer for the time being. Heaters and lights were installed, and the orphans began welding up some grilles for a proper exercise yard.

Flavio was happier than he had been for years.

Captain Routon found him a fridge and the headmaster was more than happy to open an account with the local butcher. Fresh meat was delivered daily, so the immediate crisis was over.

Millie had a new home as well, since her dormitory-shed had been burned down the previous term. It was a small classroom and the desks had been stacked against one wall. The store-cupboard in the corner had been converted to a bathroom, and a large sign saying *Girls Only* had been pinned over the glass panels in the door. She was not sure whether to be furious or relieved that she was still the only female student, and she remained extremely confused by her new title. The Head Girl badge now gleamed in the lapel of her blazer, though she despised herself for putting it there. She told herself that she would see exactly what privileges the new role gave her and balance them against any possible duties. So far there seemed to be none of either, but it was early days.

A tuck shop and a bank had opened, which was truly exciting. These innovations had been promised for some time, and Ruskin in particular was delighted as he yearned to keep his cash safe. He had paid the food bill at the Traveller's Sleepeasy; he had left the fifty pounds for the smashed burger van. He was so relieved to pass his remaining banknotes across the counter and know that it was, at last, in an account that Millie couldn't raid.

Both bank and tuck shop were to be non-profit-making and were in the hands of the three youngest orphans, who were learning to count, and therefore very diligent. At present, the tuck shop only sold a small selection of sweets and the items that Tomaz and Captain Routon cooked – but expansion was planned. The three shopkeepers had a home-made abacus and a set of old ledgers. From the first day, they demonstrated extraordinary business sense. The displays were mouthwatering and there were all sorts of inventive sales tactics, from buy-one, take-one, to a complicated credit system with sliding scales of interest according to how much you bought. Every child in the school was issued with a cheque book and a credit card (all handmade in thick yellow-and-black paper). The orphans-in-charge made endless notes and the clicking of beads often went on till well after midnight.

However, the children were ambitious and there were many things that could not be handmade or fashioned from scrap.

The concept of a Ribblestrop Speech Day circus had spread like a fire, and big plans were instantly conceived. The children needed a tent; they needed a second generator and a lighting system. They needed sawdust, pulley-systems for the opening cages, trapezes, and harnesses. Everyone wanted to buy proper cable and wire, as Flavio had been talking of his tightrope-walking days. His cannon stories had been told and retold: clearly, pipes and explosives would be needed. Meanwhile, in the evenings, Oli, Ruskin, and Sam returned to their hobby and started to sketch Millie's radio-controlled submarine – they were itching to get started. Everyone needed specialised equipment and the shopping list reached twenty pages.

One morning, Captain Routon strode into Doonan's R.E. classroom, the lists in his hand. 'Auction rooms,' he said.

Doonan didn't mind the interruption. He didn't find class control easy, and always struggled to make himself heard over the children's excitement. There was a large question on the blackboard: IS THERE A GOD? and it had provoked heated debate. Anjoli had ended up on the floor with Sanjay sitting on his chest, and most of the desks were on their sides, the children standing on them, cheering.

'Auction rooms, Captain?' he said.

The children looked up from the fight, silent and hopeful.

'In town,' he said. 'I should have thought of it before. The second Thursday of each month, there's a general-items auction. It's where we got half our stuff to start the school – it's a treasure trove! Whatever you need, you'll find it in the auction. And what's today?' he cried.

'Thursday!' chorused the children.

'And it starts at ten o'clock. So let's look lively! Get those caps on!'

It was another bright, cold day and it had snowed again overnight. Every child was ready in five minutes. Ties were straightened, blazers were buttoned, and Brother Doonan led the way. For some reason, the youngest orphans had bonded immediately with him, and Doonan wasn't sure whether to be flattered or embarrassed. They liked to hold his hands, and if fingers weren't available, they'd hold his coat. When he'd spoken at the first-night party, they'd gasped at his accent and now tried to copy it.

His popularity had been sealed forever, however, on the second night. He had visited the east tower dormitory, home to the whole orphan clan. He'd offered to read a bed-time story and was greeted with hushed wonder. A huge armchair was found and he was wrapped in a blanket. Sanjay produced cocoa and Doonan read the beginning of *The Snow Queen*, since it was snowing heavily again and a mournful wind was snaking round the tower. He came back the next night and read on. Podma cooked sweets, the parrots clucked and muttered, and Eric gave him a pair of

Himalayan-wool slippers. Even the python came close and sat on its coils as if listening.

Doonan returned on the third night to complete the tale, and – perhaps unwisely – Anjoli laced the young man's cocoa with rum. It was meant as an honour and a treat, but Doonan wasn't as used to it as the boys, so he was soon snoring, the story still unfinished. The orphans banked up their stove and carried the snoring Doonan over to it in his chair. Thus, the orphans' dormitory became Doonan's and the chair became his bed.

'Single file!' he called, as they prepared to set off that morning. The younger boys imitated him. 'When we get to town, you let members of the public pass and you raise your caps. Hush now, please! There'll be a house point for the politest boy and a sweet—'

The line galloped off over the snow. It took a good forty minutes to reach the school gates because there had to be so many ambushes and slides along the way. When they got to the road, they realised they'd be late for the 'viewing time' if they didn't run, so Doonan led a brisk canter all the way to the high street.

The auction rooms did not disappoint.

They were a magical mixture of rubbish dump and fairy grotto. Farm equipment, furniture, old clothes, mysterious boxes. Cookers, picture-frames, rugs, roller-skates, fire-irons, walkie-talkies – and the glorious thing was you could pick it all up and play with it. In fact, there were elderly porters encouraging you to do just that. Sam and Oli found radio gear immediately, which was perfect for the hobby they were so longing to develop. Asilah was led out back to a job lot of old iron-railings. Beyond this was a pile of scout tents from a troop that had given up camping. It was as if the auctioneers had assembled all the stuff in the world you needed to excite schoolchildren and said, 'Welcome, Ribblestrop Towers.'

'Millie!' said Captain Routon.

Millie turned guiltily. She was in the middle of buttoning Anjoli into a clown suit, to go with a bald wig he'd found. An amateur dramatics company had closed down and was selling off its wardrobe. The captain was beckoning her.

'You've got your head screwed on,' he said, once she was next to him. 'Come and look at this. Give me your advice . . .'

They walked with one of the porters to a storeroom just off the main hall. It was full of old bicycles.

'They'll need a bit of oil, some of them,' said the porter. 'But they'll go for a song.'

'They're ancient,' said Millie.

'Would we ever use them?' said the captain. 'When I was a kid, we loved nothing more than a good old cycle ride! But youngsters today . . .'

'No,' said Millie. 'They're clapped out. No one's going to ride things like that.'

She was interrupted by Anjoli. He had slunk in, under the captain's arm, and he was gripping that arm with all his excited strength. His eyes were glittering and his mouth was open.

'*Please*!' he hissed. 'Please buy them!'

The hammer came down.

The auctioneer got tired of saying, 'Gone to the gentleman in the black-and-gold blazer!' The wonderful thing was that none of the general public seemed to want anything that the Ribblestrop children wanted. The bikes, for example – all twelve of them – went for three pounds, and that was only because a deaf farmer wiped his eye at a crucial moment.

At the end of the morning's work, the children were drunk with happiness and shopping. The stuff would be delivered, later – it would take several trucks – but it was obvious that they'd cycle home.

Asilah did the sorting and soon the flotilla sailed out into the high street. Most riders were unsteady. Israel, for example, had never ridden, and as he had his brother on the crossbar and his cousin on his back, progress was bound to be slow.

The traffic stopped. It had no choice and the spectacle was so extraordinary the entire town seemed to seize up. The children did their best to raise their caps, which caused several pile-ups. They rang their bells almost constantly.

As they sailed back past the police station, Henry was last in line, on a bike that looked like a toy beneath him. They turned left at the lights, down a gentle slope – a flock of birds tinkling towards the snowy fields.

Behind them, a car braked sharply, the driver leaning on the horn. It was a bright red Porsche and it was itching to get past. The children moved over and it accelerated off in a burst of snowy gravel. Only Tomaz recognised the grinning face that peered out of its passenger window. He saw the hand waving and he promptly fell off his bike. He recognised the eyes, but he knew that it had to be a hallucination. The eyes had shone and a hand had pushed back long, floating hair. Tomaz lay in the snow, blinking with wonder, as the boy got the window down. He was leaning out of it, waving harder and shouting – and it looked just like his old friend! It was the image of ex-Ribblestrop pupil and expelled arsonist, Miles Seyton-Shandy – the same hair, the same voice . . .

It couldn't be true! Tomaz lay in the snow knowing that it could not be true. The school would never agree to re-admit Miles – no school would ever take him – because . . .

Because Miles was insane.

Chapter Twelve

In the south tower, Lady Vyner was putting on her coat.

'You delivered my letter?' she said to her grandson.

'Yes.'

'You gave it to the headmaster? In person?'

'Yes, Gran.'

'No reply, of course,' she muttered. 'No manners. No discipline.'

'They're too busy playing with the animals. This place is a zoo!'

'Totally, completely illegal – it breaks every rule and he will pay for it. He's late with the rent again and he thinks I don't know why. It's because he's spending every penny on a circus! Every clause in his contract, broken in a week! What's that noise?'

Caspar went to the window. 'Bicycle bells,' he said, with a sneer. 'And there's a posh car down there too.'

'I'll give him bicycle bells. I'm seeing my lawyers next Thursday – he won't have a leg to stand on! The worst school in the world . . .'

'So why have I got to go to it?'

Caspar was also wearing a black-and-gold blazer.

'Because we can't afford anything better, Caspar!' She

stared at him, rigid with dislike. 'How many more times? You don't pay fees, so you might as well get some crumbs of an education. Instead of sitting there all day getting more stupid!' The old lady shuffled over to her shoes and kicked her feet into them.

Moments later, Lady Vyner clumped off down the stairs. She'd booked an interview at two o'clock and it was her habit to be utterly punctual. She had two solicitor's letters in her hand. The first listed a week's worth of complaints; the second was an aggressive threat of instant prosecution and it had a big, red seal on the envelope.

Turning the final curve of the staircase, she emerged slightly dizzy into a connecting corridor. The light was dim and there was ice on the windows; she put her hands deep in her pockets and struggled on in the gloom. Somewhere off to the right, she became aware of running feet. In fact, they were pounding, getting louder and louder, and a shrill shriek was gathering force and volume. The bicycle bells were getting nearer too and she snarled with irritation. Cycling inside the building! It was just the kind of nonsense she hated most. So – bracing herself and getting ready to grab whatever child was hurtling towards her – she stepped round the corner, right hand upraised.

She was just in time to be knocked, reeling, into an oil painting. Lady Vyner saw a blur of grey shirt spin and zoom off. It seemed to flip and was all hands and feet, zipping down the corridor. The picture she'd dislodged came away from the wall and she was pressed to the floor under its weight.

The boy – half child, half jet – careered onwards, engines roaring. Then the bicycle bells tinkled past unseen.

The headmaster heard the howl as well and a small shock of memory jarred his bones. He stood up, putting a half-eaten cup-cake down on a plate. He removed his glasses as the shriek got louder. Then the door was flung open and he was looking into the wild eyes of the wildest boy he'd ever known.

Miles braked and skidded. He hovered. He panted for breath then stretched out his arms. His face transformed into a delighted smile and the engine-screech reached a new level of happiness.

The headmaster backed away in fear, hands upraised, and Miles leaped forward. He bear-hugged the headmaster, harder and tighter than ever before.

'Sir,' he was shouting. 'Sir! I'm back!'

'Miles!' cried the headmaster. 'No!'

He was crushed against the wall and the window. The frame was rusty and the catch broken – in a moment he was being forced out over the sill.

'Sir, thank you, sir – thank you! You are the best!'

'No, Miles! Please!' The headmaster felt a rush of cold air. He got an arm free and grabbed at the masonry, and a lump of stone came away in his hand. 'Please!' His feet weren't on the floor.

'You are my best friend! I am so, so different! You won't believe it!'

'Miles! I'm falling! Help me!'

The headmaster tried to break the boy's grip, but Miles was strong as twisted wire. He hugged his old teacher and it was only by a superhuman effort that the elderly man managed to wrench himself back to safety. He fell against his desk and the lamp buckled under him in a tinkle of broken glass.

'I thought you'd kicked me out,' said Miles, tearfully. 'I thought I was sacked!'

The headmaster couldn't speak. Broken glasses dropped out of his pocket. He was shaking, trying to breathe. He managed to get to the other side of the desk, but Miles followed him round.

'No second chance,' cried Miles. 'That's what you said, and Mum was just crying and crying . . . but then we got your letter, like you changed your mind at the last minute, and by that time we were out of the country . . .' Miles had him by the hand and was shaking it. 'It got forwarded to her office and when we read it! Wow! We just burst into tears, both of us!'

'Miles —'

The boy pushed back his hair and clutched a pair of torn shirt-cuffs together, as if at prayer. 'Mother said the first thing I had to do was write to you and say sorry – but then we got stuck on this island, so she said the first thing I had to do, to *say*, I mean, was I am so sorry!'

'Sit down, Miles – please. Let's have a —'

'Do you forgive me? I got you a present.'

The headmaster was breathing hard. Miles was fumbling in his shorts' pocket, and after a moment of searching, withdrew, amongst sweet-wrappers and tiny toy soldiers, an apple-sized lump, in tissue paper.

'It's a shrunken head,' he said. 'From the island we were on; they were selling them and they are totally real. I put it in our maid's bed, on the pillow, wearing this little T-shirt, and she went completely crazy, but I know you love stuff like this, so . . .' He unwrapped it and put it on the desk. 'Mum and I call him Gilbert.'

The headmaster managed to get back into his chair and sat staring. The little head looked as amazed as he did – it had to be some kind of nut or fruit, it couldn't be human. He tore his eyes away and looked at Miles. The boy was grinning, eagerly, and the headmaster – through the trauma of the embrace – was filled with an aching tenderness.

The child wore the regulation grey shirt, but it was three sizes too big and torn already, the collar round his ears. Two buttons at most were done up – the rest were missing; the tie was loose, the sleeves flapped, and the cuffs were gnawed and frayed. Miles drew the shirt around him like a shawl and peered from under a fringe of hair that was desperately in need of combing and cutting. In his chair he was a coiled spring – the energy was flammable, rising in waves . . .

'I've changed,' said Miles, softly. 'I am a different person now – and I've got a shrink in London too.'

The headmaster licked his lips and tried to find words. Why Miles had set fire to the dining hall was still a mystery, and he knew that he would never unpick the complexities of that strange, desperate little psyche. He realised in an instant how much he had missed him. It was for boys such as Miles that Ribblestrop had been conceived! A school of second, third, infinite chances . . .

Dr Norcross-Webb sighed. 'I'm just very glad to see you,' he said. 'Welcome home.'

'I tell you, I am so *not* the same,' cried Miles, standing up. He was breathing hard. 'I've had counselling – I've had so much work done on my head. I am going to be your best, *best* pupil. I passed them on the drive, by the way. Where's Sanchez, though?' He was at the window, pushing it wider.

'Delayed, but on his way . . .'

'Tomaz!' Miles shrieked. He was waving again. Then he gathered the snow from the sill and started to pack it. 'Ruskin! It's me! Look out below!'

'Miles, please! Come away from there . . .'

Miles turned, the snowball ready. 'I wrote to him, but he didn't reply. Where d'you get the bikes? There's loads of kids now! Oh, and where am I sleeping?'

'Miles, we have to go slow . . . The first thing is that I need to speak to your mother. We're going to put you on a *contract of behaviour*, so everyone knows what to expect. We need to establish a few ground rules and then –'

Miles turned again and threw the snowball hard. 'Tomaz!' he shouted. 'Get up here!'

'Giles,' said a voice. 'I can hear you but I can't see you . . . Oh my, now I can! Look at you!'

The headmaster stood up and peered. Without his glasses, everything was blurred. In the doorway there seemed to be a fire of red and gold, and from it came a smoky, transatlantic voice. Miles's mother seemed poised on a catwalk, a tangle of blonde hair strewn over one shoulder, wild as her son's. Peeling her gloves off she came closer, and the silk turned from crimson to wild vermilion as she came into focus, offering a long, slim hand. The headmaster wondered for an absurd moment if this was Miles's sister rather than his mother – she was thinner and younger. Above him, two parrots found their voices and cackled in appreciation.

'You have got more handsome, Giles,' said Miles's mother. 'Damn you, but you've turned into a *distinguished gentleman* – not that you weren't beautiful before, but look at that chin. Miles, you can learn even from the way this man *holds* himself.'

'I'm going down! I've just seen Tom!'

'Mrs Seyton-Shandy. It's lovely to see you. I was just saying to Miles—'

'And your school is blooming in the snow . . . Come here, you!' She grabbed her son's arm and started to haul his blazer on. 'It is a picture! We just parked up and there're so many little ones . . . Stay where you are, Miles – look at him.' Her hands were round her son's throat now, folding his collar down, and they stroked upwards to rest on his cheeks. She slid into his chair and drew him onto her lap. 'I hope this little boy has said an important word?' she crooned.

'Well, we haven't really had time—'

'Have you done that, Miles?' Miles was nodding. 'I just hope so and you look a mess again. I buy him new clothes and he turns them into rags, he just tears things up – it's a compulsion – it's a *bad* habit!' She kissed him. 'And I told you not to show him that dreadful thing,' she said, noticing the head. 'We were in the Philippines, on this crazy island – I do not believe it's real, but he's been scaring everyone on the plane. I hope he told you how he's changed?'

'Yes, he did —'

Children were shouting in the corridor and the bicycle bells were now frantic.

'We were on what they call *the island of healing*. We met a man there – some kind of witch-doctor – and he and Miles were like blood-brothers. I tell you, Giles, if you need a man to run meditation classes, I still have his number.'

The headmaster moved quickly to the door, trying to ignore the noise outside. He pressed his back to it and spoke loudly and firmly. 'Mrs Seyton-Shandy, we do have to talk about this.'

'Call me Alia, please, and —'

'Nobody is more delighted than me to see Miles back with us. However, there are a few ground rules that must be discussed.' There was hammering on the door, and cries of 'sir!'

'Rule number one —'

'Money,' said Mrs Seyton-Shandy.

'Money?'

'I'm just thinking, if we get the financial side sorted now, we can do the rest over the telephone. I was supposed to be in Cadiz by lunchtime – they will not stop calling. By the way, we left his trunk in the hallway. I asked the cleaning lady to bring it up, but she looked a little confused.'

'We don't have a cleaning lady.' Hands were now rattling the door.

Miles's mother stood, a brick of banknotes in her hand, and the door finally burst open, knocking the headmaster forwards.

'This is for the year,' she said, but the words were lost in a new din, as orphans nosed in their bikes. A parrot flapped overhead and settled on a crossbeam. It started to imitate the tinkling of a bell at a horrible volume.

'Wait!' cried the headmaster. 'There's one or two things . . .'

Captain Routon was dragging in a box that had split and a hundred ice-skates were skittering over the floor. The papers on the desk lifted and whirled as the parrot dived for the half-eaten cup-cake, and suddenly, a snow-covered Tomaz was clambering over the mess and he and Miles were staring at each other.

'Miles!' cried Tomaz. 'It *is* you, I don't believe it, what are you *doing* here?'

'Tom!' shouted Miles.

They hugged each other and then it was Ruskin's turn. Henry had to be dragged over – he was too shy to approach – and then there were introductions, and Anjoli appeared twirling on a pair of ice-skates, slicing long scratches in the granite floor. The noise was incredible and now there were two parrots, showering crumbs and ringing like telephones.

Even without glasses, the headmaster was able to lip-read Mrs Seyton-Shandy's words: 'I've got to go!'

He called out to her. He tried to get to her, but there were bicycles in the way and more boxes. He struggled after her, but hands were holding his jacket. He tripped, but was held up and turned. Oli was saying something about engines and showing him a spinning propeller. By the time he found the door, Miles's mother had gone and Millie was saying, 'Shall I show him his dorm? Is he with Sanchez?'

Doonan was there, with a child on his shoulders, and there was a large pile of animal dung in the centre of the corridor.

'Giles,' said Professor Worthington, 'can you take a telephone call from Sanchez's father?'

The headmaster tottered back to his window and was just in time to see the red Porsche manoeuvre carefully between three donkeys and a camel, and accelerate away up the drive.

Chapter Thirteen

'I can't believe he never showed you this,' said Miles.

They were climbing into the turret of the boys' dormitory – Millie, Tomaz, Anjoli, Israel, and Miles. Miles was leading. He'd unpacked, had supper, and had spent the entire time talking to anyone who'd listen. Now he clambered from chair, to cupboard, to wardrobe; at the top of the wardrobe he moved the ceiling panel. He pulled down a rope and was soon hauling himself upwards, Millie and the boys close behind.

'This is where we spent all our time,' he said. 'This was the special place, so I guess Sanchez thought it was our secret. This is where I saw the ghost!'

'Here?' said Anjoli. 'It's dark, man, I can't even see you!'

Miles hammered at something with bare fists, and there was a sudden rush of cold air and a great stream of moonlight. There was a tiny door, out onto the parapet.

'I saw him from out here!' said Miles. 'We used to sit out here and talk, Sanchez and me. This was our place, Tomaz too – remember?' He laughed. 'Little Ruskin couldn't climb the rope, but I got Caspar Vyner up here once – ha! I got him to sit up on the edge, I was going to dangle him over, but Sanchez stopped me. Remember that, Tom? Huh?'

The children crawled out and stood together in the freezing wind. Their tower wasn't the highest, but it still afforded a wonderful view. The new roof, the curling drive, the lake with its tiny bridges: the world spread beneath them, in vivid black and white. They could hear the laughter of children, floating past. There was the distant roar of an animal and the flash of welding torches. The rest of the orphans were finishing the cages with Oli.

'We've got to talk, seriously,' said Miles. 'I've done some homework and you are not going to believe what I found out. I saw the ghost twice, alright? I was the one who talked to him. I tell you what, though: we need to talk to him again . . . that ghost is looking after secret stuff. That's why he's here!'

'What stuff?' said Millie.

'Treasure. This place is loaded with treasures, some of them totally, totally priceless. You won't believe it. When is Sanchez getting back? I might wait till he's here. You went to Colombia with him, didn't you?'

'How did you know that?'

'He wrote me a letter. We were best friends, us and Tomaz. It was just the three of us, it was so crazy. I was so happy, Millie. I was going out to Colombia – he wanted me to, but I said –'

'How come you burned the school down?' said Anjoli. 'Why do you burn down a place if you like it so much?'

'That was years ago,' said Miles. 'I was so different. If I tell you a secret, though . . .' He lowered his voice. 'Will you keep it, forever?' He wrapped his blazer around himself, shivering with cold. His hand disappeared into his pocket. It came out with two toy soldiers, which he threw to the ground, then a thin bar of ivory. He pressed a switch and a knife-blade flashed in his hand, long and lethally sharp. He touched it hard to his palm and, before Millie, Tomaz or

98

Anjoli could move, he was showing them a line of oozing blood. His eyes glittered and he let a drop of blood fall on the stonework.

'Give me your hands,' he said, smiling. 'We better take some vows! Swear allegiance, yes?'

'How old are you, Miles?' said Israel.

'What? Thirteen and a half.'

'You thirteen and you're like a baby. This is the kind of baby crap I was doing five years ago.'

Miles stared at him. 'Yes, but Sanchez and I are blood brothers.'

'So what?'

'So you've got to swear to be loyal. Or you can do a dare.'

'We're not into that stuff,' said Millie.

Miles looked at her and his smile widened. He pushed back his hair and peered at the enamel badge on her lapel. 'Ah!' he said, laughing. 'I forgot! You're in charge now, huh? So you've got to be responsible! We could still be a gang, though, if you want.' He leaped to his feet and saluted. 'Protect each other, to the death. By the way, I can do curses too – I was taught. Look at this – can you see this?'

He pulled his sleeve up, revealing a thin forearm. On it, running up and down and side to side, were several scars; when he clenched his fist, they stood out vivid on his pale skin. There were strange blotches of tattoos as well, and Millie thought she could make out a large letter S curling round the boy's elbow.

'You been to prison?' said Anjoli. 'They look like jail tattoos.'

'Someone's been torturing him, I reckon,' said Israel.

Anjoli said something in his own language and both boys spluttered with laughter.

'I did a curse last term,' said Miles, loudly. 'On Caspar Vyner's gran, because of what she said about my mother.

See that one there . . .' He traced a long scar with the point of his knife. 'That means *to the death*. That one there is for *never tell, even under fire.*'

'I'm going,' said Israel. 'This guy's completely cracked.'

Miles grabbed his arm. 'No, wait,' he said. 'You want to hear the secret? I can still tell you and I bet you haven't heard it.'

Israel was moving to the door, though, pushing Anjoli in front of him. 'I think you got a problem you ought to deal with, boy,' he said. 'You've only been here half a day and you're scaring the hell out of me.'

Miles let them go and waited for the door to close. Then he sat down with his back against it and smiled again, eyes closed. 'I am so happy to be back,' he said, softly. 'You're not scared, are you, Millie? Tom?'

Millie looked at him. 'Scared of what?'

'Me.'

Millie shook her head. 'You haven't done any listening, Miles, that's your problem. Do you know what went on here last term?'

'No.'

'Sanchez didn't tell you? In the letter he wrote – *if* he wrote to you . . .'

'He said some stuff, but—'

'When I ran away,' said Tomaz, 'I found the tunnels. The treasure you're talking about – I found it.'

Miles sat forward. 'You found the treasure?'

'My God,' said Millie. 'You've shut him up.'

'I *live* with it,' said Tomaz. 'That's what Millie's talking about. I'm looking after it, down underground.'

Miles opened his mouth, but no words came. His eyes went from Millie to Tomaz, glittering still.

'Tomaz has a house down there,' said Millie. 'It's where the ghost lives – we can show it to you. It's the most beautiful place you've ever been and Lord Vyner's down there too.'

'You found it all!' whispered Miles. He licked his lips and the smile was back. 'Did you ... When you were going through stuff ... Listen. Did you find a sword?' He twisted up, onto his knees.

Tomaz nodded. 'There are six swords,' he said. 'There're suits of armour, there's a lance—'

'The special sword,' said Miles. 'One with diamonds?'

'There's all sorts down there,' said Millie. 'Tomaz has arranged it all: it's a palace. But if we show you, you've got to promise not to be weird about it.'

Miles took Tomaz by the hand and started to laugh. 'This is amazing!' he said. 'People have been looking for this stuff for years! I got a paper here – look at this ...' He searched around in an inside pocket, squirming to locate something. At last he brought out a small piece of card, folded and crumpled. 'You're not going to believe this! When we got back to London and I knew I was coming back, I went to the library, OK? I looked up *Vyner*, and the woman said I should go to a museum, if I was that interested, because I was telling her all about this place. Listen! I told her I'd been to the school, and about those monks, and so she told me about this museum in London. There was a floor where you couldn't go unless you had special permission. But they let me in—'

'Why?' said Millie.

'What do you mean, *why*? They let me in—'

'Why's anyone going to let a scruffy kid like you in? Is this all some fantasy, Miles? Just how screwy *are* you?'

Miles stared at her and grinned again. 'You don't have to believe anything, if you don't want to. But I found out secrets ...' He touched the badge on Millie's blazer. 'You'd better decide whose side you're on, Head Girl, because we are in danger.'

'We don't have sides here,' said Millie. 'And Sanchez is Head Boy, or did he forget to tell you that in his letter?'

'He told me everything.'

'Then you're a liar, because he doesn't even know himself. Don't tell us lies, Miles – we will squash you like a bug.'

'Will you tell us what happened?' said Tomaz, quietly. 'In the museum?'

Miles sat back and unfolded the card.

'OK,' he said. 'I met an old man. Professor C.W. Williams. About a hundred years old, worked at the museum all his life – and I told him all about the school and the ghost.'

'What did he say?' said Tomaz.

Miles pushed his hair back. 'He just kind of looked at me. He didn't interrupt me once, because he was interested. And after I told him, guess what? He said he had studied the Vyner family, and he said Cyril Vyner was not a thief, like some people think. He was not a smuggler, or a crook. According to the man in the museum, he was collecting up all the stuff his family used to own, because the family go back hundreds of years, and Lord Vyner was pulling stuff together. But he was looking for one thing in particular that's been lost for centuries.'

'What?' said Millie. 'What's in the paper you're holding? Get to the point.'

Miles took out a small torch and switched it on. He turned the card around, revealing a handful of lines, in looping, untidy biro.

'That's a kid's writing,' said Millie.

'Course it is,' said Miles. 'I copied it from what the professor showed me. An old manuscript.'

Tomaz peered at it. His reading was improving, but it was still a struggle, so Millie leaned in and read aloud:

'The child knows no fear . . . something.
Lion and . . . limb . . . united in this place;
After the something . . .'

'Lightning,' said Miles.

'I can't read the next bit.'

Miles took his paper back and started again. His voice took on a solemn gravity, as if the words were loaded with wisdom:

'The child knows no fear, if the tiger he rides,
And the sick can be healed through all that must pass;
Lion and lamb, united in this place;
After the lightning and the damaged face.'

'The lion and the lamb is on the school flag,' said Millie. 'It's the school emblem.'

'I know,' said Miles. 'Coincidence, huh? Listen:

St Caspar will come home; in this place he'll be sworn.
So drown the precious sword: from his heart it can't be drawn.'

'Where's it from?' said Tomaz, after a moment of silence. 'You got this in the museum?'

Miles folded the paper up. 'Yes,' he said. 'The most important thing the Vyners ever owned was the sword of a saint. Saint Caspar. The poem goes back a thousand years – it was written in French and this is a translation. The sword was given to the Vyner family, for the crusades. It's priceless and it has to stay here, in the family home.'

He looked up at Tomaz.

'You said you found a sword?'

Tomaz looked at Millie. 'I found six.'

'But is there a special one? Is there one that looks like it's priceless and was made for a saint?'

103

Tomaz paused. 'I don't know,' he said. 'We can go down and look.'

'The old man said it wouldn't be a real, fighting sword: it would be an emblem. It has jewels in it, worth billions.'

'I've not seen anything like that,' said Tomaz. 'But there're rooms I can't get to.'

'Let's go down and start looking,' said Millie.

'Hang on a second,' said Miles. 'Let me tell you something else this professor told me. You know the monks . . . the Brethren? OK . . .' He paused. 'Listen to this – and you can believe me, if you want. The reason they came to Ribblestrop is to guard the sword. There's a curse, I'm dead serious – I know you think I've got a thing about curses, but the man in the museum told me. He said that in the right hands it's good, but in the wrong hands, nothing but bad. It has to stay with the house, but people are looking for it, wanting to – '

'What people?' said Millie.

'A man. Professor Williams had a visit, about a week before I went there. An old guy, asking questions. He had a police letter, saying he was investigating the smuggling of antiques. The professor said it happens every now and then – people pick up the scent, and go looking for it. They never get anywhere, but he said this guy was desperate.'

'For what?'

'To find it, I imagine. It's priceless!'

'I wish Sanchez was here,' said Tomaz. 'I've been living down there for such a long time, and now you've got me scared. You think we should look for it?'

'If it's in your house, then it's safe,' said Millie. 'We're the only people who know how to get down. If we meet anyone snooping around, we tell them nothing.'

'I think I'm a guardian of the sword,' said Miles. 'That's what I think.'

Millie looked at him. 'What are you talking about? You burned the school down — that's a great guardian. And you're crazy and the only reason you're back here —'

'No,' persisted Miles. 'Listen. I think it's why I was brought back.' He was fumbling in another pocket. 'Maybe that's why Lord Vyner came to see me, all that time ago. Maybe I'm chosen.'

Millie was smiling.

'Israel was right,' she said, laughing. 'You are scary. And if that ghost came to see you, it was because he wanted to see a freak. How are you going to protect anyone or anything?'

'I'm here for a reason, Millie – I'm sure of it.'

'One of these days I'll tell you why you're here. You will get the shock of your life.'

'I've got a job to do,' said Miles. 'And I mean business.'

Now there was something heavy in his hand. It was wrapped in a dark grey cloth, and he let it rest on his lap. He looked up at Tomaz and smiled, peaceful and serene.

Tomaz said, 'What's that, Miles?'

'Sanchez said I should carry it,' said Miles. 'For our protection.'

He was unwrapping it, carefully, and Millie knew what it was before she saw it. She smelled it – a sharp odour of metal and grease – and she felt suddenly afraid. Miles removed the last corner of cloth and there it sat: a quiet, unassuming thing.

It was Sanchez's gun.

Millie controlled her voice. 'How did he say you could carry it, Miles? You should not have that.'

Tomaz had stood up and was backing away.

'It was in his letter,' said Miles. 'He said he wanted me to look after it, so I can protect you.'

'Can I see the letter? Do you have it with you?'

Miles looked at her, his eyes shining brighter than ever.

'Come on,' he said. 'You don't think I'd let you read my personal mail, do you? I think you're a very nice person, but I hardly know you.'

He took the gun in his right hand and slipped his finger over the trigger.

Millie could feel how frightened Tomaz was. She wanted to move as well, but something held her and she made another attempt. 'Miles,' she said, 'that's not your property. Sanchez has it for his *own* protection and it's not a toy.'

'I know it's not a toy.'

'There's no way he would let you play with it!'

Miles weighed the gun and turned it. He pressed a catch and at once the chamber was revealed. There were six bullets, snug in their sockets. He slammed it back into the breech, clicked off the safety catch, and drew back the hammer.

'We used to play with it all the time,' he said. 'Didn't we, Tom? I was the protector.'

'Please don't,' said Tomaz, very quietly.

'You need very steady hands,' said Miles. 'We used to play a game, but I don't play it any more. Didn't Sanchez tell you, Millie?'

He was aiming the gun at the low wall, opposite. The hammer stood up ready to fire and Miles's finger seemed to be uncertain. It was not on the trigger; it rested on the guard.

'Did you keep our secret, Tom?'

'Stop it, Miles,' said Tomaz. 'Please stop.'

'I played it, but I stopped. It's how I know I'm chosen.'

He laughed, suddenly, and with quick, skilful hands made the gun safe, shutting it down and folding it away.

'I guess . . . being Head Girl, Millie, you're going to have to tell on me, aren't you?'

Millie was silent for a moment. Then she said, 'Put the gun back where you found it. It's not yours.'

She would reflect on the conversation weeks later with shame. She could have taken the gun from him, by force – with Tomaz's help – and she should have done. She should have given it to the headmaster and warned him that Miles was more disturbed than he'd realised. Instead, she did nothing.

'Look at the south tower,' said Miles, softly. 'Can you see what I see?'

'No.'

'That's my little friend. I told him I'd be here and he can't wait to see me.'

He stood up and waved.

Sure enough, a window in the tower opposite opened, and Millie and Tomaz could make out the small, white face of Caspar Vyner, who was waving back.

Chapter Fourteen

Two important things happened in the next few days: one bad, one good. The good thing was that Lady Vyner fell ill and was confined to her bed. The bad thing was that Portuguese Air Traffic Control went on strike. This would have a major effect on the Ribblestrop football game.

Lady Vyner's illness meant that her legal letters went undelivered and she caused no trouble. Her collision with Miles in the corridor had unsettled her and she'd had another unfortunate encounter with a unicycling orphan the very next morning. Father O'Hanrahan made a point of visiting her regularly, but she never let him in.

In fact, Father O'Hanrahan was working extremely hard, taking an interest in everyone. He was often seen trudging around the school, trying to be cheery. He wanted to lead work-parties to the ruined chapel and set up the 'Church Renovation Club'. Unfortunately, nobody joined, and he found that however many boys he made join his expeditions, he'd always arrive at the chapel alone.

He took over Doonan's R.E. classes and put a huge jar of sweets on the desk. Nobody came, and when he asked the children why they were cutting his class, they told him that the timetable had been changed.

'We were waiting for you last night,' said Eric. 'One hour we waited.'

'Big disappointment, man,' said Israel.

'Last night at what time?' said Father O'Hanrahan.

'Ten o'clock, after supper.'

'But I was in bed.'

'It's that new timetable,' said Anjoli. 'New stuff every day.'

It was a plausible excuse, because lessons were constantly being cancelled or rearranged. Football practice was getting urgent, as the first game was looming. That had to be fitted around circus-training. Zoology continued and reproductive science classes had been doubled as Violetta was now so heavily pregnant she couldn't move. The children crammed into her den with Professor Worthington, poking and prodding, and there had been two midnight emergencies, when Flavio thought she was going into labour and had woken the entire school.

One Monday morning, Father O'Hanrahan decided to see the headmaster in person. He had been up early, clearing stone at the chapel. He had ordered Henry to attend, but there was no sign of him. He'd seen one of the Brethren and given chase: the elderly monk had simply disappeared. His hands were red and raw again. That evening he spent another hour waiting for Sam in a freezing classroom – he had organised a set of one-to-one spiritual guidance sessions, intending to interview each child alone.

Instead of Sam, Millie arrived, hot from football practice.

'What are you doing here?' he cried. His cassock was filthy and his hair was wild.

'Did I leave my credit card here?'

'What?'

'I want to buy things and I can't find it anywhere.'

'It's not time for sweets, girl – I have an appointment with Samuel! Have you seen him?'

'He's been taken by Sushamila again. He won't be free for ages.'

'I don't have a clue what you're talking about—'

'What are you going to talk about, anyway?'

'That is a confidential matter—'

'Is it like a confession? Because he won't have anything to confess.'

'What or who is Sushamila? Will you please explain what is going on in this madhouse?'

'Sushamila's the lion,' said Millie, slowly. 'She's got it into her head that Sam's a lion cub, and she grabs him now and then. He's not happy about it, but what can he do? She's obsessed and he's cute.'

At that very moment, the door crashed open and Sam stood in the threshold, breathing heavily. His blazer was sopping wet and one sleeve was coming loose at the shoulder. It gave him a lopsided look.

'I am so sorry,' he panted. 'Did Millie explain?'

Sanjay and Israel were behind him, giggling. 'She's still after you, Sam! She's right behind us!'

'It's not funny!' cried Sam, turning on them. 'You all think it's a big joke, but it's not much fun for me, you know! And look . . .' He peeled his blazer off. 'Who's going to pay for this? She must be growing teeth. Look at my shirt!'

'Sam, you stink,' said Millie. 'She's slobbered all over you.'

'I know!' shouted Sam. 'And it's the fourth time and everyone just stands and laughs.' He looked at Father O'Hanrahan. 'I'm very sorry, sir. I think I need to get changed.'

The old man could stand it no more.

He took Doonan with him and knocked firmly on the headmaster's door.

They found him in his office, cradling the telephone

receiver, unable to speak. Mr Sanchez had, at that very moment, passed on the information that Lisbon airport had been closed. Sanchez and Imagio had just landed there, for the transfer to London. The plane had docked and the boys had been taken not to their onward connection, but to a hotel. They had stand-bys for the next day's three o'clock departure, and would get the night train down to Ribblestrop, arriving Wednesday morning.

The football game against Ribblestrop High was on Tuesday, and that meant they would miss it.

When Father O'Hanrahan and Doonan opened the door, the headmaster looked haggard and bewildered.

'I understand,' he said, in a fragile voice. 'How tragic. We were all so hopeful . . .'

The two men came in softly, the anger dying on Father O'Hanrahan's lips. He had witnessed bereavement countless times before and knew its tone. He became alert.

'Of course,' said the headmaster. 'We will not despair.'

'Bad news, I think,' whispered Father O'Hanrahan to Doonan. 'Sit down and be quiet.'

'Life goes on,' said the headmaster. 'We'll do everything that's necessary.'

'It's the old Vyner woman,' hissed the old man. 'Oh Lord, I was expecting this. I managed to get into her kitchen yesterday and I thought she looked like death . . . she's had a relapse.'

'We'll carry on as usual,' said the headmaster. And he put the phone down. Brother Doonan instinctively crossed himself and the headmaster put his head in his hands.

'Is it the old woman?' said Father O'Hanrahan.

'What?'

'I was just saying to Doonan, she didn't look well yesterday. Old people often know when their time has come. She

111

was a fighter, though! She was fighting, by Jesus. Called me every name under the sun.'

'I don't quite follow you . . .'

The old man's eyes gleamed. 'She had a good innings, though, that's for sure. But everything changes now. Those monks will be cursing – they've had it all their own way till now.'

He struggled to his feet, Doonan helping him.

'I wouldn't be surprised if it's the end for the lot of us. Ha! I was going to talk to you about this wretched timetable, but that can wait.' He smiled. 'There may not be a timetable soon, eh? Might be time to start packing your things!'

'Father?' said Doonan. 'I wonder if . . .'

'What?'

'Shall I stay here, Father?'

'Yes. Offer some comfort to the man: you can see he needs it.'

Father O'Hanrahan smiled grimly at Doonan. 'I expect some of your precious little orphans will feel twice bereaved! This is a test for you, boy. But I tell you what . . .' He rubbed his hands. 'It's a blessing for some of us!'

The headmaster didn't notice the old man leave. He sat gazing out of the window, until Doonan felt he ought to say something. 'Bad news, I think, sir?' he said.

'What?' The headmaster peered and seemed surprised Doonan was in the room. He still hadn't found time to get new glasses, so everything was blurred. 'Yes, Doonan: catastrophic. Gary Cuthbertson . . . I know him too well. He's the High School's Director of Sport and he won't postpone the fixture, I know he won't. He has some talent scout coming down, apparently – one of his lads is up for a trial. And every aeroplane's in the wrong place! The children were so excited and now we'll be a dangerously weak side. It's not just the goalie – Sanchez is our goalie, you know. It's his presence on the pitch; it makes such a difference.'

'Are you talking about football, sir?'

'Not to mention Imagio – he was our secret weapon.'

'Sir, are you – ?'

'I'm talking about the game, Doonan! Eleven o'clock kick-off tomorrow and two of our key boys are stuck in Portugal!'

'You know, I think Father O'Hanrahan's got the wrong end of the stick.'

'I know what Routon will do. He'll play Ruskin in goal, and I can see the logic of that, and I am not going to interfere, but . . . Oh, Doonan! Our defence is not strong! Ruskin's brave, but he's so uncoordinated. I'd put Sanjay in goal, but Routon insists he's a winger. It's all too bad! I have every sympathy for trade unions, but . . . I'm sure if the workers knew, they'd fly one little plane to London.'

'Father O'Hanrahan got a different impression, sir. I think he's –'

'He's not a footballing man, is he? Let's be honest. We'd better find the boys and break the news. I wonder what difference Miles will make – he's fearless, you know.'

The two men crossed the lawn together.

Doonan laughed nervously. 'You know, that's why we were coming to see you, sir,' he said. 'We never seem able to find the children when we want them. We thought there were classes today.'

'No, no, no. We've put everything on hold until the match is over. Flavio's become a pretty good fitness coach, actually, which is just what Routon needed. Routon's more of a manager. This is why they'll be devastated, you see: everything's been going so well. Ruskin in goal! Can you imagine anything worse?'

'You may find,' said Doonan, 'that tragedy sometimes binds a community.' It was a line he'd had prepared and it still seemed appropriate.

The headmaster nodded. 'You may be right. So many things are not ours to control.'

113

'Prayer is action, though,' said Doonan.

'Yes,' said the headmaster. He paused and met Doonan's eyes. 'That's a useful thought. The fact is, though . . . without Sanchez and Imagio we're going to be annihilated. After so much expectation, it seems terribly cruel.'

'I'd be happy to say a few words, if that would help them, sir?'

'It must seem so trivial to you! A mere game . . .'

'No!' said Doonan. 'I was a cub scout back in Ireland – I was first reserve for the B-team. I know what it all means! Shall I tell them that story about how the Red Sea was parted for Moses? You know, even as the Israelites awaited destruction?'

'I think you should,' said the headmaster. 'It might lift them.'

'Miracles *do* happen,' said the boy.

Chapter Fifteen

The headmaster found the children practising their circus skills.

Flavio had not been keen to actually demonstrate his tightrope-walking abilities, because he didn't want to show off. However, the children had persisted and he'd slung a wire from the back of his trailer to the roof of one of the out-buildings. It was a steady upward slope if you started at the truck-end, climbing from shoulder height to about ten metres it was a sensible start for any would-be acrobat, because you slowly learned to control your fear of heights.

Flavio did it in bare feet. His toes were wide and curled around the wire. His heavy body was in strict control and he moved up it with the speed of a monkey. The orphans, of course, took to it at once. Many had worked on ships, some on lethally dangerous building sites, and they could soon run up the wire in boots or bare feet. Eric was the first to attempt it on a bike, removing the tyres so the wire could fit the groove of the wheels. It wasn't long before he and Podma could start at either end, meet in the middle, climb over the other's machine, and then continue their two journeys. Flavio would stand gazing up, realising that the mad idea about Speech Day was actually quite sane.

Perhaps the world *was* ready for a boy-circus, with animals.

The animals were all happier and healthier. Their diet was superb, as the local butcher drove in every morning with fresh supplies. They had a very fine exercise yard, now that the railings had been welded together. The tigers spent most of their time inside it, stretching and rolling; the old lion, Sushamila, was never chained or caged. She padded around the lorry, her short-sighted eyes always on the alert for a glimpse of Sam. Even the bitter-looking crocodile seemed contented, since a large stone trough had been unearthed for it. Violetta, the panther, slept most of the time and the boys took it in turns to spoon-feed her, mincing her meat so she didn't have to put any energy into chewing.

One of the headmaster's zoology-art projects had been the completion of signs about each animal, listing its habitat, its diet, and any crucial statistics. Routon had thought it wise to create warning-signs as well, and everyone had enjoyed illustrating them. There were pictures of half-eaten people and dismembered limbs. There were ferocious, snarling teeth and lethal-looking claws – everything was blood-red on a white background. Millie had drawn a fat policeman being torn apart and eaten. It was a complicated storyboard with captions, but the headmaster had vetoed it.

'Let bygones be bygones,' he had said.

'I bet he's still after me,' said Millie. 'I'm keeping ready.'

'I'm sure he's far too busy to even think about Ribblestrop,' said the headmaster. 'I'd be surprised if you ever saw him again.'

Millie decided not to mention the fact that she'd broken his window with a stone-filled snowball and made a definite sighting. She threw her pictures away and watched as Vijay, one of the leanest orphans, squeezed through the bars of the tiger-compound. Asilah passed him the biggest sign of all:

Do not come into this cage. If you do, you will die, and it will be your fault.

One of the tigers stared at him as he passed. The sign bounced over his tail and he snarled with irritation. This tiger was called Ivan and he had one fang that was too large for his own mouth: it had to sit outside his bottom lip, not unlike a cigarette. The other tiger was called Prince and was more watchful and intense. He shifted backwards as Vijay dragged the sign to the wall and leaned it proudly upright.

Elsewhere, signs were being wired to bars or hung on nails:

Do not feed us, we are fine.

I am a camel. I am not interesting. I have no point except in a dessert.

Up in the east-tower dormitory, by the scorpion's matchbox, Anjoli had written: *Don't worry! I am alive but I just don't move much. North Africa. Dangerous.*

Eric tied a label to the python: *You wanna know more about me, ssss? Just put your head in my mouth and see what you get: I can swallow you whole so don't even look at me: Sssss!*

'Is everyone here?' said the headmaster, as he called the children together. 'I'm sorry to interrupt, but I've just had some very upsetting news, and it's my duty to communicate it straight away. Sit down, children.'

Chapter Sixteen

Tuesday morning dawned and the children changed in silence.

Grey shirts, grey shorts. Ties looped through belts. Cardboard shin-pads and sensible school shoes. They were determined and they were brave: very few tears had been shed. But disappointment smarts like a wound and every child could feel it burning. Ruskin was pulling on a bright pyjama-jacket to signify his position as goalie, and it reminded them that Sanchez, and Imagio too, were a thousand miles away.

The High School team had clearly remembered the Ribblestrop facilities from their last visit, because they'd changed on home turf. Fifteen boys in blue-and-amber stripes climbed out of the first coach. The goalie was in shimmering purple. One lad was swathed in a silk tracksuit and had attendants. As the players flexed their limbs on the Ribblestrop lawns, four more coaches came to a halt and two hundred supporters moved towards the pitch. The singing started immediately.

By the fountain, Captain Routon and the High School trainer shook hands warmly. This was Gary Cuthbertson, brother to D.C.C. Cuthbertson. He was a slimmer model than the policeman, but just as bald.

'Appreciate this,' said Cuthbertson. 'There's a lot of schools can't raise a side this early in the term and those that can—' He laughed. 'Too bloody scared! Ah, now! This is Mr Scanlon, by the way, works for a rather fine London club, so a bit of an honoured guest!'

'Part-time, Gary, part-time.'

Mr Scanlon was a short man wrapped in a very big coat. He wore neat black shoes and a trilby hat. He had a thin, nasal voice and he was chewing on a wad of gum. 'Where's this lad o' yours? I hope he's not missed the bus!'

'He'll be along any sec. I told him to come and say hello. Well then, Routon, any surprises for us? I hope you've got that girlie under control – they play a young lass, right up front.'

'Do they?' said Scanlon. 'I don't like that myself. I think that's feminism gone mad, that is – oh, I say! Look at this!'

The Ribblestrop team was emerging through the main doors of Ribblestrop Towers.

'Bloody hell,' chortled Scanlon. 'Look at those shorts. We're back in the war!' He and Gary Cuthbertson laughed heartily. 'I'm going backwards – we're back in the nineteen-fifties! Ah, now, this is more like it, eh? Is this your Darren?'

The tracksuited boy appeared from a cluster of girls. He was chewing gum too and his eyes were concealed by a baseball cap.

'I told him to come and say hello,' said Cuthbertson. 'This is Darren and this is Mr Scanlon, Darren.'

'Hello,' said Darren, not knowing where to put his eyes. 'Hope you enjoy the game, sir.'

'I hope so too, lad. I hope this lot can put you to your best – you don't see much if it's a walkover.'

'I'll work hard for you, sir.'

'Dickie Rainbow saw you last month and he says you're mustard. I keep an open mind.'

The crowd had formed round the football pitch. As the Ribblestrop team ran on, there was a gale of laughter, jeers, and whistles. As the High School came out, a chant soon began: 'Dar-ren! Dar-ren! Dar-ren!'

It was a chant that would return regularly. A banner was unfurled: *Good Luck Darren*, it read. Some girls approached and Darren was carefully disrobed of tracksuit and cap. He did a quick stretch, touched his toes a few times, and bounded forward. The crowd cheered yet louder.

'I don't believe it,' said Millie, quietly.

'What?' said Miles.

'That thug they called Darren. He was in a builders' van. When I was hitch-hiking. I *knew* I'd seen him before!'

Ruskin was trotting in circles, and Asilah called him to his spot and began some practice shots. The boy took them well and passed them back. Anjoli kept his ball moving, making sure everyone got a touch. All the Ribblestrop players were working hard just to ignore the crowd.

The High School team had formed a scrum and was wrestling together, roaring. At some unseen signal, they stood up, clenched their fists, and started to chant a grunting, animal chant: the crowd went wild again and the first empty lager can flew onto the pitch. The players broke into an orgy of fast passing, hard and intense. Shots at goal became constant and the High School goalkeeper was soon twirling and diving. One cannonball shot bent the goalpost out of square, and Flavio and Captain Routon moved in quickly to repair it. The High School players started jumping on the spot and that was the cue for Gary Cuthbertson to blow for the start. It was ten past eleven.

'My, my, my,' said Cuthbertson, as Darren and Millie approached the centre spot. 'Old friends meet again. Remember me, girlie?' he said.

'You're a bit balder,' said Millie. 'Just as dumb.'

Gary Cuthbertson gasped. He licked his lips. 'Am I really?' He was bright red, instantly.

'Breath's about the same,' said Millie. 'I can't forget that.'

The man could hardly speak. 'Heads or tails? In fact . . . forget it.' He found his voice. 'I'll choose for you, you rude little . . .' He was getting blinding white flashes across his vision: how could a child so small and frail have such an effect on him? He managed to look squarely into Millie's eyes. 'You're gonna lose *everything*, girlie: what's the toss of a coin matter? My brother's back and he means business.'

'He's still a policeman, isn't he?' said Millie.

'He's working on a very nice little deal and he will close you down!'

'My word,' said Millie. 'A bent cop and a bent ref. Are your kids all benders too?'

Cuthbertson fought to keep his hands down. He had a vision of his fingers tightening around her throat. 'I tell you what,' he hissed. 'You're going to wish you'd died in that freezer. We've got plans for you!'

He looked up at Darren. 'Let's keep this to thirty minutes – our kick-off, playing downhill.'

He blew his whistle, waved for a change of ends, and jogged off.

Darren spat a big globule of spittle and it landed on Millie's shoe. 'Time to die,' he said.

Chapter Seventeen

A tall, shaven-headed boy with the numbers 666 on his forehead kicked-off. Immediately, the High School came forward like a wave, to the roaring of the supporters. They were colossal and had a new strategy, devised specially – no doubt – for the Ribblestrop side. They kept the ball moving in short, hard, accurate passes, drawing their opponents and then slotting the ball around them. In seconds they were dangerously close to the goal. A forward pushed it sideways; it crossed the pitch in three quick zig-zags, and came to Darren.

The chant started, fast and frenzied. Miles came for the tackle and Darren dummied it past him – the crowd was delirious and they were just thirty seconds into the game. Darren stayed in control, his nerves under an iron hand, and he unleashed a comet of a shot. It was cruel. It swerved towards the goal: it would take the bar off if it struck.

Ruskin didn't flinch: he'd learned to stand firm. He just got his hands up, but the ball went through them and hit him full-square in the face, knocking him backwards. The rebound was cleared by Israel, who found Sam; Sam played it forward, dodging a scythe of a tackle, and Ribblestrop were out of danger.

Millie ran to Ruskin, who sat bloody-faced in the goalmouth.

'That was superb!' she said. 'If you can do that, we're laughing.'

'Millie. . .'

The boy seemed to be having trouble breathing. There was something wrong. Israel had dropped back as well and saw the problem at once.

'Oh man,' he said. 'Look at his specs.'

A nosebleed had started. But worse than that, Millie saw that the two lenses had been knocked from Ruskin's spectacles. They were on the ground at his feet.

'What can you see without them?' said Millie.

Ruskin simply shook his head. There was a shout from Asilah: the High School had possession again and were breaking through.

The crowd was starting a new chant and it was very unsettling: '*Have* them! *Have* them! *Have* them!'

It got louder and louder. Same tactics, they kept passing along the line. The orphans were failing to predict where the ball would go. Miles was yelling at them, trying to keep them back and mark rather than run, but he couldn't make himself understood. Then he intercepted a pass himself and flicked it forward, leaping a dangerously high tackle. He got it to Asilah, who got it to Anjoli, and for a moment the Anjoli-Sam double act was there, both boys perfectly positioned. Number 6 came carving in and Sam went head over heels, at least – thank goodness – landing on his feet.

'*Have* them! *Have* them!'

The chant got into Ribblestrop's ears. It was like listening to your own death sentence. The High School were over the centre line, pushing down, same tactics. They were very, very good at it: the ball shot from boy to boy and, just like

123

last time, it went to Darren. The chant rose into a monstrous wailing. Eric was there and saw the identical feint to the left: he whisked it off the monster's feet, but was too weak to clear it. He passed it limply to Millie, still hanging back, and she booted it up the field as Darren came at her.

She went down and he simply rode over her.

How had she forgotten?

It was a war, brutal and terrifying. She lay there, the breath knocked out of her, her arm on fire. She rolled back her sleeve and there were a dozen stud marks on her forearm, several of them leaking blood. When she stood up, she noticed that another Ribblestrop player was down.

The referee didn't appear to be interested.

It was Miles on the ground. He lay on his back, holding his face. Asilah had the ball and booted it out of play: there was a chorus of booing and whistling. Millie and Henry got to him together.

'You didn't warn me,' he said.

'What about?'

Captain Routon was running on with a carrier bag in hand. He had a sponge and various creams. Miles was sitting up, holding his eye. There was blood in his mouth and the cruel bruising around the eye was purple and yellow already. His shirt was ripped wide open.

'They're big, rough boys, aren't they?' said Miles. He was smiling through the blood. 'I thought we were here to play football. I didn't realise they wanted something else.'

'What happened?' said Routon. 'I didn't see.'

The crowd was whistling. Routon started to sponge Miles down. Henry knelt beside him and stared. His own nose was bleeding, but he seemed more interested in Miles, who was spitting red mucus onto the turf.

'Their number 6,' he said. 'He didn't like the way I tackled him so he elbowed me in the face.' Miles sounded

124

amused. 'And just in case I didn't get it, he punched me in the mouth. I think most people saw.'

'Is he on or off?' shouted Cuthbertson. 'You've had your time!'

'On, thank you,' said Miles. He smiled at Millie, with bloodied teeth. 'It's fine. I don't mind a bit of violence.'

Henry helped him to his feet and the game restarted.

From that point on, it was Miles who kept Ribblestrop alive. He was everywhere, fast and fearless. He was cut down regularly, but rose again, leaping into the most dangerous tackles. He threw in every ounce of his minimal weight, jabbing and snatching at the ball, ignoring the countless blows he received. Indeed, it was as if he sought them. He was headbutted and body-checked to the ground, but was always there, wide-eyed and manic. His team-mates picked him up, Routon sponged him down, and he was back in the fray.

Ruskin had rescued his lenses and held them to his eyes. This meant he could follow the play, but that his hands were unavailable. He shuffled up and down his line peering at the action, calling and encouraging.

In defence, Henry was like a large, faithful dog, and remained in the goalmouth as the final obstacle. Despite it all, the High School were dominating – and it was only a question of time. They came in waves, again and again. The passing was the same and, though it was predictable, the ball came dangerously close to goal. At last, Darren found his space; the ball soared high and he chested it down. Miles was there, but he was giddy and weak. He got it away from the boy's left foot, but then his legs were hacked from under him and he was flat on his face. The ball trickled and Darren was ready again. Ruskin peered and scuttled, but there wasn't much hope. Darren slotted the ball precisely into the lefthand corner of the net.

One-nil.

A clap of thunder seemed to roll over the world. The crowd swarmed onto the pitch and Darren found himself borne aloft and bounced. His team-mates crowded around him, leaping, punching the air, and Flavio could stand it no more. He'd been watching the game and the crowd with growing disbelief: now he went onto the pitch himself and let forth a torrent of Portuguese abuse over the referee. Gary Cuthbertson only smiled and took a long time recording things in his notebook. It was a full five minutes before play could continue.

The High School boys were also smiling. They rubbed their hands and took possession almost immediately. In seconds, they were close to goal, confident of their plans.

Ribblestrop – if truth be told – had gone to pieces. Apart from Henry and Miles, the defenders had lost their nerve. Henry was slow and Miles was limping. Darren relaxed and began to show off. Twirls, knees, intricate little flicks of the heel – he saw he could enjoy himself and the crowd went wild for it. The 'Darren!' chant started again, and ten minutes before half-time he'd scored his hat-trick.

Worst of all, some of the Ribblestrop players now began to pick on each other. Millie cursed Asilah for a dismal pass and Anjoli suddenly lost his temper with Sanjay. Taunting laughter gusted from the crowd. Some of the boys by the High School goalmouth unfurled a banner: *Private School Snobs Go Down* and the ref ignored it. The Ribblestrop tactics were forgotten and, despite Sam's cries and pleas of encouragement, his axis with Millie and Anjoli collapsed. The closest the team came to a goal was when Millie made a breathtaking run past three players and crossed perfectly to Tomaz. The goalie was committed right; the goal was open. Tomaz shot and the ball spun crazily from his shoe way over the bar. The scorn, laughter, and whistling from the crowd was ear-splitting. At just that moment, the ref blew for half-time. The High School was laughing and high-fiving. Darren disappeared under a crowd of girls. It was a rout and the Ribblestrop players staggered to the touchline.

The score now stood at five-nil.

Chapter Eighteen

They sucked oranges.

Brother Doonan said, 'There's no shame. They're a strong bunch of boys and they play well.'

'They're dirty sods,' said Millie. 'And they don't play well.'

Israel said, 'Look at this.'

His left leg had a cut all down the inner thigh, past the knee. It was black with congealed blood. Other orphans showed their injuries. Sam had a black eye coming and Millie was having trouble walking. As for Miles, his swollen mouth hung open, and his eyes were dazed and exhausted. His shirt had long been ripped off and his arms, face, and torso were a mess of mud and blood. He sat quietly, too weak to peel his own orange. Henry was feeding him segments from his own.

'There's no shame,' said Doonan. 'We're doing our best. I just wish Father O'Hanrahan was here to give a little . . . boost.'

'We're crap,' said Sanjay. 'Five-nil!'

Flavio said, 'I never see football like this, an' I see some tough games. Is the ref, I wanna . . . Man, I wanna to talk to him properly, just him and me.'

'Who cares?' said Millie. 'If we do get a chance, we waste it. Give up.'

'Hey, you gotta fight,' said Flavio. 'I learn that in the *favela*: you give up, you die.'

'Listen,' said Brother Doonan. 'You might think this a little bit inappropriate, because I know not all of you share the faith. But I think we should say a prayer. Together.'

Millie happened to be kneeling, attending to her laces. She put her hands together and said, in a voice so heavy with contempt Brother Doonan winced, 'Dear God. Where were you?'

Miles laughed.

Asilah said, 'Maybe He's playing for the High School. Maybe they say *their* prayers.'

'No, listen to me,' said Brother Doonan, gently. 'I'm quite serious. If we were to hold hands for a moment . . . just a moment of contemplation —'

Millie interrupted again, with withering scorn. 'If God sends us a miracle, I'll become a nun. I'll give up smoking; I'll never do a bad thing and Miles won't, either.'

'Look at Darren,' said Sam.

They looked over at the High School team. Cuthbertson had separated his striker from the crowds and he and Mr Scanlon were deep in conversation. Darren himself was sitting tracksuited, in a folding chair. A girl was massaging his shoulders as Scanlon put some papers in his lap.

'Well then, boys and girls,' said a voice.

They all looked up. Gary Cuthbertson was standing close by. He was smiling and he winked at Millie. 'Shall we abandon the game?' he said.

Captain Routon said, 'Abandon it? It's only half-time.'

'I know, but to be honest, the fixture was for Darren really, and Scanlon says he's seen enough. Says the boy's ready to move up, which we all knew really – he needs to

129

play a bit of serious football.' He raised his voice. 'So, if you want to call it a day . . .?'

Somewhere, an engine was roaring.

'Speak louder,' said Millie. 'We can't hear you!'

'I said, shall we abandon the match?'

A number of people had heard the helicopter, but nobody had thought much about it. Helicopters are not uncommon. However, the engines of this particular craft were getting ear-splittingly loud, to the point where many people were wincing. Hair was becoming tousled and clothes were flapping.

Captain Routon had to shout to be heard. 'I say play on!' he roared. Cuthbertson couldn't hear and had his hand cupped behind his ear.

'What?' he was shouting. 'What do you say?'

The helicopter was getting yet lower. It was looking for somewhere to land. The pilot had seen the football pitch and swung his machine closer. It was dropping fast.

'Back! Get back!' shouted the headmaster, rushing at the crowd.

Professor Worthington was anxious. 'It could be an emergency!' she shouted. 'Can we all get right back?'

She was inaudible. The helicopter was getting bigger and yet louder, and floated down within its own tornado.

Millie found herself clutching Sam.

Sam found himself clutching Brother Doonan – who was the one person not standing. He was on his knees, deep in prayer. The undercarriage bounced gently on the rippling grass, taking the strain, and the door in the side flipped upwards.

'I don't believe this,' said Millie. 'This is not possible.'

As one, the Ribblestrop team moved in. The hurricane didn't matter, nor did the shattering noise. They moved in because they could see a boy who looked just like their dear friend Sanchez. There was another boy with him, but hidden in the aircraft. Sanchez was in the doorway, pulling himself up and out. In a moment he was on the grass, his goalie's shirt rippling emerald-green.

He turned and the other boy pushed out a cardboard box. Then another, then another. Sanchez set them on the grass and kit-bags followed. The luggage taken care of, the second boy emerged. He wore black shorts and a football shirt that gleamed with golden stripes. His long hair flew under the rotor-blades and he held it to his head with both hands. It was the boy from the film. It was Imagio, but he might have been an angel.

Brother Doonan looked up and promptly fainted.

The helicopter door slammed and, as if released on elastic, the craft shot upwards, taking the noise with it. The sun chose that moment to break through a cloud and the two boys shimmered like apparitions, caught in a shaft of light. Then they were lost in a frenzy of hugs and handshakes, dances and kisses.

Millie could not get to Sanchez: the orphans had him for themselves, sweeping Imagio up as well in their joy. When they finally broke away to look at the boxes, Millie found he was in front of her.

'Hello,' she said. He held out his hand and she shook it.

'How are you?' he said.

'I'm fine. We're losing.'

'What's the score?'

'Five-nil.'

She looked into his eyes and he looked into hers. 'Do you remember Miles?' she said, after several long seconds.

'Yes.'

'He's amazing.'

Miles was right behind her and heard. He grinned and put out his hand; Sanchez put out his arms and hugged his thin shoulders to him, hard.

Then there was Sam to be embraced, and then there was Ruskin, moist behind a pair of glasses that were almost obliterated by sellotape. Finally, there was Tomaz and the hugs could get no tighter.

Behind them, the team was getting changed. Imagio had taken charge and was dishing out boots, shorts, and shirts. Plastic bags were ripped open and left to sail off in the breeze. School uniform was being flung into a bloody, muddy pile. In seconds, black-and-gold warriors were emerging. In the space of five minutes, ten children were changed and ready: ten hornets and their goalie.

Captain Routon stood close to Gary Cuthbertson and said in his ear, 'Two subs. Ready when you are.'

Chapter Nineteen

That night, when Sam and Ruskin were together, they opened a brand-new exercise book and looked at the bright, white pages. How would they describe the game now that it was over? Even a heading was impossible. Ruskin wrote the date. Sam underlined it. They then simply looked at the empty lines.

Millie was sitting with a Bible. She had decided to read it, convinced at last that it might have something to say about the world. Page one was long and tricky, but she persevered. She had asked Doonan about confirmation classes.

Amazing scenes, wrote Ruskin.

The miracle from the skies, wrote Sam. He sucked the fountain pen and pulled a thread of blotter from its golden nib. *The Turning of the Tide . . .*

Anjoli crept over to them as they contemplated their work and leaned between them. He had a big, fat felt-tip with chisel-edge, and he simply wrote the final score in letters as high as the page. Then he climbed onto the table and danced.

Sushamila crept in and gazed at Sam from the doorway, purring longingly.

* * *

The Ribblestrop teachers yelled support as the teams returned to the pitch, but their voices were lost in the tide of hooting laughter and derision that came from the High School crowds.

Mr Scanlon was about to leave, but he paused. The Ribblestrop team was transformed visually. He'd watch for five minutes, he decided – he was due back in London, but his taxi could wait a moment.

Ribblestrop kicked off and lost possession immediately. A long pass went out to the High School winger, who booted it midfield again: same tactics, no surprises. Their triangles formed efficiently, but the Ribblestrop players were anticipating and watching. They were controlling themselves. The passes continued, Ribblestrop holding back; the ball fell for Darren and the supporters' chant kicked in as usual. He took it past a defender and shot a hard, curling ball. The Ribblestrop goalie snatched it from the air and brought it to his chest.

Mr Scanlon liked Darren's play and would certainly call him up for a trial in the next few weeks. But he was aware the lad hadn't been stretched. It would be nice to see him under a bit of pressure. He folded his arms and went back to the touchline.

Sanchez rolled the ball briskly to Israel, as the crowd bayed and hooted. Israel found Anjoli. Anjoli's confidence was back: he took it past two of the High School players before trickling it to Sam, who dummied neatly and got it to Asilah. Asilah found Miles, up front again, and he found Millie; by this time Anjoli had made the run and was dangerous. Millie got it to him. All through this, there was one boy, not running. Imagio was still and simply watched. He looked a little tired from his flight and he sat down on the grass. He was pulling his hair back with both hands, lazily twisting it into a plait and slipping a sweatband around it.

He watched as Anjoli was surrounded. He watched Anjoli panic and boot the ball anywhere. It ran in his direction and he idly punted it to Millie without even standing.

Millie got the ball to Sam, who crossed hard. It was only the second Ribblestrop attack and the High School goalie seemed unable to believe it. The cross was low and Miles was there. He dived headfirst and the header cracked the post. There was another thunderclap of jeering and another beer can was hurled onto the pitch. Goal kick.

Imagio had seen enough. He trotted into midfield and – inevitably – the magic started.

The High School goalie played a long ball and, as if Imagio had called it like a dog, it bounced straight to him. He trapped it, turned, and waited for attack. Number 666, it was; he came in hard and saw a football disappear. It was simply gone. He turned fast, caught sight of it, lunged; it flipped over his head. He chopped at the player's legs, but they too were suddenly in the air. Another High School boy joined the assault, leaping up to head it: Imagio's head was faster and higher and harder, and clicked the ball to Anjoli, who simply back-heeled it to Sam.

Sam and Imagio decided to play football.

Imagio just wanted to feel the space, of course, and acclimatise himself. He'd been crammed under boxes in the helicopter for two hours; prior to that was a crazy car ride from Lisbon to Malaga, to the Sanchez jet, scrambled from North Africa. Now he limbered up and cleared his head. The High School boys reminded him of South American buffalo: dangerous if mishandled, but slow, stupid, and utterly predictable. They were like the tourists on the beach ... the men who thought they could play football. There were seven of them now, all rushing from point to point, snorting and booting at the ball.

Imagio started to smile, and when he smelled in his

nostrils the heat of the boys' anger – and their terrible sweat – he started to enjoy himself. He flicked and tucked, stood on the ball, played wild dummies in which the ball rolled slowly on its own, untouchable under his dancing feet. Then he'd twirl it to Sam, who'd rest him, and flick it back. In this way the two boys edged from side to side and a minute passed. The crowd had started whistling, but it petered out. There were just a few cries now: 'Come on the High!' 'Close him down!' But most of the supporters were silent.

The ball was still around the centre line when Imagio spun round and knocked it to Miles. Miles played it to Anjoli, who was grinning, and he passed it back to Imagio. Imagio broke.

A whippet? A missile? A stone skimmed on water? Imagio was a blur of black-and-gold, poking the ball through legs and over shoulders: the goalkeeper came at him – why? Imagio simply let the ball bounce and the goalie was too low, it fell over his head tenderly for the volley and it was five-one. Imagio raised a hand.

Then he was shoulder-high.

He was up on someone's back, but felt his feet grabbed and he was hoisted higher; when he let himself fall, it was into the arms of all his team-mates, who threw him up again. He spun, they caught him, he was kissed and patted, and was finally allowed to stand. Sanchez had both arms round him, hugging him tight. 'Oh man, we want ten,' he said, in the boy's ear.

'*Te doy cinquo, y me voy a dormir*,' Imagio said.

'What did he say?' cried Sam.

Sanchez said, 'He said, "I'll give you five, then I'm sleeping." Five's his lucky number.'

For the next quarter of an hour, the High School team watched a display. They took no real part. They ran about and kicked hard at space. They had possession immediately after the goals they conceded, and at the free kicks they were awarded for a rash of theatrical dives. But in fairness, they were spectators; Imagio simply danced amongst them. The ball zig-zagged one minute, if he played close with Sam or Anjoli. The next it was long balls, Miles, Tomaz, and Millie all crucial to the routines. Suddenly, it was the extended run: the dribble. He was a spiralling fighter jet and he simply cut through everything. The High School goalie spent as much time in the back of his net as in front of it; the shots came long and short, the woodwork was cracked again and again, and the net was torn from its hooks. The High School collapsed and their supporters went silent.

Three goals were disallowed for no reason. Nobody cared: the score was still five-all, with twenty minutes left. Imagio had scored them all: could Cuthbertson disallow any more? He called fouls at whim, offside at random, throw-ins that weren't. He lost his temper and yellow-carded Sam for smiling. He shouted at Darren and Darren shouted back.

Poor Darren was helpless and he'd barely touched the ball.

It wasn't just the two newcomers: every Ribblestrop player now seemed to whisk the ball from his boot. He tried to fight dirty, of course, but neither blows nor kicks connected. He ran up the field, sweat and tears blinding him: he couldn't get back in time. All the High School could hope for now was to keep the draw. They piled back into defence and built walls in the goalmouth. Imagio was lethal, though – however many defenders cornered and surrounded him he'd still poke the ball through. Five minutes from the end, he had closed in again. Ten men opposed him, but he juggled it to Sam. Sam took it backwards, into the centre; Anjoli was waiting and lobbed it. A lob was a dangerous move considering the height of the High School players, and time was ticking. They took possession but muffed it, two boys struggling for the same ball. It was Miles who nipped it from their toes and sprang like a deer, into the penalty area. He drew back his right foot, and for a moment time froze.

It was a photograph: a blood-stained Miles Seyton-Shandy, about to shoot at goal, not wanting to shoot. It was five-all and he wanted the moment to last forever. That night, when he talked about it with Millie and Sanchez, he explained the pain and the joy – the knowledge that the goal was wide and the goalie on his knees. He'd thought: *Sam should score this goal – or Millie, or Tomaz, or anyone else. Why me? How can I deserve this*? And then, for a ridiculous moment, he had thought of his mother, and wondered why she wasn't on the touchline, watching.

He shot, hard and true.

To watch – not the goalie, he was nowhere near – but the perfect swish of the net, as it sighed with satisfaction. To turn and see the firework display of joy from his own side. To see Imagio handspring back to the centre line. To see Millie run the length of the pitch and meet Sanchez in the centre and embrace, Sanchez swinging her off her feet and kissing her. It was six-five, six-five, six-five to Ribblestrop. The headmaster and Professor Worthingon were in each other's arms. Flavio and Routon were dancing together. Just one little kick and the world had changed.

Those who saw Miles fall to his knees and cry never mentioned it. He was picked up and carried, carefully: every part of him, it seemed, was cut and bruised and he could no longer stand.

Six-five and five more minutes left. Gary Cuthbertson blew for full-time there and then, and nobody cared. The High School boys staggered off the pitch, heads down.

Darren's girlfriend was there with the tracksuit, but the boy didn't want to know – he was making straight for the coach.

The Ribblestrop Towers team stayed on the field.

By some instinct, they collected in their own goalmouth and simply sat down. There was nothing to say. Individuals went to speak, but it was as if they were dumb. Some held hands. One by one, they lay down.

The teachers stayed away and left them to their time of grace.

The teachers cleared the refuse. The teachers took down the nets. They left the children out there on the sacred ground until the moon rose.

That very night, Violetta gave birth to six panther cubs. The children watched, in the candlelight and straw. Six healthy parcels of fur, with snarling, yowling mouths and needle-sharp teeth. Professor Worthington was midwife and managed a fascinating lecture on the muscles of the uterus as she delivered them.

Chapter Twenty

Had Father O'Hanrahan been a little less impetuous, he might have saved himself a great deal of trouble. Had he only chosen to go slow and, for example, enjoy the football game, he might have avoided some unfortunate blunders.

When he left the headmaster's office, he had convinced himself that Lady Vyner had just died. Naturally, he telephoned D.C.C. Cuthbertson with the wonderful news and the two men arranged to meet the next day in a quiet Ribblestrop bar.

'It's just what we hoped for,' whispered the old man. He'd allowed himself a glass of whisky in celebration and he gulped it down in a single mouthful. 'You told me here in this office. When she goes, the contracts go with her. The Brethren will be forced to move out and—'

'It also means,' said the policeman, 'that you can search her rooms. See if there's documents and keys.'

'I'll talk to the monks first. Vow of wretched silence, I'll give them silence now!'

'Still no communication, then?'

'No, but I had a bit of luck the other day. I found a set of stairs! The artful swine: they've been coming and going and

I couldn't work out how they popped up and disappeared. There's a little staircase, all hidden with bushes and – oh, they're a clever little outfit!'

'That will be the staircase down to the pump-room,' said D.C.C. Cuthbertson.

'What are you talking about? What pump-room?'

'There's a pump-room underground. That's how the Brethren get down.'

'When the devil did you find this out?'

Cuthbertson laughed. 'Police work at its finest,' he said. 'I called up some old friends at the Water Board. Said we had some problems at the lake. They sent me maps, yesterday. Pipe diagrams as well – if I was a plumber, I think I'd be in heaven. It's a staircase down, isn't it? Seventy-two steps, then a door with a mortise lock.'

'Yes.'

'I've got a copy of the key as well – here it is, oiled and ready to go.'

Father O'Hanrahan looked bewildered.

'You do know what a pump-room is, Father? Let me tell you all about it, then you'll know as much as me. Now you know that this lake is an artificial one?'

Father O'Hanrahan sighed in frustration. 'I don't know what you're talking about – how can a lake be artificial? There are things swimming in it!'

'It's a *manmade* lake. It was dug, years ago, by human beings. Countrymen of yours, funnily enough. Check out our tourist information centre, Father – it's a goldmine. That lake, and a lot of the tunnels, were dug two hundred years ago. The Vyners were so rich they thought they'd give the grounds a face-lift, and putting in a lake was the fashionable thing. So they imported two hundred potato-eaters to do the job. No – calm down, Father. I will get to the point in a moment. Get yourself another drink.'

Cuthbertson supped his beer and the old man looked at him with dislike. He slid back to the bar and replenished his glass. When he sat down again, the policeman was sitting back, smiling. He had a large sheet of paper in front of him, with a labyrinth of pipes traced out in blue ink.

'Why is a pump-room relevant?' he said. 'Well. The Water Board boys explained everything. An artificial lake needs to be topped up. In the summer it gets dry and the level goes down. Then, when it rains, it gets too full. The pump-room, therefore, is the underground chamber that controls all that. And you have to be able to get to it, and that's the little staircase you've discovered.'

'And the monks live in a pump-room?'

'I doubt if they *live* in it. But they must live nearby, because according to my sources, they look after the pipes.'

Both men were silent.

'So . . . the Brethren are a bunch of handymen-plumbers?' said Father O'Hanrahan.

'No,' said Cuthbertson. 'But I imagine that's all part of their duties. It can't be the most difficult task, polishing a few pipes – but the point is that if they have access down there, then there's a strong chance they get through to all the tunnels. They must interconnect, and they might well know about young Tomaz and the wine cellars. And everything else besides. How are you getting on with Tomaz, by the way? Have you had your little chat?'

Father O'Hanrahan looked uncomfortable. 'I'm afraid I've barely spoken to him.'

'Oh, for goodness' sake! I thought that was your priority.'

'I told you before, getting to sit down with those children is impossible. They have no timetable – it's a wretched free-for-all.'

'What about in the evenings? Are you the housemaster now?'

'No.'

'Oh, Father! I thought you were going to move in with the little wretches and read them Bible stories!'

'*The job went to Doonan!*' hissed the priest. 'At the age of seventeen, with a brain the size of a pea! He's a child himself, but he gets the job, over a man of my experience! The headmaster says I've got too many duties as chaplain.'

'I didn't think you had any duties.'

'I have no duties at all! I call them for interview: they don't turn up! They're all heathens. All they do is mock and sneer. I hate the lot of them. All I do is break my fingernails moving stones around, and all that turns out to be for no reason because you knew about the stairs and have the wretched key!'

'I found out yesterday, Father –'

'Have you been down?'

'No!' I was going to tell you, so calm yourself down – I'll give it to you later and you can go exploring.'

'I'll go see the Brethren first, then –'

'You have still got the radio set, haven't you?'

'Yes.'

'Is it charged?'

'Yes!'

'What about Lord Vyner? Any news on the ghost?'

'I've seen nothing. Tomaz won't talk about it. I tell you what, though . . .' He patted a small satchel that hung over his shoulder. 'I'll be ready for him if he does show up. Him or his missus – I can deal with ghosts.'

'What's in there?'

'That's my exorcism kit. I'm taking no chances now the old witch has gone as well.'

'You're not a priest any more. What good's that going to

do?'

Father O'Hanrahan took a long mouthful of whisky, licked his lips, and smiled. 'I remember the basics. I got some fresh holy water, mail order. I got it all written down, and anyway – it's like riding a bike. Exorcism is something you don't forget.'

'Drink up, then. Sounds like you've got a lot of work to do.'

Professor Worthington was in the Tower of Science with the headmaster and noticed a flashlight bobbing over the grass. She had brought the python up to her lab and it lay coiled around her chair, hoping for some scraps of toast. The two teachers always met last thing at night to discuss the day and review progress.

'Father O'Hanrahan's out and about,' she said.

'Is he?'

'What could he be up to at this time of night?'

'I think he's looking for a purpose, Clarissa. I don't think he feels connected to this community just yet.'

'I wonder if you should have invited him.'

'He invited himself. I think I have to get better at saying *no* to people. Having said that, Doonan is an absolute blessing. He's just the sort of teacher we need.'

'He's very good with Caspar, I've noticed. Even Miles gets on with him.'

'Why do you say *even Miles*? Miles seems to have calmed down.'

'Miles won't ever be calm. Have you seen the way Henry's behaving, by the way?'

'No. Not particularly.'

'You don't notice things, do you, Giles?'

'How is Henry behaving?'

'He's always watching Miles. Something's brewing.'

144

'Something's always brewing, that's the nature of a school . . .'

'Yes, but Henry feels things. Henry's on edge and I don't know why.'

'Clarissa, I'm sorry to interrupt – but is that snake trying to hypnotise me, by any chance?'

Professor Worthington scratched the python's head gently, but it didn't take its eyes off the headmaster's.

'He's probably wondering if he could swallow you. That's our next project, you know. Once we've finished reproduction, the boys want to do digestion. It will mean ordering piglets, but I think we should follow enthusiasm when it's shown.'

Chapter Twenty-one

It was pitch dark when Father O'Hanrahan reached the chapel. He was in a hurry, feeling at last that there was progress to be made. He had a torch in his hand and the key in his pocket. He descended the steps slowly and tapped at the door.

'Hello?' he cried, softly. 'Is anyone there?'

He went to knock more loudly, but hesitated. He didn't need to announce his arrival and it might be better to approach secretly. He fitted the key as silently as he could and the mechanism turned. Masking his torch with one hand, he pushed it open to reveal a tiny landing and another set of steps descending into darkness. There was a scent of wood smoke and incense.

Holding his breath, he thought he could detect a very faint chanting. His heart leaped – he could see a candle in a small stone recess. This was a breakthrough moment and he descended the steps, holding tight to the iron rail. He was underground at last! After so much searching and expectation, he was close to the secret tunnels. The pump-room didn't interest him at all: what thrilled him to his bones was the knowledge that he must be so close to the whole tunnel network and all the Vyner chambers.

He could hear the chanting still, getting louder.

He came to a passage and a dozen more candles; he walked along it, gingerly. It widened and turned, and at last he came to what had to be the Brethren's chambers. The ceiling was low. He passed a number of small cells that might have been bedrooms. A golden glow gleamed up ahead and he was drawn to it, the music slow, peaceful, concentrated.

Six figures, all in brown robes.

They sat with their legs crossed, their hands upon their knees. Father O'Hanrahan waited another five minutes, until there was a pause. Then he spoke.

'Gentlemen,' he said. 'I'm sorry to startle you.'

The monks did not react.

'Forgive the intrusion,' he said. 'There's bad news up at the house and I thought you ought to be the first to hear of it.' He looked round for a chair and there wasn't one. He was about to speak, when one of the monks resumed the chant, in a high-pitched, quavering voice.

The priest raised his voice. 'If you wouldn't mind just pausing for a moment? I'm all for a bit of worship, but business is business.'

The chant stopped and six heads turned to look at him. The monks wore their hoods up, so their faces were in shadow.

'Serious business, gents. And it hasn't been easy tracking you down. By God, you can run like rats.'

He paused and nobody moved. The monks looked identical. Having moved their heads, they were now motionless.

'I understand a chat is not easy for you and I respect that. A vow is a vow and we're all holy men together. So what I thought I'd do, was organise a little code system, which we used in Ballybeg when these situations arose. I did a few of these silent routines myself, so I know where you're coming from. No one will think any the worse of you if we bend the rules a little bit.'

Father O'Hanrahan chose a monk at random and walked across to him. He put his stick in front of the old man's nose and said, 'Would you be so kind as to take a hold of this stick, mister?'

The monk seemed not to have heard. The seconds passed and Father O'Hanrahan repeated himself. 'I know it's a distraction, sir, but the sooner we do business the sooner I'm out of your way. News is news and it affects your future.' Very slowly, the old man's hands came up from his knees and gently took the stick.

'I'm sure you know the form,' said the priest, with a certain relief. 'You knock the stick upon the ground. Once is yes and twice is no. I'll sit down, if you don't mind – try and make myself a bit more comfortable. Then we can – ouch! – get on with what we all need to get on with.'

He placed himself opposite the monk with the stick. He was surrounded and their concentration was intense. Even so, the priest had the sensation that in a strange way the monks were unaware of him. He coughed.

'Lady Vyner has passed away,' he said, grandly. 'In the last forty-eight hours. I was not at the bedside, but you will be pleased to know that I was there a short time before. I had the feeling then that she knew her time was upon her and I was able to be of some comfort. Her loss will leave many of us devastated. You, most of all. Would you mind knocking if you're taking this in, sir?'

There was a pause and the listening monk knocked once upon the floor.

'Well, thank you for that, it's nice to know this *is* a conversation. What does the sad and tragic death of the old girl mean to us? Well, it means there's bound to be a few changes – and I want us to get ahead of the game. The estate trustees are going to want to work out just how much stuff you're sitting on, down here – they'll be adding things up even as we speak. We, therefore, need to move fast. Would you just mind knocking again, so I know your mind isn't wandering?'

Again, there was a pause. Again, the stick moved once.

'OK,' said Father O'Hanrahan. 'I'm not one to be mealy-mouthed. I don't want to be the bull smashing at the china shop, when you boys have been here so long, getting your feet under the table. But I'm looking for the sword of the Order. The Order of St Caspar. Shall we just nail our colours to the mast – is that what you're looking for too?'

'No,' said the monks.

The old man shouted in terror and clutched at his chest. His gasped for air and crossed himself, peering around behind him.

'For the love of God,' he gasped. 'You nearly gave me a heart attack! Could you not have spoken up before? Oh my word . . .' He found a handkerchief and mopped his brow. 'I'm glad of the breakthrough, but that was a shock. We can talk at last, can we?'

'We are allowed to speak of the Order,' said a monk to Father O'Hanrahan's left. The old man spun round to look at him.

'And of the Vyners,' said the man with the stick.

'Lady Vyner's dead?' said someone softly. 'Are we sure about that?'

Father O'Hanrahan realised that there appeared to be no ultimate spokesman. This meant he would never be sure who he should be looking at. It didn't matter a great deal, since he couldn't see faces – but it was disorientating.

'She's tough as boots,' muttered somebody. 'I don't believe it.'

'Let's focus on the issue,' said Father O'Hanrahan. 'You can do your weeping and wailing a bit later, because I want to get something clear. Whilst I am looking for the sword, I want to check that you are *also* looking for the sword. Is that what you just said? Because I have assumed, up to now, that your Order was formed in honour of the sword. The Brethren of the Lost were looking for –'

'You're right and you're wrong, Father,' said one of the monks.

'So . . . very well.' Father O'Hanrahan licked his lips. 'Am I right that you are *looking* for the sword?'

'No, sir. We are not looking for anything.'

Another monk spoke. 'What we were looking for, we found. Our search ended some time ago.'

'Yours has ended too.'

Father O'Hanrahan felt a little pulse of hope beating within. He'd never been good at reading subtexts or hidden meanings, but the answers he'd heard could suggest extremely good news.

'We're talking about the sword of St Caspar – can I get that absolutely straight?'

Six voices said, 'Yes.'

'Which means . . . it's here. In Ribblestrop?'

'It was brought here by Lord Vyner. It's been here for more than half a century. Now it has its guardian.'

'And Lady Vyner was a guardian?'

'No, she was not.'

'The sword is held for the grandson,' said a quiet voice. 'He will inherit everything.'

'But the sword itself,' said Father O'Hanrahan. 'Can we stick to the point here?'

'Our Order traced its journey in the same way that you did,' said another monk. 'There was a sighting in Villeneuve. It is written about in a private diary, in nineteen hundred and seven, and the writer refers to it being displayed at a supper.'

'Then it was moved to a bank, in Switzerland,' said someone.

'From there it was moved to Rouen,' said the first man, 'and the intention was to get it out of the country during the war.'

'But where—'

'One of our own Order gave it to Lord Vyner, in person, and helped him bring it here.'

'Of course, he was given it with many other items. Even Lord Vyner didn't know its full importance. The guardian need not know the worth of what he guards.'

'But where is it now?' cried the priest. 'You're telling me it's here? Here at Ribblestrop?'

'Yes.'

'Then whereabouts? In this room?' Even the priest realised that he sounded too anxious. His voice betrayed a certain desperation and terrible yearning. He discovered he was standing and sweating heavily.

'Father,' said a monk, 'the sword is in its rightful place. Our job is to stay close to it. We draw great spiritual comfort from it.'

'We're all old men,' said another. 'To be close to it is enough.'

The priest could stand it no more. 'Have you seen it, though?' he shouted. 'Have you actually touched it?'

Nobody spoke.

'I must assume you have! Is it as lovely as we're told? Tell me the truth. Does it have the gems intact – does it have the twelve stones?'

'It's in safe hands, Father.'

'Are the stones – the apostles – are they there still? I've seen it in glass. I've seen the replica.' His voice was trembling and high-pitched. He didn't know who to look at and he dropped to his knees. 'Show it to me!' he cried. 'Show it to me!'

Chapter Twenty-two

'Can I ask you, Father: what is your interest in the sword?'

The monk's voice was gentle and courteous, but Father O'Hanrahan was trembling all over and was less ready for the question than he might have been.

'My interest,' he said, 'is that . . . a sacred article – one that so many hold in such high esteem – is where it clearly shouldn't be. Neglected. Unseen. My interest . . . is to return it.'

'To what place?' said a voice. 'A bank vault?'

'The sword has reached its home,' said somebody. 'It cannot be moved.'

'And it's not neglected, sir. It's in regular use.'

The soft voice from behind spoke again. 'To answer the question that you put earlier, Father. Only Brother Rees has seen the sword and he only saw it once. He touched it, I gather. And then he came away.'

'*Where is it?*' hissed Father O'Hanrahan. 'Who's Brother Rees? Where is he?'

'Close by.'

'Oh, will they not answer a simple question?' howled the priest. 'Must I tear this place apart and find it for myself? Where is the sword of St Caspar? Where is this Brother Rees?'

There was a long silence, as Father O'Hanrahan's fury soaked into the stonework.

'You asked if it is as beautiful as the reports suggest,' said a voice, at last. It was of a higher pitch than the others and hesitant; Father O'Hanrahan found himself spinning round again. A seventh monk had entered the chamber and there was an eighth behind him.

'I am Brother Rees.'

'We didn't mean to startle you,' said the other. 'I'm Brother Martin, by the way. We were sleeping, but we heard the voices. I'm sure we can answer all your questions, given time.'

'Sit here, Brother.'

'Oh, we're happy standing, thank you,' said Brother Rees. 'I've had a full six hours.'

'I'm going to get a little broth,' said Brother Martin. 'Would anyone like some? Or a cheeseboard, maybe?'

There were various replies, as orders were placed, and then the silence settled again.

'Funny,' said Brother Rees, with a chuckle. 'Our work is done without the need for conversation, but now you'll find us quite the chatterboxes. It's why we have the vow of silence – we'd never get anything done without it! But we do allow ourselves to speak of the sword and, yes, as my brother explained, I was the one privileged to see it.'

'We teased him rather,' said a monk opposite. 'We called him *nosy-parker*.'

'Oh, I was certainly teased!' said Brother Rees and the soft laughter pattered around him. 'But the fact is, I did not mean to walk in on it —'

'Some of us, you know, still aren't sure of your motives!' There was another flutter of laughter, louder now.

Father O'Hanrahan groaned with frustration and the laughter died.

'*Where* did you see it?' said the priest, slowly.

'It's in Tomaz's home. He lives in the old storage chambers and it's in his dining room.'

'But where – please God – is Tomaz's home?'

'Close by,' said Brother Rees. 'Just above the Churchill bunker, if you've been down there. The access is blocked, though, and I'm afraid that was because of me poking my nose in. Tomaz must have realised I'd got in and he rather prudently changed the entry system. We couldn't get in now, even if we wanted to. Lady Vyner had a map, I believe. Whether or not it still exists is—'

'But how *did* you get in?' cried the priest. 'Where's the access?'

'Well, that's a bit of a story. I discovered the boy's home quite by accident, when I was rambling. I was a geologist before my calling – I say a geologist, I mean by that I was a geology teacher. And one of my passions was to take the boys and girls potholing, which I don't suppose you can do any more – but I used to enjoy it and so did they. It's a craze – once it's in your blood, it never leaves you. So unlike my respected friends here, I would do a little exploring in the Ribblestrop rocks – there are some splendid fissures up on the Edge and they go hundreds of metres down. I'm not advising you to try, by the way, Father – they are very dangerous.'

'There have been casualties,' said another monk.

'Oh yes. If the waters are high, the whole area becomes *lethally* dangerous. There's an underground lagoon and they say it's claimed a number of lives—'

'I am not about to go swimming in a lagoon!' said Father O'Hanrahan. 'All I'm asking is how you got into the boy's home.'

'Well, I'm not sure I could find the spot again, but I was accessing a bottle-neck, which after about fifteen metres got much tighter and turned into a spigot. A bottle-neck is an opening in the rock that gets narrow. Well, the one I found was a beauty and it led me into an unusually tight, cantilevered elbow – easy to get down, but harder on the ascent. It was the spigot that took me down to Tomaz's beautiful home. We'd been aware of him, of course, and we knew he'd found the treasures—'

'Oh!' cried the priest. 'Praise be! He *has* found them . . .'

'Yes, and if you can persuade him to show you round, then you must let him. We have never intruded as a brotherhood, because it seemed wrong – he's a nervous child. But – as I told you – I found myself climbing down through the spigot and, suddenly . . . I was in one of the chambers. Years ago I could have got back the way I'd come in, but . . . I suppose I gave in to temptation and sought the easier path. The way through Tomaz's home and out of the door was a simpler option.'

'Which is why young Tomaz made the door rather smaller,' said a monk and there was laughter again.

'Now it's like a rabbit hole.'

'Will you finish the story?' said Father O'Hanrahan. 'Did you see the sword or not?'

'By coincidence, I did,' said Brother Rees.

'It was not coincidence,' said another. 'It was the Lord's doing.'

'It was ordained,' said another. 'You're quite right.'

Brother Rees took over again. 'Who knows?' he said. 'We will argue about that until Doomsday. The important thing was that I saw it. I went through Tomaz's lounge and he'd left it out. I admit I inspected it. As far as I could tell, the stones are in place – that was the geologist in me again, I'm afraid. I said a prayer – and I left. So to answer your final question, *is it beautiful*? Well. Its beauty is concealed. The impure can never bear true perfection, so the stones are

155

covered.' He smiled. 'But the sword has come home, Father, and that boy is one of its guardians.'

Father O'Hanrahan thought he might sob. Hope and frustration churned his entrails and he was giddy. 'You say it is in its rightful place . . .' he whispered.

'We do,' said the monk to his left. 'It is. Ribblestrop Towers.'

'But. If I understand you . . . I'm sorry, this is astonishing news, to be told everything at once like this. If I understand you correctly, it is in a cave. And the cave is the . . . dwelling of this little long-haired fellow – this Tomaz – a little foreign orphan from nobody quite knows where. He broke into the chambers used by Vyner – himself a criminal – and is fooling about with the plunder. Selling wine at knockdown prices and goodness only knows what else! The sword of St Caspar, therefore – which must surely belong in the church – is in the care of a thieving child. We must remove it from him!'

'The sword,' said Brother Rees, 'is where it should be. I can see we're going to differ on this point, but hear me out, Father. The sword comes from Jordan, and tradition says it was blessed by St Caspar as a sword of healing and reconciliation. Traditionally, it brings peace, to lost individuals and—'

'I don't need a history lesson! I need the sword!'

'And you're not familiar with the rhyme, I take it?' said Brother Martin. He had returned with a plate of cheese and was chewing thoughtfully.

'What rhyme?' said Father O'Hanrahan.

'I used to have it by rote,' said Brother Martin. 'Something about a tiger . . .'

'I can remember it,' said another voice. 'I've always thought it very pretty:

> *'The child knows no fear, if the tiger he rides,*
> *And the* something *shall be healed, for all that has passed;*
> *The river shall run . . .'*

He stopped.

'Sorry, I've lost it. I know there's a river running . . .'

Another voice took over, lower and stronger. The temperature dipped, though only the monks noticed. They drew their robes a little tighter and did not look at the one who spoke, from the shadows. It was a low, heavy voice. It was as if whoever spoke had difficulty forming the words:

> *'The child knows no fear, if the tiger he rides,*
> *And the sick can be healed through all that must pass;*
> *The river shall run full, that the valley be watered – at last*
> *Will the labyrinth come straight, though the sword hides.*
> *Lion and lamb, united in this place;*
> *After the lightning and the damaged face.*
> *Seek not for the children that choose to be lost: realise*
> *That the world still weeps, but must one day dry its eyes.*
> *St Caspar will come home; in this place he'll be sworn.*
> *So drown the precious sword: from his heart it can't be drawn.'*

'Tomaz is not a thief,' said Brother Rees. 'He is a custodian. And we will protect him.'

'I don't understand.'

'I'm sure you don't,' said Brother Martin. 'But let's have some broth, before you go.'

Father O'Hanrahan was on his feet. He had spied a passageway behind Brother Rees, half concealed by an old curtain. He clicked his torch back on and shouldered his satchel.

'Oh no,' he said. 'You can sit chuntering all day. You can eat your broth till you burst! I'll find the damn thing myself . . .'

157

Chapter Twenty-three

'How's it feel to be back?' said Millie.

'Good,' said Sanchez. 'It feels like I was never away.'

'The film went down a storm. The little ones thought it was magic. They cried when you disappeared.'

Sanchez smiled. 'You haven't asked me about my mother.'

Millie hesitated. 'I know. I suppose I never really understood what you were doing. It was her ... birthday? But she's dead.'

'It's just tradition. You don't stop having a birthday party just because someone's died. You have it at the graveside.'

'With presents? With a cake?'

Sanchez smiled again. 'We have food, yes. We give each other presents. The main thing is you just sit with your mum. Keep her company.' He looked at Millie. 'Did you see your parents at all?'

'No. Easter's the next meeting. Maybe.'

Sanchez paused. 'Do you miss Colombia?' he said.

'Yes,' said Millie. 'I think about the mountains. The horses. But I suppose the best thing . . .'

'What?'

'Wow.' Millie laughed. 'I was about to say something really nice to you, then, and I just managed to stop myself.'

'In that case, I won't say what I was going to say.'

'Deal.'

It was evening. The children sat in a blaze of candles in the cathedral home of Tomaz. Like the headmaster, he'd found it impossible to pull the Christmas decorations down – the orphans had made them so lovingly. Shards of mirror hung on a thousand invisible threads. Nightlights had been laid along the fissures of rock and the mirrors threw their flames in a slowly turning cosmos of tiny stars. They'd painted tree branches white and positioned them with such skill that the grotto took on the magic of a fairy-tale forest. If the snow queen was out there with little Kay, and if Girda was still searching, she might pass at any moment. The children lay back in their seats, hot and fat. The wood-stove blazed and they fanned themselves as Tomaz stirred the embers with the poker. The feast was done. His moussaka had been rich, his salad cool.

Bottles of wine were moving rapidly up and down the tables, most children heaping sugar into their glasses and stirring vigorously. They all found the Clos de Beze way too dry, though with chilled lemonade it was refreshing. Tomaz had no fridge, but an underground spring kept essential items ice-cold.

Why an underground feast? Why the celebration? They needed no excuses – most evenings were celebrations of some kind. But this one formally marked the return of Sanchez. It marked the arrival of Imagio and the six baby panthers. It marked a football game that would never be forgotten or surpassed, and another overnight snowfall with a refreezing of the lake. Millie suggested they should celebrate the recent disappearance of Father O'Hanrahan, who had not been seen for two days and two nights, but nobody else felt as cruel.

159

Sanchez said to Millie, 'What do you think of Miles, by the way? Are you glad you brought him back?'

'He's harmless enough. I can't make up my mind. He's funny, but he's such an attention-seeker.'

'I guess you don't like attention-seekers?'

Millie narrowed her eyes. 'Let me ask *you* something – and this is serious. Did you write to him over Christmas?'

'No.'

'Have you ever written to him?'

'No.'

'He said you did, you know. And I saw you kiss him, on the football pitch. If something's going on, you ought to tell me, Sanchez.'

'Millie,' said Sanchez. 'You spent three weeks in South America – we kiss everyone.'

'You didn't write to him?'

'You are such a little English girl, sometimes. What does a kiss mean? Are you jealous of him?'

'Hi.'

Oli had appeared behind Millie, with a cigar in one hand and a candle in the other. He presented the cigar to her and waited until she leaned in for a light. Three puffs later, she said, 'Thank you, Oli. An ashtray and you're dismissed.'

The little boy walked off and Sanchez stared, expressionless. 'You still amaze me,' he said. 'You still take such advantage, every time.'

'Sanchez, it's the first time that boy's been truly needed. A child like that is born to serve.'

'Is it true he brings you breakfast every morning?'

'Every morning, nice and hot.'

'Ruskin told me. I couldn't believe it. He's the cleverest kid in the school and you treat him like a slave.'

'It's a deal we struck. And he's a lot less geeky than he was – just like Sam. My mission is to help these boys become useful human beings . . . So Miles is really a liar – I did know it. Why isn't he here?'

'He's with Caspar. They've become friends again.'

'I thought they hated each other.'

'Yes, they do. And then they don't. You don't understand Miles at all, do you?'

'Are you sure you didn't write to him?'

'And he really bothers you, doesn't he? He wrote to me twice, if you want to know. They were weird letters, they were . . . You don't know how lonely he is, alright?' Sanchez took the cigar and inhaled, long and deep. 'I should have written. But I'll tell you something about Miles,' he said. 'He is actually incapable of telling the truth. He lies all the time, by accident. Half the things he says, you can pretty much guarantee are a lie.'

'He told me about a game you used to play. His "favourite game".'

'We played football. Scrabble, I think – which he cheated at. Conjured a ghost . . . I'm not sure what his favourite was.'

'He said it involved a gun. He called it his "favourite game" and asked did I want to play.'

Sanchez sat up.

'Millie, if that boy came near a gun, it would be time to run away very, very fast.'

'He was telling Tomaz too—'

'He's past all that. That was last term and I told him he had to stop.'

'Stop what?'

'All that stuff about games. He's happier now, you can see it.'

Millie went to speak, then changed her mind. 'He's special to you, isn't he?'

Sanchez looked at her. 'Yes, of course. He's a special guy.'

Millie frowned.

161

She wanted to tell Sanchez about the conversation up on the tower. She wanted to unload and was almost prepared to risk Sanchez's fury when she brought up the gun. But at the same time she didn't want to break the mood they'd created. The cigar smoke smelled so old and wise – she would never admit it was making her feel sick. Once again she was torn between weakness and strength. Oli brought the ashtray and the moment passed as he leaned between them.

'How's my submarine?' said Millie, hugging him to her. 'You were going to build me the best submarine in the land.'

'Mmm,' said Oli. 'I've made progress. We had a maiden-voyage yesterday, but the radio signals were being interfered with. It's watertight, but I'm not sure . . .'

He faltered. There were raised voices at the end of the table.

'I can't hear you,' said Millie.

'I'm not sure what depth we can go to.'

Sanchez was standing up. There seemed to be an argument raging and a flurry of angry hands. 'It's just not on! It's not on at all!' cried a high-pitched voice.

It was Ruskin and he was surrounded by the littlest orphans. He broke free of them and moved swiftly to Sanchez, choking back a sob. 'Hold me back, Sanchez!' he was saying. 'I can no longer be held responsible . . . this is an outrage!'

'What?' said Sanchez.

Asilah was on his feet too and the smaller orphans looked very crestfallen.

'It's the wretched, blasted bank!' cried Ruskin. 'I thought it was all sorted out, but they've just told me I have no credit left and I can't have a chocolate! I am the only person who put money in and now they won't let me take it out again.'

'Ruskin,' said Sam. 'If you want a sweet, I can lend you money!'

It was the wrong thing to say. Ruskin clutched his head and shouted: 'I do not want your money! I do not want anybody else's money! I want mine!'

He plunged into a chair and put his face on the table. A young orphan put his hand on the boy's shoulder and Sam sat down next to him.

Asilah spoke curtly in his own language and the younger orphans all started talking at once. One held a file of papers and another the abacus.

'I knew this was a bad idea,' said Millie. 'Money and children: a recipe for disaster.'

It was true that the school bank and tuck shop had become remarkably complicated. The orphans that ran it had learned arithmetic with record-breaking speed. Now their arithmetic had mutated into interest calculations and profit projections. Eric's younger brother had been at the helm – a sweet-faced boy of six by the name of Kenji, who'd spent two years of his life sweeping the floor of a bank in Western China. In between sweepings, he'd read financial newspapers, and he now looked after all the children's accounts as credit-controller. His team carried the tuck shop around, erecting it in corridors, classrooms – anywhere the children went. Right now they were selling homemade chocolates for a penny each or three for two, or five for three with a free gift and loyalty card for ten. The children ate them with the thick coffee that Podma was cooking.

'How is it I have no money?' moaned Ruskin. 'The only one . . . Thirty pounds I put in!'

'You have money but we moved it,' said Kenji, softly.

'I don't understand!'

'Look, Jake . . . your investment's growing all the time,' said another boy. This was Anjoli's cousin – a tiny, black-eyed boy called Nikko. He flipped the beads on the abacus, his fingers a blur. 'We got you, listen . . . twenty-eight per cent over ten days. That's not bad! Same as everyone. You're totally protected, Ruskin – your portfolio's solid.'

'But you can't withdraw at the moment,' said Kenji. 'The dollar's too strong – you'd be cutting your own throat.'

'All I wanted was a chocolate. One chocolate!'

A ring of chocolates was quickly put around him.

'All I was saying,' said Nikko, clicking quickly, 'is to put the purchase against someone else's account, just for the time being – just till Hong Kong closes. It's for the good of the school – we got a vineyard in Argentina going up like a rocket. We don't need instability.'

'If you really want to use your own credit,' said Kenji, 'we can authorise it, but it's going to be three over base.'

'Crazy,' said someone.

'Eat your chocolate, Ruskin,' said Millie. 'There's no point arguing.'

'I've lost everything,' moaned Ruskin.

'No, no, no!' said Kenji, calmly. 'Nobody's lost money – we just *moved* your investment and, as everybody knows, it costs money to move money.'

His friends were nodding.

'He'll be better off in the end,' said one. 'You've got to take a few hits up front.'

'When you sign up with the syndicate, your investment may go up – it may go down . . .'

Ruskin tried one more time. 'Please tell them, Sam. I did not sign up with any syndicate!'

'Jake, maybe you didn't read the small print . . .' said Sam. 'I remember now, you'd lost your glasses – it was after supper.'

Kenji smiled sadly. 'Everyone signed,' he said. 'Including you, Millie – and you're a lot better off than you were. We've invested part of your capital in gemstones, making three hundred per cent in a fortnight.'

'Not after the commissions,' said Nikko. 'Two seven zero, net.'

'I don't have any money,' said Millie. 'I never gave you any.'

'Ah, but that's why we used Ruskin's!' said Kenji. 'We put his money into a communal pot and we struck lucky in the first week. The headmaster put in a fair sum as well – the numbers are pretty sweet!'

They were interrupted by dessert.

It was a Podma-Tomaz speciality – a dish they'd created together, with Captain Routon, for the New Year party, and were now repeating by popular demand. They had constructed a long platter of fresh fruit and chocolate, and sculpted it into the shape of a Viking longboat. The oars were gingersnaps and the figureheads at either end were dishes of meringue, loaded with cherries. It sat in a sea of neat brandy, which they now ceremonially set on fire.

Ruskin sat up and wiped his face. The blue flames blazed, illuminating nineteen eager children. The confection collapsed into a mess of molten chocolate and sweet, roasted fruit, and it was scooped into bowls. It was the closest most had come to paradise. When Tomaz appeared from the kitchens to sit down at last, he was cheered. The poor boy had been working all day: he looked exhausted, but happy. He sank into a chair and smiled.

'How's the ghost of Lord Vyner?' Millie asked, a little later.

It was nearly midnight and they knew they ought to be leaving for their dormitories soon. Sanjay had wound up the gramophone and sweet, crackly jazz was playing. Boys lay on sofas and rugs, some chatting, others simply gazing at the flickering lights above them.

Tomaz closed his eyes. 'He's good.'

'You know, Miles said he saw him again.'

165

'Really? He's been here all day, Millie – not Miles, I mean the ghost. Miles could have had a long chat – I just wanted to get on and cook.'

'Seriously? You've been with a ghost, all day?'

'This is his home, I told you that. He's always around at the moment. And I tell you, there's something weird going on. I thought I heard digging noises earlier and voices.'

'The monks, maybe?'

'No, they leave me alone. There's other people, but I don't know who. We had to open up the entrance to get Henry in – we need to shut it right down, tonight if possible. And there's something else.'

'What?'

'Did Miles tell you? He says he's lost Sanchez's gun.'

'That's completely impossible. He's lying.'

'He says he put it back in the hiding place and now it's gone. Do you think we ought to tell Sanchez?'

'Miles is a complete liar—'

'He shouldn't have that gun. He's still scary.'

'Tom, this is just his way of getting attention. Like not being here tonight, he wants everyone to talk about him. He's cracked!'

Tomaz sipped his wine. 'He might not tell the truth all the time, Millie. But he saved my life.'

'When?'

'I told you. He's a lot braver than most of us and Sanchez knows that. You saw him at football—'

'Oh, come on, you heard him on the tower! He's a nutcase!'

'No. Don't say things behind his back – he's my friend.'

They were interrupted by a tinkling sound. Asilah was rattling a spoon in a glass and the grotto fell silent. The boy stood straight and tall – flushed and happy. He had pulled on his blazer and buttoned it.

'I want to make a little speech,' he said. 'I don't want to be a bore, 'cause I know we get a lot of speeches, but . . . My friend Tomaz, down there, has cooked about the best meal I've ever eaten in my life. He made this place, and he invites us to it, and he does all the cooking, and I think he's one of the best people in the world!'

There was a storm of cheering and applause.

'I want to say that we're glad to have Imagio too. And Imagio doesn't want me to talk about this, but I think everyone needs to know . . . Imagio, don't go! Get him!'

Imagio had made a leap from his chair, but Anjoli and Sanjay were too quick for him. They held the squirming boy by his arms and pinned him down on a rug.

'We know he's the best footballer in the world,' continued Asilah. 'We all saw that.'

There were murmurs of support. Imagio lay back, with his eyes closed.

'And we know he saved us from defeat. But the thing is, something happened. I think we all ought to know about it, because it's good news. Sad news, but—'

'What's happened?' cried Sam, impatiently. 'Get on with it!'

Asilah stopped. He delved into his pocket and brought out a piece of grey paper. It had various official-looking stamps and he opened it carefully.

'Sorry – I'll just say it. Stand up, Imagio – come on.'

Anjoli and Sanjay hauled him to his feet and Imagio stood staring at his shoes.

'They've offered him an immediate contract,' said Asilah. 'It's fantastic news, but it means . . .'

'Who's offered?' said Millie. 'When?'

'The old guy,' said Sanchez, proudly. 'The talent-scout who came down to watch that guy, Darren.'

'This telegram arrived this morning,' said Asilah. 'And

167

Imagio's not too sure, but . . . well. It's big money. They want him in London. Formal offer. They want him immediately. He's gonna be a professional footballer.'

There was a silence as the enormity of the news crept over each child. Many remembered the video they'd watched, of a street boy in tatty shorts, dancing with a Coke can. Some could even recall Sanchez's words, 'so all you dream about . . . the richest boy in Colombia . . .'

Imagio sat up. He didn't know where to look, though. He was smiling, but nervously. Grey shirt, black-and-gold tie. He looked so different already: he'd been turned into a Ribblestrop schoolboy and was soon to be stolen away again. Anjoli had his arm round him.

'He can't go,' said Millie. 'He's only just got here!'

Imagio said something softly in Spanish.

'He's going to be a pro,' said an awestruck Sam. 'He'll play for Arsenal maybe. Chelsea!'

'He'll play for Colombia,' said Sanchez. 'I guarantee that.'

The applause started again. Sam was on his feet, his eyes moist. It had dawned on him that he had experienced a privilege he would never have again. He had played with a superstar. The child standing opposite was a genius and that had been instantly recognised. Sam started to sing and, before the first line was done, the whole school had taken up the tune. Imagio was set on his feet, and he stood there, in a tangle of hair that hid his eyes, his hands over his nose and mouth. Three times through they sang it, and everyone rose up, one by one, to honour him.

> *'Ribblestrop, Ribblestrop, precious unto me;*
> *This is what I dream about and where I want to be.*
> *Early in the morning, finally at night,*
> *Ribblestrop I'll die for thee, carrying the light.'*

Father O'Hanrahan heard the song. He was lost – more lost than he had ever been, clambering in the terrible circles of the labyrinth. The song came drifting from a fissure in the rock above his head. His hands were damp with sweat and blood, and his cassock was covered in sand. The tunnels ran up and down, round and round. Some were blocked, others simply looped back to his starting point, and the poor man was exhausted.

'Ribblestrop, Ribblestrop, precious unto me!'

He leaned against the wall and a sob escaped his lips. From the same rock, he thought he caught a sweet smell, thick and sugary like burnt fruit . . .

He sank to his knees and hauled out his radio. 'Cuthbertson,' he whispered. He wasn't even sure what button to press, he was so tired. 'Come in, Cuthbertson.'

He could hear people clapping and cheering.

'Please answer! I'm so close. I'm so close!'

Chapter Twenty-four

The next morning, the temperature dropped still lower.

It meant that working in the classrooms was almost impossible, for there was no heating system. This meant no R.E., no art class and no handwriting practice. Routon simply lit a bonfire and upped the intensity of the circus-construction. Flavio organised braziers and the tent-stitching continued.

Professor Worthington lit all the gas-burners in the Tower of Science and refused to cancel nature study. She got the headmaster to help her with a large vat of hot chocolate and the lab slowly warmed up.

She looked down from her window and saw the boys capering towards the building. The snow was thick again and they never seemed to tire of it.

'We must get into a proper routine,' she said to the headmaster. 'The term is slipping away.'

'I agree, Clarissa,' he said. 'But one has to be spontaneous. They've nearly finished the marquee, you know. I thought we could start the speeches inside, with a little demonstration of gymnastics –'

'I'm sure we could!' said Professor Worthington, with a touch of bitterness. 'I get a demonstration every day – Anjoli can do three trapeze-somersaults before Eric catches him by the ankles. He was showing off yesterday.'

'Where?'

'Here. He's a menace.'

'But . . . there's no trapeze.'

'From the rafters, Giles – above your head! This is what I mean: I'm all for spontaneity, as you call it, but some of the boys lose all self-discipline. If Anjoli had fallen, he would have broken precious equipment, not to mention these beautiful models.'

'Yes, I've been wondering what they are.' He peered again at the cardboard and plastic. 'What are they meant to be?'

'The arches are pelvic bones.'

'Pelvic bones?'

'They constructed the pelvis first, before putting in the uterus. We've used plasticene for the muscles –'

'And rubber bands, my word . . .'

'The uterine sac was Sanjay's work, and the umbilical cord. See that tube there? Turn the pump on and you get the blood supply, all the way to the infant. That vessel there is the placenta.'

'Well, well.'

'That child could be a surgeon. I tell you, he's got the most delicate fingers I've ever seen and a complete understanding of musculature. I've offered him evening classes.'

'Sanjay's . . . eleven, isn't he?'

'Yes, and his dissection is quite superb. I tell you who else has impressed me and that's Imagio – another little medic in the making. You've got to put your foot down about this wretched football nonsense: we can't let him go.'

'What exactly are you dissecting?'

'Rats at the moment. We're infested again, luckily, and the orphans are a dab hand at catching them. They use the scorpion.'

171

'What do you mean?'

'They use the scorpion to sting them and we can get them onto the slab with their hearts still beating. By the way, Doonan fainted the other day.'

'When? Why?'

'It was Sanjay again. His rat was pregnant and he was separating out the foetuses – so we'd all gathered round. I don't think young Doonan's a very *worldly* young man . . .'

'But what was he doing here?'

'Oh, he always joins the science classes. He's had no education, you know. It's criminal what some schools get away with. Do you want to start pouring the drinks? I can hear Miles.'

The door burst open and the room was suddenly full of excited snow-monsters. Doonan was in the centre, head and shoulders above most, with an unnatural glow of desperation in his eyes. Miles was pushing him from behind.

'Oh, Professor!' he said. 'Headmaster . . .'

'What's the matter?'

'The lake's frozen.'

'Of course the lake's frozen; it's been frozen for weeks.'

'But Captain Routon's done some checks with Oli,' said Doonan. The children were silent. 'He's taken some samples and . . . he says . . . He says . . .'

'Spit it out, Doonan – what does he say?'

'He says it's safe for skating, Miss,' said Asilah, quietly. 'But only with your permission being as it's your lesson. We don't want to cut classes . . .'

Professor Worthington looked at the headmaster, who was looking at his hands.

'I see,' she said. 'You don't want to cut classes, but the lake's frozen and perfect for skating.'

Sam said, 'We could do an extra session tonight. After tiger-taming.'

'These classes are important,' said Professor Worthington, softly. 'Captain Routon knows how I feel about ice: I will not tolerate aimless sliding about – that's for playtime. If you had ice-skates, it would be different. We could call it sport.'

'Er . . . we do, Miss,' said Asilah.

Shyly, each child revealed what they had, until this moment, been concealing: a pair of antique ice-skates, courtesy of that early trip to the Ribblestrop auction house.

'But do they fit?'

'Yes, Miss,' said the children.

'And you're saying that despite being in the middle of a fascinating science project, you would prefer to waste your time chasing each other, falling over and generally messing about on a frozen lake?'

'Yes, Miss,' said the children.

'Very well. The headmaster and I will join you in five minutes.'

The children were out like a flock of squealing, howling birds. Some grabbed their bikes; others grabbed useful toys, such as tea-trays, sticks, and odd bits of furniture. Sam, Ruskin, and Oli were carrying their most prized possession, finished only the night before: Millie's radio-controlled submarine. How they had found the hours would always be a mystery, but somehow the soldering had been completed – they'd had a bath-time trial – and it was now ready for the lake.

An interesting sight was Flavio, in a thick fur coat. He was exercising Victor, which was the name that had finally been chosen for the grumpy crocodile. The beast slithered miserably on the ice, then rested. It was showing more animation that it had ever shown back in its trough, but it still looked sour.

'He likes the cold,' said Flavio. 'I don' know why, but he's more restless now than he ever was.'

'I expect he wants a good swim,' said the headmaster. 'Has he been in the water?'

'I was trying to find some. The ice is too thick.'

Victor made a sudden break for freedom, but Flavio had the leash firmly and held him back. His claws scudded uselessly, and Flavio dragged him gently backwards. Victor was less than two metres, tip-to-tip. He rarely opened his mouth, and when he did it was an unspectacular centimetre or two, as if eating was an effort. His teeth ran around his face in a crooked zip, some in, some out; his eyelids slid open and closed, but he never seemed particularly aware of the world around him. Flavio had secretly been hoping he'd die; he longed for a pair of crocodile-skin boots and knew just how to make them.

'I'm going to show these miserable children how it's done,' said Professor Worthington, staring at the skaters. She had her own skates on and was experimenting with a few slow moves out from the bank.

'You skated before, huh?' said Flavio. 'It looks tricky to me.'

'Figure-skating champion, University of Geneva. I was sixteen, so I'm well out of practice. Are you up for a spin, Giles?'

'I'm afraid not,' said the headmaster. 'I think I'll stay back and watch Oli.'

Professor Worthington launched herself into a long, graceful arc, her arms horizontal and her right leg raised. She managed three quick pirouettes, then shoved off again in an elegant bounding motion. In seconds she was in the centre of the lake, in the thick of a racing mob. Before long, she and Millie had divided everyone into teams and a bizarre ice-hockey game was raging. One group kept its blazers on; the other side stripped them off and piled them up as goalposts. The puck was a punctured football, beaten flat, and Henry had soon broken enough tree branches so that everyone had a suitable stick.

Meanwhile, the engineering party had chosen a site and it was over there that the headmaster tottered. Oli had made some adjustments to the craft's buoyancy and, with a recharged radio, he was keen to put it through its paces. It had a set of bright halogen lights and he had the idea that he could use it for underwater exploration. His dream was to rig it up with a camera, but that would require a few more days' construction. It was long and sleek: sharp as a torpedo.

Sam and Ruskin trundled the mobile-drill into position and it was soon boring through the ice.

'Hey!' said Sam, looking down. 'What on earth is that?'

'I don't know what you're looking at,' said Ruskin. Ruskin's face was still a mass of sellotape and crooked lenses.

'Underneath us. Look! Oli, come and look at this! Sir! I can see gold!'

Sam had noticed something wonderful. It was a whirl of white ice, rising from the depths of the lake. The white water seemed to be locked inside blue ice – a form within a form. Jets of bubbles were corkscrewing from below, and they had been caught and frozen. It was a frozen whirlpool: a vertical torrent, twisted around itself and held absolutely still. At its base was a bar of shining gold.

'It's like a tree,' said Sam. 'It's an ice-tree . . .'

'Quite beautiful,' said the headmaster. 'It looks like an underwater fountain.'

Oli eased the submarine in through the hole that they'd cut. In seconds, lights blazing, it was nosing amongst the branches of the ice-sculpture, illuminating its blues and silvers. The controls were definitely more responsive and he was confident enough to plunge it deeper and deeper, so that it circled the torrent.

'Thermo-dynamics,' said Professor Worthington. 'A miracle of science.'

Chapter Twenty-five

'It's what happens when waters of varying velocities and temperatures meet,' continued the professor. 'They freeze at a different rate. Gather round, everyone – we can learn a lot from this. Oli, see if you can get the light to its root – where the bubbles start. You'll have to go deeper.'

The hockey game had finished, and most of the children were wet and bruised. Some had chattering teeth and most were exhausted. Miles, inevitably, was bloody. He was wet through, wrapped in Henry's blazer.

Oli did as he was told, dropping the sub another five or six metres until its pool of light seemed worryingly dim. The radio-control crackled with static, as if it was frightened.

'Yes,' said Professor Worthington. 'I've got a feeling about this. Just turn her round, turn her round a bit . . . there. What do you see?'

'Is it gold?' said Sanjay.

There was a little tremor of excitement. Most of the children were on their knees, staring through the ice. The submarine turned again and, sure enough, the flash turned itself into a long, solid bar of precious metal.

'It's a sword,' said Miles.

'Don't be fanciful,' said the professor. 'I don't want

anyone diving for that. What you're looking at is brass and it's just unromantic old pipework. You've discovered a pump and a drainage system, Oli.'

'What does it drain?' said Millie.

Professor Worthington looked around. 'Where's Tomaz?' she said. 'He'll know.'

Tomaz blushed. 'I think there's a way of draining the lake,' he said. 'But I never found out how it was done.'

'He's absolutely right, of course. You see? We can have a lesson after all! This is an *artificial* lake, children. Any artificial lake or pond has either to be aerated – Sanchez, that's one for you.'

'Um, aerated, Miss – to add air, or refresh.'

'Very good – in other words *oxygenate*, to stop it dying. Either that, or its waters must constantly be replenished. Now we're fairly close to Neptune, which may contain some of the switches. But I would say that we are also very close to the lake's pump-room. There's a castle in Kent that has some of these features and I wouldn't mind betting its pump-room is just the same. What's the name of the local river, someone? Anjoli?'

Anjoli jumped in surprise. 'Pardon, Miss?'

'You're not listening at all, are you? You were poking Brother Doonan.'

'Sorry, Miss, I—'

'What river takes the excess water from the Ribblestrop lake and supplies water when the level gets low?' There was a forest of hands, but Anjoli was clueless.

'Is it the River Strop, Miss?' said Kenji. 'We put it on our map – it's a tributary river.'

'Excellent, Kenji. How old are you?'

'Seven, Miss.'

'Anjoli, how old are you? Stand up straight!'

'Ten and a half, Miss. Ten and—'

'He puts you to shame, doesn't he? Three years younger and he has a power of concentration I think you leave in your dormitory. I've been watching you this term, Anjoli – I was hoping for a bit more application. Put your tie on properly. I hate this habit of wearing it round your head. Miles, as well, you look like a pair of tramps.'

There was a crackle of static. It was like a cough. Then, as everyone turned to look at Oli's radio, a soft voice emerged from the little speaker. 'Cuthbertson! Please . . . help me!'

Everyone crept closer.

Oli clicked switches and twiddled a knob. He put his ear to it, listening intently.

'I thought this was just a transmitter,' said Ruskin.

'No,' said Oli. 'I adapted it from a receiver. I get a few odd voices now and then. I got Radio Afghanistan once.'

'Someone needs help,' said Asilah. 'Can you send a message?'

'Or they're fooling about,' said Sam.

Oli groaned. 'We're losing the sub again,' he said. 'This happened last time! It's because the frequency's so dodgy.'

'Give it to me,' said Sam. But Oli wouldn't. He pressed more switches and changed position. The radio started to cough and buzz, and all at once there was another horrible cry. It was if somebody was trapped inside the box, breathing hard. Then the same desperate words: 'Help me . . . help me, Cuthbertson!' But it was faint and failing.

'Who's Cuthbertson?' said Doonan.

'It's interfering!' cried Oli. 'We're going to lose Millie's sub!' He was on his knees. Far below, the toy submarine was rising, but its course was erratic. Sanjay knelt by the ice-hole next to him and rolled up his sleeves. The lights were a long way down still, but at least it was moving upwards.

'She's coming,' cried Sanjay. Sam and Ruskin leaned into

the hole, ready to retrieve the precious craft. At last it broke the surface and the boys grabbed at it with relief.

At exactly that moment, disaster struck.

First Flavio's crocodile slipped its leash. He would never work out how it happened, but at least he learned never to trust bored-looking reptiles. The creature rolled a full circle on its back, snapped its jaws, and the leash was off – then it simply ran. It didn't run far, because it knew exactly where it was going. As the submarine was lifted from the ice-hole, the crocodile slipped underneath it, under the boys' arms, and into the freezing water. Flavio leaped, but was way too slow. As that happened, the headmaster shouted in surprise and stepped backwards. He trod hard on Sanchez's foot with his ice-skate, grabbed him, and both were suddenly slithering on the ice on their backsides.

The assembled crowd looked to where the headmaster was pointing, horror in his eyes: the great head of the Neptune statue was moving. The children were used to it; the teachers weren't. They stared awestruck, as the chin tilted upwards. Oli's radio stuttered again, a strange cry of effort or triumph; the head fell backwards so it was staring at the sky and out of the neckhole emerged a wild-eyed Father O'Hanrahan.

His cassock was in shreds. His face was a horrible mask of blotched red and terrified white. As if this wasn't enough – as everyone stared, not sure whether to think about crocodiles, secret tunnels or strange-looking priests – there came the unmistakable sound of a loud, sharp gunshot. In the still of the winter air it seemed to ricochet left to right; it was caught in the hills and bounced from sky to lake, gradually disappearing into another, more horrible silence.

Finally, from the south tower – home of Lady Vyner and her grandson Caspar – came the most awful scream.

Chapter Twenty-six

'An intruder,' gasped the headmaster. 'Children – stay here!'

He jumped to his feet and slipped straight onto his face. Skates were torn off and everyone was running.

The sun was low, so there were lights on in the south tower. There was a crash of glass or crockery, and another scream. Asilah was the fastest, closely followed by Tomaz and Imagio. They raced up the winding staircase and reached the top landing in time to see Crippen – the elderly servant – stagger out of the door. His face was a mask of horror and he was breathless. He leaned against the wall, gasping – there was yet another scream from inside and then it softened into a desolate wail.

The children dashed inside, piling through the Vyner rooms. Turning into the lounge, they came upon a terrible sight. Lady Vyner was on her back. The sofa she'd been sitting on had been upended and her right hand clutched either a neck or shoulder wound. Her face was grey and her lips translucent – she was squawking and flapping weakly, in an old white nightgown, like a broken-winged bird. The orphans gasped as one: the upper half of her nightie was drenched in blood. She tried to sit up and there was an awful sucking sound; there was a puddle of blood underneath her and it was spreading rapidly.

The next moment Routon was there. 'Scissors!' he shouted and he knelt down close. Somehow scissors were found. Whatever he was saying to the old lady was inaudible – just the murmurs of comfort one tries to offer.

Lady Vyner seemed delirious. 'Get off me!' she cried, flailing at the man, but Routon's powerful hands were too strong for her. He was snipping at her clothes, gently pulling the fabric back, probing with careful, professional fingers, even as he caught a stinging slap across his cheek.

'I want everyone outside!' said the headmaster, panting and wheezing. He came in close and his hand sprang to his mouth; he seemed about to faint. Nobody else moved. Lady Vyner's pale shoulder was coming into view and it was soaking red. You didn't need any training to recognise – at once – the black mark of a bullet-hole.

'Ambulance and police,' said Professor Worthington – and raced from the room.

'The intruder could still be at large!' cried the headmaster. 'Back to your room, boys! Asilah!'

Routon had ripped the sleeve from his shirt and was attempting to stop the exit wound.

'Fool!' cried Lady Vyner. 'Fool!'

'I need sheets from the bed,' Routon said to Millie and she sped off in search of them.

'Where's Caspar?' said Israel. 'What if they shot Caspar too?'

Sanjay and Podma raced up the hall to check bedrooms.

But little Caspar Vyner was sitting under a table, not two metres from his grandmother's body. He still held the gun, as though it was welded to his fingers – he could not shake it loose. His sobs had run out and he'd pushed himself back as far as he could go into the darkness. He was making small noises and rocking backwards and forwards. 'Bubb . . .' he said. It was a little bleep of a sound, like a sick machine.

The headmaster and Doonan were at the child's side, immediately. As they lifted him, he made the same noise three more times. When his gran came into view, he went rigid with fear and then he was in spasm.

The men steered him from the room as the word 'M . . . m . . . murderer!' was hurled at his head in a long, terrible scream.

'Hush!' said Routon.

'Don't you hush me, you ogre!'

Routon had bound pads of sheet to both sides of the wound. He tightened the bands that held them, making the old woman wince with pain.

'Is there anything we can do?' said Sanchez.

Routon tightened the bandages a little more and sat her up. 'It's a flesh wound,' said the captain. 'Nothing broken. No vital damage.'

'But the blood,' said Millie. 'Look at it.'

'Don't you worry about blood.' He dragged one of Lady Vyner's arms over his own shoulder. She gasped with pain. 'She's alright. The more they scream, the more life they've got. It's the quiet ones you worry about. Hold this pad in place, Millie. I'm going to get her up.'

'Should we move her? Shouldn't we wait?'

'She's a trooper – you can walk down a few stairs, can't you, love? See if you can find her slippers.'

'Caspar,' said Doonan, softly. 'I need you to put the gun down.' He stroked the boy's hair with one hand, so gently. With the other he kneaded the child's wrist. 'We're going to put the gun down, Caspar, aren't we? And we're going to go downstairs and everything's going to be fine.'

'Ba!' said Caspar. 'Mmah!'

'We're going to stretch out our fingers. We're going to get this nasty thing down on the table. What a great heavy weight it is! Let's see if we can get our fingers out of the hole . . .'

'I *din* . . . I din!'

Doonan spread his own fingers and held them in front of the terrified Caspar. 'Can you just do that for me? Let's touch fingers, come on, Caspar!'

Caspar blinked and licked his lips. Gazing into Doonan's eyes, he finally opened his fingers and the gun slipped onto the kitchen table. The headmaster removed it. The boy then watched as his gran limped from the flat; he was shaking, and her threats and abuse echoed all the way up the stairwell.

After some time, Doonan managed to soothe him into a chair and Flavio made a pot of tea. The children were finally sent away and there was calm.

The story came tumbling out. It was short and it was sad.

The gun belonged to Sanchez: everyone knew that. But how had it found its way to Caspar? According to Caspar, another boy had loaned it to him. Caspar admitted he'd been hunting for the weapon all over Christmas, so it was a joyful moment when this kind, generous, friendly boy knocked on his front door and put the weapon in his hands. The boy had even given him advice, which Caspar had listened to, carefully: the gun is not loaded, said the boy. It's a harmless toy, so you can point it at anyone. They'd even tried out a few combat manoeuvres together, on the landing.

'What do you mean, *manoeuvres*?' said Doonan, gently. Caspar was on his lap now, slowly recovering.

'Cowboy,' said Caspar. 'We did cowboys.'

'Did you really? That's very good – and he showed you

how to hold it, did he? Did you try any others? Talk me through it, take your time.'

'Then we did cops, because he said cops were more fun. He said it was more fun, because cops have to . . . have to burst in and shoot. So he showed me how to . . . burst in and shoot.'

'When was this?'

'This morning. And we were playing. We were pulling the trigger and it was an empty gun! I shot him and he shot me. But I said cops was more fun, so he said fine and he went away. And I had lunch. And then . . .'

'Go on, Caspar.'

'Gran was having a nap. I was only to have the gun for the day so I was just stroking it. I waited for her to wake up. I was just going to show it to her! She likes weapons, same as I do. She was on the sofa . . .' The boy started to cry. 'I pretended to be a cop. I had it all ready, like Miles had shown me. I just . . . pointed it at her.' He stared into Doonan's eyes, a new wave of horror rising as he relived the moment. 'I just pulled the trigger.'

Caspar dissolved into sobs again and it took another ten minutes to quieten him. When he was able to go on, there wasn't much more to the tale.

'He said I could have it till teatime. He said Sanchez knew and everyone wanted to be friends with me. I was really happy, because he'd taken a curse out. He'd said he wanted Gran dead, but now he said the curse was over . . .'

Inspector Cuthbertson did not attend the crime scene. He was alerted, immediately, and sent a handful of trusted men. He asked for a full report, subject to a government H.O. He tried to contact Father O'Hanrahan, but the man wasn't contactable.

Blue lights winked for several hours as darkness fell and

statements were taken. Caspar was taken to a police station and Doonan stayed with him.

The headmaster now sat in his study, with his head in his hands. He had sent for Miles.

Chapter Twenty-seven

'This might be the most important conversation you're ever going to have,' said the headmaster. 'So I would advise you to think carefully about everything you say.'

'If you think it's my fault,' said Miles. 'Why don't you just send me to the police station?'

'Because you're a child.'

Professor Worthington served tea and then withdrew.

The headmaster looked at the boy in front of him and hunted for an opening. After a long minute of silence, he said, 'When you came into my study, on your first day back at Ribblestrop, you told me that you had changed.'

'I have.'

'Those were your very words, Miles: "I have changed." And yet, it would appear that you were handling – and offering – a loaded gun to another boy.'

Miles was silent. He let his chin drop to his chest and his hair covered his eyes. He pulled his shirt around him like a shawl.

'Why is your shirt so torn, Miles?'

'Because I tore it.'

'Yes. Why are there cuts on your forearms?'

'Football.'

'Those are tattoos, aren't they? Professor Worthington says you do them yourself. With a compass.'

Miles stared at him. 'I don't,' he said.

'Did you give Caspar Vyner that gun?'

Silence.

'Will you please answer my question?'

'Yes,' said Miles. 'Yes.'

'You loaded it?'

Miles nodded. 'Yes.'

'If I know Sanchez, it would have been empty when you found it. Sanchez left it unloaded, true or false?'

'He left it unloaded. It was in his hiding place and I took it out. Ages ago and I told everyone.'

'You gave it to Caspar and you loaded it at the last minute.'

Miles licked his lips.

'You told him the gun was empty,' said the headmaster. 'But you had secretly loaded it.'

The silence stretched between them.

'Is that the case, Miles? Can you confirm or deny what I have just said?'

'If you want to expel me again, you can do it – you don't need to go through all of this.'

'I am not interrogating you. This is a conversation.'

'You're asking all the questions! How is that a conversation?'

'Are there questions you want to ask me?'

'Yes.' The boy sat up. 'For a start, why do you allow a gun to be in a kids' dormitory? That little freak was after it – he would have found it in the end.'

The headmaster picked up his cup and sipped his tea. 'It's Sanchez's gun, as you know. It saved lives last term. And his father insists that he keep it.'

'Not very safe, though, is it?'

'No, it's not.'

'Weird school that lets its pupils have guns.'

The headmaster looked at him. 'You have a point,' he said. 'Ribblestrop is an unusual school and some of its pupils are also unusual.'

It was Miles's turn to sip tea. 'I didn't mean to give Caspar a loaded gun,' he said. 'I thought I'd taken all the bullets out, but sometimes they get stuck.' Suddenly, there were tears in his eyes. 'This is the last thing I wanted to happen! Everyone's going to think I did it on purpose. Sanchez is going to go crazy – he's my best friend! I love him!'

The headmaster watched carefully. There was a single tear rolling down the boy's nose. Miles wiped it away angrily.

'If you expel me, I'm going to kill myself.'

'Oh, Miles, what a disgusting thing to say!'

'It's true! If you want to—'

'It's absurd and obscene!'

They sat in silence.

'We're halfway through the term,' said the headmaster. He was breathing heavily. 'I have a casualty in hospital, with gunshot wounds. I have a boy threatening suicide. I have a traumatised child in a police station. Less than six weeks, Miles! When, not just two hours ago, we were enjoying ourselves on the lake! You come to me: "I've changed! I'm healed." You shouldn't have even been *touching* Sanchez's gun! Not after last term!'

'But I didn't know there was a bullet in it.'

'What difference does that make?'

'He begged me to borrow it, Caspar did!'

'Yes. And Caspar is one of our most vulnerable children. He's completely isolated! Are you proud of tormenting him?'

'I didn't torment anyone!'

'Is this the new Miles? Are you gloating, now? Are you proud of yourself?'

Miles was turning red. '*I didn't mean to do it!*' he hissed.

'You gave him the gun,' yelled the headmaster. 'You put bullets in the chamber – just like last term! You showed him how to shoot and you told him – !'

'I thought it was empty!' screamed Miles. He was on his feet. 'I thought it was empty! Empty! Empty!' He smashed his teacup onto its saucer, breaking both. A lake of hot tea spread over the table and Miles's right hand was suddenly red with blood. He grabbed the teapot and turned wildly around, and then crashed it through the window. The blood now ran freely from his injured arms and he howled suddenly, like an animal. Once, twice – he stood and howled, and then the sobs took hold and shook him like a doll.

The headmaster sat in horrified shock. He forced himself to be calm. Despite the blood and the screaming, he had to be calm. There was a box of tissues nearby and he slowly laid them over the boy's injuries. Miles leaned forward, gasping. Blood leaked through the tissues. The headmaster pressed a napkin, gently, firmly. His own hands were shaking.

Miles quietened. 'No . . .' he moaned. 'I don't want to go. I have to stay!' It was a whine and he seemed to be five or six years old suddenly. 'You never heard what she said!' he shouted.

'Who?'

'Lady Vyner. Last term! You never heard what she said about my mother!'

'And you're telling me . . . Miles, are you telling me you've been holding a grudge for all this time?'

Miles said, 'She got what she deserved!'

The headmaster sat in silence for a moment.

'You're cut,' he said. He knew his voice was trembling.

Miles shook his head. 'I've had deeper than that. This is nothing.'

'Let me see, please.'

Miles sat down and laid his arms on the table. The headmaster removed the napkins and tissues, peeling them back. He felt utterly sick. The child's skin was ruptured in several places and he clearly needed stitches. Even that could wait, though: this moment was too important and he needed time.

'I'm going to tell you about one of my problems, Miles,' he said. 'Can you hear me?'

'Yes.'

'How much pain are you in?'

Miles met his eyes.

'No pain,' he whispered.

'See if this makes sense to you, because I need your advice. I'm going to tell you something that I think is true and important. Throughout my life, I have never been able to recognise truth from lies. One of my worst failings is that I find almost everyone I meet plausible. And I am cursed with an imagination that understands people who do awful things. It's why I was sacked from two schools. It's why I lost my family, I think – and it's no doubt why Ribblestrop will fail.'

'I'm telling the truth,' said Miles. 'If you don't believe me, there's nothing I can do about it.'

'But we can't go there, can we? We can't talk about truth.' The headmaster paused. 'Don't you see? Liars lie to themselves. The need to survive is such that we *believe* our own lies – just to keep going. Do you understand me?'

Miles said nothing.

'I've got one more question for you, then I think we ought to look at your cuts. I want you to think about the answer – alright?' The headmaster paused. 'I want to know,' he said, 'what you would do, if you were me?'

Miles still said nothing, and the only sound was a very soft drip of blood and tea from table to floor.

The headmaster continued. 'Would you believe this boy sitting opposite me? Would you say, *This wonderful boy. He must be telling the truth. It's all a horrible accident that we can learn from.* Or would you know in your heart that he's just done a wicked thing and is now lying about it? Lying to himself, even.'

Miles went to speak three times and each time nothing came. He had sucked his injured flesh and, just like at the football match, there was blood on his lips. His eyes were wide and luminous, and he was staring at the little shunken head that was still on the headmaster's desk.

'That's my head,' he said.

'What do you mean?'

'That's the head I gave you. That's what I feel like, that's how it feels.'

'Miles, you can't go on like this.'

'Don't tell her, please—'

'Look at me!'

The boy's eyes lifted and stared without blinking into the headmaster's.

'Oh, Miles – I don't know what to do. If you're lying . . .' The headmaster paused and then his voice shook with new passion. 'If you're lying and deceiving, then you'll do something like this again, I know you will. And someone will die – possibly you. If you're lying, then you need help, urgently. Where can you get that help? We are not equipped to help you here. We haven't the expertise. Tell me what I should do!'

'If I were you,' said Miles, 'I wouldn't know what to do.'

'So what would you do?'

'I'd expel me.'

The headmaster sat still and silent. After some time, he

picked up a piece of china. 'Yes,' he said. 'That's a very good answer.' He sat back in his chair and the silence went on. Suddenly, he stood up. 'And that's why I can't. I cannot expel you, you're too precious.'

He strode across the room, to the door. 'You're going to make your peace with Caspar and his grandmother. You are going to put things right. You are going to change. You are going to amaze yourself.' He pointed at the boy. 'That is my promise to you.'

Chapter Twenty-eight

D.C.C. Cuthbertson had no sympathy for Father O'Hanrahan. He despised weakness and stupidity, and it was with great difficulty that he concealed his fury at the man's recklessness. He heard all the news by telephone and gave him a few days to recover. Then – his own sense of greed now fully aroused – he called a council of war.

First he picked up his brother, Gary Cuthbertson. They drove to a small country pub, six miles outside Ribblestrop.

Father O'Hanrahan arrived a little later, his fingers still covered in plasters from clawing at stone. His hands were shaking visibly and he wore a bright white bandage around his head.

'I can hardly drive a car,' he said. 'Why do we have to meet miles from anywhere?'

'Because secrecy is now more important that ever.'

'This whole thing is turning into a nightmare!'

'And whose fault is that?' replied the policeman.

'Excuse me!' exclaimed Father O'Hanrahan. 'Who was it who confirmed the existence of the sword? Who put their own life at risk, eh? So I don't need any smart-alec criticisms—'

'You have also alerted the Brethren to your own personal interest.'

'Ach, they're a bunch of old women!'

'And made a fool of yourself telling one and all that Lady Vyner was dead.'

'Which I thought was the case! How was I to know he was talking about a wretched football game? The man looked traumatised. I put two and two together—'

'And made a very wrong number.'

'Alright, I jumped to conclusions . . .'

'You go charging in, getting yourself lost. And what's wrong with your head?'

'What?'

'What happened to your head?'

The old man took a long pull on his whisky.

'I got hit by a piece of flying china.'

'Flying china?'

'That is the kind of school I am working in!' cried the old man. 'I'm on my way to see the headmaster, to see if I can help. I stop for a nip of something strong and someone tips crockery out of the window. The place is a madhouse – all I want is to get out of it, the sooner the better.'

The policeman sighed. 'Your job was so simple. All you had to do was see what the Brethren had to say, not lose yourself in the tunnels. I could have told you that you stood no chance of finding the chamber. I've been looking for months, before the entrances were blocked. We tried maps, we went down with metal-detectors—'

'And this pump-room –?'

'We only just found out about it! So we have to go slower than ever – but you're still our man with access. We still need you in there, more now than ever before. You found out that the sword is safe – that is a big step forward.'

'It's in there, alright!'

'Shhh! Keep your voice down.'

The policeman looked around him, but the pub was empty. 'You've identified the location. We treat that as one hundred per cent positive: we are on the right track, so that's good.'

'Can I say something?' said Gary, leaning in. 'I say it's time for the next move. If this old boy's made everyone suspicious, then we ought to move fast. Now I suggest a speedboat is the priority. For that we're going to need –'

'What?' said O'Hanrahan. 'What do we need a speedboat for?'

'Hold on, hold on – both of you,' said Cuthbertson. 'We're all jumping the gun and putting carts before horses. First thing, Father, is this: how suspicious are the children?'

'Of me?'

'Of anything.'

'I don't think they're suspicious of me at all. They think I'm some kind of clown – they probably want me for their damned circus . . .'

'Then we still go softly. Alright, Gary?'

'Fine. No problem. But Darren's in, I can tell you that. Confirmed today.'

'Good.'

'Who's Darren?' said Father O'Hanrahan.

Gary supped his beer. 'Darren,' he said, 'is a rather disappointed lad who's been preparing for a football contract. And then in came Ribblestrop Towers, and took it from under his nose. He hates those kids more than I do, so he'll drive the speedboat.'

'We're a team of four,' said the policeman. 'But we're still not going to rush into anything. The Brethren saw the sword – that's what they said. Therefore, we can assume it's sitting there, waiting for us.'

Father O'Hanrahan nodded.

'I've got a man in London, ready to receive it. Three million, in cash. There'll be a down payment of a half-million.

The rest as soon as the authenticity is proved, and I don't think that will be difficult.'

'What's he going to do with it?'

'What does that matter?'

'I'm thinking if he's going to sell it on, it won't be long before it's recognised for what it is . . .'

'He's buying it for a private collection. Middle East, that's all I know.'

'Alright. Good.'

Gary Cuthbertson unrolled the pipework blueprint, setting down the beer glasses to keep it flat. 'Getting the sword out,' he said, 'will be easy – once we've got it. We need a boat waiting here.' He put a fat finger close to the Neptune statue.

'We don't know where it is!' said Father O'Hanrahan.

'Shh! We *do* know where it is. It's in Tomaz's house.'

'*Yes, I know that,*' hissed the old man, his eyes closed in frustration. 'But we don't know how to get there. I spent two days trying and you wander in circles! All we've got is what you gave me: this blessed map of the blessed pipes. And that's no good to anyone.'

'No,' said the policeman. 'You're wrong. If you'd taken this drawing with you, you could have found your way to the pump-room, and you could have got out much quicker than you did. Where is it, by the way – the copy I gave you?'

'In my room, where else would it be?'

'Locked away?'

'It's secure, if that's what you mean. I'm not a complete idiot. But I still don't see what a load of pipes and pumps have to do with anything. The sword is somewhere in a place we can't get to.'

'The pump-room's important,' said Gary, patiently, 'because it's our best way out. This is what I've been saying all along. There's a way up from the pump-room through what's called a dry dock, just here.' He poked at a jumble of lines and boxes. 'You get out in a little rowing boat, rising with the water level right up to the lake. We row a few metres and transfer to a speedboat. That's where Darren comes in.'

'Our man from London's waiting on the far side of the lake: the handover takes half a minute. So what we've got to do, if you'll let me finish . . .'

Father O'Hanrahan sat with open mouth.

'What *you* have to do, I should say, is find out from little Tomaz how to get into that home of his. You said you could hear them having some kind of party?'

'Yes.'

'Then you must have been close. We play it soft and slow – see what he'll give you . . . any clue at all. Meanwhile, Gary is researching the potholing and caving side of things, in case we have to go down that way. Have you got anything yet?'

'Not yet,' said Gary. 'I've sent letters to the main clubs. There's a man called Spedding, used to be in charge of mountain rescue – I'm visiting him tomorrow night. The thing is, the Ribblestrop estate is private property, but the Ministry of Defence took some of it. So the routes haven't been listed officially. And we can't go exploring at random; it would take forever.'

'I've got a couple of contacts who might help out.'

'Listen,' said Father O'Hanrahan. 'I had better tell you something. I'd better come clean about something right now.'

'What?' said both men, together.

The old man took a long pull on his whisky. 'You're asking me to talk to the little long-haired boy, young Tomaz.'

'Yes.'

'In my role as chaplain.'

'Yes,' said the policeman. 'You were going to make it a priority, remember? To have one-to-one, soul-baring sessions with each of them.'

197

'And I did make a start. But to be honest . . . they didn't go too well.'

There was a silence.

'What's been the problem?' said Gary.

'There've been several problems. One is that they keep changing the blessed timetable, so the children hardly ever show up. The other problem is when they do show up, they don't seem to take me very seriously. I told you before, I can't talk to children!'

The policeman sighed. 'That was your job. You said you would win their trust.'

'*You* try doing it! Half of them are psychopaths! They spend their time playing with tigers – the rest of the time they're running wild.'

'So try again.'

'Who's going to bare their soul to me, looking like this?'

'Look,' said Cuthbertson. 'What if I was with you?'

'You? How?'

'There is a way —'

'You said you couldn't come near the place.'

'Not in person, no. But what if I was on the end of a wire? Would that make you feel any better?'

Father O'Hanrahan thought about it. 'So you'd be listening in? Guiding me?'

'Yes. I can fix you up with a surveillance radio. Earpiece, microphone. I could feed you a few ideas if you get stuck. Keep you calm if you got a bit flustered.'

The old man nodded.

'Would that help you?'

'I think it might be a good idea,' he said.

'In the end,' said Cuthbertson, 'you're looking for a simple clue. You must never forget: you're dealing with kids. Kids respond to discipline.'

Chapter Twenty-nine

Father O'Hanrahan let several days pass.

He was aching and bruised, so he let the days go by, spending most of his time in his room. When he did venture out, he made a point of smiling regularly and being particularly nice to those he met, even Doonan. He constantly reminded himself that there was no hurry. The school was getting back to normal after the shooting of Lady Vyner. She had checked out of the hospital and was back in the south tower. Her first act had been to evict her grandson, who was now sleeping in a small bed next to Sanchez. Miles had asked if he could move out, temporarily, and was sleeping in a store-cupboard used by Professor Worthington. She was keeping a close eye on him.

The old man studied the new timetables as they were produced and tried to get into the swing of the school day. Circus-skills, gymnastics, science, football, and art – they seemed to run from one thing to another almost at random. The initials R.E. occasionally appeared, but nobody ever showed up.

One Friday he did manage to teach a class, but that was almost by accident. He came upon the three youngest orphans who had laid out their abacus and ledgers under a staircase. Father O'Hanrahan found a stool and joined them. He talked at length about bread and wine and the importance of the incarnation. The boys thanked him politely when they left, and he felt as if he'd made a breakthrough.

At mealtimes, he watched Tomaz.

Now that he knew that Tomaz was chief cook, he started to compliment the food.

One lunchtime he took a chance: he took hold of the boy's sleeve and asked about the recipes he used. He even asked how Tomaz had mastered them and managed nearly a minute's worth of normal conversation.

The boy was polite and self-contained. He was small and quick. He didn't have the horrible confidence that some of them had, and didn't find eye-contact easy. Father O'Hanrahan began to wonder why he'd ever felt nervous. The boy was thin: if it came to it, he thought, he could get the child in a headlock and squeeze. On the other hand, that would simply cut off the air-supply, which would be foolish. A few sharp slaps would be better. A twisted arm . . .

Alternatively, he could administer the currency of his own boyhood – a sound thrashing with a belt. Hands first, then the backside – he could remember even the toughest boys sobbing like babies after a strapping. It was a last resort, but the idea was comforting. He would talk the talk, but if it came to it, well . . . he wore a thick leather belt that would do the job beautifully.

He would have the map in his satchel and a pen. All Tomaz had to do was mark his home with a cross.

Encouraged, he created a new interview schedule and posted it on the notice-board. He decided not to use his classroom, which was drafty and doorless. He chose the stationery cupboard, at the back, which had one small window and was about the size of a church confessional.

He blacked out the window and put a small table and two chairs inside. Inspired, he found some candles. Inspired further, he fetched his cassette recorder and put on one of his relaxation tapes. When he closed the door, the room took on a calm, almost magical ambience. He unpacked his surveillance kit and put it on as he'd been shown – earpiece and microphone. Then he prepared for his first customer. Wisely, he had chosen Sanchez, who he knew would keep the appointment.

The meeting went well. The boy was civilised, and when Father O'Hanrahan offered a can of Pepsi-Cola – yet another inspiration to put the children at their ease – he accepted it. The old man quite enjoyed the exchange and Cuthbertson – listening in and offering encouragement through the earpiece – was very positive.

Fired by this success, he waited forty-eight hours and summoned Asilah. Asilah was another pleasant, responsible member of the community, and though he was more skittish than Sanchez, nothing terrible took place. The chaplain managed three minutes of easy conversation and Cuthbertson didn't intervene once. He felt calm and professional.

The very next day was Tomaz's day. He reminded him at breakfast and then, just after lunch, he waited outside the kitchen.

'Tomaz!' he cried, rubbing his hands and smiling. 'You've not forgotten our appointment, I hope! Shall we walk together?'

'Oh,' said Tomaz. 'No. I mean . . . yes.'

'Two o'clock on the nose – let's be punctual.'

'It's just that we're . . . I think Professor Worthington needs us for a –'

'Oh, I've had a word with her,' Father O'Hanrahan lied. 'She knows it can't be helped! You can do your science any old time. Spiritual matters come first, everyone knows that.' He put his hand on the boy's neck and got a firm grip of his collar. 'We're talking about your soul, son. Your immortal soul.'

He pushed, noticing how light the child was. Tomaz had no choice but to walk. 'I'll tell you something, Tom: when I was your age, it made my day when the priest had a moment to spare. I did not keep him waiting, or he'd make me dance, I can tell you! That was a splendid bit of beef you did for us last night, by the way. Roast potatoes to die for and that's an Irishman speaking. I've eaten a few potatoes in my time and you've got a magician's touch, Tom – a magician's touch . . .'

The cupboard was ready, candles flickering. Fizzy drinks were on the table. Father O'Hanrahan had gone through his tape collection and found *Whales of the Antarctic*. He switched it on and the lonely cries, over the hum of an organ, seemed friendly and gentle.

'Sit yourself down, boy,' he said. 'This needn't take long at all. It's a formality, really, but I believe that all children have the right to speak up about spiritual matters. I was chatting with one of the little foreign boys, yesterday – Ashlah or something similar. Quite a lot to say for himself, he had. Surprisingly ignorant of the Bible, though – and that's one thing about these interviews, my boy.' Father O'Hanrahan picked up a small, plastic Bible. 'You don't go away empty-handed. I'll be giving you one of these to keep at the end of this little chat, and they're not as cheap as they look.'

He closed the cupboard door and shot the bolt.

'Fitted that myself,' he said, smiling proudly. He fingered his microphone and turned the battery pack on. 'The last thing you want is interruptions when you're baring your soul, and I do find children here have no sense of privacy. What's the little long-haired fellow, wears his tie like a bandana?'

'Imagio?'

'No.'

'Miles?'

'No, not that monster. This one's a foreigner.'

'Anjoli maybe?'

'That's the one! Always in my face, jumping around me. The devil's own, in my opinion.'

'Receiving,' said a voice in his ear. 'Proceed.'

'Are you sitting comfortably, Mr Tom?' said Father O'Hanrahan.

'Yes, sir.'

'Then what we need, now that we're ready – one to one like this – is a nice refreshing glass of the old *Pepsi-Cola*.'

'No, thanks,' said Tomaz, as the can was offered. 'I don't drink it.'

'Oh.'

'I don't think it's good for you.'

'Well, I'm sure you're wise. Tastes like muck to me, but most kiddies seem to like it. Now, Tomaz . . . do you want to kick-off, or shall I?'

Tomaz hesitated. He tried to smile, but he was sweating already. His eyes danced round the little cell and he was dreadfully conscious of the bolt on the door. Father O'Hanrahan seemed much bigger in a cupboard. He was all black cassock and lobster-like hands.

'I'm not really sure what to say,' he said, politely. 'I don't believe in God, you see.'

Father O'Hanrahan nodded. 'That's a very good start,' he said. 'I like a boy who thinks before he speaks and says things frankly. Some of your friends, they don't ever shut up – that Millie girl, for instance: she's got a mouth on her.

203

But you're a thinker, I could tell that straight away. You're an orphan, aren't you?'

'Well. Yes.'

'You see, death gives us stability. If your parents are dead, you know your own mortality.'

Tomaz went to speak, but the old man interrupted. 'A bit of tragedy is actually good for you, in my opinion. It leads to a certain seriousness, especially if your folks pop off when you're young. You must have been glad to find a home in dear old Ribblestrop, eh, after that kind of suffering? How did they die?'

His earpiece buzzed. '*Stick to the point!*' hissed Cuthbertson.

'How did they die?' said Tomaz. 'They were living in—'

'Ah, it's not important,' said the old man. 'Get over it, that's my advice – once they're gone, they're gone. And I tell you another thing, you can think of me as a second father. And I won't let you down.'

Tomaz was silent.

The old man smiled. 'Of course, you don't actually live at the school, do you?' he said, slowly.

'Don't I?' said Tomaz.

'Go careful,' said Cuthbertson, softly. 'Don't rush it.'

Father O'Hanrahan smiled even more broadly. 'If the rumours are true,' he said, 'I hear you have your own little retreat. A second home, as it were. You can tell me, you know! There should be no secrets between a boy and his Father.'

He leaned forward and patted Tomaz reassuringly on the knee. The boy leaped to his feet as if he'd been stung, crying out.

'What in God's name's the matter?'

'I thought you touched me. I felt something on my knee!'

'I did touch you. To make you feel safe, you idiot. Sit in your chair.'

'Go gently,' whispered Cuthbertson. 'Keep it relaxed.'

'I'm trying,' whispered the old man. 'He's like a scalded cat!'

'What?' said Tomaz.

'Nothing! Mind your own business and sit yourself down.'

'Can I go now, please?'

'No, you can't go, we've hardly started! Where have you got to go to?'

'I told you, Professor Worthington's running an extra class. I didn't want to miss it.'

'Sit.'

Tomaz slid back into his seat. There was a long silence.

'You don't actually live inside the school,' said Father O'Hanrahan, at last. 'Do you? Come clean.'

'Yes,' said Tomaz. 'Yes, I do.'

'Do you?'

'Yes.'

O'Hanrahan smiled as broadly as he could, showing all his teeth. He chuckled and said: 'You have a bed elsewhere. That's what I heard. I believe it's underground?'

There was a longer silence now. Tomaz was looking into the old man's eyes.

'Let him sweat,' said D.C.C. Cuthbertson, very softly.

'Either you do or you don't,' said Father O'Hanrahan, after a moment. 'I'm just asking out of fatherly interest and it's not a difficult question. I'm trying to build up a picture, Tomaz. You see, I was told you were a nice polite, honest boy who didn't want any trouble. But if I've got that wrong . . . If you're a boy with something to hide, then . . . maybe I should be taking a different approach.'

'Let him dangle,' said the voice in his ear.

Thirty seconds passed.

'I'm going to ask you again,' said the old man, slowly.

'And I want you to think hard about your answer. Do you have a home, under the ground, that's part of the Ribblestrop tunnels as once used by a gentleman called Vyner? Yes or no.'

Tomaz was white. 'Yes,' he said.

'Then you'd better tell me everything about it.'

Chapter Thirty

Up in the Tower of Science, Professor Worthington had not noticed the absence of Tomaz. The children were used to him missing lessons for special kitchen duties, so they said nothing. It was on with the project of the day.

The reproduction module was over now that the baby panthers were up and running and though the professor was keen to work with the python and explore digestion, she was always equally keen to take opportunities when they presented themselves.

That very morning Doonan had given her a set of blue-prints, clearly labelled *Ribblestrop Pumping Station*. He had been tidying Father O'Hanrahan's desk and had remembered the science teacher's excitement when they'd all looked down into the swirling water together. He'd borrowed them, vowing to replace them the same evening. Better still, young Caspar Vyner – who had become a permanent member of the class – remembered that a key to the pump-room hung in his kitchen. He had produced it at lunchtime and an expedition was planned for that very afternoon. First, however, was the removal of Miles's stitches and the children had their books and pens out, ready. Miles had become a quiet student. He sat in his chair, still and nervous, looking at the expectant class.

Imagio had the job. He stood ready with mask, gloves, and a plate of freshly sterilised tools. His hair was neatly tied back and he wore a white coat.

Miles had his hands on a stool under a pair of desk-lamps, his elbows held gently by the clamps of a retort stand.

The rest of the children sat as close as they could, Doonan at the back, peering nervously.

'The healing of the skin,' said Professor Worthington, with a hand on Miles's shoulder, 'starts as soon as a cut occurs. A mixture of corpuscles and "clotting factors" join together. The other blood cells fight off the bacteria trying to get into the cut, and meanwhile, the *dead* bacteria, the immune cells and the blood all clot together to help form a scab. If the cut is too big for a scab to form, that's when stitches are required. That's why we had to stitch Miles.'

She used a pointer and touched the top of a wound. 'Are you alright, Miles?'

'Yes, Miss.'

'We'll be as gentle as we can. Now, who can explain scar tissue?'

There was a forest of hands.

'Podma?'

'The scab does only a temporary job,' said Podma. 'It seals things up, but once the normal skin grows under it, it dies and turns to crust.'

'Very good, but what do we mean by "normal skin"? Eric?'

'The white corpuscles that repair the damage at the slower rate, Miss.'

'Good. Now, let's give that a quick wipe with antiseptic. Is that hurting, Miles? You're looking a little bit sick.'

'A bit, Miss. But it's OK.'

'You're a brave boy and this won't take long. Now, what do you think the function of pain is? I'm asking you, Miles, as you're experiencing it.'

'I don't know, Miss.'

'That's not an answer I can accept. Try again.'

'To . . . alert the body to something that's wrong?'

'Very good. Pain is very important. Pain alerts us to the fact that our body is under threat, and it becomes important to remove the *cause* of the pain. If you lean in, children, you can see – just where Imagio's tweezers are, by the first stitch – keep them still, Imagio . . . Can you see? That's the first sign of infection – and *that* is what is causing Miles pain. It's nothing serious, but . . . Anjoli: identify it.'

Anjoli looked nervous, but he did his best. 'It's the . . . redness, Miss, and the slight swelling. Possible secretion of pus, Miss.'

'Ah, very good. You're redeeming yourself. Snip it, Imagio, then pull the thread,'

Miles gasped as the first stitch was eased from his flesh.

'Good,' said Professor Worthington. 'We're being very careful, Miles.'

'I know.'

'Define pus, quickly!'

She put her hand gently on Miles's shoulder again.

Miles looked as if he was about to faint, but he thought hard. 'It's an emergency . . . fluid, Miss.' He swallowed. 'It removes antibodies that are hostile to the body.'

'Absolutely right. The body heals itself – the body is determined, always, to live and reject anything threatening to life. Caspar, how would you treat Miles's infection?'

Caspar was staring at Miles.

'Miss?'

'How would you treat the infection? You did a lovely picture last week, remember?'

'Antibiotics!' he cried.

'Excellent,' said Professor Worthington. 'Removal of dead tissue and antibiotics. I'm impressed, Caspar. You've only just joined the class – you're doing better than some. This, of course, is not gangrenous – there's no need for Miles to be worried. It's a mild infection and we've caught it in plenty of time. Are you enjoying Miles's discomfort, Caspar?'

'No, Miss. Of course not.'

'You think we should we treat his infection?'

'Treat it, Miss, yes,' said Caspar.

'Of course we should. Suffering has to be kept to a minimum. We are all about healing, not destruction. In my experience, we very rarely enjoy another person's pain. And yet we always think we will. Millie, I want you to remember that too.'

'Me, Miss?' said Millie.

'Note it down, in large letters. Write it on your wall.'

'I don't understand, Miss.'

'Write down what I said and learn from it. Next one, please, Imagio – you have a beautiful touch and I think Miles can bear it. Miles is stronger than he knows.'

Miles gasped again and changed colour. The whole class was rapt, aware of the sweat springing out on his forehead.

'I can see tears, Miles,' said the professor. 'Tears of grief? Or pain?' She put her hand on his shoulder.

'I don't know, Miss,' whispered Miles.

'They're probably both. Those tears are a result of a hormone produced when the body is in distress. Your body will do everything it can to keep you alive – am I making my point, Miles?'

'Yes, Miss.' He nodded and a tear dripped into his lap.

'*We* will do everything to keep you alive. Now put your head up, please – I want the class to see. Tears, children, clean the eyeball – everyone knows that. The cornea has to be lubricated as well as oxygenated. However, we also—'

'Excuse me, Professor Worthington?' said Brother Doonan. He was standing excitedly. 'We were reading *The Snow Queen*, me and the little ones, and there's a scene when young Kay gets a piece of glass in his heart and it's washed out by tears.'

Miles cried out again and Doonan hesitated.

'Go on. We're nearly there, Miles. You're doing very well.'

'The glass was washed out via his eye by his tears,' continued Doonan. 'Is that scientifically possible?'

'No, it's not.'

'Oh. I thought it . . . probably wasn't.'

'Tears come from tear glands and have nothing to do with the bloodstream. What you were reading was a fairy story, and in my experience fairy stories have very little connection to science.'

She turned back to Miles and put a hand on his forehead, pushing his hair back. 'Now, class – can you see how much sweat Miles has produced over the last two minutes? You can see his shirt is quite wet with it. Sanchez, we did this in the reproduction project . . .'

'It's because his nerves are being overstimulated, Miss. That leads to heat. He's trying to keep his body temperature normal and the sweat helps that.'

'Very good. And what is the normal body temperature, Nikko? Put the abacus away.'

'Ninety-eight point . . . six, Miss?'

'Spot on. Another example of the body working to keep itself safe and alive. Are you all right, Henry? You're looking very anxious – there's no need to be. Now, Miles. I'm going to ask Caspar to apply the iodine, is that alright?'

'Yes.'

'It will sting, you know.'

'I know.'

'And well done, Imagio. You have the hands of a surgeon: that was beautiful work.'

The final stitch came out and Imagio dropped it into a dish to a smattering of applause. Miles was rocking slightly and his face looked grey. Caspar stood beside him and applied the iodine gently. Miles gasped and went totally rigid.

'Very painful stuff,' said Professor Worthington. 'Put more on – don't worry, Miles, we're very nearly there.' Miles cried out yet again, through gritted teeth. The veins stood out in his neck. Caspar kept the wad of cotton-wool firm against his wound, staring anxiously.

'Any questions?' said Professor Worthington. 'Miles?'

She freed Miles's arms and took over. She mopped the excess alcohol off and, with a clean bit of cotton-wool, she dabbed away his tears. The room was silent, and Miles looked drained and exhausted.

'What questions do you have?'

'None, Miss.'

'Are you sure?'

'Yes, Miss.'

Another tear ran from his eye.

Professor Worthington turned back to the class. 'I have to say that this is an extraordinarily brave boy.' She stroked Miles's cheek, gently. 'I was a field-doctor for a while, in Beirut, and we had to do similar things – no anaesthetic. Grown men would scream the place down, so I was predicting a fainting.'

She moved her hand to his chin and tilted his head up. 'Promise the class that you will never hurt yourself again, Miles – not on purpose.'

'I promise,' said Miles, softly.

'Keep yourself safe,' she said to the children, slowly. 'If you want to experience pain, I can organise it: you don't need to inflict it on yourselves or each other. I don't usually dictate notes, but I want that in everyone's book. Ruskin, did you get it down? I will repeat: Keep. Yourselves. Safe.'

She waited as the children copied down her words.

'Right: blazers on, all of you. We have a treat in store and I want us all to stay together. You have that key, Caspar? Good boy. Off we go, then – line up outside.'

In half an hour they were at the top of the Brethren's secret staircase. The air was instantly clammy as they descended and the darkness was soon total. Every boy – and Millie – had a torch ready.

Caspar fitted the key proudly. The door swung open with a satisfyingly ghoulish creak and some children screamed.

'Is anyone scared of the secret tunnels?' cried Professor Worthington.

'No!' cried the children.

'Well then, let's see what's underground.'

Chapter Thirty-one

On the lawns, Captain Routon, Flavio, and the headmaster were pacing out the site of the big top. The scout tents had been tailored and stitched, and Sanjay had cut sixty tent pegs from an old set of railings. The three men started at the circumference and met in the centre.

'There's something on my mind, sir,' said Routon.

'I thought there was,' said the headmaster. 'I can always tell, Flavio. When this man has something on his mind, I lose sleep myself. It's about Speech Day, isn't it?'

'Yes. It's something you mentioned yourself, sir, and it's been nagging at me. Flavio too.'

'I don't think it's gonna work,' said Flavio. 'Who's gonna come? Most of them don' have no parents.'

They stood in silence.

'You're quite right,' said the headmaster. 'The audience *will* be a bit thin.'

'I just think it might be seen as a bit insensitive, sir. I mean, who can we actually invite? Sam told me his dad can't travel at the moment. Miles's mum – where's she now?'

'Tokyo. Making a commercial.'

'What she say about his accident?' said Flavio.

'She said she was going to have a serious word. I'm not altogether sure she understood the gravity of the situation, though. She was calling quite late, from a bar.'

'Flavio's had an idea, sir. I think it's one in a million.'

Flavio looked embarrassed. 'I don't know anything, OK? And it's your school, so if I'm out o' line, you just gotta say so. But I never seen nothing like these boys. That little one, Anjoli – he's the best acrobat I ever see and I see all over the world. Look.' He paused and went slowly. 'What about we take the show on the road?'

'On the road?'

'On the road. We practise. We get it ready. We load up the truck, take it to the people. Make a poster, make up a load o' tickets. Make a fortune.'

'What do you think, sir?' said Routon. 'I think it's a winner.'

The headmaster was silent, pondering quickly.

'Circus Ribblestrop,' he said. 'Touring the south-west over the Easter holidays. We could play in the park, here in the town.'

'Play anywhere, sir. Take it to the coast and play on the beach.'

'And that way, of course ... the orphans would get a proper holiday. I was talking to Professor Worthington, only last night – they're so cooped up here. Nothing to do, nowhere to go. They could see a bit of England – spread their wings a bit. You know what the problem's going to be, though? You know what we're dangerously short of at the moment?'

'Money,' said Routon and Flavio together.

'It's those animals,' said Flavio. 'They eat through everything!'

'It's not just the animals,' said the headmaster. 'A school is an expensive thing to run.'

'I turned all the boilers off, sir,' said Routon.

'I didn't know they'd been on. Oh Lord . . .'

'What, sir?'

'Don't turn round. Don't look.'

'What's the matter?' said Flavio.

The headmaster was peering short-sightedly into the distance.

The two men turned and followed the headmaster's gaze. A small figure was crossing the gravel drive in a strange, lopsided walk. It struggled down the steps and a thin voice floated over the lawn.

'Don't you run away from me, headmaster! I've got you this time!'

'Lady Vyner,' said Routon.

'She's got a legal summons for me. I don't think I can avoid it this time, unless I run.' He waved, cheerfully. 'Good afternoon, ma'am!'

He sighed. 'It's the one thing I always leave until last: the wretched rent. We simply don't have it.'

Lady Vyner reached them at last, white-faced. She was wrapped in an old fur coat, buttoned crookedly over her wounded arm.

'I'm here to serve you notice,' she said, breathing heavily. 'Two weeks. Final demand for a full cash payment. Then you're all out – all of you. Down the road and gone, back to your cesspools.'

She produced a bottle of rum. 'The end of the road, headmaster. Shall we celebrate?'

Tomaz, meanwhile, was sitting all alone.

D.C.C. Cuthbertson had been clear and firm. 'Let him think about it,' he'd said.

Father O'Hanrahan stood outside his cupboard, his back against the door. He pressed the earpiece into his ear and pulled up the microphone.

'How long shall we give him?'

'The longer the better. Believe you me, a bit of solitary brings them round. I'd say to my junior officers, "Why use your fists? Let them sweat." There's nothing worse than waiting for pain. Give him time, Father, and then show him that blueprint.'

'Ah,' said Father O'Hanrahan. 'I haven't actually got that with me.'

'What do you mean, you haven't got it? Who has?'

'It's in my room, but in all the hurry of the morning, I couldn't lay my hands on it. It's not a problem. I've done a little sketch of the tunnels as I remember them—'

'Not a problem? What do you mean, it's not a problem?'

'It's in my room, man! Don't panic. Doonan was clearing up and he must have popped it in a drawer. I'll find it tonight when I see him.'

'I don't like the risks you take,' said Cuthbertson, quietly. 'We are on the edge of something very special and I don't want it blown.'

They were silent for a while.

'Go on, then,' said the policeman at last. 'Get back to your man. And don't overdo it. I had a prisoner once so scared he died of heart failure. That was a paperchase, I can tell you – it would be worse with a kiddy.'

Father O'Hanrahan breathed in and out a few times, and pulled his satchel round. Opening the flap, he pulled out his own sketch of the tunnels. A green leaf fluttered from his fingers and he sighed in irritation. The children were constantly interfering with his things.

'How are you feeling there, Tom?' he said, from the doorway.

'I'd like to go now, please,' said Tomaz, in a small voice.

'I'm sure you would. I'd like to let you go as well. But I've just been talking to the headmaster and he said to me that these sessions have to take priority. That captain fellow too. Respect your elders, that's what he said. So if you know what's good for you, you're going to answer my questions. I'll ask you again: how do you get to that house of yours?'

The old man sat down heavily in the chair and bolted the door.

'Through Neptune,' said Tomaz.

'That's a start, that's a start.'

'He knows you know about Neptune,' said Cuthbertson, through the earpiece. 'He's given you nothing.'

'But I think you know that I know all about Neptune. So I don't think you're giving me much by mentioning him. Once you're down the Neptune fella, where d'you go then?'

'Along the tunnel.'

'To a secret door?'

'No.'

'What, then? Some kind of passage?'

Tomaz licked his lips. He was hot in his blazer and he was sweating all over. 'I don't really remember,' he said, at last.

'Little liar,' hissed Cuthbertson, through the earpiece.

Father O'Hanrahan leaned forward and took a gentle hold of Tomaz's tie. He wrapped it round two of his fingers and drew the boy just a little closer. In the candlelight, Tomaz noticed how the man's hands appeared to get lumpier: they threw awful shadows. Then he caught the subtlest whiff of alcohol on the man's breath. He tried to sit back and the tie grew tight.

'How do you get to your house?' said Father O'Hanrahan. 'I'm asking as your spiritual father and as a friend. I want to know where your home is and how a man gets in.'

Tomaz nodded. He could think of nothing to say.

'I was hoping you'd give me a little help, Tom. I didn't think I'd get the *I-don't-remember* treatment.'

'Careful,' said the voice of Cuthbertson. 'You've got him where you want him. Go easy.'

The old man released the boy's tie and smiled. 'So, let's start again,' he said. He unfolded his paper and spread it on the table.

'Help me with my little survey,' he said. 'I've drawn the Neptune thing there. There's a tunnel coming off him, isn't there? So what I want you to do is draw me the best route.'

'I can't draw,' said Tomaz.

O'Hanrahan sucked in his breath and stared. The boy met his eyes.

'He's playing games,' hissed Cuthbertson. 'Time to be firm.'

Father O'Hanrahan slapped Tomaz hard across the face. The weight of the blow spun Tomaz in his chair and he nearly fell. The old man's voice changed and the new regis-ter was deep and hard.

'What I want you to do,' he said, 'is draw me the route. If you don't want to do that, my friend, I'll thrash you. And then you can draw it.'

Tomaz closed his eyes, briefly, and discovered he was trembling all over. He could not marshal his thoughts and he could not think of a way out. He knew that the next remark he made would be very important. Before he could speak, though, the man had his tie again and was drawing him forward, half out of his chair.

'Will you tell me where the door is?'

'No, sir,' he said. 'Please don't—'

'Smack him,' said Cuthbertson.

The blow came from above this time – another stinging slap that whipped the back of his head. Tomaz was knocked to the floor. The table was on its side and the candle flames were dancing. Worse, the chaplain was now bending over him, a huge shape in the darkness. Tomaz curled up out of instinct.

'I didn't want it to be like this!' cried the voice. 'I gave you every chance, but I don't have time to waste!'

Tomaz peered up and hunted for a way out: there wasn't one. He could see the man's hands and, before he knew it, they were coming at him again. He was lifted. He was back in his chair. He put his arms up, fearing another blow from the side, and received one between his shoulder blades. He was knocked forward and winded, totally helpless.

'How do you get into your house, boy?'

'I don't know!' It was all he could think of.

'What's going on?' hissed Cuthbertson. 'Play your advantage – is he scared?'

'What you little fellows need is a bit of discipline,' said the chaplain. 'Where is your house? Where is your house?'

Tomaz felt a hand on the collar of his blazer. He rolled by instinct and the blazer came off – but the hand moved to his hair, and he was lifted onto his toes. 'You'll talk, sonny Jim. Once I've whipped you, you'll be pleased to talk!'

Chapter Thirty-two

'Stop, everybody,' cried Professor Worthington.

They were in a long, curving tunnel. Water gurgled along its centre, in a wide gully, and the torch beams were scattered crazily over the stone. 'Look at this – this is a marvel. This is the kind of thing I was hoping for!'

The children pointed their torches and made out the shape of a long barge. It lay sadly on its rotting keel, tipped over in an ungainly sprawl of broken wood. There were oars and an old life-belt, and everything was coated in dirt, sand, and dust. It was turning into a skeleton.

'How did they get that down here?' said Sanjay.

'I would imagine it was *built* down here,' said the professor. 'Some of these passages could be flooded and used as canals. What you're looking at is one of the boats that used to transport materials. The lake was dug, don't forget, by men, women, and children.'

'Wow,' said Anjoli.

'These tunnels are the equivalent of storm drains. They take the excess water away when the lake floods. Whoever designed this was a genius. You should be proud of your relatives, Caspar.'

'Um, do you mean this could all be underwater?' said Oli.

'Yes. The taps and valves will be in the pump-room, which is why it's so important.'

'I would have put pumps and stuff above ground,' said Anjoli, as they set off again.

'Yes,' said Sanjay. 'Why put it all underground so you have to come all the way down?'

'A very good question,' said Professor Worthington. 'It's because the engineers were making use of *hydraulics*: I'll explain later. Why have we stopped?'

They had stopped because the passage was completely blocked by a grille of metal bars. An ancient sign was just legible: *DANGER. NO ENTRY.*

Caspar was looking at his keyring, nervously.

A circle formed around him.

'Don't forget you're the boss,' said Sanjay. 'This is your house, man.'

'Yes, but I may not have *all* the keys.'

'I could get through there,' said Anjoli. 'Breathe in and someone push me.'

'Yeah, you're just a stick,' said Israel. 'What about Henry?' He was holding Henry's sleeve, as the giant boy always got nervous underground. Miles was holding his hand.

'It might be this one,' said Caspar, holding up an old, chocolate-coloured key. His voice had little confidence, but he pushed it into the keyhole. Asilah helped him twist it and, suddenly, the mechanism clicked. The gate swung back and they were through. They turned to the right and came upon a steep circular staircase. There was a noise of rushing water.

'We are close!' said Professor Worthington, studying the map.

They descended, chattering with excitement. Soon, their footsteps had taken on a new echo; their voices were suddenly louder as the acoustics changed. Turning on the last

222

step, they came under a low beam and looked up. *Pump-room*, said the sign.

It was as if they had stepped into a musical instrument.

It was as if they'd walked into some infinitely complex body-part of tubes and pipes. There were pipes everywhere – thin and thick, straight and swooping. They soared overhead and then you saw them under your feet. They were lost in impossible knots and then everything was untangled, running straight and parallel. The air was thick with water vapour, and the children's torches cut through it like searchlights, striking the brass to be reflected back and forth. It was a spaghetti so intricate that the eye was lost and confused. Some tubes were thin as straws; some were great columns, thick as trees. Valves, nipples, and tees; spiders, spigots, tanks, and stopcocks – everything was polished and you could hear constant water, frothing inside.

The children moved forward into it, as if into the jungle. The noise was fabulous – all around them, drippings, high and low, and the echoes of those drippings. There were groans and throbbings. There'd be a sudden whoosh and whirl – but the overwhelming sound, deep and constant, was of roaring water, hurtling unseen, ferocious as rapids or waterfalls.

The children touched, stroked, and gaped.

Gradually, as if drawn by a magnet, they came to the central chamber and gaped again.

'Oh my word,' said Professor Worthington. She brushed away tears with the back of her hand and started to laugh. 'I so hoped they'd have one of these . . . I didn't dare believe they would . . . Caspar, this is priceless. What did I say about tears, Miles?'

'They clean the eyeball, Miss.'

'Yes. But they are also a hormonal reaction. My goodness . . .'

Again, every torch was focused on it and some dared a gentle touch. 'We are so lucky,' she whispered.

It was a giant column, made of glass. There was a brass frame, but the overwhelming impression was of a long, crystal shaft sinking into the ground and rising way up out of sight. Within the cylinder were four smaller glass pipes, full of bubbling water. It looked like an ultra-modern lift shaft, or a glass syringe. There was a glass door in the nearest panel, so you could step into it. There was also a set of dials beside the door, inscribed with fine calibrations.

'It's an elevator,' said Millie, with wonder in her voice. 'Isn't it? It's a lift.'

'It's a . . . it's a kind of lift,' said the professor. 'I've seen one other. They are extraordinarily rare – this is engineering at its most miraculous. I think there are four, in the whole world.'

'But why do you need a lift . . . in a lake?'

'Why do you need a lift? Why would anyone need to ride a lift car, to get to the bottom of a lake?'

'Fishing?' said Ruskin. 'Swimming?'

A number of children laughed, but professor Worthington silenced them. 'He's right,' she said. 'He's absolutely right. There was – how can I explain it? – a certain vanity when these things were constructed. Don't forget that every archi-tect likes to push himself and try new things. Let me try the control . . .' She touched the knob, gently. 'These little dials, children, control about three million metric tonnes of water. And look at them: they're the size of a teacup.'

She turned the top dial, gently. The bubbles in the four pipes slowed down in their journey. She turned it another degree and they stopped altogether. From over their heads there came a vibration and the sound of a tide slowly, laboriously turning.

'This is weird,' said Sam. 'The ground's shaking.'

A water-lift was descending. They all recognised the principle at once: it was a lift-car, dropping in a glass shaft. But as it came into view and hovered in front of their gaze, they could see it was different. It was two-thirds full of murky green water and there were three platforms, like diving boards.

'It's a ride!' said Anjoli. 'We could get in, through that door! We could go for a ride!'

'Absolutely,' said Professor Worthington. 'It takes a while to get used to – but yes, one could empty the water, so the space is dry. Climb aboard and . . . up you go. It's about displacement. If you were to step into this chamber, you would have controlled access to the lake. It's the most beautiful thing – it's both a pumping mechanism and a kind of decompression chamber. You can get into the lift and find yourself at any level of the lake that you choose. Then: touch the controls and you can step out into a boat. You can go swimming, if that's what you prefer. Or you can stay inside, safe and dry, and observe the fish. I would imagine the lake has underwater electric lights. In the days of your ancestors, Caspar, they probably came down here for pre-dinner cocktails, to watch the mysteries of the deep.'

'Let's do it!' said Israel. 'We can swim home!'

'It's so beautifully maintained,' murmured the professor. 'Someone must come down here . . . there must be a team. Where's Tomaz? He should know . . .'

Nobody answered.

She raised her voice. 'Where's Tom?'

'He might be with Father O'Hanrahan, Miss,' said Sanchez. 'His interview was this afternoon.'

'How do you know that?'

'Um . . . he told me, Miss. Is everything alright?'

'No. Who said he could cut my class? Was he there for the stitching? I thought I saw him.'

The children were silent. At last, Asilah said, 'I don't think he wanted to go, Miss. But Father O'Hanrahan was pretty fierce about it. He came and got him, just as we were lining up.'

Professor Worthington was staring into the glass, tight-lipped. She was clearly trying to conceal her anger, but wasn't succeeding. She turned away from the group. 'Get your notebooks out,' she said. Her voice was thin and clipped. 'I want you to sketch this mechanism – we need to discuss hydraulics . . . Israel, what are you doing?'

'Swimming,' he said, hopefully. 'I thought—'

'Put your clothes back on. And you, Anjoli! Honestly . . .'

Suddenly, there was a shout. It was Eric, and he had his hands at his mouth, and was staring at the glass with mesmerised eyes. 'Victor . . .' he whispered. 'I just saw Victor!'

The children moved quickly round to where he was standing and peered into the chamber. The water was murky and there was weed floating in it – some kind of log as well.

Sam crouched down and peered upwards. 'He's right,' he said. His eyes were wide. 'It's the crocodile. He's in the lift!'

Professor Worthington went back to the dial and lowered the car so the waterline was under the children's noses. The crocodile lifted its nose two centimetres and the dark crenellations of its back came into view. It turned itself around and scrabbled up onto the muddy platform.

Chapter Thirty-three

'I'm lost for words,' said Professor Worthington.

The children pressed their noses to the glass and the little ones knocked violently. The crocodile lifted an eyelid and closed it again. His zip of teeth appeared to be smiling smugly. He turned and started nosing into the mess of mud and grass that had accumulated.

'There's eggs, Miss,' said Sanjay.

'What?'

Sanjay had his hands cupped around his eyes and was down on one knee. He was peering into the crocodile's lair and he started to count. 'Two, three . . . I think there's about seven, Miss.'

'He's got a nest!' said Ruskin. 'He's got a nest!'

Professor Worthington brought the lift lower still and the children pressed right round it, straining for the best view. Sure enough, half buried in the silt they could see ivory-coloured spheres. Victor moved his body up and over them and closed his eyes dismissively.

'I have to say I am . . . bowled over,' said the professor. 'They say that all animals have an instinct, but this is remarkable. The temperature of that water is probably higher than any other part of the lake. What a survivor – what a parent! I am filled with admiration.'

'But where's the mother?' said Millie. 'I don't understand.'

'I think we're going to have to tell Flavio that Victor's a girl. I had my suspicions, you know! I thought she was acting strangely.'

'How does she get in and out though, Miss?' said Kenji. 'Is she trapped now?'

'We'll put her back up to the top before we go. It's only at the top you can get out, so – yes, she's trapped at the moment.'

'You could drown in there,' said Miles, quietly.

Everyone looked at him. He'd been noticeably keeping back and saying nothing. Henry stood next to him, in shirt-sleeves. He had given Miles his giant blazer again and the boy was wrapped in it, perched on a pipe. He looked uneasy, staring at the murky water.

'Why do you say that?' said Professor Worthington.

'I don't know,' said Miles. 'I've seen this before.'

'Liar,' said Millie.

Somebody pushed her, hard, and she nearly tripped.

'. . . I don't know when,' said Miles. 'Can we go back up, please?'

'In a moment, of course. I'm interested in what you say, Miles – there's one other, to my knowledge,' said Professor Worthington. 'It's sometimes open to the public.' There was a squirt of radio static. 'What was that?' she snapped. 'Was that you, Oli?'

'Yes, Miss.'

'Why have you brought a radio down here?'

'It's Millie's submarine, Miss.'

'Have you been carrying that for the last half-hour? You amaze me, you boys. Turn the wretched thing off and listen. What was I saying? Yes. The other model – it's in a castle, in

Kent. Maybe you've seen that one, Miles? Have you ever been to Kent?'

'I don't know.'

Miles looked troubled. 'The controls are on the outside,' he said. 'They should be on the inside.'

Professor Worthington looked at him more carefully. Apart from Henry, the children had moved away from him and his eyes looked slightly glazed. She wondered for a moment if he'd heard the story.

'I think you must have seen the other one, Miles. It's a famous story – they call it *the housemaid's revenge*. Eight people were drowned – is that what you're thinking of?'

'No.' He seemed distracted. 'I want to go back. I want to go up.'

'Tell us, Miss,' said Anjoli.

'No, it's far too grim for children. It will give you nightmares.'

There was a chorus of disappointment. 'Tell us! Tell us!' The cry was repeated and she felt hands tugging her coat.

'Alright,' she said. 'But if you can't sleep tonight, don't blame me. It's all to do with gravity-fed water systems. Miles is absolutely right. He's spotted the flaw in the design – the fatal flaw. These dials can lift and lower the car, as you saw. But they can also fill it full of water and empty it. It doubles as a pump, you see – to drain the lake – and it's a crucial part of the machinery. I could fill that car with water and anyone in that car would be helpless. How long can you hold your breath, children?'

'Five minutes,' said someone.

'Three minutes!'

'I did seven last term – that's my record.'

Some of the younger orphans immediately filled their lungs and stared at their watches. Oli's radio crackled again and Professor Worthington did her best to ignore it.

229

'Well, I can tell you that the average for a human being is between twenty-five and forty *seconds*. Less if you're panicking, and a lot less if you know they're the last seconds of your life.'

She saw that she had the children's attention again. 'Now the system in Kent was almost certainly built by the same team – it controls a large, ornamental moat round a castle. One of the reasons very few of these pumps were made is because of the problem Miles has identified. When one steps into that chamber, one is entirely dependent on those controlling the dials outside. I'm sure you can understand the logic: when this thing was made, the people who used it would have had total faith in their servants. Those servants were loyal and did what they were told. However, it is open to abuse – as the family in Kent found out, to their cost.'

She paused.

'What happened?' said Kenji.

'Well. It appears that the family had trained up a young girl called Ethel Mosse. Ethel was, apparently, an expert in handling the equipment, though it's not hard to master – the principles are very simple. She was very skilful and she certainly seemed trustworthy. The family who trained her got used to showing the pump to their guests and demonstrating the wonders of the journey to the moat's bottom. Unfortunately, on one occasion, Ethel decided to take revenge.'

'For what?' said Millie.

'Nobody quite knows. Some say she'd had her wages stopped. Others say she'd been, er . . . molested by the father of the family. There were all sorts of rumours – there always are. The events that followed, though, are quite straightforward: for whatever reason, the girl responded to her ill-treatment in spectacular style. It was a Saturday evening and the family had decided to demonstrate their toy to some visiting big-wigs. They were a fabulously wealthy family – the castle was just their country home. The lift-car was full. Eight people – four adults, three children, and a baby. It was the summer and they were in their bathing costumes, Anjoli. Just as you would so like to be. They were going to plunge to the bottom of the moat, then finish with a swim. The butler was going to meet them in a rowing-boat, with a picnic. Young Ethel was at the controls.'

She paused. The children were silent and enthralled. Those that had held their breath had let it escape, quietly.

'She ushered them into the car,' the professor went on. 'She sealed the door, as was customary. Then she dropped them to the bottom. She let them see the . . . fish, I suppose. There was an intercom system, but whether it was used nobody knows. She brought them back to the starting point and it would appear that she turned the bottom dial, which controls the pumping mechanism. Do you want me to go on?'

The silence convinced her she had no choice.

'Ethel pumped a thousand gallons of water over them. There were no witnesses, of course – I mean no survivors. But when the police pieced things together and interviewed her – she admitted it. She stood there and watched them drown.'

Professor Worthington closed her eyes. 'Can you imagine it? Trying to keep your nose above the waterline, as the water rises and rises? Ethel stood and watched them. And then . . . and this is the detail that has always haunted me. She raised the car and sluiced the dead bodies into the moat. The butler found them as he rowed up with the champagne and strawberries.'

Professor Worthington paused. 'The girl was found guilty, of course; she was hanged. It's the reason why these contraptions went out of fashion. What's the matter, Miles – you look like you've seen a ghost.'

'I can hear one,' he said. 'I think he's talking to me.'

Miles was standing, looking at Oli's radio. The boy had turned it off, but for some reason it was crackling again and there was a sound like grunting. Oli put his ear to it.

'I'm sorry, Miss,' he said. 'It *is* switched off, definitely.'

'Then what's that noise?' said Professor Worthington. The grunting had turned into deep breathing.

'It picks up strange things. I think—'

'Shhh!'

A low voice came through, loud and clear. There was hatred in every word and some of the younger orphans pressed together for comfort. 'I've been wanting to do this to one of you for weeks!' said the voice. 'This is going to do me good . . .'

In Father O'Hanrahan's confessional, Tomaz was fighting for his life.

He had managed to grab the bolt, but his hands had been snatched away and he'd been thrown across the table. Squirming like a fish he'd managed to get free, but there was simply nowhere to go, and when the belt hit him across the back, he was stunned by the pain. O'Hanrahan grabbed him by the neck and the fight was over. As he did so, the window shattered.

It simply blew inwards and shards of glass were whirling in a blizzard, dancing between the walls. Father O'Hanrahan felt them on his hands and face, and had no choice but to cover his eyes. Then, before he or Tomaz could move, the door was rattling in its frame. The handle was turning back and forth, and all Tomaz could think of was Captain Routon. He slipped to the ground in a ball, hoping with all his strength – and he heard the wood splitting as if an axe was hacking it to pieces. The bolt burst and the door crashed open with such force that one hinge was torn loose. The tape recorder was lifted to the ceiling and plunged onto the floor where it exploded in fragments.

'Help!' cried Father O'Hanrahan.

'What's happening?' shouted Cuthbertson, down the wire.

The priest was standing still now, too shocked to move. The cupboard was a destroyed wreck around him and the violence had lasted no more than five seconds. The candles were out.

That was the moment the wind started.

It came through the window and it came through the door. It rose quickly to a hurricane and spun into a whirlwind. The old man's paper was lifted and torn to confetti. Tomaz crawled away from it and found a tiny space where it was calm; the old man, however, was caught in its frenzy – he was spread-eagled against the wall, his robes flattened and his face buffeted by freezing air. For the wind was Siberian, and the old man felt his eyes smarting and his teeth aching in his gums. He knew then what it was, and though he was frightened, it stirred an instinct in him. His right hand fought the vortex and he got it to his chest. He needed his crucifix! This was a haunting more powerful than any he'd experienced. For a mad second he'd assumed it was children's games. Then, like Tomaz, he'd wondered if Routon or Flavio was behind it. Pressed to the wall, feeling the agonising chill, he knew something far more powerful was in the room, and he was fighting for survival.

'*In nomine* . . .' he whispered.

The chairs and table disintegrated. The wooden pieces clattered round the walls. The cans of drink spun on the floor, the liquid foaming out of them. Tomaz was on his feet, somehow, staggering wildly. The old man could only watch as the boy was blown through the doorway, his blazer flapping after him. Then the broken door took on a life of its own and smashed back into its own frame.

He was sealed in.

Father O'Hanrahan clung to his crucifix, but couldn't speak. He was dimly aware of Cuthbertson's voice in his ear, shouting and cursing: 'What are you doing, man? Don't kill him!'

He knew that all he could do was sit it out – the ghost was roasting him. It was a trial of strength he had not been prepared for. He had holy water with him, deep in his satchel, but there was no way he could get to it. He mouthed the words again, '*In nomine* . . .' but they seemed to make the furious presence even more violent.

His belt was lifted from where it had fallen. It sprang upwards and came down like a whip. He was caught a stinging blow across the face, then two more across his hands. The wind continued to blow and he sank to his knees to endure it. He had no idea how long he knelt there, whimpering into his microphone.

It was dark when he crawled out of the cupboard and across the classroom. He got to his room, somehow, and used his remaining strength to pack a holdall. Then he limped to his car and fell into the driving seat. He could stay at Ribblestrop Towers no longer.

Chapter Thirty-four

'It was Lord Vyner,' said Tomaz. 'I know it.'

They were in the orphans' dormitory, up in the east tower. The boy had refused to speak about his experience all through supper.

His friends waited patiently. When he asked for a meeting, everyone went straight to the orphans' dormitory. The only problem was the presence of Brother Doonan.

Asilah had taken him to one side. 'Just now and then we have to meet alone, sir,' he said. 'It's not that we don't trust you, and we don't want to hurt your feelings. . .'

'You don't want me in the room?'

'No, we want to talk together.'

'I don't understand – you want to talk to me on your own? In the room?'

'All the kids want to talk. Alone.'

'With me?'

'No, Father. Would you mind leaving us on our own for about two hours?'

Doonan laughed. 'I'm so sorry to be slow, Asilah.' He patted the boy's shoulder. 'It's just as it should be and it's

235

kind of you to explain. I'll go round the lake and I'll knock before I come in.'

Asilah shook his hand and kissed it.

Once they'd heard the full story, Millie swore.

A number of orphans moved closer to Tomaz and Sanjay put his arm round him. 'That old ghost loves you, Tom,' he said. 'He's looking after you, boy!'

'What's the priest up to?' said Eric.

'He's never a priest,' said Sam. 'I do not believe he's a priest!'

'Yeah,' said Anjoli. 'If that old skrag is asking about Tomaz's house, it's because he's after something. We've been so slow! He was coming out of Neptune that time – now how did he find out about that?'

'Yes!' said various children.

'That's all true,' said Asilah, holding up a hand for quiet. 'We never found out what he was doing down those tunnels. He's got something on his mind.'

'Did you tell him anything?' said Sanchez.

'No,' said Tomaz.

'You stayed silent under torture,' said Ruskin. 'Because that's what it was – torture.'

There was a buzz of indignation all around the room.

'He smacked Tomaz,' said Eric, shaking his head. 'That's as bad as it gets, man.'

'Sounds like the ghost gave it to him, though,' said Podma.

Imagio smiled a thin, cruel smile. 'Where I live,' he said, 'he'd be in the ground by now out in the damn desert.'

'Let's go see him!' said Anjoli. 'We need weapons!'

Everyone stood to leave and it took Sanchez half a minute to get their attention. 'Listen!' he said. 'Listen!'

The children were calm.

'We made a big mistake last term. We did everything by ourselves, when we should have talked to the headmaster.'

'Oh, come on!' said Millie. 'Are you serious?'

'Of course I'm serious! We always think we're best handling these things alone. But all we have to do is say Father O'Hanrahan assaulted Tomaz. He'd be sacked, immediately.'

'He would not!' said Millie. 'Our headmaster can't sack anyone – look at Miles, how come he's still here?'

Miles was sitting on the floor, legs crossed. He did his best to smile as the children laughed.

'Miles is loaded!' said Anjoli. 'His ma just shells out the cash.'

Sanjay said something in his own language and there was applause.

'What did he say?' said Millie.

'I said she pays a million to forget she's a mother!'

'Shut up!' said Sanchez, fiercely, looking at Miles. 'That's a dirty thing to say, Sanjay! You apologise right now.'

Sanjay's smile had died. 'I didn't mean it, man. All I meant—'

Asilah was standing and administered a stinging slap. He said something fierce and furious in his own language, and Sanjay put his hands over his mouth, the tears welling. 'I am so sorry,' he said, quietly. 'I don't know why I said it.'

There was a terrible silence. At last, Oli said, 'Can I ask a question?'

'Yes,' said Sanchez.

'I've been thinking. Tomaz was being interrogated and tortured. And the ghost of Lord Vyner helped him get out of it. That must mean the ghost will make sure nothing bad happens.'

'True,' said Eric.

'So why don't we try and talk to Lord Vyner?' said Sam.

237

'I wanted to do that at the start of term,' said Millie. 'So let's go down with Tomaz, have a little consultation with the ghost.'

'What does this ghost look like?' said Imagio. 'You're all talking like you believe, but how many of you have really seen it? I've never seen no ghost.'

'He's real,' said Ruskin.

'What's he look like? Who's seen him?'

Tomaz hesitated. He'd got so used to the ghost of Cyril Vyner: they'd kept each other company in a strange, silent, shy kind of way. He had reason to be very fond of him and he didn't want to show him any disrespect now.

'It's hard to describe,' he said. 'I never saw him full on, but I know exactly what he looks like.' He paused. 'You see him, but then you think it's because you were expecting to see him. And his face is . . .'

'Damaged,' said Miles, quietly.

'Yes,' said Tomaz.

'Is it true he's had half his head blown off?' said Eric. ''Cause that is grim.'

Tomaz winced. But it was clear that everyone wanted to know.

'Like I say, you don't see him full on. I think he knows he's a mess and doesn't sort of . . . want to upset you. Maybe – I don't know – he's sad a lot of the time. They shot him in the head, so of course he's a mess.'

Anjoli said, 'Where I live we got a ghost. By the river. And he takes little children and he cuts them up.'

Israel punched him. 'That is such crap!'

'He chased me! You don't even know —'

'Baby crap, from a baby!'

'OK, so why do you always run in the dark, huh, big boy?'

'Shut up, both of you!' said Sanchez. He had his hand

over Anjoli's mouth and Asilah shoved Israel onto the floor. 'The important thing is that Tomaz is safe. The ghost sorted that out, whatever he looks like and for whatever reasons. What we've got to worry about is what this man's next move might be.'

There were grunts of approval.

'Yeah,' said Israel. 'We gotta find out why he's so keen to get into Tomaz's house.'

'But that's obvious,' said Sam. 'We all know Tomaz's house is full of beautiful things. He must be a robber, and that's —'

'That's why he was poking around Neptune,' finished Oli.

'So what do we do?' said Asilah. 'If Sam's right, he's going to find a way in sometime. Isn't he?'

'Oh my,' said Millie.

Everyone looked at her.

'I've just thought of something else. We are stupid – we are *slow*.'

'What?' said Sanchez.

'When I was in the car with him and Doonie – first day, travelling down. They told me something important. Father O'Hanrahan is an *exorcist*. And it's one of the reasons he's here.'

'What's an exorcist?' said Imagio.

'Imagine you get possessed by an evil spirit,' said Sanchez. 'Or if you buy a house and it's haunted – with a ghost or an evil presence. You call in an exorcist and that person is skilled at saying the right prayers and doing all the holy water stuff. Until the ghosts are driven out.'

'Seems like he's not much of a match for Lord Vyner,' said Asilah. 'At the moment it's one-nil, easy.'

'Yes, but he was unprepared,' said Tomaz. 'Next time he might do better. I mean, if he comes down to my place

239

with Bibles and holy stuff, Lord Vyner might not stand a chance!'

Sanjay laughed. 'He's gonna get a shock when he looks in that satchel of his.' He caught Anjoli's eye and they both grinned at each other.

'Why?' said Sam. 'What's the joke?'

'You seen little Joe lately?' said Anjoli. 'The scorpion?'

Some of the other orphans were smiling.

'You did it?' said Eric. 'Good man.'

Sanjay said, 'It was my idea. After we stung that camel's arse, Anjoli put little Joe in the old man's satchel, with a few leaves. He's gonna get a nice surprise, sometime.'

'Unless Joe's asleep,' said Anjoli. 'I shouldn't have put the leaves in. He eats and sleeps for days.'

'Look,' said Sanchez, when the laughter had died. 'We'd better decide what we do. Who votes we go to the headmaster?'

Not a hand was raised.

Millie smiled and took off her enamel badge. 'That's the power of democracy, Head Boy. And if you tell him anything, we'll put that scorpion right up your—'

'We need an action plan,' cried Asilah. 'I'm with Millie. We can handle this on our own.'

'First idea,' said Ruskin. 'I vote we put a guard in Tomaz's house.'

Millie nodded. 'That is surprisingly good for one so slow.'

'We make sure Tomaz is never alone,' said Israel. 'Always in threes.' He went and sat next to Tomaz and put his arms round him.

'Get radios,' said Eric. 'Sort out the tools – just like last time. We don't wanna be caught short.'

'Maybe a few *different* plans,' said Oli. 'So we can adapt, according to what he throws at us.'

'Weapons,' said Anjoli. 'You can't beat a good weapon.'

Millie looked at Miles. 'Why did you muck around with Sanchez's gun?' she said, tiredly. 'We're going to need it again and the police have taken it.'

'Yeah,' said Eric. 'If we all get killed, whose fault's that gonna be?'

'It doesn't matter,' said Sanchez.

'Of course it matters!' said Millie.

'I know where the gun is,' said a voice.

Everyone turned. The voice belonged to Kenji, the orphan in charge of the school tuck shop and bank. He was cross-legged on the floor with his fellow infants, and had been following the debate with interest. His hand was now raised.

'Where?' said Asilah. 'How do you know?'

'You said the police had taken it, but that's not true. Lady Vyner never pressed charges, so the gun was returned.'

'It's a Thirty-Eight Special, isn't it?' said Nikko. 'Snubnose?'

Sanchez was nodding.

'I saw it this morning,' said Kenji. 'It's perfectly safe.'

'Saw it where?' said Millie. 'You're wasting time. If it's locked up somewhere, it's not going to help us. Sanchez needs it in his pocket – or I do.'

'That's the point, though,' said Kenji. 'It's in the head-master's safe. And we run the Ribblestrop Syndicate, and that means holding the bank's investments.' He was pulling a chain out from under his shirt. 'We have to have a secure storage area and that . . . well, that happens to be the head-master's safe. I'm the keyholder. I can get it for you any time, if you want.'

Sanchez felt Millie's gaze upon him and blushed. 'That would be very useful,' he said, quietly.

'I think so too,' said Anjoli. 'I don't feel safe any more – this is all getting freaky.'

'Tomaz,' said Millie. 'At the moment, is there any way the priest could get into your home?'

241

Tomaz thought and shook his head. 'I've been wondering about it. You all know the way – you know how it looks . . . it's just a rabbit hole. Even if he found it, he's too fat.'

'Could he dig it? Make it bigger?'

'It would take a while, but . . . yes. We do that for Henry. I guess so.'

'Any other way?'

'Only by caving. That was how I got in first, from above. I blocked the way as best I could – it's not easy to spot.'

'Ruskin's right: we better get guards down there,' said Asilah. 'Groups of three. Through the night.'

'Oli,' said Millie. 'Draw up a rota.'

'Set spies,' said Anjoli.

The meeting was breaking up. The children hauled themselves to their feet and there was a flurry of high-fives and hugs.

'We're at war again,' said Israel. 'Feels good to me.'

Chapter Thirty-five

'Millie,' said Miles, later than evening. 'I want to ask you something.'

'What?'

They were alone in the boys' dormitory and Millie was wondering if she should have brought Anjoli or Sanjay with her. She wasn't frightened of Miles, but there was something about him that disturbed her.

'I want to show you something as well.'

'Go on then?'

'You know you asked me if Sanchez ever wrote to me? I said you couldn't read the letter, because it was personal. You didn't believe me.'

'I still don't.'

'Do you want to read it now?'

'He didn't write to you, Miles. He told me so himself.'

Miles pulled a piece of paper out of his blazer pocket.

'Anyway, what's it matter?' said Millie. 'Why are you so obsessed?'

'Something bad is coming,' said Miles. 'But I want you to know that I'm going to look after you.'

'*You're* going to look after *me*?'

'Yes.'

Millie sighed. 'You are seriously cracked – you can't look after yourself, we've all seen that. Show it to me.'

She took the letter and held it to the light. It had clearly been folded and unfolded many times. It was in a childish hand that she didn't recognise.

She read it aloud.

'*Dear Miles,*

I can't make this a long letter. Of course I miss you and I understand what you say but you still shouldn't have done what you did. I don't know what you mean about coming back to Ribblestrop. I can't see the headmaster changing his mind, but I will talk to him if I can. So will my dad. We all want you to come back.

Your best friend: Andreas Sanchez

'You wrote this yourself,' said Millie.

Miles shook his head. 'I didn't.'

'It's not even his signature. Anyway. . .' She passed it back to him. 'What am I supposed to say? Big deal. Well done.'

'Listen, Millie. The ghost comes to see me. Every night. If we climb up on the tower, like last time—'

Millie sighed and turned away. 'I'm going to bed,' she said. 'I'm not staying alone with you – you're too creepy.'

'There's something written on the wall. I want to show it to you . . .'

'You're writing on the walls as well? I am not climbing that tower with you, Miles. I saw what you did to Caspar.'

'I'm a guardian. You're safe if you—'

'I don't want to be around you!' shouted Millie. 'What are you turning into? You were freaky before, but this is a new . . . zone of freakiness. You need a shrink.'

'Sanchez brought me back here and I think there were reasons!'

'What?'

Millie laughed sharply. She stared at Miles. He was in shirt-sleeves, and she noticed the grey cotton was ripped and frayed. He was twisting a cuff in his fingers.

'I think Sanchez must have spoken to the headmaster,' he said. 'He wanted me back here, badly. And I think it was for a reason. I think—'

'Wait a moment,' said Millie. She laughed. 'Look, I don't want to disillusion you, but . . .' She shook her head. 'They say never indulge the fantasies of dangerous lunatics, so I better set you straight. The reason you're here, back in Ribblestrop, is because of something I did last term. I changed the letter that was expelling you and I did it as a joke. Total spur of the moment, off the top of my head decision because your photo made you look a lot sweeter than you are. The letter was on the headmaster's desk and I scribbled on it. Posted it. Back you came. Your "best friend" Sanchez didn't want me to – he said you were a dangerous liar.'

Miles blinked.

'If you want to look after someone, practise on yourself. No one else is going to.'

Miles stood for a moment, watching Millie as she walked away.

Then, slowly, he climbed onto the desk. He moved to the wardrobe. From there, mechanically, he opened the loft-hatch. With practised ease, he hauled himself up to the roof space. In a moment, he was out on the parapet, the freezing wind rioting around him, lifting the shirt from his body.

He put his back to the battlements and hugged himself, shuddering in the cold. The stones were covered in scratch marks. They had been getting more intricate each night. He had wanted to show her, but she'd gone, and he was alone.

Now he simply read them again, to himself.

> *'The child knows no fear, if the tiger he rides,*
> *And the sick can be healed through all that must pass . . .'*

He crawled further round the tower, for the next section.

> *'The river shall run full, that the valley be watered – at last*
> *Will the labyrinth come straight, though the sword hides.'*

The next part ran over the door, sliced in the old paintwork:

> *'Lion and lamb, united in this place;*
> *After the lightning and the damaged face.*
> *Seek not for the children that choose to be lost: realise*
> *That the world still weeps, but must one day dry its eyes.*
> *St Caspar will come home; in this place he'll be sworn.*
> *So drown the precious sword: from his heart it can't be*
> *drawn.'*

There were lights on in all the towers and a sprinkling of stars. Miles closed his eyes and stood up. Then he opened them and looked down at the lawn.

The ghost of Lord Vyner was standing below him, as Miles knew he would be. He was still as a sentry, arms by his sides. He was dressed in a black tailcoat, as if he'd been called out of a cocktail party. The face was pale, and even at this distance you could see the horrible distortion of the bullet wound.

Miles swallowed and stared at him. Then, carefully, he

sat up on the parapet and swung his legs over the edge. The wind was now freezing his body and he was starting to feel the numbness he craved. As he stared, the ghost did what it had done last night, and the night before. It clasped its hands slowly together and raised them above its head. Its gaze did not leave Miles's face.

Meanwhile D.C.C. Cuthbertson, Gary Cuthbertson, Father O'Hanrahan, and Darren were sitting around the same barroom table as before. They surrounded a single piece of paper.

'I can't see it,' said the old man. 'You'll have to read it to me.'

Cuthbertson held it nearer. 'Can you read the title?'

'No, I can't read the blessed title! I've still got a headache from hell.'

'It's *The Potholers' Gazette.*'

'Why have you brought it?'

'Can't you guess? I'm always proud when a little police work pays off.'

'Just tell me what you've found out.'

'That's the difference between us, isn't it? Gary and I, we go slow and steady; you move in like a bull. I get results; you get a broken head. *The Potholers' Gazette* closed down twenty years ago. This is an old edition.'

Father O'Hanrahan went to speak, but the policeman rode over him. 'Gary tracked it down, from nineteen fifty-one.'

'Go on.'

'You'll be wanting champagne at the end of this. There's an article here by Barnaby Phipps, who was one of those lads who went rambling and cycling and then wrote all about it. This is May, and he found himself on our doorstep. Listen.'

Cuthbertson licked his lips and tried to catch the jaunty tone of a fifties youth hosteller:

'Cycling up from Taunton, one has several choices. The majestic peaks of Exmoor rise seductively to the north, but there are interesting geological formations to the west as well. I fortified myself with a foaming pint of scrumpy cider and opted for the latter. What a happy choice it was! I found myself pedalling towards the sleepy town of Ribblestrop, and just before I got there, a kindly farmer directed me to a spectacular viewpoint, the Ribblestrop Edge. (A word to the wise: once you've seen it, replenish that flask with a bottle of Williams's ginger-beer, available from 36 Ribblestrop High Street – quite the finest in this sceptred isle, and a snip at threepence halfpenny.)

As I ate my sandwiches, who should appear but a gamekeeper. Now I'm for it! I thought. But not a bit of it. The fellow sat with me – shared a sandwich, in fact – and told me a few yarns.

"Ever done any potholing?" he said.

What a question to ask Barny Phipps. "Not half," I said and he took me along various paths to a grassy knoll (map reference OS344993). An unlikely-looking tumble of rocks opened quickly to a substantial bottle-neck, and that led to a cantilevered elbow. A very promising start. Cursing the fact I had no ropes, I drew back – no point putting oneself at risk without the proper equipment.

It's the ideal spot, though, and I will return. Any readers interested in joining me for a proper Ribblestrop expedition are invited to write in immediately. Potholes don't get more promising than this one – it's crying out to be mapped!'

There was a silence.

'Are you awake, Father?'

'Stop calling me *Father*.'

'The map reference is one hundred per cent accurate. We've found our way.'

'How do you know?'

'We visited last night,' said Gary.

'You think it's the one the monk was talking about?' he said.

'We don't think,' said the policeman. 'We *know*. The magazine uses the same words you did: "bottle-neck" ... "cantilevered elbow". It's the same.'

'And it's open? We can get down?'

'It's tight,' said Gary. 'It won't be easy and someone's tried to cover it up. But with the right gear, we can get it open.'

'Oh, and listen to this, by the way,' said Cuthbertson. 'It's in the next edition of the magazine – this is June nineteen fifty-one, just one month later. Editorial apology. Looks like young Mr Phipps got a bit carried away. Listen:

> *'The editor would like to apologise for, and withdraw, the invitation made to readers to explore potholes situated on the Ribblestrop Edge. We have been informed by the Ministry of Defence that the land referred to in the article is strictly private, and off limits to the general public. The estate of Ribblestrop has long been under the control of the War Office, and the pothole referred to has been sealed. Ground staff are not allowed to discuss the topography of the area, and the gamekeeper who extended a wholly inappropriate welcome to an unwelcome trespasser has been disciplined.'*

'When do we go down?' said Father O'Hanrahan, after another silence.

'Darren and I are going to clear a bit more stone,' said Gary. 'We'll do a few "explorations". But I'd say next week.'

'You still with us, are you?' said Cuthbertson.

Father O'Hanrahan looked up and his eyes had brightened. 'Oh yes,' he said. 'By next week I'll be ready. I'll be prepared for that ghost, as well. He is going to be annihilated.' He tapped his satchel. 'I'm almost looking forward to a showdown. With Vyner and all of them.'

Chapter Thirty-six

Darren wore a black tracksuit with a hood and he carried a dark sports bag. He took his dad's van and drove across town to pick up Gary Cuthbertson. There was just time for a quick beer, so they studied the map of the school one more time. Conversation hadn't been easy since the disastrous football game and the collapse of Darren's professional hopes – though, in fairness, conversation had never been easy, as Darren tended to grunt rather than speak. Now, even the grunting was strained. By an unfortunate coincidence, they had run into Mr Scanlon, the football scout, that very afternoon on Ribblestrop High Street. He'd checked into the local hotel – tomorrow he'd be driving up to London with Imagio, so he was in buoyant mood. He hadn't noticed Darren's smouldering fury.

Gary and Darren drove to the High School and loaded the van with climbing equipment. Climbing Club had folded a few years before, due to health-and-safety legislation, and Gary had sold off a lot of the gear. There were ropes, though, and a few spigots. There was also a wire assault ladder – the sort you could roll up and put under your arm.

Gary locked up and directed Darren out of the school

onto the Old Taunton Road. They turned into a farm, crossed its yard, and took a track through a bit of scruffy woodland. Soon they were crossing the railway line and coming under the Ribblestrop Edge onto Lady Vyner's land.

It was another night of spectacular stars, so Darren drove with his sidelights only. At exactly ten o'clock, he saw a torch flash and he spotted the D.C.C.'s police car. Father O'Hanrahan sat in the back and Percy Cuthbertson was in the driver's seat. Both men were dressed in black.

The first thing everyone did was share a thermos of coffee. A half-bottle of brandy went round with it and the policeman rubbed his hands.

'How are you feeling, Darren?'

Darren grunted.

'Good lad. I want to stress the need for *calm* on this job. We're going in at about eleven. It's an hour's climb – I think we cleared most of the debris last night and we did a bit of a recce. But tonight it's the real thing, and I want to stress something else. If there're kids, and believe me, there's always a chance –'

'This time of night?' said Gary. 'They'll be asleep by now, surely?'

Father O'Hanrahan chuckled bitterly. 'Not these children,' he said. 'They don't behave like any children I've ever met.'

'He's right. You can't keep tabs on them. We might encounter individuals; we might encounter groups. If we do, we use reasonable force. We are not going to be thwarted this time, alright? This is an in-and-out job and we want no trouble. But if you encounter a kid, don't let it run.'

'What do we do?' said Gary.

'Immobilise it, fast. Then handcuffs. I've got a dozen pairs. We handcuff them to something, knock 'em out if you have to. I don't mean we go looking for trouble. But we don't go soft, either. If some little devil raises the alarm, all hell could break loose. Darren, you're our timekeeper. What's the time?'

Darren held up his watch.

'Everyone comfortable with that? Ten-oh-seven. Rendezvous by the Neptune statue, one-thirty. You'll have the boat by the bridge, Darren. Yes?'

Darren nodded.

'No lights. No engine. Float in her while we're underground. We'll be up from the pump-room as soon as we're done – if we're ahead of time, I'll flash you two short, one long. You've got to be by the *first* bridge. As soon as we're up – home we go.'

'What about Crowther?' said Gary. 'Have you seen him?'

'Yes,' said Cuthbertson.

'Who's Crowther?' said Father O'Hanrahan.

'Mr Crowther's in position and he'll be straight off to London. Crowther's the antiques man, Father. I told you about him.'

'And has he got the cash?'

'I saw it about thirty minutes ago and it looked crisp enough to me.'

Father O'Hanrahan felt his mouth go dry.

'We settle up, as discussed – then separate ways. I'll drop you by the boat now, Darren. Crowther's in a BMW on the far side of the lake. The three of us have a bit of a hike – how long, Gary?'

'Forty minutes.'

'Forty minutes. In that case, let's get going. Let's get rich.'

They transferred the bags and D.C.C. Cuthbertson started the engine. He slid his vehicle through the darkness, down to the lakeside. He drove carefully and slowly, picking his way over the grass. Ribblestrop Towers appeared on their left, half the windows lit. Dance music came from one of the towers and the policeman shook his head in disbelief. They drove carefully round and the speedboat appeared just as they'd moored it, bobbing in the water.

Darren climbed onboard, black from head to foot.

The other three shouldered their bags and struck off for the Edge.

The children of Ribblestrop had no idea what the next six hours would bring.

Chapter Thirty-seven

In Tomaz's home, ignorant of the movements above ground, night-watch number 901/7 were playing chess. Oli had created the schedules and changeover was midnight. Sam and Ruskin were completing what they hoped would be the last game. It was Imagio's final farewell party and they were itching to get back to school to attend it.

'Your move,' said Sam.

'I thought it was yours,' said Ruskin.

'No. I had to move my knight. Your humbug was threatening.'

The children always used sweets as pawns – it was a nice little treat when you captured one.

'You know, I've lost the plot a bit, Sam. To be honest. I'm completely shattered and my eyes . . . How long have we got?'

'Eric should have been here twenty minutes ago.'

'This really is the graveyard shift, isn't it? At least the midnight team gets to sleep. We just have to sit and . . . I'm not complaining, I mean it's a very nice place to sit. Shall I put another log on the fire?'

'No, it's too hot as it is. D'you want a cup of tea, Oli?'

'No, thank you.'

Time meant very little to Oli. He had brought Millie's submarine with him and was resoldering its propshaft for greater speed. He would work through the night, if allowed to, and wouldn't think of moving. He was hoping to present it to his friend at the end of term, all trials complete.

'Shall I check in with the boss?' said Sam. 'Where did you put the radio?'

'It's on charge,' said Oli. 'In the kitchen.'

Up in the south tower, Lady Vyner had poured herself a large glass of rum. There was little chance of sleep without it. The tower opposite – the orphans' tower – was throbbing with music again and lights were flashing. As far as she could tell, the children seemed to have parties most nights and her insomnia had got progressively worse. Tonight, the racket seemed particularly extreme. She glanced out of her window. She could see boys on the roof again, but she had no reactions left – they'd been doing it for weeks. Recently, there had been a spate of tightrope-walking, and because of this, one of the power lines into the school had come down. She could not believe what she was expected to endure. She could make out dancing shapes in the windows.

She looked at her grandson. She had formally forgiven him a week ago and he had moved back into his bedroom – rather reluctantly, she had noticed. Now his nose was pressed against the glass.

'You want to join them, don't you, my little viper?'

'No,' said Caspar, guiltily. He turned to face her. 'And I am not a viper, Gran.'

'You seemed to be getting along with them nicely enough. Made a few friends, did you, after the assassination attempt? I'm not surprised –'

'I am not a viper! I thought that gun was empty and it was not an . . . an assassination attempt!'

'Yes . . . well, there's many a murderer's gone to the gallows claiming he thought the gun was empty. I could press charges yet, you know – there are care homes for boys like you.'

'Gran! I thought the gun *was* empty! Miles told me—'

'Yes, I know. I've read your letters of apology, every one. They make a fat file.'

'I don't know how many more times I can say it.'

'I read your cards, I . . . arranged your flowers. I appreciated all your efforts to atone, Caspar. It's rare to see you feigning affection.'

'I did *not* mean to shoot you.'

'Of course you didn't, darling. It was a mistake any unloved, friendless child could make and I do not reproach you.'

As they watched the east tower, a window opened. A boy – naked apart from shorts – clambered out and reached up to the guttering. Doonan was there too, trying to reclaim him, but the boy was up onto the roof in a moment, a bottle in his hand. Someone threw him what looked like a firework and the bottle was placed up by a weather-vane, then lashed to it with a school tie. A match was struck and explosions ricocheted over the roofs. Arcs of silver were shot in a giant umbrella of phosphorescence.

'It's Imagio's last night,' said Caspar. 'It's his special send-off.'

'Imagio's last night. On his deathbed, is he?'

'No!' said Caspar, trying to keep calm. 'I told you. He's a nice boy—'

'You say he's *nice*, Caspar. But that, to me, suggests your loyalties are now divided. I thought you were the spy behind enemy lines, and now you appear to be turning your coat.'

Caspar writhed with frustration. 'Oh, Gran, honestly!

Leave me alone! Some of them *are* nice! Even Miles, when you talk to him – he's been nice to me. Oh! Listen, it's the school song.'

Lady Vyner closed her eyes. 'Jungle music.'

'Can I go? Can I go to the party? Please?'

Caspar turned, his eyes burning with longing. He stared at his gran and put his hands together, as if in prayer. 'Just for half an hour, Gran,' he whined. 'Just to say goodbye to Imagio?'

'No, darling. You can't.'

'But – please! Please!'

'I am an invalid still and your place is at my side. Anyway, they'll all be on the road soon. Their deadline is approaching – let's look forward to the eviction party.'

Chapter Thirty-eight

Gary Cuthbertson was the most experienced climber, so he had led the way.

He wasn't fit any more, but he was strong and he still had a certain technique. He knew how to keep his balance, and shift his weight, and having run Caving Club he was very good at leading others.

'Right foot down, Father.'

'Down where?'

'Down to your right. Take it slow – feel the rock-face. Just a bit lower . . .'

'The rope's tangling.'

'Don't worry about the rope. Ease yourself down, right side. I'm right underneath you.'

D.C.C. Cuthbertson was above, his teeth gritted with impatience. He shone a flashlight down, careful to avoid the old man's eyes. Gradually, painfully slowly, they descended another two metres.

It was past midnight already and progress had not been quick. They were through the worst of it though: the cantilevered elbow had nearly defeated Father O'Hanrahan and they'd had to haul him like a roll of carpet, bending his fat body over a shelf of limestone that threatened to cut him in half. His rucksack had got stuck, he'd got dirt up his nose, and he'd lost a glove. Cuthbertson waited and heard his brother whistle. He let himself down on the rope and bounced inelegantly down to the next platform.

'We can't be far,' said Gary.

They were staring into a dark chamber. Their torches picked out swirls of rock, folding and stretching. For fifty metres or so, they followed a trail of loose scree, hearing the stones they dislodged skitter and tumble either side of them. The rope gave out and Gary paused to tie the next. As he did so, he heard his brother gasp.

'What's the matter?'

'Look this way. Look at this!'

Percy Cuthbertson was pointing his torch into a grotto. The sides of the rock were pale pink; the colours flowed in a corkscrew pattern, plunging down. Then they seemed to open up, suggesting bottomless caverns.

'Turn your torch off,' said Gary.

The policeman did as he was told; so did Father O'Hanrahan.

The darkness seemed total. It seemed to jump at the men and press itself against them. Each man blinked and stared, astonished that such darkness was possible. Then, at first like a trick of the brain, they saw a flicker – a very thin glow, that suggested candles. It might have been a hundred metres below them, but in that overpowering darkness, the glow leaked upwards without a flicker.

'That could be it,' said Gary. 'There shouldn't be a light source down there.'

'How do we descend?' said Father O'Hanrahan.

Gary switched his flashlight back on.

'We drop. Ever tried an assault ladder?'

The man had his rucksack open and was pulling a large coil of wire from it. The policeman seemed to know what to do as well. He had a metal stake in one hand, a hammer in the other. In seconds the air around them was throbbing to the sound of iron blows, and the old man watched as the wire was bent and tied, tested, and double-tied.

'It's a knack,' said Gary. 'Put your torch round your neck.'

He flung the coil into space and it unfurled downwards into the corkscrew. The ladder was the width of a hand. The wire was so thin as to be invisible.

'I'm not a spider, sir,' said the old man. 'You won't get me down on that!'

'Your choice,' said Gary, getting his boot onto a rung. 'It's a lot easier than it looks and the alternative is staying up here.'

He swung himself into the void and, with surprising speed, started his descent. Ten metres below, he paused and looked up.

'Gentlemen,' he said. 'I can hear jazz. I think we might be close.'

In the orphans' east tower dormitory, the party was getting yet louder. Doonan had tried to call for hush, but the boys didn't seem to hear him. It was pyramid time and that meant a great deal of drumming. Biscuit tins had been saved for several weeks and a substantial kit had been created. Sanchez started the first roll and Henry moved to the centre. Two pairs of sturdier orphans flanked him, and then – one by one – as the cymbals crashed, boys leaped and scrambled. Within seconds there was a second tier. The third tier was easy too, especially as Flavio had coached the team in handsprings and backflips. Anjoli and Sanjay were still the stars and could fly upwards, somersaulting twice into position on the shoulders of their cousins.

As the party was in Imagio's honour, he was allowed pride of place at the apex. He couldn't jump that high without the trampoline, but he could flip into eager hands, which then flung him up another level. The pyramid stood firm, Imagio's head way up in the conical tower amongst the drying socks and hammocks.

Sanchez changed the drum rhythm. Millie was trying to make herself heard, but was having as little success as Doonan. The boys now started to change position. The four at the base dropped to their knees and crawled backwards. This meant that the formation was now centred around Henry only. On his cue, Henry started to turn and the structure turned with him – the boys had their arms outstretched.

'I can't hear you, Sam,' said Millie into a radio set. 'It's completely crazy! Wait!' She took the unit out of the dormitory and closed the door. She still couldn't hear – she had to descend a dozen steps. 'Right. How's it going? Over.'

'Pardon?'

'I said "How's it going?" Over.'

'Oh, it's not bad at all,' said Sam. 'We've had our supper. I'm making some tea and we've put a record on.'

There was a pause.

'Say *over*,' said Millie. 'If you say *over*, I know you've finished speaking. It makes it easier. Over.'

'OK. Over.'

'So what are you calling about, Sam? Is there a problem? Over.'

'No. It's just that . . . well, it's gone midnight and there's no sign of Eric.' He paused. 'Over.'

Millie checked her watch and cursed. Asilah had insisted on rigid timekeeping, so far, and everyone had been very conscientious. Eric, Podma, and Israel should have left half an hour ago. Without them, however, the pyramid had no centre. There was also the obvious fact that nobody wanted to miss Imagio's farewell – the boy was a much-loved figure.

He had been in tears twice already during the day, dreading the farewells that were now so close. Mr Scanlon was arriving the very next morning and a limousine would take their friend away to London. The deal was done.

'Are you there, Millie? Over.'

'We're running a bit late, Sam,' said Millie. 'Over.'

'Yes,' said Sam. 'It's just that . . . I played football with Imagio too, Millie. I was hoping to see him.'

Millie knew this and cursed under her breath. If there was one boy desperate to say goodbye personally to Imagio, and spend time with him, it was loyal little Sam. She could feel the guilt rising, so she moved swiftly to aggression.

'I'm afraid you have to make sacrifices sometimes,' she said. 'There's a party going on: you'll see him in the morning.'

'I know, over. It's just that —'

'Life isn't always fair, Sam. Sometimes you get the short straw.'

'Millie . . .'

'What? Say *over* if you've finished, or we just sit here interrupting each other. Look: we'll send Eric as soon as we can, alright? Open another bottle of wine and make Imagio a nice card.' She clicked the radio over Sam's clicking. 'See you later. Over and out.'

'Millie . . .'

Sam clicked the radio more urgently, stepping back as he did so.

'Millie! Wait . . .'

He was in Tomaz's kitchen, beside the charger. As he spoke, he had glanced up into the lounge area, where Oli and Ruskin sat. He had seen something and it had made him go cold.

It was a man, wearing black. He was standing on a

sideboard, with his back to Sam. He was staring at Ruskin, but Ruskin was dozing over the chessboard. As Sam watched, he let himself down noiselessly onto the carpet. Sam had no idea what to do. He stepped sideways, into the darkness, and hugged the radio, quivering.

'Sushamila's gone,' said Flavio, standing by the cage.

'That's not a problem, is it?'

'Is not a problem – everyone else accounted for . . . I jus' don' know how she does it.'

'Well,' said Captain Routon. 'She's harmless. She pads about on her own from time to time – let's leave her to it.'

'It's like magic,' said Flavio. 'How can she chew her way out o' here when she's got no teeth?'

'Do you want to go looking for her?'

'I think she misses that damn crocodile. She was by the lake yesterday. And the day before. That's the thing about these animals, you know – I guess it's after all that time on the road. They like a little family. They *care* about each other.'

Routon checked his watch.

'She'll be back,' he said. 'If we're going to see the headmaster, we ought to be moving. He said he'd be brewing the cocoa just about now.'

'You're right. Shall I bring a bottle?'

'Always wise. I've got a feeling it's bad news.'

'Still no money?'

'Things are grim. Unless something comes up, Circus Ribblestrop will fall at the first fence. I just wish I had some ideas. Or some savings.'

Captain Routon spent a lot of time down in Flavio's cab. It reminded him of the services and time under fire, warm as toast in a dug-out. He didn't miss the bombardments, of course, but he did miss the easy comradeship of soldiers together. He put his coat on and they set off together.

'Talking of the circus,' he said, 'did I ever tell you about the time my corporal got trampled by an elephant?'

Flavio sucked in his breath. "That happened to a friend o' mine. Where was yours?'

'Sri Lanka.'

'Mine was a wedding in Pakistan. The bride's father, man – got drunk and tried to swing on its trunk.'

As the two tales unfolded, the men wandered to the building. They did not go past the lake, or even look towards it. If they had, they might have seen Darren paddling the speedboat with silent oars. He was thinking about betrayal, turning his rage over and over in his empty head. He would have liked to use the motor – he liked noisy things. But his instructions had been clear: *Total silence.*

It wasn't hard work: the boat was light and handled nicely. Landmarks were easy to see in the starlight and the water lapped softly under him. Far off he could hear the clatter of drums. His brain went back to the chance he'd had and the chance he'd lost. He'd heard about Imagio's luck, of course, and his loathing for every member of that cursed Ribblestrop team caused him to grit his teeth. To be here, on their territory, made him feel even worse. If the opportunity came – if he met up with any of the kids – he'd do more than *immobilise.* The thought of pounding the face of a Ribblestrop child made him grin for a moment.

He came round to the first island and sighted the white shoulders of Neptune. He paused and wondered if he had tools to vandalise it. He brooded, floated, and lit a cigarette.

Who knows how many birds or beasts noticed that small flaring of a match? Who knows how many fish felt the vibrations of that matchstick as it landed on the water? One thing was for sure: a crocodile noticed, because the night was so still, and it was hanging motionless and hungry not five metres from the boat. It had followed its wake and it turned now, slowly, and rose to the surface to open a single eyelid.

On the edge of the woods, meanwhile, a larger animal had seen the flame. Her old eyes were poor, but the match had still been like a flare in the darkness, and she paused in her drinking. Darren didn't hear the low, anxious growl. He pressed on into the shallows, and reaching the bank, clambered out to wait under the statue.

Chapter Thirty-nine

Gary Cuthbertson's ladder had fallen amongst the shards of mirror that the orphans used as Christmas decorations. They swayed on their cords and a couple of them clinked.

As he climbed down, he was so astonished that he wasn't sure what to do. He'd emerged from darkness and here he was in a forest of fairy-lights: it was some kind of palace, and his thoughts were racing so fast he could only gape at the treasures around him. He could see tapestries and a suit of armour. There was a picture in a gilt frame; in fact, there were several pictures. There was what appeared to be the chimney of a stove – but there were so many tree branches it was hard to see what was where.

His instinct was to call up to his brother, but he checked the cry in his throat and climbed a little lower, holding his breath. Clearly, there was someone down there – and at the moment he still had the advantage of surprise. He hoped the old man above him wouldn't slip or shout. Decision made, he went down another few rungs, doing his best to be silent. He found a ledge of rock and stepped onto it. Then it was easy: he found two good footholds and lowered himself onto a sideboard. The Vyner collection was laid out as if it had been waiting for him.

He saw the child at the same moment it saw him. It was Oli, and they stared at each other.

The boy licked his lips and put down his soldering-iron. He looked utterly bewildered.

'Jake,' he said. 'There's a man.'

Gary Cuthbertson moved fast. He was a ruthless soul and had played rugby for years, specialising in the illegal tackle. The adrenaline flared up in him and he leaped. He had Oli by the arm before he could flinch, jerking him out of his chair and swinging him round. There was another boy at the table, so he picked the little one up in both hands and shoved him onto the big one, hard. The larger one buckled under the impact, grunting with pain, and they were both on the floor. Then the little one took a deep breath and screamed.

Gary Cuthbertson found the two heads and slammed them into each other. Then he moved his hands to their necks. He pulled and pushed until they were under him. He got his knees on top, pressing with all his weight, and he shoved the two faces into the rug. No more screaming, no more moving. He didn't have the handcuffs or any way of restraining them, but he could hold them until help arrived.

'Percy!' he yelled. 'Get down here, now!'

He glanced around the room, fearing witnesses. They seemed to be alone. He pressed the faces down, harder. Then, as he got his breath back, he allowed himself another look around the astonishing room. There were stuffed animals, statues, and more suits of armour. The furniture was polished wood, reflecting the silverware – there was cut-glass on the shelves and a white rabbit standing in terror on an armchair.

His eyes were drawn to some kind of pedestal. Then, upwards, to the thing on the pedestal. It was turned away from him – he hadn't seen it at first. Whoever had put the place together had an eye for display, for it stood against a background of dark greens – it was a golden suit of armour and it stood at ease, shoulders back, surveying the chamber. Its gauntleted hands came together in front and they clasped . . . a golden sword.

One of the boys made a frantic bid for air or freedom. Gary Cuthbertson changed his grip and got more weight on him. He didn't want to kill them, but he had no anxiety about causing them pain. Not when he was so close to success.

He had to look again. Was that the sword they'd come for? If so, they were now so close . . .

'Percy!' he shouted. 'Where are you?'

D.C.C. Cuthbertson appeared on the ladder. 'This is it!' he cried. 'This is it!'

'Help me,' said Gary. 'We've got visitors to deal with.'

It was another few minutes before the policeman was on the ground. He had taken it slowly, because his hands were shaking and his feet couldn't find the rungs. When he made it to firm earth again, he staggered and his legs buckled. He took in his brother and the two captives, but he too was lost in the wonder of the treasures around him. He saw the knight immediately and its beauty left him speechless. He reached up and touched it.

'Give me your handcuffs!' shouted Gary. 'Let's sort these kids out first.' The policeman didn't hear him. He had to say it again, louder.

D.C.C. Cuthbertson turned. His brother was sitting back and the two boys weren't moving. The skinny one was crushed under the larger one and his nose was bleeding.

'Oli,' said the larger boy. 'Oli? Are you alright?'

'Shut up,' said Gary.

'My brother,' said Ruskin. 'You've hurt my brother!'

The policeman fished out two sets of handcuffs. He brought Ruskin's arms roughly behind him and slapped them on. He jerked the thin boy into a sitting position. His eyelids fluttered.

'You've hurt my brother,' said Ruskin. 'If you've hurt Oli, you're for it. Do you understand me?'

'Shut your mouth,' said Gary Cuthbertson. He shook Oli by the shoulder, dragging him into a sitting position. 'Say something, you!'

'I think you've . . .' Oli's voice was very quiet. 'I think you've broken my arm.'

'Nobody's dead. Not yet, anyway. A broken arm won't kill him.'

'You brutes!' cried Ruskin. 'You just let us go, right now. He needs an ambulance and you know it!'

D.C.C. Cuthbertson had handcuffed Oli as well, threading the cuffs through those of the older boy. The child cried out as he was moved: he appeared to be only semi-conscious. They were back to back, and as the policeman lifted them, Oli could hardly stand.

'Who else is down here?' said the policeman. He punched Ruskin hard in the small of the back. 'Where are the others?' he shouted.

'There are no others!' said Ruskin.

'And what are you doing here? Why aren't you up at the school?'

'I'm not in the school because . . .' Ruskin couldn't put his thoughts together. 'Because here is where me and Oli . . . are. I'm not telling you anything, anyway! My father, when he hears about this . . . You don't want to get on the wrong side of our father. There would not be one bit of you left, I can tell you.'

'I know . . . both of these,' said an Irish voice, softly.

The words came between long, panting breaths. 'I don't know . . . their names, but I can tell you . . . they both need a damned good thrashing.'

Father O'Hanrahan was covered in dirt. Trembling from his descent on the ladder, he had managed to clamber to the same shelf of rock that Cuthbertson had used. Now he slithered down onto a table and sat there swaying.

Oli was hurting too much to raise his eyes, but Ruskin looked up. When he saw the face of the ex-priest, his anger rose to a new level. The old man's face was red and it was running with sweat. The mouth was open, the yellow teeth bared like fangs as he sucked in air. The exertion of the climb had almost killed him, but the treasures he could see had set his heart pumping so his eyes bulged from their sockets.

'You!' said Ruskin, softly. He shook his head and from the depths of his outrage managed to say, 'And I thought you were a man of God.'

Even Father O'Hanrahan managed to laugh.

'A so-called policeman!' cried Ruskin. 'A referee! Ha! So biased and unfair . . .'

Both Cuthbertsons were chuckling. They had moved back from the boys and their eyes were travelling round the chamber again.

'All I can say is you've opened my eyes. I am innocent no more.'

The ex-priest, however, came closer. He climbed down from the table and stood over Ruskin, smiling broadly. 'You'd better keep that mouthy gob shut tight, boy. I nearly died up there and I'm just in the mood to batter someone. Have either of you seen the ghost? Is he down here?'

The old man was pulling his satchel round to his stomach

271

and opening the flap. He removed a whisky bottle first and swigged deep. Then he took out his holy water and looked up defiantly. 'I'll lay that miserable spirit any time he likes – he won't get me this time!'

Chapter Forty

In the kitchen, it had taken all of Sam's courage and self-control not to panic, not to scream, and not to cry. He was just hidden in the doorway, by a curtain of catkins and pine-cones. He had made it with the little ones only a week ago.

He had to stand and watch the assault. Somehow, with a supreme effort of will, he managed to stay silent. Somehow, he managed to take another step back. Contradictory thoughts were clashing in his skull. To run in and intervene – to save his friends! To stay back and call for help. To pull out a kitchen knife and steam in, as he knew Anjoli or Miles or Millie would. Alas, he was not made for such attacks – he'd be swatted in an instant.

He started to shake. Surely they'd come into the kitchen soon and he'd be trapped! He could hear the struggle and the horrifying fear in Ruskin's voice and the agony in Oli's, but he found the calm to make his decision. To raise the alarm, that was the important thing. By radio? Not by radio.

He backed away further, thanking his lucky stars that he knew the layout of Tomaz's house. There was a passage by the toilet and that ran to the little area Tomaz called his 'hall'. That was where the boys left their shoes and hung their blazers, and it was where the exit was. He found his legs were heavy – they seemed to swing crazily from his hips, but he managed to make his way round. He clutched the radio to his chest, stamped his shoes on, and sat down. Then he scooped himself through the hole into the tunnel and he was running.

He stopped once, to try the transmitter. Nobody answered his cries – the party was too loud, he presumed. He had made the right decision, then: he would have to raise the alarm in person. The way was familiar: two lefts and a right, then through another hole – Tomaz had been so careful! – and he was in the Neptune tunnel. He shoved the radio down his shirt and he was climbing the ladder. The exit mechanism was oiled and simple to operate. Oli had helped there, setting up counterweights so the giant's head tipped back easily – and as he thought of his friend Oli, Sam found a new burst of adrenaline. Everything was down to him – Sam Tack. He had to run like he'd never run before!

He balanced on the giant's shoulder and jumped. As he hit the ground, he stumbled and he saw a pair of legs. Instinctively, he tried to swerve – it had to be the enemy, for the legs were black and the boots were huge. He changed direction, but he was off-balance and a hand grabbed him by the arm. He snatched his arm away, flailing wildly, and the hand came again and this time got him by the hair.

Darren had seen the giant's head open and was ready.

Strong fingers transferred to the boy's shirt collar. He shoved forwards and then jerked back hard, so the kid's tie cut into his windpipe. He slammed Sam onto his back and dropped his knees onto his shoulders. The little boy looked up, hopelessly caught – a rat by a cat – and Sam recognised his assailant.

He tried to roll and kick, but the older boy had all his weight on him; one hand came under his chin and the face loomed down, eyeball to eyeball.

'I know you,' said Darren, slowly.

'No you don't!' said Sam.

'You're that little scumbag from football.'

'I may be,' said Sam. 'What of it?'

'What of it? I'm going to kill you.'

Sam yelped. 'You can't,' he said.

'Yes I can. I hate your guts.'

Sam thought hard and fast. 'If you let me go,' he said, 'you can have my radio-controlled digger.'

Darren seemed to think hard for two or three seconds. Then, with the practised ease of a thug – a thug who specialised in hurting small children – he gave Sam a jaw-breaking slap. Then he was up and he was lifting his victim by the collar again. Sam knew that escape was impossible and he also knew he was in for a beating he'd probably never recover from. His teeth would be smashed. His bones would be broken – he might even be crippled forever. You heard stories about backs being snapped and parts of the brain switched off forever by hard kicks – boys like him lying in lonely hospital rooms breathing by machine, their parents weeping.

He cried out once and found that his tie was tight round his throat again. He saw a fist drawn back and he tried to get his arms up, closing his eyes, waiting for the crunch of knuckle.

At just that moment, the ground under him seemed to somersault. One second he was being strangled and the next fragment of the same second he was flying. Then he was turning over and the lake was up on its side – even the stars were wheeling around under his feet. The side of his face landed in soft mud and his legs collapsed over his chest to land in icy water. There was a very powerful smell of wild animal, but then it was gone in the breeze.

Darren was nowhere to be seen.

The radio was smashed into Sam's ribcage and it was agony. When he was able to look up, he realised what had happened. The world had righted itself, just about – the lake was under the sky again. And Darren had reappeared, kneeling in the shallows of the lake. The only reason he was upright at all, however, was because his head was in the mouth of a lioness. It was Sushamila and she was shaking Darren like a rag. The High School striker had been turned into one of those toys Sam's gran bought for her Jack Russell to dismember.

Sushamila seemed uncertain whether she wanted to shake the boy's head off or drown him, and she spun round in fury so the boy's legs swung clear of the water. She spun him three hundred and sixty degrees and then shook him again. She dunked him in the water, and it occurred to Sam that she was reviving him for another bout of punishment.

Sam stared in horror and Sushamila – as if suddenly ashamed – threw the limp body sideways and turned towards him.

She then padded proudly onto the shore and put her huge muzzle against Sam's chest.

'Good girl!' said Sam, as firmly as he could. 'Good girl!'

He stood up, painfully, and backed away. His body hurt all over, but he tried to speak both gently and authoritatively. 'Stay back there, now. Stay back . . .'

Sushamila wasn't listening. 'Please!' cried Sam. 'We don't have time!'

The lioness nosed under her favourite's chin, then she licked his face lovingly, removing the few hairs that had grown back in his eyebrows. Then, with a mother's infinite patience, she nudged him hard, so he was knocked off balance, and caught him by the back of his shirt. Sam was lifted off the ground, totally helpless.

He did his best to talk his way out of the situation, but he knew from experience what would happen. He would be taken to Sushamila's cage and washed; nothing he could say or do would prevent the beast from doing its duty. This was now the sixth time it had happened.

As they made their way towards the school building, Darren floated in the water. It was lucky for him that he'd been dropped on his back. It was even luckier that that the pumps were working in the pump-room and there was a very gentle current pushing to the bank – otherwise he would surely have been drowned. He lay there, looking at the stars, gradually getting his breath back. Three ribs were broken and he was in such pain he couldn't even whimper.

Chapter Forty-one

Beneath all this, Brother Rees – superintendent of the pump-room – was closing the final valve.

'I think we're done for tonight,' he said.

He wiped his hands on a rag and took a last look at the bank of dials. His assistant, Brother Morgan, was making a note of the numbers on the various gauges. A silent, grey-shirted child sat on the pipes, some distance off, watching quietly.

'What's the time?' said Brother Rees.

'It's exactly . . . one-ten. There's rain forecast by noon, so that should bring us back to normal. One of these days . . . Just look at it.'

He moved to the glass cylinder, in the centre of the room. He played with the knob, gently, and after a few seconds of distant sluicing, the capsule descended into view. The bubbles in the four pipes around it shot upwards.

'One of these days we're going to have to strip this master-piece down and give it a good old greasing. I doubt if it's been taken apart for a hundred years.'

'Is it showing any signs of age?'

'No. No, it's as smooth as it ever was. It's the engineer in me, I suppose. I'm so keen to see exactly how it works.

My brother was the real craftsman. He ended up driving trains and I used to watch him stripping down steam engines.'

'Is he local?'

'Oh yes – he lives in Taunton.'

'He could come and give us a hand if you think he'd like to.'

Brother Morgan shook his head. 'He had a bit of an incident just before Christmas, unfortunately. He was driving the train that . . .'

'Ah! The one that . . . had the incident. Yes.'

'His hands are a bit shaky now. Still, he's got his garden – he's happy enough.'

Brother Rees opened the chamber and stepped into it. He looked at the schoolboy sitting quietly on the pipe opposite and smiled at him. The boy stared back, white-faced.

'Have you seen this, son?' he said.

Miles nodded. He stared into the capsule and remained still.

'Come and have a look. If you'd been here last week, you would have seen something truly remarkable – come over here.'

Miles stood and picked his way carefully to the door of the capsule. Brother Rees was holding up a large, broken piece of egg.

'Six baby crocodiles,' he said. 'We watched them hatch last week. The babies are gone – they've found somewhere more private, I should imagine.'

'We saw the eggs,' said Miles, softly.

The two monks looked at each other, relieved to hear him speak. 'Ah, well! *We* saw them hatching,' said Brother Morgan, cheerily. 'Truly miraculous.'

Miles stared at the chamber and blinked.

'Are we done?' said Brother Morgan. 'Shall we lock up?'

'I think so. Are you ready, son? What's your name?'

Miles nodded.

The two men looked at each other again, then looked at the child. He'd been with them all evening and he'd barely spoken. His shirt was torn and he had a wild-eyed look, as if he hadn't been sleeping properly. He'd simply appeared underground and walked into their circle. He'd listened to their chanting and sat down. He'd taken some soup, but refused to say a single word.

Brother Rees put his hand on the boy's shoulder. 'I think we need to get you back to school,' he said, gently. 'They're going to be wondering where you've gone.'

'I'm not going back,' said Miles. 'And nobody cares.'

The monk smiled and patted him. 'You know that isn't true. And you can't stay here, can you? Your friends will be worried.'

'I'm a guardian, though. And I have no friends.'

'Guardian of what?'

'She changed the letter,' said Miles. 'Millie changed it, but that doesn't mean anything – I still had to come back.'

'Why don't we walk you up to the school?' said Brother Morgan. 'We could have a nice chat with your headmaster and hear all about it. Shall I turn the light off, Brother?'

'Yes, please do.'

They emerged into the passage and began to climb the stairs. Miles let himself be led by the hand. 'Do you want me to call your home?' said Brother Rees. 'Is something going on that perhaps your parents should know about?' Miles walked on. 'If you're upset about something, I'm sure they'd want to know. Where's your mum?'

Miles stopped. He was at the top of the stairs now, looking down.

'What's the matter?' said Brother Morgan.

Miles looked at them, silently.

280

'I think you need a doctor,' said Brother Rees, slowly. 'There's something wrong, isn't there?'

'No.'

'You can tell us, you know. We might be able to help.'

He went to touch Miles's shoulder again, but this time the boy backed away from him and stood poised, ready to run.

'Don't be frightened.'

Miles stared at him. 'I'm not,' he said.

'There's something wrong, isn't there? Tell me your name.'

'Miles. I'm a guardian.'

'Miles, I think we need to talk to your parents . . .'

He went to touch the boy again, but Miles simply dived to the side and fled.

'Miles!' cried the monk. 'Come back!'

By the time he reached the top of the stairs, the boy had disappeared. They could hear his feet drumming along the tunnel, until they were lost to the silence.

'Brother Morgan,' said Brother Rees. 'I want you to go up to the school and find that headmaster. The boy's in grave danger, I can feel it. Go at once, please.'

Chapter Forty-two

'We should have brought a trolley,' said the policeman. He was rubbing his hands and flexing his fingers. 'There's a small fortune down here! This is the most remarkable find!'

'There's rooms everywhere,' said Gary. 'We need a truck! You look for the sword, Father. We'll get other stuff together, anything that looks valuable.'

'The sword's the most valuable item—'

'And you're sure it's not that gold one? That suit of armour must be worth—'

'You don't pay three million pounds for one of them, I can promise you. The sword of St Caspar has twelve priceless diamonds – I showed you the pictures!'

'So go and look for it!' said the policeman. 'Look at this . . .' He turned and yanked at a tapestry.

Gary laughed, 'And to think a little foreigner's been sitting on all this. It's enough to make you weep.'

D.C.C. Cuthbertson turned to the boys. They were sitting quietly, back to back, their handcuffs tight on their wrists. 'This where you have your midnight feasts, is it? You're more daft than you look, if that's possible. You could've made millions out of this.'

'Oi!' shouted Gary. 'Here's the wine cellar! How much did you say a bottle would fetch?'

'A thousand pounds.'

He stood in the kitchen doorway with a bottle in each hand. He smashed the neck of one against a nearby table and the wine foamed over the carpet. 'We can afford a glass each, can't we?' he laughed. 'Celebration time?'

He pulled two of Tomaz's best wine glasses from their cabinet and glugged the wine into them. The two men gulped a mouthful down.

'This is to you, boys,' said Cuthbertson. 'Thanks for being stupid. And thanks for being our guides out of here.'

'We won't be guiding you anywhere,' said Ruskin, bravely. 'And my brother needs urgent medical attention – that is the priority.'

'The priority,' said Gary, kneeling beside Ruskin, 'is that when the time comes, you get us straight down to the pump-room. Or I'll break his other arm.'

'Cuthbertson!' called the old man.

The policeman looked up. 'What?' he shouted. 'What have you found?'

'Come and see this – you won't believe it.'

The two men trooped out of the lounge and down a passage. They entered another grotto – the chamber Tomaz used as his bedroom. The old man was standing by a long rosewood table and on it was a hexagonal chest. It was Indian sandalwood, clearly carved by a craftsman. Its drawers got progressively smaller as they rose to the apex and every face was inlaid with marble. Father O'Hanrahan had removed a drawer and revealed the contents to his colleagues: a diamond, the size of a pea. He set it down and removed another. Two emerald earrings lay on a bed of red velvet. It was a jewellery chest that all the children had seen and admired. They had taken turns polishing the gems and rearranging them in different sized drawers. Anjoli had once sat down to dinner wearing the rings, two on each finger, so that his hands looked like they were in flames – but Asilah had made him put them back.

'I'll take care of that,' said Cuthbertson. He was smiling broadly. 'You look for the sword.'

'I will do – but this in itself is a million! We're rich . . .'

'I'll take care of it.'

The policeman pulled his rucksack off and opened it wide. It took him two minutes to go through the chest, and by the time he was finished he was ankle-deep in empty drawers. His brother, meanwhile, had started work on the oil paintings. He stripped the larger ones from their frames and rolled the canvases. He laid them gently in a leather trunk, interspersed with wine bottles. Now he stared around the room, wishing he knew more about antiques – wishing he knew what was really worth stealing.

Father O'Hanrahan, meanwhile, made his way back to Tomaz's kitchen. He pulled out the drawers, hurling everything onto the floor. He moved to the larder and upturned trays of vegetables and fruit. The sword was in use, every day – that's what the Brethren had told him. Assuming they were telling the truth, that must mean it was a tool – so why not a kitchen implement?

He swung his torch into the recesses, muttering greedily.

'Something that is used every day . . . A spit, maybe? A carving knife?'

He searched the kitchen methodically, but found nothing of value.

'Think!' said Father O'Hanrahan.

Cuthbertson walked in. He had a large stone Buddha in his arms.

'Is this worth anything?' he said.

284

The old man ignored him. 'The monk told me he saw it,' he said. 'It must have been in the main room, not in here . . . Why am I wasting time in here? Where would you put a sword? Why would he be using one?'

'It's not on display,' said Cuthbertson. 'We would have seen it. And you're sure it's not the gold one?'

'I showed you pictures, man. It's a small thing.'

The old man stood still. 'What do you use a sword *for*? What is a sword, eh? It's a stick. A walking stick? A lever – something to lift things with?'

'A toasting fork?' said the policeman. 'What if he toasted things on it, by the fire?'

They moved quickly, back to the main chamber. Gary Cuthbertson joined them at the stove.

'We're so close,' said the old man. 'I can feel it. It's getting cold as well, isn't it? The temperature's dropping. That's a good sign!'

'Why?' said Cuthbertson. 'What does that mean?'

'It means that wretched old ghost's around, I reckon. It means he's not happy – and it means we might be right on top of what we're looking for.'

He went right up to the stove and opened the door.

'See if there's a poker, or something,' said Gary. 'That would be used every day, wouldn't it?'

Cuthbertson felt his heart lurch: there *was* a poker and it lay discarded on the flagstones. He put his hand on it gingerly and it was warm and heavy.

'Give that to me,' said Father O'Hanrahan.

'It's small enough, isn't it?'

'Give it here.'

Cuthbertson held onto it, weighing it in his hands. 'I think we're in business,' he said. He was grinning again. He took out a penknife, and as he did so, the mirrors above started to move. They knocked gently together, as if

285

shifting in a breeze. The temperature had dropped again and the men found that they were shivering and rubbing their hands.

Cuthbertson handed the poker to his brother, who held it firm. He stroked one of the sides with a blade and started to scrape carefully at the coating of coat dust.

'Harder,' whispered O'Hanrahan. 'Scrape it there, on the . . . Just there!'

The policeman pushed the point in and twisted. Then he levered up and a lump of black came away, like crust. A precious stone winked up at them and – unseen – a wall mirror split with a silent crack, top to bottom. In seconds, throughout the chambers, every mirror shattered. The three men were too intent to notice. They didn't hear the deep, angry rattling of glassware.

Underneath the crust of carbon, shining like pure, silver fire, lay walnut-sized diamonds.

'Oh my word . . .' whispered Father O'Hanrahan. 'We're touching it.' One by one, the policeman exposed them.

'This is it.'

'This is it – you're holding it!' The old man started to laugh. 'Find something to wrap it in! Quickly. On the chair – look . . .'

There was a red velvet cloth, draped over a fallen table. The policeman grabbed it and watched as the old man took the sword and wrapped it. He held it to his chest, laughing softly. 'What did they say? Too beautiful to be looked at, that's why it's concealed. Gentlemen, we have what we came for – the sword of St Caspar! The job's done.'

He stopped and looked up.

'What's the matter?' said Cuthbertson.

'The ghost.'

'What about him? Where is he?'

'Somewhere close. Oh, he doesn't like us, that's for sure. Can you hear him? I can . . .'

Father O'Hanrahan looked carefully around him. 'You can feel him, can't you?' he said. 'He's wanting that show-down I promised him.'

The policeman took the sword and pushed it firmly into his rucksack. As he was clipping it shut, he saw the old man move into the middle of the room. He was looking up, now, for the shards of glass were dancing again, louder, and the noise they made could not be ignored.

Father O'Hanrahan held up his crucifix. 'In the name of the Father,' he said, firmly. 'In the name of the Son. I command you . . . to leave this place.'

On the far side of the room his bottle of holy water stood on the sideboard, next to the whisky. He moved towards it and, as he did so, it broke apart and the water ran harmlessly over the wood.

Father O'Hanrahan chuckled. 'Oh, I see,' he said. 'That's your game, is it? We're having a stand-off are we? Well, you won't get the next one, Vyner, old chap! And you will not resist me, for I am here by the power that *no* spirit can resist. I am here by the Spirit—'

'You're not a priest!' cried Ruskin, from the floor. He was craning his head to see what was going on, peering through his sellotape and spectacles. 'You're just a crook and a fake.'

Father O'Hanrahan's right hand was moving slowly to his satchel. His left held the crucifix high and he was turning in a circle, knowing the ghost was about to attack. He ignored Ruskin and cried out again in his deepest register: '*In nomine Domini et in nomine Christus!*'

He loved to use Latin.

He remembered the pulpit vividly. He remembered the incense and the choir singing – he remembered the robes. His fall from grace had been swift and total, but the memory of the church was still there. He opened his satchel and reached for the second bottle of holy water. He had three in all.

'*In nomine Christus!*' he cried again. '*Res mea, occupa – et exit in nomine Deus!* I, as a servant of the Lord, command you!' He took a deep breath for the climax, his confidence at its peak. Exorcism was all about showing strength. Ghosts would fight to distract you. They would try to terrify you. The secret was to be focused and remember that you wielded ultimate power. He grinned in satisfaction as the glasses burst in the cabinet – as an armchair leaped backwards and the chimney wrenched itself free of the stove. Lord Vyner was getting violent and that meant he was scared!

There was a vibration in the ground and he could hear the tinkling of little rock falls. All he had to do now was spray the holy water round the chamber and that would force the old ghost out, once and for all. He would be sealed out – and a homeless ghost could be vanquished in seconds. He felt for the third bottle – it was entangled in some kind of foliage, so he delved deeper, pushing it clear. He shook the satchel and pulled.

'I say it again!' he cried. 'In the name of the Father!'' He shook the satchel and pulled, and that was the moment Joe the scorpion decided he'd endured enough. He'd been woken by the cold and was in the foulest of moods. The satchel was flapping open and rocking about – the light had scared him. Then a thumb had pushed him roughly to one side and four fingers seemed to be scrabbling around in his nest. Using all the instincts he possessed, he backed into a corner and arched his tail. Then, as the hand continued to jostle him, he slammed his sting right into the back of it. A spurt of poison followed, jolting into the vein – then Joe stabbed again and, clenching his pincers and closing his eyes, stabbed once more for luck.

Father O'Hanrahan was rigid and silent.

'Has he gone?' said Cuthbertson.

The old man couldn't speak.

'Have you won, Father? Why the silence?'

Father O'Hanrahan staggered, swallowing. He pulled his hand out of his satchel and stared at it, unable to believe that pain could be so intense. He opened his mouth to scream, but no sound would come. The worst thing was that the pain was increasing, as if some fuse had been lit and was igniting pain cells up his arm, and across his chest. It was as if his heart was pumping not blood but some dreadful acid. He sank to his knees and felt his brain boiling. At last, he managed a whimper. Then a cry. Then at last, as the steam of the poison built its intolerable pressure, he screamed. He screamed and screamed, and when the policeman and Gary ran to him and tried to hoist him back to his feet, he was violently sick and the screams turned into a terrible gurgling.

The sting of a North African Death-stalker scorpion, they say, is one of the most painful in the world.

Chapter Forty-three

Meanwhile, Caspar Vyner was making his escape from the south tower.

His grandmother had closed her eyes at last. The mouth was open and there was drool – but she had been known to fake all that in the past, so he was rigid with tension. A glass of booze had been upended over her knees and her breathing was turning into a noisy snoring – these were encouraging signs. With a trembling hand, he squeezed her nostrils together and waited for the startled grunt. It came and she didn't wake up. That meant she really was unconscious.

He let himself out of the front door and ran briskly down the staircase, pulling on his blazer. He had so enjoyed his fortnight as a true Ribblestrop pupil! Home, now, was a prison – he had never wanted to return to it. He remembered Doonan's kindness; he remembered Imagio in the Tower of Science, sharing his rat on the dissecting bench. He had learned so much! He had *done* so much. He was soon at ground level and his excitement was rising. He would not miss the party!

Lady Vyner kept the tower door locked, but he knew the window was loose and it was a small drop. He let himself out over the sill and did a neat paratrooper's roll – Sanjay had taught him that. Sanjay had taught him to ride a bicycle too, though he hadn't dared tell his gran. As he came across the courtyard, the noise from the orphans' tower was still blaring. The drumming had stopped and they were singing. Caspar hurried round the corner and gasped in shock. He stopped dead and found himself staring into the eyes of a lion.

All he could do was gape.

'Caspar?' said a voice.

Caspar didn't move. Nor did the lion. The creature was so big! Dimly, through his terror, he remembered a much-loved storybook with a talking lion. It had been kind and comforting – wise, even. This one looked senile and the voice had sounded rather reedy and tired.

'Caspar! Is that you?'

The boy stared harder, wondering whether he should bolt, or move away slowly. Then he saw that there was something in the creature's mouth, dangling between the monstrous forepaws. It was a mess of grey and black and . . . Caspar found a tiny fragment of courage and went slowly down on his haunches to get a better view. It was a boy and the boy was Sam Tack.

'Sam,' said Caspar.

The lion growled and Caspar whimpered. He took a few steps back and found himself pressed to a wall.

'Caspar, don't be scared!' squeaked Sam. 'It's Sushamila – she won't hurt you. Look: you've got to help me.' His voice sounded tearful. 'We're in a mess, Caspar. You're the only one who can help us. Raise the alarm!'

'What alarm?' said Caspar.

'I can't do it myself. She usually lets me go after about twenty minutes, but it might be different tonight. Look, Caspar – I'll do anything you want – you can have my . . . digger. But this is the most urgent thing I've ever asked you. Can you find Sanchez?'

'That's where I was going,' said Caspar. 'Imagio's party!'

'Find him immediately. Tell him . . .' Sam struggled. 'Sorry, it's hard to talk in this position. Tell him that Ruskin and Oli are prisoners. OK?'

'Ruskin and Oli are prisoners.'

'That's right. Tomaz's house is being burgled. I saw a man and it was that referee – the policeman's brother. There might be more. And there's a boy by the Neptune statue, but I think he's probably dead.'

'OK,' said Caspar. 'Tomaz's house is being burgled.'

'And they've got Ruskin.' The enormity of the situation suddenly hit Sam again and he started to cry. 'I'm not joking, Caspar, this is the most serious thing ever. They've got my friends and they were *hurting* them – Ruskin and Oli. Please help us!'

'But . . . what about you?'

'Don't worry about me! Run, Caspar. Run!'

Chapter Forty-four

The expression on the child's face killed the singing dead. A silence fell, worse than deafness. Even the hissing of the cooker died and every eye bored into Caspar Vyner.

Sanchez was upside down, dangling from a trapeze. The rest of the children were on the ground, looking up. He swung himself upright and dropped. Imagio steadied him and everyone's eyes were fixed on Caspar.

'Ruskin and Oli are prisoners,' he said, breathlessly. 'There's a man down there: the referee called Cuthbertson, but Sam thinks there may be more. He thinks one of them died, but he's not sure. Tomaz's home is being burgled and Sam was very upset because his friends are being hurt. That's the message.'

'Where's Sam?' said Millie.

'He's been taken by a lion. He hopes to be free in about twenty minutes.'

Sanchez looked at Asilah. Asilah looked at Millie. Tomaz looked at the ground.

'This is it,' said Anjoli. 'What are we waiting for?'

Sanchez said, 'Caspar, are you absolutely sure —'

'Of course he's sure,' shouted Millie. 'He wouldn't lie about it, would he? Sanchez, where are the plans? Get the plans . . .'

Vijay dived to one of the wardrobes and came back with an armful of papers. The older children huddled around them.

'Plan E,' said Asilah. 'If they've taken hostages, it's Plan E – no other option.'

'I agree,' said Millie.

'Plan E's major,' said Anjoli. 'We wrote that one after three bottles: we better be sure, because that is . . . *ultimate*. Ultimate force.'

Everyone now looked at Sanchez.

'Ultimate force,' he said. 'If they've touched Ruskin or Oli . . . God help them.'

He turned to Brother Doonan.

'Brother Doonan,' he said. 'I'm really sorry about this, but I don't think we have any options right now, so please don't take what we're going to do personally.'

Brother Doonan laughed. 'I'm afraid that most of this is going over my head,' he said. 'Is this one of those pranks you boys like so much?'

'It's the first part of Strategy E,' said Asilah. 'We have to be independent now.'

'Yeah,' said Sanjay. 'We like you a lot. That story, man, about the mirror – I still can't sleep . . .'

Doonan was confused. All the children were moving towards him and their expressions seemed so tender. He realised something was wrong, but he hadn't quite digested the substance of Caspar's message.

He smiled happily. 'Boys,' he said, taking charge, 'I think it's time for bed. If Imagio's off tomorrow, it'll be an early breakfast!'

Suddenly, he found that he was being lifted. There were hands holding his arms and legs, and supporting his back, and he was being moved swiftly towards a cupboard. He cried out, 'No, boys!' but it did no good. He'd been the victim of practical jokes all too often over the last few weeks. He'd had his socks sewn up; he'd had chilli powder mixed into his toothpaste. Nikko had hidden in his pillowcase one night and frightened the life out of him as he dozed off – but imprisonment seemed unusual. And it was odd to see Asilah and Sanchez joining in.

He decided to be firm. 'I'm going to count to three, children,' he said. He was now inside the cupboard. They were sitting him on a chair. 'One.' He was wrapped in a blanket. 'Two – I want you to think very hard about this . . .'

There was a rum truffle on his lap and a candle between his feet. The door closed and he heard the key turn. 'Three,' he said, quietly.

Then he listened hard and heard a multitude of feet padding out of the dormitory.

The children formed into groups, dragging on blazers and stamping into shoes.

There were to be three detachments and each had a commander and a radio-man. Henry was designated a 'special weapon' and could be called upon by all three companies. To start, he'd be with the Sanchez contingent, which would attack through Neptune as the advance party. Asilah led the tools and hardware group, whose brief was flight prevention. They were down the stairs in seconds and on their bicycles. Within minutes they'd skidded up to the circus tent. Flavio and Routon had left, so they set to work at once.

Eric moved to the cages and dealt with the animal chains. The tigers sensed the excitement and it was all Podma could do to control them. He led them out onto the mud and Ivan sniffed the air hungrily. Prince strained at the leash, pulling the boy forward so that Eric had to run ahead and seize him by the collar.

Meanwhile, Asilah supervised the truck-loading.

He found the explosives and took three coils of wire. The concrete pipe required block and tackle, but that was one of Kenji's specialities. It was swung onto the truck and Nikko secured it. Israel revved the cab unit and reversed it to the trailer. It took two minutes to check the coupling and another one to manoeuvre the thing back through the cages, to the track. At last the truck was on its way to the lakeside, its giant wheels hammering over the mud.

'We're rolling,' cried Asilah to the radio. 'Come in, Sanchez! Unit two reporting, over.'

'Unit one receiving,' said Sanchez. He confirmed his position. 'We'll be by Neptune in two minutes, over.'

'Tigers on their way. Truck to lakeside reconnaissance, over.'

'Unit three's on its way to the pump-room, Millie's leading. Have you seen Miles? He's the one person missing. Over.'

'No. Over.'

'Was he at the party? Did you see him at the party?' Asilah asked the boys in the cab.

'No one's seen him. Israel thinks he's run away. And another thing – your gun. Over.'

'It's too late for that. I forgot all about it—'

'No, listen. Kenji's just told me. He says it's gone.'

'Gone where?'

'Someone took the key to the safe. Yesterday, when he was in the shower.'

'Are you saying it's been stolen? Over.'

'Sanchez, let me finish.' The truck reared up onto the school lawn and picked up speed. Asilah had to shout. 'Kenji says it was taken yesterday, but he didn't notice 'cause whoever took it just changed keys – put a locker key in its place. So Kenji didn't notice. Over.'

'And that somebody?'

'He thinks it was Miles.'

'Oh boy . . .' muttered Sanchez. 'Miles with a gun. Again.'

'Miles was around,' shouted Asilah. 'Now he isn't. All I'm saying is, it's possible.' The truck jolted again and Asilah was thrown against the dashboard. 'I have to go!' he shouted. 'We can see the lake, over and out . . .'

'Come in, Millie,' said Sanchez. 'Unit one to unit three, are you receiving, Millie?'

'Yes,' said Millie.

'We've got problems. State your position, over.'

'I'm on my way to the pump-room. Where's the freak?'

'Are you on your own, Millie?'

'Yes. Miles is missing and so are Ruskin and Oli. I'm by myself.'

Chapter Forty-five

Professor Worthington had spent the evening reading the drafts of an article she was writing and was now ready for her usual nightcap with the headmaster – she always enjoyed the end-of-the-day chats. It was very late, but she could see a light on in his study. She noticed with approval that the east tower was now in darkness. Doonan had been told to end the orphans' party soon after midnight: he'd been as good as his word and it seemed every boy was in bed – there wasn't a sound. She knew that a special farewell breakfast was planned for Imagio, so that probably explained it.

She knocked lightly on the headmaster's door.

'Clarissa!' said the headmaster. 'Come in!'

She saw at once that there was something wrong. There were papers all over the floor and both Flavio and Routon looked tired and sad.

'We're having a wretched time,' said the headmaster. 'We've been looking at the bank statements and . . . we need inspiration.'

'We need cash,' said Flavio.

'Things are looking bad,' said Routon. 'But the truth has to be faced.'

'What about the loan?' said Professor Worthington.

'Used up. Gone. And the bank's calling it in.'

'I feel so bad about this,' said Flavio. 'I was jus' saying, I know where all the money's gone – it's those damn animals again.'

'No, Flavio—'

'I tol' you before this thing started, they use up every penny you get . . .'

'A school is an expensive thing,' said the headmaster, soothingly. 'I don't want you blaming yourself.'

'The root of the problem, surely, is fees,' said Professor Worthington. 'So few children are actually fee-payers.'

'Did you see the solicitor today, sir?' said Captain Routon.

'Yes, I did.'

'Could he see a way forward?'

'Not really, no. He said we ought to close immediately and auction our assets. Then we should file for bankruptcy and come to terms with Lady Vyner to avoid immediate prosecution. Then he advised me to leave the country.'

There was a silence.

'We are in a serious situation,' said Professor Worthington.

'What did you say to your solicitor, sir?' said Routon. 'I hope you didn't stand for that kind of nonsense. Surrender and retreat – that's not a strategy any of us would even consider.'

'I said giving in was out of the question, of course I did.'

'I can take a cut in salary!' said Routon, standing again.

'Sit down,' said Professor Worthington. 'There *are* no salaries – none of us are paid.'

'The kids come first,' said Flavio. 'We cannot close.'

'It's two weeks before the end of term,' said the headmaster. 'I told the solicitor that the children look to us as their guardians, and we will not be interrupting their education, simply because of a . . . . cash-flow crisis.'

Everyone was nodding.

'Stick to your guns, sir – always.'

'We've been up against it before,' said Professor Worthington. 'Surely Lady Vyner can wait?'

'What's that noise?' said Flavio.

'Someone at the door, by the sound of it.'

They listened again and three heavy blows of a door knocker echoed up the stairs and corridor.

'It's not those parrots, is it?' said the headmaster. 'They imitate everything.'

'No, sir – they're asleep.'

The headmaster looked nervous. He stood up and peered out of the window. 'I just hope it's not bailiffs or debt collectors. She warned me they'd be showing up soon, and once they're in . . .'

'Don't answer the door then, sir,' said Routon. 'Sit tight.'

'Sometimes it's the best thing to do.' The door was hammered again. 'Ignore it. Now can I tempt anyone with a little more whisky?'

Meanwhile, under the ground, things were getting ugly.

Gary and Percy Cuthbertson had been walking for twenty back-breaking minutes, supporting the groaning figure of Father O'Hanrahan. The policeman was holding Ruskin – their guide – by his collar and progress was pitifully slow. The two boys were still handcuffed back to back, so they moved sideways, like an injured crab. Oli was constantly tripping and his brother would become entangled. The old man had foam round his mouth and could hardly walk.

'My feet are numb,' he said. 'I can't feel my feet!'

'Keep going!' hissed the policeman.

'I might be dying! People die of a scorpion sting!'

He had seen Joe crawl from his satchel, so he knew what had happened. His hand had swollen and there were red pimples over the back of it. One minute he was freezing cold – the next he was feverishly hot. He felt like his throat was closing over his windpipe, and had to stop and suck at the air.

D.C.C. Cuthbertson had a hand under his arm, but he was also trying to drag the large trunk full of tapestries and wine. Gary Cuthbertson had the roll of oil paintings, but the stone Buddha had been abandoned. Both were weighed down by rucksacks full of plunder.

'Please,' said Oli, softly. 'I need water. I can't go on . . .'

'I'm on fire!' whispered O'Hanrahan.

'Please unchain us,' said Ruskin. 'We are all suffering!'

The policeman put his hand on the boy's neck and squeezed. 'You'll walk as you are, son. So will your squib of a brother.'

'Left or right?' said Gary. 'Where is the pump-room?'

'I'm pretty sure it's to the left . . .' said Ruskin.

'No, Jake,' said Oli. 'Show them the quickest way. It's right, then right again. Then up the steps.'

'Oli, no – that way was bricked up. It's a left, then a right, and then you're in the Neptune corridor – then it's *down* the steps.'

The hand on his neck squeezed tighter. 'Don't waste our time, boy. I will break you if I have to! Which way? That statue's supposed to be five minutes from where we were, so how come we haven't reached it?'

'I don't know,' said Ruskin. 'It does seem strange.' He paused and looked about him, holding his lenses close. 'You know, I'm sorry to say this,' he said. 'But I think Oli might be spot on. I think I've made a bit of a gaffe. It's an awful confession, but . . . I have a feeling we should have gone right when we came out of Tomaz's house.'

There was a long silence, interrupted only by the heavy groaning of Father O'Hanrahan.

'I can only put it down to disorientation and these wretched specs.'

301

Oli slumped to his knees and then lay on the sandy floor.

Father O'Hanrahan leaned against the wall and retched. D.C.C. Cuthbertson closed his eyes and fought to control his temper. He had a brief vision of smashing Ruskin's skull hard against the rocky wall, but he knew it would do no good. 'How do we get out, then?' he said, quietly. 'Try and think where we are.'

'I'm pretty sure we're close. I need to look at my map.'

'You have a map?' said Gary.

'We've got a very detailed map. Sam and I put hours into it.'

'They've got a map,' said Gary. His voice was dangerously low.

'We colour-coded it,' said Ruskin. 'It's like the London Underground, only clearer.'

'Well, perhaps we could take a look at it, son. Maybe it would help us?'

'I wish we could. I keep it in my blazer, you see. And of course . . . my blazer's hanging up in, um . . . Tomaz's hall.' He attempted a laugh. 'We didn't expect to be leaving in such haste.'

'Let's keep calm,' said Cuthbertson. 'Panic leads to disaster. Can you get us back to Tomaz's house? From here?'

'Yes,' said Ruskin. 'I think I can.'

'Are you sure you can?'

'Uncuff them,' said Gary. 'We've got to move faster than this.'

'You don't uncuff prisoners,' said the policeman.

'They're kids, Percy! The little one's half crippled, his brother's not going to run off anywhere.'

Still Cuthbertson hesitated.

'I think he's right,' whispered Father O'Hanrahan. 'They can carry some of the load as well. Take the risk, man, otherwise we're all dead.'

The key was produced. The handcuffs were removed and the boys rubbed their sore wrists. Oli staggered to his feet, cradling his damaged arm, and stifled a sob. Father O'Hanrahan forced himself upright and the party set off the way it had come, Gary Cuthbertson's torch illuminating the long, gentle curve of the tunnel.

Chapter Forty-six

'Come in, Millie,' said Sanchez. 'Where exactly are you, over?'

'I'm five minutes from the pump-room. Where are you? Over.'

'We've just got to Tomaz's house.'

'You're inside? Is there any sign of Ruskin or Oli?'

'No. And still no sign of Miles.'

Millie caught the subdued tone in Sanchez's voice.

'Is Tomaz's house OK? Over.'

Sanchez paused. 'No. It's been smashed up pretty bad. Millie . . .'

'What are you going to do?'

'You shouldn't be on your own, Millie.'

'I know, but the pump-room's a quick exit, isn't it? Right up to the lake.'

'But you shouldn't be alone! You were supposed to be with Miles.'

'Where are the cats?'

'Through the railway entrance, moving in.'

'Everything depends on how well they know the tunnels,' said Millie. 'Or if they've got guides – they've probably got the boys as prisoners. We can still get them – is Asilah outside?'

'Yes, he's covering the lake.'

'Sanchez, we better face it – and you better tell Tomaz. If they've found the pump-room, they'll be gone by now. We should have checked it first.'

'I'm worried about Miles, Millie. He was acting strangely . . .'

'He's always acting strangely!'

'What if he's run away? We've got to look for him too . . .'

'He could be in on this, Sanchez, have you thought of that? I'm coming down the steps, over.'

'He's got my gun again.'

Millie cursed quietly. 'He got your gun?'

'I need to tell you something. Last term, he took it twice . . .'

'So none of us are armed?'

'Millie, I'm worried about him . . .'

'I'm worried about *us*! I tell you, Sanchez, when I see that freak again, I'm going to shoot him myself. He's putting everyone in danger. We don't know whose side he's on any more.'

'He has this obsession with guns . . .'

'Let's hope he shoots himself and gets it over with. I'm going to have to go, I'm close to the pump-room. I'm turning the radio off.'

'No, Millie! Don't!'

'Over and out.'

Up by Neptune, the injured Darren had managed to get back into the speedboat. He'd paddled it right back, under the bridge, and drawn it close into the shadows. He was in great pain and he lay on his back, shivering with cold, trying not to make a noise. There were children all around him and he hardly dared breathe. They'd clattered over the bridge and he'd seen them streaming down the neck of the statue.

He had no idea what to do, so he lay there and did nothing. He could hear the sound of a truck. He could hear machinery moving and the shrill voices of children shouting instructions in a foreign language. Chains were clanking and at one point there was an explosion, like a rocket, and he saw sparks travelling over the lake. He was aware of someone, or several people, in the water. Any minute now he knew he would be discovered, so he lay silently and closed his eyes.

What, meanwhile, had happened to Doonan?

The boys had left him with a candle so, as his eyes adjusted, the cupboard didn't feel quite so lonely. There was a window high above, letting in a little starlight, and at least he wasn't cold. He sat and thought hard, trying to suppress his disappointment that even the oldest children should behave so childishly.

They'd given him sheets and a pillow. Did they really mean to keep him here all night? No prank could go on as long as that . . . He turned over Caspar's words in his head. The little chap had seemed very serious and the reaction he'd caused has been pretty major. Doonan found himself wondering if something serious was going on.

He stood up and rattled the cupboard door. It was locked firmly and the wood was far too thick to break. He looked up again at the window, and a plan formed. He had a penknife – he wasn't helpless. He made two little cuts in the edge of the cotton and, after a good deal of ripping, he had three sheet pieces. He knotted them together and had a rope some six metres long. It wouldn't be enough to get him down, but it might be enough to get him up – if he had a grappling hook. He didn't, of course, but the chair might do. He lashed the sheet around its back. Then, using muscles he hadn't had to use for some time, he made his way to the top of the cupboard, bracing himself against a shelving unit, until he could hang upon the window.

It opened just wide enough for the chair.

He let it through, then he put out his arms and head. Not three metres above his head projected a gargoyle – he'd seen Anjoli swinging on it a number of times. It was a place that most of the orphans liked to sit, so it had to be pretty secure. He swung his sheet and threw the chair – on the fifth attempt, the chair went over the gargoyle and lodged itself securely in the guttering. A series of hard tugs reassured Doonan that he now had an exit of sorts.

He muttered a prayer and heaved the rest of his body out of the window. For thirty dreadful seconds he was suspended over nothing, clinging to the sheet. Terror gave him strength and he clawed his way up, legs kicking, feet grabbing at the knots. At last he had the gargoyle in his arms and a foot on the roof. The drop, as he accidentally looked down, made his stomach heave and for a moment he was paralysed. It occurred to him that he had taken a ridiculous risk and that his journey over the wet roofs of Ribblestrop was going to be lethally dangerous. That was always assuming he could get onto the roof, because at that moment, he was completely stuck.

Someone had to raise the alarm, though. Something was wrong and the headmaster needed to know. As he sat, he too heard the revving of an engine down on the lakeside. Like Darren, he also saw a rocket burst and zoom across the lake in a flurry of sparks. He knew in his bones now that the children were not playing games.

'I'm sorry,' said Oli. 'It's my arm. I can't go on!'

'Shh!' said Gary. 'Yes you can.'

Oli crumpled to the floor. His brother knelt beside him.

'I think he's fainted.'

'We'll leave him here,' said Cuthbertson. 'We must be at the blessed statue – we must be!'

'My arms are numb,' whispered Father O'Hanrahan.

'Shut up!' said Gary. 'I can hear something. I don't know what it is . . .'

He bashed his torch hard and the weak beam brightened for a second or two.

They listened to their own breathing. Then, just as Cuthbertson went to pick up his bag, the sound came again. It was a deep-throated animal growling.

Everyone stood still.

The tunnel they were in had a sandy floor and curved sides. Just ahead, it was bisected by another tunnel: Gary's torch illuminated the corner of the stonework. He found himself backing away from it, because the growl had come from that passageway and it was amplified and sinister. It was like an engine, throbbing. When it came again, it was nearer and it was followed by a steady, heavy panting.

'What *is* this place?' whispered Gary. 'Where have these kids brought us?'

'That is not a human sound,' hissed Father O'Hanrahan. 'That is the sound of a beast. I've left my Bible . . . I left it on the chair!'

Gary kept his torch on the intersection. The panting was regular, but in the strange echoes of the labyrinth, it seemed to come from in front and behind. It could only be seconds before the thing appeared.

Sure enough, as they watched, a huge head and a huge pair of shoulders moved around the corner, into the beam. The creature stopped and everyone stared at its profile. Then the great head turned and two green eyes flashed like emeralds. They could see a fang, too large for the creature's mouth – then more teeth as the thing licked its lips. Its fur was black and white and then, like a crack of flame, they saw the burning stripes of a tiger.

Nobody moved a muscle; nobody breathed. It was as if the three men hoped they might not be seen behind the torch. For the tiger peered, but seemed to be dazzled. It took another two paces, revealing its monstrous chest. Most strange of all – and most terrible, because it sent the scene falling away into the horror of true nightmare – there was a child on its back. The child held the fur in both hands and his knees clamped the animal's flanks. He wore his shirt open and there was a black-and-gold tie around his head.

'Israel,' said Oli. 'You're just in time.'

'So's Ivan,' said Ruskin. 'These men are bad.'

The tiger and its rider stared, expressionless. Israel kicked at the flanks and moved closer to the torch. The child stared forward, as a king might stare from a throne.

'That's you, Ruskin, right?' he said. 'I can't see nothing, man – turn off the torch. Pod's got Prince, but he's doubling back.'

And the tiger chose that moment to roar, bucking its great shoulders so that Israel nearly fell. The sound filled not just the tunnel, but the labyrinth, and seemed to blow the three men backwards. They dropped everything and fell against the walls. Father O'Hanrahan spun, and even in his pain grabbed, instinctively, at Cuthbertson's rucksack – the bag with the sword. He heaved it onto his shoulder, desperate and driven. He was poised to run, and would have done so, had not an answering roar echoed even louder and frozen him. It was in front and it was behind. Ivan roared again and went into a crouch. The three men screamed and from the far end of the tunnel, behind them, cutting off their exit, came the second tiger – Prince. He was moving at a lolloping run, with Podma standing on his back. The child had his arms out and was bare-chested. His skin shone and he looked like an avenging demon.

The three men clutched each other and stumbled again like drunks. They were united by one simple, human desire: the desire not to be eaten. Ivan roared, Prince roared, and they moved in for the kill. Gary Cuthbertson led the way, plunging down the one open tunnel, not caring where it might lead.

The tigers came together and leaped into a snarling, joyful fight, Ivan rolling Prince easily onto his back so that Podma had to somersault to safety.

Ruskin had his arm round Oli.

'You poor thing!' he said, earnestly. 'Can you walk? I can carry you if —'

'Jake, you twit!' shouted Oli, scrambling up. 'I was pretending! It was my way of slowing them down. Like you, pretending to be lost.'

'We *are* lost.'

'Of course we're not – that's the tunnel to the pump-room.'

'Go!' shouted Podma. 'Let's get after them!'

Chapter Forty-seven

Millie entered cautiously, radio in hand, relieved to find the place empty. She clicked the switch. 'Come in, Sanchez. I'm in the pump-room. Over.'

'We've got the boys!' said Sanchez. 'Ruskin's OK, so's Oli – they got them lost in the tunnels and Oli pretended to be injured . . . but they're fine! We're all here with the tigers . . . and, Millie! Positive identification of the intruder. It's Cuthbertson again.'

'I knew it.'

'Cuthbertson, the priest – Father O'Hanrahan – and the bent ref: Cuthbertson's brother.'

'I told you, Sanchez! Anjoli told you as well!'

'We think they're heading towards you. They could be there any minute – you've got to get out!'

'How do you know?'

'Eric thinks so and so does Oli. When they saw the tigers, they legged it. The tunnel they took leads straight to the pump-room and if they've been there before, they'll recognise it. Remember that barge?'

'Yes. Hang on, I can hear something.'

'It's the tunnel with the barge. If they see that, they'll have their bearings. Have you seen Miles?'

'No. Forget him.'

'Millie, I don't like you being in there by yourself! Are the monks around?'

Millie wasn't listening. There was a noise outside and it was growing louder. Running feet. She could hear somebody gasping and she slid back between the pipes, instantly on her guard.

'Millie, where are the monks?'

'Shhh!'

It wasn't just one man: there were several.

'Millie, will you please come in? Over.'

'Shut up! They're here.'

'Who? The monks? Come up to the lake. We can get them on the lake – Asilah has everything rigged –'

Millie frantically turned the volume down. She was looking at the policeman and he was as big and as ugly as she remembered him. Her palms were suddenly sweaty and a wave of fear rose up in her belly. She watched him as he staggered, wheezing, through the doorway. Behind him came his brother and, seconds later, stumbling, unable to stand upright, came the old man. He carried something in a red cloth and it looked heavy. They were all desperate and shaken, and they piled back against the door.

'Get it closed!' yelled the policeman. 'Get the door closed!'

'It is!' gasped Gary. 'We're OK, we're OK ... Nothing's coming! Calm down ...'

The old man was on the floor, racked by a coughing fit. He looked utterly wretched.

Millie drew the radio to her mouth, her hands trembling. She turned the knob a fraction.

'They're here, Sanchez,' she whispered.

'Who? The monks?'

'I'm turning off.'

'I can't hear you!'

312

But now Millie didn't dare speak. The policeman was staring around the room into the infinite tangle of the pipework. She turned the volume down to minimum and crouched in the darkness. She had no idea what to do.

There was silence but for the orchestra of drips and surges.

Millie put the radio to her lips again, wondering if she dared speak. Then, carefully, she turned it off. As the connection was broken, the receiver let out a shrill squirt of static.

'What was that?' said Cuthbertson.

'What was what?' said Gary.

'I heard a radio.'

'I'm not interested in a blessed radio,' said Father O'Hanrahan. 'We've still got the sword. Let's just get ourselves out.'

'It's a sound I'm used to,' said the policeman. 'We've got company.'

Millie took another step back and felt a pipe behind her legs. She carefully stepped over it and retreated, ducking under another.

She could see the policeman's brother again. He too was staring around, up and down. The pipes took your eyes off into random corners – it was hard to focus. As she watched, he seemed to lose interest – he moved off to what Professor Worthington had called the dry dock.

Millie's heart was beating fast. She could see that the man knew the system. He was hauling at the rowing-boat, preparing his exit.

'Give me the sword,' he said.

The old priest seemed to wake up. He was clearly exhausted, but he got to his feet, leaning on pipes, moaning. The red bundle was on the floor and the old man could barely lift it. He half dragged it and soon it was in the boat.

'Percy?' called his brother. 'What are you doing?'

There was no answer.

Millie stared at the radio switch and made her calculations. To raise the alarm and be discovered alone in this room: that was frightening. Not to raise the alarm, however, and risk them getting away, seemed even worse. They were so close – she could see Gary Cuthbertson's bald head staring down at a stopcock, twisting it open. The dock was filling and the boat was floating.

'Percy!' he shouted. 'We've got no time to waste!'

'Come on!' cried Father O'Hanrahan. There was desperation in his voice. He so wanted to be gone.

Millie turned on the radio again and put her mouth close to the transmitter. 'Sanchez!' she whispered.

And that was when she felt a huge hand cover her face.

Her arm was wrenched behind her back and the radio skittered away from her. Then the arm was twisted and bent in the Cuthbertson technique she had experienced once before: terrifying strength. Terrifying malice. And worst of all, no chance of escape. She smelled breath she had hoped never to smell again.

Then the voice was in her ear.

'Oh my,' it said. 'Of all the people I hoped I might run into.'

Chapter Forty-eight

'Has the party finished, Clarissa?' said the headmaster.

'Yes. They're quiet as mice.'

'That's good. Doonan seems to have those boys well and truly under his thumb. He was quite a find, wasn't he?'

'He's doing well,' said Professor Worthington. 'Now ... Sanjay gave me some of that lovely cake from teatime.'

She brought a heavy triangle out of her handbag, wrapped in a napkin. The icing was black-and-gold and there were little meringue footballs embedded in the sponge.

The headmaster produced a knife and it was cut into four.

'I'm going to miss Imagio,' said Captain Routon. 'It was a privilege to coach him.'

'I never see skill like that,' said Flavio. 'Genius.'

'He's going to leave a hole here that will be hard to fill,' said Professor Worthington. 'He's as tough as they come – I mean, a real street boy. But the most delicate hands and an absolute thirst for knowledge.'

The headmaster was nodding. 'It's going to be a sad farewell. I was writing the goodbye speech this morning. Do you remember that section in Virgil when Aeneas kisses Dido? I thought I'd quote it: *Tu nobis memorabilis es caelo paterfacto.*'

'What's it mean?' said Captain Routon.

'*You showed us heaven,*' said the headmaster. '*We will not forget you.*'

'That is beautiful, sir. And very true. We had a commander-in-chief in the Falklands, stood on a grenade. We sang a song at his funeral and—'

'You got someone on the roof,' said Flavio.

'I'm sorry?'

Flavio had been distracted and was half standing. He was staring over the headmaster's shoulder, out of the window.

'There's a man on the roof. Debt-collector, maybe?'

'Surely not,' said Professor Worthington.

'He's waving,' said Flavio. 'I think he's in trouble.'

The headmaster stood up. He still had no glasses. 'No,' he said, peering. 'Can't see anyone.'

'He's gone again,' said Flavio. 'I think he slipped, maybe.'

'Who was it? Man or child?'

'Not a child.'

Flavio had the window open. 'I think I better go see,' he said.

Flavio's days as a wire-boy stood him in excellent stead. He kicked off his slippers and was onto the sill in a moment. He ran briskly up the hip of the roof. The slates were wet with spring dew, so he kept his toes splayed. He ran along the ridge tiles towards the orphans' tower, but stopped almost at once. He could hear somebody calling and a choked sob. He followed the sound and peered carefully down.

Brother Doonan was spreadeagled on the slope beneath him. He was holding himself still, arms and legs open to maximise friction. But he was gradually slipping and as Flavio watched, his feet and then his knees pushed past the guttering.

'Oh God!' he cried, staring up at Flavio with desperate

316

panic in his eyes. 'Please help,' he said. 'I knew I shouldn't have done this.'

Flavio went into a low crouch. It wasn't difficult to pad down to the frightened boy and, after five minutes of careful shuffling, he was out of danger. Doonan was shaking and he wouldn't let go of Flavio's arm. It took longer to get him to the headmaster's window, but then there were many hands to help him in and soon he was in a chair with a large glass of rum by his elbow.

'I'm so sorry,' said Doonan. 'I had to reach you. I think we may have a major crisis on our hands.'

'Hello!' shouted a voice.

The headmaster went back to the window.

'I don't believe this,' he muttered. 'This is harassment.'

The headmaster leaned out of the window. He could just make out the robed form of of a monk. He had his hood off and was looking up, his hands cupped round his mouth. 'Can you hear me up there?'

'It's one of the Brethren!' said the headmaster.

'Answer him,' said Professor Worthington.

'Yes!' called the headmaster. 'How can we help?'

'I've been trying to raise you for quite some time. I'm sorry to bother you, but we think one of your little chaps might be in danger. A little long-haired fellow, name of Miles.'

Cuthbertson swung Millie round and held her by the chin. He stared into her eyes, and in the half second before he spoke Millie recalled a huge, mad mastiff-dog that one of her relatives kept. A guard-dog that barked and bit. Cuthbertson's eyes were mad as a dog's and his teeth were exposed in a smile that made Millie turn away and jerk for freedom. She kicked wildly and screamed, but the hands were used to restraint and they bashed her hard against a nearby pipe, so her skull burst with lights.

317

The voice again close to her ear. 'We don't need weapons, Millie Roads. Not in the police force. That's what we used to say: *Who needs a weapon?*' He cracked her again, so that it was the back of her head this time, smacking hard against a stopcock. 'Use what's around you. I had a chap try to get loose from me on Ribblestrop High Street. I broke him round a lamp post. Now . . .'

'We've got to go!' hissed the old man. He was now sitting in the rowing-boat, the sword across his knees.

'If your friends are on their way,' said Cuthbertson, 'you'll be rescued, won't you? You'll live to tell the tale. But to give ourselves a sporting chance . . .' His hand moved to the back of her neck. 'To keep them at bay . . . I'm going to flood the tunnels. Do you know how to drain the lake? I do.'

He was opening a spigot with his left hand. Immediately, there was a vibration in the floor. Forces were coming to life under their feet. He dragged Millie round a corner and there was a box she'd never noticed before. No lock, so the lid flipped open to reveal four enormous valves, all painted red. Without hesitation, Cuthbertson spun each one of them, one-handed. They were so well greased they flew like propellers and the roaring under their feet doubled in volume. The rowing-boat joggled in its dock.

Millie struggled again and tried to bite, but the policeman had both hands free again and she didn't stand a chance. He turned her to the central shaft – the glass elevator. The four pipes in the corners were bubbling furiously and, as if on terrible cue, the floating chamber drifted into view.

There were fifteen centimetres of water in the bottom and a mess of weed and driftwood.

'My only regret, my friend,' said Cuthbertson, as he opened the door, 'is that I don't have time to watch you drown.'

Millie managed to speak. 'Please!' she said. It was the only word she had time for, though, because he pushed her hard. She fell sideways into the chamber – an awkward fall into mud and water. By the time she'd scrambled up, the door was closed and sealed.

Cuthbertson allowed himself a few seconds to look at her. Then he spun the dial.

Millie's hands went to the glass wall. She felt the chamber shift, up a few centimetres then down again. He was working it out. Moments later, she felt the water at her feet start to froth and bubble, and she knew what he was doing. She knew that the chamber was filling from the bottom upwards. From where exactly, she couldn't see – there appeared to be various inlets and they were gushing. The housemaid's revenge. The family. Millie never forgot stories, and Professor Worthington's story had been so horrible it was etched in her memory: '*dead bodies, sluiced out into the moat . . .*'

She hammered on the door, knowing it was useless. She cried out, knowing that cries were even more useless because the glass was so thick. There was the noise at her feet, but more terrible was the thunder of thousands upon thousands of gallons that were sluicing through the giant pipes around her. If the tunnels were filling, her friends would be fleeing. If her friends were fleeing, who would ever reach her?

The door to the dry dock was closing; the rowing-boat was rising and, even as she watched, it disappeared.

She was reminded of waterfalls, and the strange thing was she now felt a curious stillness. This could not be death, she thought. You didn't die like this. She beat the glass again and it was obvious that no amount of kicking would even so much as crack it. The ceiling was more than a metre above her head and that was sealed with brass bands. The water was over her feet, past her ankles. She could stand on one of the platforms, but ... the level was rising. There was no space for doubt or dispute: the water would rise steadily.

The pump-room was empty. They'd bolted the door. She was alone.

Chapter Forty-nine

'Brother Rees?'

'What?'

'Brother! I'm sorry to disturb you – I know you've only had an hour or so . . .'

'What's the matter? Have you found Miles?'

'No.'

'What's the time?'

'It's two a.m. and I hate to wake you, but we might have a problem. Brother Joe heard the noise and he woke me. It would appear that somebody's got into the pump-room and I think they might have done something rather foolish.'

'What have they done?'

'They appear to be draining the lake. The tunnels are flooding.'

'That's impossible. That was . . . I had a dream . . .'

Brother Rees was sitting bolt upright in his bed. He fumbled for his glasses and said a number of very quick prayers, bobbing to the crucifix in the alcove.

'Is the sword in danger?' said the other monk as he hastened after his friend.

Brother Rees was moving swiftly in the direction of the pump-room. 'Technically, no,' he said. 'As I understand it, the sluicing tunnels would not interfere with Tomaz's home. Therefore the sword is not in any danger. We clearly have a situation, though. This could be very, very dangerous, so I think we need to get everyone up on the surface. When was the lake last drained, Brother Joe?'

The monk shook his head. 'Certainly not in my lifetime,' he said. 'I saw a chart once and nineteen hundred and two rings a bell.'

'Is everyone up? Is everyone awake?'

'Yes, Brother.'

'Good . . .' He thought hard. 'We need to close the valves, obviously. Oh my word, who on earth would have opened them?'

'Brother Rees!' said a voice.

It was Brother Martin. His hair was wild and the bottom of his robe was soaking wet. 'You've heard the news?'

'We need to close the valves —'

'It's not possible, Brother. I've just tried. The pump-room's cut off.'

The three men continued, climbing the steps as quickly as they could. They could hear the drumming of water above them and as they turned onto the platform, it became a roar that was frightening.

'Oh my word! I see what you mean!'

The tunnel was no longer a tunnel. It was a canal and the water was racing. As they watched, they saw pieces of the old barge – a section of rib and a length of gunwale – spin madly, sink and then rise again. The velocity of the water was terrifying and its colour was filthy brown.

'What can we do?' shouted Brother Rees. 'We'll have to go the long way round!'

'I think it's a lost cause!' yelled Brother Martin.

Brother Rees hitched up his robe and tucked it firmly into the cord.

'What are you doing, Brother?'

He put his spectacles in an inside pouch and kicked his slippers off.

'Brother, what are you doing?'

He put his mouth against Brother Martin's ear. 'I'm going to take a chance,' he shouted. 'I'm a strong swimmer – I might just do it.'

'You're joking! You're mad!'

'I want you to get everybody else up through Neptune; something very serious—'

'No, Brother, this is suicide!'

'Leave me alone. I'm worried about that boy.'

He closed his eyes, wondering if he was making a wise decision. 'Miles,' he said. 'I've got a bad feeling about him.'

'Brother Rees, you are far too old for this and I will not let you put yourself at risk.'

He saw his friend move to the edge of the platform and put out a restraining hand. Too late: Brother Rees had jumped, as far as he could, into the centre of the torrent. His friends gripped each other in astonishment and watched as the old grey head dipped beneath the waters. Ten metres on, it rose again, and they saw him breasting the waves making for the opposite bank. The water turned him like a stick, but he fought. There was an iron post driven into the wall and he fumbled at it, but the water had him again and drove him away. In seconds, he was swept round the curve of the tunnel and his chance was gone.

Just around that very bend, Sanchez was shouting into his radio. 'Asilah, come in, please! Asilah, come in. . . . It's Sanchez, over!'

He turned to Sanjay. 'He's not answering.'

Imagio snatched the radio and pressed a different switch. 'Asilah, are you receiving, over?'

There was the buzz of static.

'Asilah here – what's happening down there? The lake's moving. Over.'

Sanchez took the radio back. 'We've got floods,' he shouted. 'There's water in the tunnels. Ruskin and Oli are safe, but there's still no sign of Miles. Have you seen him? Over.'

'Nothing,' said Asilah. 'We're just sitting waiting and we can hear . . . it's like someone's pulled a plug.'

'No sign of Millie? Over.'

'Negative. Where are the tigers?'

'We sent them back – job done.'

'What now, then? Over.'

Sanchez looked haggard. He hated indecision, but what was the best move? Instinct told him to get everyone back up onto dry land, but all he could think about was Millie, cut off and alone – it was like a headache, getting worse. 'We've got to get to her,' he said. His fury got the better of him. 'Why does she have to do everything on her own?'

'The monks might have found her,' shouted Ruskin. 'Maybe they did this—'

'There's someone in the water,' said Sanjay.

'Where?'

His sharp eyes had picked the figure out long before anybody else. It was rushing towards them, and it was only the quick thinking of Henry – always a boy to work by instinct – that saved the day. He stepped out into the water, holding the rail tight with one hand; as the body came by, he lunged and grabbed it with his left. Fighting the current, he drew it back and in, the railing bending under the strain. But he was held by many hands, and in a short while the bedraggled form of Brother Rees was up on the platform. The old man coughed up lungfuls of river water, wiped the weed from his face, and managed to sit up.

He looked up at Henry. 'Thank you,' he gasped. 'Who's draining the river?'

The boys looked at him.

His eyes went from face to face. 'What's going on? Why are you all down here in the middle of the night?'

'My house has been robbed,' said Tomaz.

'Did you see Millie?' said Sanchez. He was clutching the old man's robe. 'Were you in the pump-room?' he cried. 'Did you see Millie?'

'What do you mean, *robbed*? Is the sword safe?'

'Millie!' insisted Sanchez. 'Is she still in the pump-room?'

'I don't know who you're talking about,' said the old man. 'I don't know anyone called Millie and I haven't been to the pump-room. It's cut off, and we—'

'But she said you were there!' said Sanchez.

The water surged and a wave drenched them all. Nobody could speak for a moment and then it was Oli who said it. 'What if the policeman got there? What if they're the ones flooding the tunnels?'

Sanchez's face lost the little colour it had. The water was now over the platform and over their ankles and the noise was unbearable.

'Let's go!' shouted Sanjay. 'What are we waiting for? We can swim.'

Brother Rees clambered to his feet. 'Impossible,' he said.

'We have to try!' yelled Sanchez.

The monk closed his eyes and thought a moment. 'There's another way,' he said. 'But it won't be passable, it's madness . . .'

He moved to a side tunnel and up some steps. The noise reduced in an instant, falling to a low throbbing.

'I did it years ago, in the summer,' he said, softly. 'It wasn't easy then, and it won't be passable now, not—'

'Another way? What do you mean?'

325

'Another way to the pump-room. But it's a long shot. I don't hold out much hope . . .'

'Why not?' said Sanchez.

'Because the caves will be submerged.'

'We can try.'

'There's nothing more dangerous than an underground lake. Follow me!'

He continued, fast, along the tunnel. As he went, he tore off his saturated robe. He wore a black vest and shorts underneath, and soon he was half running. The boys jogged after him, their torches bobbing.

Chapter Fifty

The tunnel zig-zagged madly, for there were extrusions of rock. They ducked and grovelled, and at last came to a wall. It had crumbled and behind it was yet another rocky passage; they moved along it, as quickly as they could. There was hardly room to crawl.

'I've been here once before,' said Tomaz.

'When?' said Ruskin.

'I came with Miles.'

'Miles,' said Brother Rees. He stopped. 'Did he go back?'

'From where?' said Sanchez.

'He was with me. This evening. Then he ran away and I–'

'We haven't seen him,' said Sanchez. 'Did you talk to him?'

Brother Rees closed his eyes and muttered a prayer. 'I'm not sure this can get any worse,' he said. 'Let's keep going – we're nearly there.'

The passage got tighter and it was impossible to talk. They trained their torches forward and crawled. At length, out of breath and covered in dirt, they clambered up to a sharp lip in the rock.

'Careful!' said Brother Rees. 'There's quite a drop – we call this a drowned cave.'

They dragged themselves slowly forward and trained their torches down. The rock hollowed beneath them into an enormous chasm. Had they had time, they might have admired the swooping columns and the folds of quartz. As it was, they simply stared at the jet-black water, spreading before them, and making further progress impossible.

'We're way too late,' said Brother Rees, in a voice heavy with distress. 'I've never seen the water as high as this.'

'I can swim,' said Sanjay.

'Oh no,' said the monk, grabbing the boy's arm and holding it. 'Nobody swims here. You can't even think of swimming.' The chamber gave his voice an echo and the grotto was full of whispers.

'The caves will all be flooded now,' he said. 'They're a labyrinth when they're dry – imagine them full of water. There are currents down there too. You wouldn't stand a chance.'

'We've got to get to the pump-room,' whispered Sanchez. He had tears in his eyes. 'Mille's there. She might be . . .'

'We can't go any further!' said the monk. 'You see that column?' He trained Sanjay's torch onto it. 'Just there and the pink arch under it. That's where the passage starts, but the passages are low. The water sits in them – fills them. There's no air.'

Oli said, 'If they've got Millie, they'll kill her.'

'We'll find a way up,' said Brother Rees. 'And call the police.'

Then a soft voice from the other side of the lagoon said, 'Sanchez?'

Every torch shifted and every beam came to rest on a sharp rock rising out of the water. A boy was perching on it, wearing a tattered grey shirt and a black-and-gold tie.

He blinked in the light and put his hand over his eyes.

Sanchez said a prayer quietly in Spanish. 'Oh, Miles,' he said. 'Oh thank God.'

'I used to come here with Tom,' said Miles.

'I know,' said Sanchez.

'This is where I played the game.'

He had something in his hand. It was Sanchez's gun.

'I know,' said Sanchez again. He spoke as softly as he could. 'Come over here now. You shouldn't be on your own.'

Miles stood up. 'They've got Millie, haven't they?'

'No,' said Tomaz. 'We don't know that.'

'You're going to fall,' said Sanchez. 'Sit back down. I'll come to you.'

He could see the boy more clearly now, poised on the rock. He felt a sob rising in his throat. Miles's shirt-sleeves were gone and his arms looked bruised and thin. His hair was a bird's nest and he was shoeless. He balanced on bare feet.

'I'm coming to get you,' said Sanchez.

Miles smiled. 'You're too late,' he said.

'How can I be too late?'

'You didn't want me back, did you?'

'Of course I did!'

'This is my job.' He pushed the gun into his belt. 'I'm a guardian.'

'You're talking nonsense! Stay where you are, Miles! Stay—'

Miles slipped off his shirt and dived into the water.

Brother Rees cried out in pain and his howl echoed in the chambers above. He put his arms tight around Sanchez, who moved to jump too, and dragged him back. 'Suicide!' he shouted. 'Suicide!'

Sanchez was screaming, Sanjay was on the edge, and Ruskin held his wrist. The water was churning and as they searched the surface, there was the most monstrous splash of all. Henry had seen at once that Miles would never come up. He shrugged off his blazer and threw himself after him.

* * *

329

Miles was in a darkness more total than he had ever known.

He had dived and then turned underwater, and for some seconds he didn't even know which way was up. He opened his arms and legs; he kicked, knowing that this must push him to the top, but he had the curious feeling that he was moving downwards. There was a weariness in him, as if he had been running a long distance, and the water felt warm rather than cold. He sank, and sank, and he knew suddenly that he didn't ever want to come up. The weightlessness was beautiful.

He felt rock under his feet. He opened his eyes and saw nothing. He pushed off, gently, and pulled with his arms. Now he was rising, picking up speed. He kicked again, surprised at how little he cared. He knew his lungs would burst soon and that he would gulp only water. He knew the bubbles would not be seen, because by now he had to be under the rock. He was aware of tunnel walls around him and a current taking him.

One more kick and he was moving faster still – the water was cold, swirling green. He could see a shape in the distance, swimming towards him as if from a mirror, and they were on a collision course. It was a boy, just like him, coming to get him. It too had floating hair and wild eyes, and he knew immediately that he was seeing himself. Closer and closer and they were looking into each other's eyes, and they came together, rose together, and Miles broke the surface, gasping.

As he did so, another figure emerged, and this one was spluttering and coughing as much as he was. This one lunged for him and caught him by the shoulder. A torch came out of the water and Miles saw Henry's huge face, racked with fear and desperation, the staring eyes made all the more mad by his slicked-back hair. They trod water together.

After some time, Miles said. 'I don't know the way.'

Henry pointed with his torch and they saw together that there were no options. The cave they were in tapered to a tunnel and, after ten metres or so, that tunnel submerged. They would have to swim blind, hoping that the roof would rise before they ran out of air.

Miles smiled at Henry and shook his head. 'Suicide,' he said.

Chapter Fifty-one

Above ground, Darren was making his move. He had realised that the level of the lake was going down. This exposed
some of the pipework around Neptune and he could see a
small, concrete platform, which had not been there before.
There was a stone wall next to it, circular – it looked like a
well. As he stared, trying to work out what it might be for,
he saw a rowing-boat float up out of it and he was able to
recognise three hunched figures.

He looked about him, stealthily. As far as he could tell, he
was alone. The children he'd seen had gone down the
Neptune statue: he'd heard nobody for a long time. He was
bitterly cold and horribly bruised. Breathing was painful
and he felt he had very little strength in his right arm. Still,
he had done his duty by waiting; now, at last, it was pick-up
time.

He lifted the oar of the speedboat – wincing as he did so
– and pushed off from under the bridge.

D.C.C. Cuthbertson saw him and waved frantically.

Asilah crouched on the bank, observing everything.

'Come in, Sanchez,' he said.

There was no reply.

'Sanchez, are you receiving? Over.'

'Asilah, it's not Sanchez. It's Ruskin.' The boy's voice was cracking. 'We've lost Miles and Henry. They jumped in! They just went and jumped!'

'There's movement on the lake, Ruskin,' said Asilah. 'There's a boat coming over the lake. Over.'

'Who's in it?'

'I can't see who's in the little one,' said Asilah. 'There's no hurry – they're not going anywhere. They're . . . moving towards each other. I don't think it's kids – they're too big. Unless one of them's Henry . . .'

'It must be Cuthbertson,' said Ruskin. 'Get him.'

'What are you thinking, boss?' said Anjoli. He had slunk up beside Asilah and they watched together as the two boats came together. Vijay was on the bridge and waved an arm. Two more boys ran silently to him and knelt by his side.

'What are we waiting for?' said Anjoli. 'We gotta take 'em.'

'What do you think, Israel?' said Asilah.

Israel chuckled. 'He wants to fly, you let him fly. We'll lose them if we don't move.'

'You sure?' said Asilah. 'We never did this in water.'

Anjoli said, 'I'm Icarus, man.'

The decision made, the three boys moved back to where the concrete pipe stood ready, the charge packed in a water-tight skin. Anjoli put on a crash helmet and buttoned up his blazer. Then he took up the asbestos tray and clambered up the pipe. Seconds later, he was folding himself into its aperture. He got the tray under his backside and hugged his knees.

'Ready,' he said. His voice had a strange echo, emerging from a gun barrel.

Israel took a bearing and shoved the pipe sideways. He jammed a rock into the soil to stabilise it.

Asilah knocked on the pipe. 'Anjoli – I don't want to hurt you.'

'Light the fuse! It's what I was born for.'

Israel grew impatient – he was a practical boy. Most of the orphans carried cigarette lighters and his had a healthy, five-centimetre flame. He touched it to the fuse and watched it burn, fast. Asilah heard the hiss and moved away: it was a ten-second delay, and that gave them time to get a little distance and crouch with their backs to the pipe.

The detonation rocked the peace of the night and was bounced back from hill to hill. The pipe itself burst, sending several shards of concrete zipping over the grass. Anjoli, however, was borne up in the most beautiful of trajectories. The tray saved his flesh and as it fell away, he was a diver rising in the starlit night, somersaulting higher and higher. He saw Orion's belt and opened his arms to swing on it. For several seconds he seemed to hang in the air and enjoy weightlessness.

He got his bearings and sighted the two boats beneath him. They were touching. Anjoli gritted his teeth and became a weapon, pure and simple. He drew his knees to his chin – Flavio had coached him, so he knew the drill. His elbows gave him some control over direction and he fixed his eyes on the target.

'My God, what was that?' cried the headmaster.

He was standing in the deserted east tower dormitory; everyone crowded to the window. They missed the flash of fire, of course. All they saw was a black speck rising.

'I'm very concerned,' said Professor Worthington.

'Let's get down to the lake.'

Before they reached the door, Anjoli had smashed between the Cuthbertsons, turning their rowing-boat to matchwood. He plunged almost to the lake's bottom, lucky that he'd hit a deep patch, as the level was falling fast. He revolved, got his bearings, and struck out for the surface. Through the murk he saw a pair of kicking legs and he knew someone was in the water.

It was Father O'Hanrahan.

The Cuthbertsons were grabbing at the speedboat – the policeman had the precious sword and managed to pass it to Darren. Gary Cuthbertson rolled himself into the boat and went straight to the engine, to yank at its cord. Father O'Hanrahan managed to grab the policeman's leg and then he too had the side of the boat.

Anjoli hauled at him, but he desperately needed air, so he couldn't hold on for long. He kicked away and burst onto the surface, laughing and gasping at the same time.

Then, from the other side of the lake, came the children's own rowing-boat, concealed for counter-attack. Nikko was in the bows and his thin voice came floating over the water: 'Stroke! Stroke! Stroke!' The oarsmen were pulling hard and still the speedboat's engine would not fire.

'Get in!' roared Cuthbertson, and by superhuman effort and a great deal of luck, the old man hauled himself up; the policeman wrestling him onto the boat's floor.

All at once, there was fire in the air. Kenji was throwing fire-bombs and one hit the side of the speedboat, splashing burning rum across the gunwale.

'Stroke! Stroke! Faster!' yelled Nikko.

Gary Cuthbertson almost fell, for the craft was rocking more madly than ever. He leaned heavily on Darren's shoulder, which elicited a hideous scream, and tried once more at the engine cord.

'My goodness,' said the headmaster, pausing on the lawns. 'They're on the lake! This is an outrage!'

As he spoke, the speedboat came to life and its chainsaw screech blotted out further comment. Gary Cuthbertson was an adequate climber, but he was no boatman. He dropped the propeller way too fast, before he had control of the rudder, and the boat spun in dangerously fast circles, the flames now fanned by the breeze and taking hold.

Anjoli dived out of the way for safety.

'Hard to starboard!' shrieked Kenji. He had one more bomb to lob and aimed it at the engine. The rowing-boat was moving at speed, though, and it was an impossible shot. It fell harmlessly into the water.

The rowers were tearing at the rowlocks. Their vessel had been patched up with bits of timber and canvas, but there was no way it could stand the strain it was under: holes were appearing where their feet were braced. They hoped to ram the villains broadside and then, like marauders of old, they might have jumped onboard for a total rout. Sadly, it was not to be. The policeman grabbed the tiller and righted his craft. The engine howled and the boat swept forward out of the smoke. The boys' boat rushed by, just grazing the motor. Israel lunged at the policeman with an oar, but the blow glanced off the side of his head and Cuthbertson stayed upright. They pulled Anjoli out of the water and sank in the wake of the disappearing speedboat.

'Damn!' cried Asilah. 'We need that gun, man! Why did Miles take it?'

'They're getting away!' wailed Israel. He was up to his knees in water.

Sure enough, Percy Cuthbertson – even whilst clutching his ear – had brought the boat under control and was turning it in a graceful curve. Somehow they'd put out the fire and were on their way.

'What *is* going on?' cried Professor Worthington. She too was in the water and was panting hard. Flavio and Routon were soon beside her.

'They're getting away,' said Anjoli.

The speedboat was almost out of sight and the misery of defeat rolled in like a fog.

Then a curious thing happened. The speedboat appeared to stop.

'It's stopped,' said Asilah.

'What's it doing?' said Kenji.

Flavio's eyesight was good. He peered into the moonlight, the white of the boat vivid against the dark water.

'I think they're grounded,' he said. 'They're just standing there.'

Anjoli gasped. 'Of course!' he cried. 'The water level's dropped, man. They're stuck in the mud.'

At this point, the head of Neptune opened and the rest of the children poured out onto his shoulders, led by Brother Rees. The old monk saw the teachers and clambered through the mud to get to them. He nearly fell into the headmaster's arms. 'There are two children, sir!' he gasped. 'Underwater.' He fell to his knees and the headmaster crouched beside him. 'There's another one . . . lost, sir. Millie, I think.' His eyes were wild and the headmaster could only stare. 'You're going to need divers!' cried Brother Rees, finding a last morsel of energy. 'Fire crews, sir! Air ambulance. I've afraid you must expect casualties, sir. I did what I could – I tried to . . .' Brother Rees had started to cry. Sobs were choking him, as he saw again the black water and Miles's face as he dived.

The headmaster, meanwhile, started to run. He reached his study in record time and snatched up the telephone receiver. 'Emergency . . .' he shouted. 'Emergency!'

Above his head, two parrots woke up and flapped angrily. One let off a volley of gunshots, whilst the other roared like a tiger.

The headmaster swore and dialled firmly: nine-nine-nine. 'Ambulance,' he cried. 'Fire crews too! Police!'

*　　*　　*

337

'Everyone in the lorry,' said Professor Worthington. 'We'll go round!'

'No!' said Asilah. 'We stretched a wire across. We can walk.'

Flavio saw what he meant and his eyes bulged with wonder. They had fired a wire right across the island and used the truck to stretch it. It was secure and tight, and they could simply stroll into the middle of the lake.

Imagio led and soon there was a queue of schoolboys making their way behind him.

Chapter Fifty-two

The water level had risen to Millie's shoulders.

She stood on the top platform, her eyes fixed on the pump-room door that remained so completely closed, just ten steps away. When the level rose to her neck, she started to pray. When it got to her nose, she lost her footing on the platform and had to float. She tried to keep calm.

There was less than a metre of air above her, and when she kicked to locate the platform, she couldn't find it – it was out of reach. She bobbed in the water, her nose just above the surface, still hoping. Soon, the effort was unbearable and she was gulping river water. She had to cough it out and replace it with air – air that was becoming fetid and thick. She needed all her strength to do that and yet her real strength was needed to keep herself afloat.

She tried to lift herself up and stretch out in a star shape. When she did this, it was a little easier, but the horror was looking only at the ceiling, as it came closer and closer. She realised she was crying and she thought of Sanchez.

Miles was also floating.

The tunnel had seemed endless and, again, it had been like swimming in oil or ink – the blackness seemed to get thicker. He knew, like Millie, that panic of any kind burned up oxygen, and he knew that to get into difficulties now – to suddenly lose confidence – would kill both him and Henry. The thought of dying, though, had become too attractive to resist and he knew it was why he was here. He would not panic: in a strange way, he was in slow-motion, and the fact that he had no idea of his direction and therefore could not worry . . . it kept him calm. Then he saw himself again, but the phantom boy was underneath him now, and it was younger. This one was wearing baggy red swimming trunks, which Miles dimly remembered were the ones he learned to swim in, when he was six years old. He saw his mother, then, at the far end of the tunnel, stretching out her arms to him, because it had been she who had taught him. She was laughing, he was laughing.

He kicked once more and the six-year-old rose so that Miles could get his hand on his shoulder. He was drawn through and the little boy pulled him into a new cave, down through rock, and over a ridge that scraped his belly. His mother loomed closer and she was calling out to him as his face broke the surface. Air cascaded down upon him and there was light from somewhere as she hugged him.

Henry was there again too, though Henry's face was unrecognisable. Something had happened to Henry's face. Maybe he'd caught it on the rocks as he swam, but his jaw seemed to be dark with blood and he looked like an old man. He'd lost an eye and he was wearing a suit and holding Miles up. The light swung away and Miles knew he was in the arms of Lord Vyner and that he had to dive again.

Tomaz swam with him this time. It was the Tomaz he had known at the start of last term – the shy Tomaz, who spoke very little English. It was the Tomaz he'd looked after and they swam well together. They could hear Sanchez's voice calling them and they raced towards it. Miles felt stronger and when he kicked his legs, he seemed to shoot forward at amazing speed. He followed Tomaz, who was quick as a tadpole, and when the cave divided into two, he had no choice to make – he followed the racing boy. He just had to hope that Henry was following.

When he broke the surface again, he knew he was nearly done. These great feats of endurance, they took their toll and he was shivering. He had drunk so much water and his strength was leaving him. He could barely tread water; he had to lie back and float – and thank goodness for Henry. Henry was there again, his face repaired, and he held him up. Then Henry was shaking him, because he was suddenly sleepy. His big friend was slapping him gently. He was wrapping a tie around his wrist. Then, instinct taking over, he took a great lungful of air and was diving for what had to be the last time.

This time Henry was leading and Miles was tied to him. He hardly had to do anything; it was as if he was under the boy's arm, drawn onwards. Then the inky water around him seemed to catch fire and he was hallucinating more violently than ever. All around him, fire was rolling and it was the roof of Ribblestrop. He'd set it ablaze; he had no one to blame but himself. He had packed the broken-down organ with paper and paraffin rags and it had gone up like a torch. So much anger and anger burned best of all! The whole cave was on fire and Miles was a bullet in a gun, shooting through it. A black-and-gold tie tugged at his wrist – if he could only slip it off, undo the knot . . . but Henry was pulling hard and the waters were rushing.

He saw Sanchez now; he saw Ruskin. The headmaster was by the side too, cheering him on, and out of nowhere a boy in the luminous strip of Ribblestrop High came at him.

It was a swinging tackle, but Miles swam over it, the ball miraculously still at his feet. His mother was waving, on her feet with excitement, because he was going to score again – the winning goal was his. Still there was fire and he knew he was the one burning. He was flying forward like a comet and the water could not extinguish him.

Someone had a handful of his hair.

They were dragging him and the pain of his torn scalp cut through the hallucinations. He was on his knees in mud and Henry was standing, pulling him up.

In his hands, Miles felt a thick, brass pipe.

He managed to look up and he saw that it ran through a low arch of rock and he glimpsed more pipework.

The two boys dragged each other, and though there was such stillness in the pump-room, and though they were half-dead, they both were overwhelmed by a feeling that time was against them. Just as they wanted to rest, they knew they had to be fast. They crawled and staggered, using the pipes for support. The plumbing was thick about them – it was a maze. But soon they were at the centre and there was the great glass column.

The chamber it held was full of brown water.

Miles would return, to contemplate it. Unknown to anyone, he would bring a small bottle and preserve some of that water. It would always be holy to him.

Because Millie had no more air.

The water was so dirty that they didn't see her at first. But Miles saw movement.

If he had not, then Millie would have drowned: she had another thirty seconds of life – forty-five at the most.

He saw a hand, fluttering at the very top of the water. Then he saw a shoe kick the glass about halfway up. At once, he threw himself against it.

Henry leaped into action too. They both moved round

the chamber, in an agony of helplessness, shouting – screaming. They saw Millie's face and her eyes were closed.

Then Miles had the gun, as if someone had put it there.

He had forgotten that he had it. How had it not dropped as he swam? He had pushed it hard into his belt and it was heavy. He pulled off the safety and the mechanism ran with water – it would not fire, but he had to try. He had a moment of terrible indecision. To shoot the lock? The lock was a wheel and the wheel had been bent. No: he would have to shoot the glass.

He did so and the first bullet ricocheted straight off and punctured pipes above his head. Spouts of water cascaded from ceiling to floor.

He tried to aim straight, but the second bullet did the same, and he feared for Henry, who was moving somewhere behind him. Again, punctured pipes sprayed over them both. Millie was helpless at the top of her deathchamber, her face crushed against the ceiling. Miles held the gun close and fired three more times. At last the glass was broken.

It was Henry who knew what to do next. After the second gunshot, he took hold of the nearest pipe and wrenched it from its stopcock. The brass fittings were sealed and bolted, but he simply tore at them, ignoring the new geysers that sprang up around him. With a metre of metal pipe in his hands, he set to work on Miles's bullet-hole. The glass around it cracked, and he twisted his weapon and attacked the centre of the crack. As Miles fired again, he had a hole as big as his wrist and water was gushing from it. He fired one more time and the glass split like an egg, the deluge of water knocking Miles backwards.

Henry attacked the brass seals. Inspiration seized him and he leaped upwards and hung from a convenient pipe, so that he could kick with his big boots. The first kick produced a crack from top to bottom. The second opened the chamber in half – the two sides simply came apart and the water cascaded out in a river. Millie was sluiced out onto the pump-room floor and she lay with her hair plastered over her face, like a dead thing. Her skin was white and rubbery and she was covered in algae and weed. She was a creature of the lake; it was as if the waters had claimed her and released her only with reluctance.

Miles lifted her carefully. They were surrounded by broken glass. He checked her airway and laid her in the recovery position.

Then he and Henry sat, dazed, unable to speak, watching her breathe. The miracle of her chest, rising and falling, drawing in air . . . it was almost too much to look at. The wonder of her face, gradually taking colour – Miles sat close, but dared not touch her again. They were surrounded by water and glass, and the glass was like ice.

It was some ten minutes later that Brother Rees arrived.

He had led Sanchez over the lake, wading in mud so thick it threatened to suck them down. At last they got to the dry dock – the well, through which O'Hanrahan and the Cuthbertsons had made their escape.

It was a difficult climb, but they were both desperate and fearless, and they braced themselves against the walls, helping each other. At last they found the remains of a rusty ladder, bolted in place, and they descended to the pump-room.

The devastation was tremendous, though most of the ruptured pipes were now only trickling. They didn't see Millie at first and stood there, astonished, trying to make sense of the wreckage.

Miles looked up and saw his friend. Sanchez saw Miles and limped over the mess towards him. When he saw Millie, he cried out and dropped to his knees. He cried out again and again, and Miles had to hold him tight, for he looked desperate.

'It's alright,' said Miles, when he could make Sanchez hear. 'Everything's alright.'

Chapter Fifty-three

On the lake, things were getting more complicated.

For the four men in the boat, it was an experience of the most terrible despair. They were wet, cold, and in pain. There had been the one moment of joy, as the boat catapulted them to what they thought was safety: now they were frightened. A hundred metres away, a car was on the lakeside, flashing its lights. Behind them, they could hear their own engine revving uselessly.

Gary Cuthbertson was up to his chest in cold water, feeling the mudbank that gripped the keel of the boat. Darren and Percy were trying to rock in time together, to dislodge it that way. The old man simply sat with chattering teeth, clutching the sword. After his tenth mouthful of muddy water, Gary gave up.

'We'll have to wait for it to drop further,' he gasped. 'Then we can get off. It's either that, or swimming.'

'We're in the middle of the lake!' hissed the policeman. 'Can *you* swim that far? With half a tonne of metal under your arm?'

The policeman threw his weight against the side of the boat, hoping to dislodge it. He tripped on Darren's legs and was a hair's breadth from going overboard. He sat down again, his head in his hands.

'I can't shift this bloody thing with you three sitting it!' shouted Gary. 'If you get in the water, we might have a chance!'

Their shouts drifted over the water, like the calls of furious birds.

It was at that point that Sam reappeared.

He had squeezed out from under Sushamila's paw at his first opportunity, having been washed three times over. Once out of the cage, he was running. He took the same route as the tigers, following the disused railway into the labyrinth and soon he was pelting up the tunnels towards Tomaz's house. He stood in his friend's ruined chambers, numb with shock, and turned in confused circles, helpless and confused. On the floor lay a soldering-iron and next to that the radio-controlled submarine. At least he could salvage something, so he gathered it all together and hurried on to Neptune.

The relief as he clambered out and saw his friends nearly made him faint. He slithered wearily down the giant's shoulder and the boys were reunited.

Oli stared at what Sam was carrying.

'Jake. What did I just say?' he said, in a voice squeaking with astonishment.

'You said you wished you had your submarine,' said Ruskin. 'Oh! Sam! What an inspiration! Sanjay! Plan E, section thirty-two. We can do it! We've got the sub.'

Sanjay squelched back to the shore, rubbing his hands.

'You sure about this, Oli?' he said.

'Yes. I'm sure Millie won't mind when I explain. You see, it's hers really.'

'There won't be anything left,' said Sanjay. 'You clear about that?'

He picked up a watertight package and Ruskin directed

the torch. Oli went down on his knees and started to unscrew a nose-panel. He had pliers in his pocket, so the wiring alterations were not a problem.

'She's going to lose buoyancy,' he said. 'The charge is going to weigh her down. Mmm, it would be best if I swam with her, till we get the speed up.'

Sanjay started to strip. 'You can't even swim,' he said.

Sam packed the explosive and Oli improvised a fusing system. He hated working at this kind of pace and was horribly aware that if he pressed the switch by accident, there'd be a huge detonation immediately under his nose – a detonation that would take his head off. However, he was not going to confess to these fears and he carried on cutting and fixing.

They could hear the shouts of the men getting louder and louder. It looked as if three of them now were in the water, dragging at the boat. Meanwhile, the rest of the orphans were walking out towards them on the wire.

Sanjay was shivering as he took the sub. Sam started the motors and, once the propellers were spinning, they lowered it into the shallows of the lake. It did feel heavy, but Sanjay kept pace with it, taking some of its weight. The little craft picked up speed and Sanjay started to swim. A few metres more and it was on its own; soon it reached maximum velocity and that was just enough to keep its central-stack proud of the water.

Oli walked out into the mud, his eyes only on the vessel. He balanced the motors so that it followed a gentle curve out towards the stricken speedboat.

As they watched, the speedboat started to move.

The shouts of rage had turned to cheers. The Cuthbertsons had tried one last time to heave the vessel upwards and – astonishingly – they must have timed it perfectly with Darren's pressing on the throttle. The keel was suddenly hauling itself through the mud, upwards and onwards. It took a good ten seconds to get completely clear and then it shot forward. Darren eased the rudder round, to return for the swimmers – and so for another half-minute the speedboat was still.

Oli, Ruskin, Sam, and Sanjay were all gathered by the radio set. They watched the boat rock and right itself – the four men were inside. Oli adjusted the starboard motor and the sub veered to the left a little. He could see how critical it was. The tightrope-walkers were coming, but they weren't going to make it. The speedboat was turning away from them. He pushed the sub's motor to maximum and its mosquito-whine screeched out over the lake. It was so close!

Had Father O'Hanrahan been able to help, they might have won those critical seconds – they may have just got away with it. It was not to be.

The submarine hit the port-side of the speedboat just below the waterline and Oli detonated the explosives. There was a burst of fire and water and the tail of the boat was lifted high. Fragments of fibreglass were blown upwards and the engine simply dropped away.

The four men were back in the water.

Imagio stopped in the smoke and the line of orphans gathered behind him, to stare as the swimmers floundered beneath them.

The youngest one – Darren – struck out for the nearest shore, immediately. The policeman and his brother turned and seemed unable to decide what to do – then they also started to swim.

The old man, however, was having problems staying afloat. He was holding something in a red cloth and it was dragging him down. As the orphans watched, the red cloth came away in his hands and something heavy slipped into the depths of the lake.

The old man looked stricken and he flapped helplessly in the water.

Anjoli sat down on the wire. 'Anyone want to rescue him?' he said.

'No,' said Israel.

'I don't,' said Vijay.

'I want to watch him drown,' said Eric.

'Come on,' said Asilah, shrugging off his blazer. 'We'd better get him.'

'No way,' said Anjoli. 'He called me a dumb heathen. I asked him one little question.'

Asilah said, 'Doonie liked him. Let's get him out for Doonie.'

He stepped over Anjoli and walked along the wire. Father O'Hanrahan was gasping below him, too weak to use his arms. The boy prepared to dive, when a curious thing happened.

Father O'Hanrahan was treading water and he might have lasted. He was cold and seeing the sword slip from his hands had broken his heart. Asilah would probably have got him to the shore, though, and he would have survived.

It was Victor the crocodile who did for him.

She had been nosing around constantly, ever since Darren threw the lighted match. So many legs had appeared, creating so much disturbance. She'd seen Anjoli and backed off – Anjoli had kicked her too many times already, trying to motivate her. She'd been very tempted by Gary Cuthbertson and his meaty calves, but the whining engine had unnerved her. The old man, however, was kicking gently and the engines had stopped. It was peaceful in the gloom and the legs had a slow-motion attractiveness. He was likely to be a fatty dish, but there was plenty of him: that, to a crocodile with babies to feed, was important. She came from the depths, and waited till the man's legs were wide apart. Then she slammed upwards into him, grasping a thigh in power-ful jaws.

Crocodiles do not kill their victims by tearing them to pieces. The tearing comes later. They kill by rolling their prey deep underwater; they use their jaws to grip and hold – they need only hold for a minute and the victim will drown. The lungs fill and the body sinks. It's an easy job, then, to drag the meat deeper still, and nose it into a suitable shelf of rock, where it will lie until it's needed.

Father O'Hanrahan drowned quickly and not a mouthful went to waste.

Epilogue

I

Time passed and the end of term approached.

Professor Worthington supervised the refilling of the lake with Brother Rees. Only half had been drained, and as there was a heavy rainfall for the next five days, it was soon full. The swollen River Strop had done little damage, so what could have been a disaster for the town was averted.

Meanwhile, the headmaster interviewed each child in his study.

He was determined to build up a narrative so as to understand the extraordinary events, and might have done so had he not been constantly interrupted by Lady Vyner. She haunted his office demanding not just her rent, but interest and compensation. After one particularly difficult meeting, Captain Routon and Flavio found the headmaster with his head in his hands. On the rafters above, the parrots were pretending to be both ringing telephones and shouting old women, and the poor man was nearly in tears.

'I can't even pay the butcher,' he cried. 'The tigers alone —'

'We'll be on the road soon,' said Flavio. 'We'll be making money.'

He was referring to the circus, of course. The orphans were packing the tent even as he spoke.

'Maybe, but it's all a question of cash flow . . .'

'We've been in tighter spots than this, sir?'

'I'm just longing for a little good news.'

'Well, the Cuthbertsons have disappeared – that's pretty good. Seems like they had a car waiting and there's no trace at the moment. Course the police look after their own, we all know that, but –'

'That's good riddance. Let's hope they've gone for good.'

'We do have another little complication, though, sir.'

'What?'

Captain Routon paused and looked at Flavio. 'We didn't want to worry you with it, but . . . it's becoming major.'

'Scanlon,' said Flavio.

'Who on earth is Scanlon?'

'The football scout. He was supposed to take Imagio last week, sir, but what with all the excitement, we've been putting it off.'

'Absolutely right. The boy was exhausted – they all were.'

'He's downstairs, sir. Yesterday, as well. He's got that contract in his hand and he says he wants the handover – or we'll be in breach and liable to . . . litigation. He says we're now holding the boy against his will.'

The headmaster closed his eyes. 'Oh dear. Where's Imagio?'

Flavio looked at Routon again. 'This is the problem,' he said. 'We can't find him nowhere.'

'What?'

'We've been looking for him for two days. One boy says he's in one place, so we go there. Then Anjoli says he's just left and goes off to fetch him and he never comes back. We go down to the lake, we go back to the tent. He's disappeared.'

'Have you asked Sam? They were playing football together this morning.'

'Sam says he's with Tomaz. And then Tomaz say he's with you.'

'Oh Lord . . . What's the time?'

'Ten past ten.'

The headmaster turned to the latest timetable. 'I know exactly where he'll be right now. It's Clarissa's science lesson and she wouldn't let him miss that – let's bring Scanlon in and get the job done.'

The three men walked down to the courtyard and there, in the back seat of a large black car, sat Arthur Scanlon. He wound down the window.

'At last,' he said. 'I'm sick to death of this town and this school.'

'We've had rather a lot going on.'

'I just want to be on my way. It's a big day for the boy, I'll say that – he's bound to be nervous. It's a big day for football, as well. Where is the little chap?'

'I'll show you.'

'Packed and ready, is he?' Mr Scanlon climbed wearily onto the drive. 'My phone has hardly stopped ringing – he's a valuable commodity, you know.'

'He's with our Director of Science at the moment, so you might have to hang on for half an hour.'

'I wish I could, sir, but I've just rearranged his press call in Exeter. Then we'll drive on to London; we've lost far too much time.'

They made for the Tower of Science, Flavio leading.

'We're getting the press in right from the start,' said Scanlon. 'He's the youngest we've signed, you see, so we're going to splash it about a bit. One of the TV companies is

354

interested too, which is nice. There's a dinner at seven, which is more press again. He's a handsome lad, isn't he? We've had a lot of sponsorship interest, already, just from the photos. Do you know that outfit in Malaysia, *Toy Factory*?'

'No, I don't.'

'Biggest toy manufacturers in the world. Not just sporty stuff, all sorts. They've made a bid for some TV ads. That boy's face is going to be all round the world.'

Mr Scanlon had to stop for breath. 'Fair few stairs, eh? By the way . . .'

'What?'

The party set off again.

'We're not going to say much about Ribblestrop. We've changed the story a bit – it's for the press mainly and this documentary they're making. We're going to say we found him in a Brazilian slum. Rio de Janeiro.'

'He's from Colombia,' said Captain Routon.

'Ah, but he's got no passport, has he? So what we're going to do is say he's Brazilian – fix him up with papers, make it all legal, and that way we get sponsorship from *FruitiFibro*, that's the Brazilian drinks company. You see, the only thing people know about Colombia is drugs – we can't have that.'

'Nearly there.'

'Back to school, eh?' laughed Scanlon. 'What lesson's he in at the moment?'

'Science,' said the headmaster.

'Poor kid. Nice day like this, he must be bored out of his skull.'

Captain Routon knocked and the four men stepped into the room. Every child looked around, abruptly, and there was total silence.

'Headmaster,' said Professor Worthington, politely.

'Clarissa. I'm so sorry to interrupt.'

'You've come at the perfect moment. The digestion project's really taken off. Good morning, everybody – boys?'

'Good morning,' they said, in chorus.

'We were looking for Imagio,' said Flavio. 'Mr Scanlon's been waiting for him.'

'Oh,' said Professor Worthington. 'How unfortunate.'

It wasn't quite clear what the class was up to, but it appeared to be in the middle of something unusual. The desks had been pushed back and Professor Worthington was in the centre of a scrum of children. Whatever she was demonstrating was concealed by the crowd. Some boys were kneeling and appeared to be holding stethoscopes.

'I never understood science,' whispered Scanlon to Flavio. 'I was a bit thick.'

'We've got an unfortunate clash of interests, Mr Scanlon,' said Professor Worthington. She was trying not to smile. 'I'm afraid Imagio's rather involved in an experiment at the moment.'

Scanlon laughed. 'Where is he?'

'He's . . .'

'He's in a rather awkward position,' said Sam.

Anjoli said, 'I wouldn't try moving him. Not till we sedate her.'

Mr Scanlon was intrigued. He stepped forward to see and the circle of children shifted. The headmaster, Flavio, and Captain Routon also moved in, aware that there was something big and cylindrical laid out on a bench. A number of wires hung from the ceiling, attaching themselves to what looked like a very large pair of jaws.

'Move back, Vijay. Caspar, get out of the way.'

The four men saw it then. It was the python and its mouth was gaping so wide that its jaws were dislocated. Its eyes were wide, as if it was straining. They blinked once, then bulged a little more.

'It's a snake,' said Scanlon. He took a pace back.

'It was his turn, Mr Scanlon,' said the professor. 'I'm very strict – they all get a chance. There is no other way to understand how a snake absorbs its food.'

'So where's the boy?' said Scanlon. His eyes were darting from the snake, around the circle. He noticed Millie, who was grinning at him. He went forward again and peered nervously into the python's mouth. A brown face stared back at him, taut with concentration.

'Hi,' said Imagio.

The man looked around the circle again, totally at sea.

'I'm OK,' said Imagio. 'You can feel the acid though, man. It's all down my back—'

'He's being eaten! Do something!' said Scanlon.

'I got the mandibular raking too,' said Imagio. 'It's . . . wow. Like a massage.'

'That's the ribs,' said Caspar.

'Get him out!' shouted Scanlon. 'The car's downstairs! He's got to be in Exeter . . . Get him out of there!'

He spun round again, astonished that nobody was moving.

'Get this boy out of that snake,' he hissed.

'Imagio,' said Professor Worthington, 'I think you'd better tell him.'

'Tell me what? You're insane, all of you . . .'

Imagio tried to roll his shoulders and he felt the python's muscles convulse. He wormed his way forward a couple of centimetres, but was suddenly drawn back by a powerful force. His face had almost disappeared.

'Mr Scanlon?' he shouted.

'What?'

'Can you hear me?'

'Of course I can hear you. Give me your hand!'

'Sorry, man . . . look . . . I can't hear you too well, it's all kind of . . . slimy down here. But . . . I've been turning it over. I've been thinking and thinking, and . . . I just don't think I can do it.'

Mr Scanlon stared. 'What can't you do?'

Imagio managed to get his nose up, so he could look at the football scout properly.

'I want to stay here,' he said. 'I want to go to college and stuff and . . . I'm probably not smart enough, but what I really want to be is a doctor.'

Mr Scanlon was speechless.

'Sorry, man. It's my decision. The world needs doctors more than footballers.'

II

Millie asked Miles if he would go for a walk with her.

He said he would but he'd like Sanchez to come. Sanchez said he wasn't sure he was wanted, so Millie told him not to be stupid.

Then they weren't sure where to go. They talked about it: the Edge was a lovely viewpoint, they said, but too familiar. The lake was still muddy and there was debris from the smashed-up boats. There were no new walks and it was steady drizzle.

Eventually, they pulled out three bicycles and cycled into Ribblestrop town. There they found a tearoom and ordered cream teas. When the scones came, they were hot to touch. The jam was pure, fresh strawberry, the butter was soft, and the waitress was huge and maternal.

'Now if you want anything else, my dears, you just ring this bell,' she said. 'You warm enough? What's your name, dear?'

She was looking at Sanchez.

'Andreas,' said Sanchez.

'You look just like my youngest,' she said, unexpectedly. 'Now you stay long as you like and eat as much as you want – no rush. I'll be downstairs.'

'Thank you,' said Sanchez, blushing heavily.

Considerable time was spent buttering the scones. Miles was scientific in his pouring of the tea and the adding of milk and sugar took forever.

After some time, Millie said, 'I'm sorry I said those things I said, Miles.'

Miles said, 'You don't have to say sorry.'

'I do.'

'You've got nothing to say sorry about. I was . . . bad.'

'Yeah, but the thing is, you saved my life. You and Henry.'

'Henry saved your life. I was just there. Have more jam, look. Shall I ask for more? We're running out.'

Millie went to speak and stopped. She was looking at Sanchez. They sorted out their scones again and discovered how long it took to divide cream fairly.

'I've been working on a speech,' said Millie. 'Will you let me read it?'

Miles stared at his knife. When he tilted his head forward, his hair hung so low his eyes were completely masked.

'*Dear Miles,*' said Millie. '*I said the most awful, terrible, horrible things. I don't know why. I just wasn't ever sure about you and all the things you said. I liked you from the first time I saw you and I like you even more now, even though – obviously – you can be really stupid. Changing that letter to get you back to Ribblestrop was the best thing I ever did. I am not fit to be Head Girl because I am a liar and very mean and jealous, so I have resigned the post, though I don't know who else they will get to do it and I'm not sure if I ever had any duties anyway, but I am definitely not fit to be someone that is a role model. I hope you are not going to leave this school because I really want to get to know you better. From Millie.*'

Miles said, 'Thank you, I . . .'

'I wrote you a letter too,' said Sanchez. 'It's quite long though, so I can just give it to you.'

He passed an envelope to Miles and Miles slipped it into his blazer, his face burning red.

'How did you swim under those rocks?' said Millie.

'Brother Rees says it's completely impossible. He says nobody could do it.'

Miles picked up his teacup and it trembled in his hands.

'I just swam,' he said.

'You saw Lord Vyner, didn't you?'

'Yes.'

'If I ask you a question, will you tell me the truth?'

Miles nodded.

'What was the "favourite game"?'

Miles looked down. He looked puzzled, as if he was trying to remember.

'Why are you scrunching up your eyes?' said Sanchez. 'Why don't you just tell her?'

'You said it twice, or three times,' said Millie. '"My favourite game" – were you talking about what I think you were talking about?'

Miles looked at his plate. He went to speak and stopped. He reached for the teapot and Sanchez took it away and put it out of his reach.

'Alright,' said Miles. 'It's no big deal. I used to take Sanchez's gun, OK? I used to play Russian roulette with it.'

'You did it twice,' said Sanchez, angrily. 'Twice you got my gun and you went underground, and you made Tomaz watch!' He paused and Miles simply stared at his plate. 'It's not a secret any more.'

Millie leaned over and took hold of Miles's tie. She wound it round her fist and put her face close to his.

'I knew,' she said. 'It was easy to guess.'

She touched his ear and held it, softly, between her fingers. She moved her lips close and spoke very slowly. 'Promise me you'll never do it again.'

'I promise,' said Miles, quietly.

'Promise me.'

'I just did: I promise.'

'Promise you'll stop, Miles – please.'

'I'm promising.' He would not look up from the plate.

'Promise me, looking at me.'

'I promise!'

'Promise Sanchez.'

'I promise. I promise! I promse you both.'

'We don't want you dead. Do you understand that? We want you alive. You were in the water, Miles – didn't you think, *I don't want to die*?'

'No,' said Miles. 'I've never thought that.'

'What about now?' said Sanchez. 'Here. Now. With us?'

Miles looked up and the dullness left his eyes. He found he was staring at Sanchez, and then he swivelled his gaze and it was Millie's face, still centimetres from his own. 'But this won't go on,' he said.

'What do you mean? What won't?'

''This won't go on,' he said again. He swallowed and there were tears now, rolling down his cheeks. 'Because ... this ends, doesn't it? This is just an afternoon and things change and you'll leave. You'll go off to South America together, and you'll be friends, and I ... Because I don't know. I just don't know and I don't have anyone – do I?'

There was a pause.

Sanchez said, 'We're staying here for Easter, just us three. We're going to go somewhere nice, with Doonan. We're just going to go for walks and read and do ordinary stuff. 'You, me and Millie. You have loads of people, Miles.'

Miles stared.

'Is that a good idea?' said Sanchez.

'Yes,' said Miles. And the tears dripped slowly onto his plate.

They got back to school late, because they decided to wheel their bicycles rather than ride them, and when they got to

362

the school gates, they walked on to where someone had tied a rope to a tree and they mucked about on that until it got dark. Then they decided that a quick stroll to the Edge would be good, because it was warm and the air was full of the scent of spring flowers.

Supper was over, so they went up to the east tower, where the orphans always had food. They were surprised to find everybody there, including all the teachers. They'd completely forgotten: Kenji had asked to make a presentation.

He coughed nervously and they sat down, unnoticed.

'Thank you very much, Nikko,' said Kenji. 'Your introduction was very clear. I am now pleased to present the accounts of the Ribblestrop Towers General Holding Company, which is the name we've been trading under. I have the figures, if you'll just . . . could you do the lights, Podma?'

They'd found an old overhead-projector from somewhere. Grey columns of numbers appeared on a bedsheet draped over a wardrobe.

Eric was passing the rum truffles. Anjoli came round with the hot chocolate and slipped onto Millie's lap. Tomaz, Caspar, and Oli sat together. They had spent the day redesigning the secret doorway into the underground chambers, which everyone had been restoring.

'I won't go through all the ins and outs of this,' said Kenji. 'The details are . . . sorry, that's the second page. The details are available if anyone wants to go through them.'

'Just tell us,' shouted Sanjay. 'Is Ruskin bankrupt?'

Kenji laughed nervously. 'Well. The items of interest are on the third sheet – that's this one – and this is when we really started getting lucky. Ruskin, your money moved in and out of bonds for a while, which is what enabled us to offer credit to everyone, and it was that credit we put against the headmaster's investment.'

The headmaster smiled. 'I'm a little lost already,' he said.

'Our first real coup was the investment in the vineyard – it just took off and we were able to shift most of that money away to a little diamond mine. That little diamond mine . . . well, you can see on the final column. It's now rather a *large* diamond mine. So we moved half of that to a whole basket of what you call high-risk enterprises, which is exactly what they were – but we did pretty well. We took a big hit on the mortgage market, but so did everyone. Where we really scored was in a natural spring in Switzerland. We bought in just before a couple of the big boys crashed – there was that bottled water scandal, you may remember it. And that's why I can tell the school that . . . hold on.'

He searched for his final sheet. He put it on the screen. It was upside down. He snatched it off and righted it. It was a childish hand, but the numbers were clear. Seven four four, then a slash that may have been a comma. Seven nine nine, and a point. Seven. Two.

'That's net, after commissions.'

Ruskin said, 'I don't understand. What *is* that number?' He was peering through his latest attempt at glasses: the lenses were taped to a coathanger that had been shaped around his head. It was working well.

'That's what we're holding, as of close of play last night,' said Kenji.

'But is it . . . what is it? Pounds? Pence?'

'Sterling. That's what's in the tins – we don't use the safe any more. Seven hundred and forty-four thousand, seven hundred and ninety-nine pounds and seventy-two pence. That is the net profit of the company, which I would like to formally hand over to our chairman, the headmaster. And we invite him to address us, of course.'

Everyone turned to look at the headmaster.

They waited for him to speak, but he remained sitting. The biscuit tins of cash were passed to him and he held them between his hands. They waited a full minute. He stood up and said, 'Boys.'

He looked at Millie. 'Millie.'

Thirty seconds passed.

'I'm going to have to . . . Excuse me. Routon, could you . . .? I'm not sure what to say. Would you mind, um . . .'

A full minute went by and the children waited.

Finally, and very quietly, he said, 'My dear friends. Thank you.'

III

It was the very last day of term.

Professor Worthington had not been popular when she insisted that her morning science lesson would take place, as timetabled. The orphans were particularly cross.

'We don't cut classes,' she said, as they protested.

'But, Miss, we're loading the truck! There's so much to do . . .'

'You can do it this afternoon.'

'The clown costumes . . .'

'You can finish your clown costumes tonight. The fact that you're off to . . . where's the first night?'

'Budleigh Salterton, Miss.'

'Budleigh Salterton. Well-known for its elderly population – what *will* they think of you?'

'It's going to be the best!'

'You can play at acrobats and clowns all over your Easter holiday. I am running a science lesson and we are all meeting – that's your teachers as well – in the pump-room at ten-thirty.'

At this, the children changed their minds and cheered. They were off like a flock of birds, knowing that something exciting lay in store. The pump-room had been out of bounds ever since the destruction of the elevator, but they knew the Brethren had been working down there, night and day. They were desperate to see the results.

*   *   *

Twenty minutes later, the whole school filed in. As before, the room cast its magical spell and there wasn't even a whisper. The air was full of vapour and the pipes seemed to be breathing like some great organism. The ruptures had been repaired, the debris shifted, and in the central column stood a new lift-car. It wasn't made of glass, though – it had a rough, homemade look about it. There were steel hoops and a mass of tarpaulin and plastic.

'This is purely temporary,' explained Professor Worthington. 'We will replace the glass unit, but I'm sure you can imagine, it's a very specialised job. This, however, will do for one quick trip – are you going to be alright, Millie?'

Millie nodded.

'If anyone's fearful, then go back up the steps and meet us by Neptune in about fifteen minutes. If you want a ride, step in – carefully, Anjoli! There is absolutely no need to push.'

Asilah held Anjoli back and allowed everybody else to climb aboard, teachers first. It was a tight squeeze, but with the little ones on the older ones' knees, they were reasonably comfortable. Captain Routon sat next to Flavio, covered by six orphans. Henry and the headmaster carried another four. Professor Worthington sealed the door and studied a control panel. Millie was pleased to see that it was *inside* the car and tried to keep calm.

There was a dramatic bubbling and they rose up slowly. Soon, the sound of roaring water filled their ears. They moved through darkness and then the light was strangely blue. The car hesitated and bobbed.

Professor Worthington crouched to one side and turned a valve. She drew a hosepipe over her shoulder, and though everyone strained to look, it was hard to see what she was doing. The noise of water made questions impossible.

She beckoned the children to her, Millie first. Mille was followed by Sanchez and behind him came Miles. They stepped out of the lift-car into a large, glass viewing platform. They were still far underwater and the lake looked murky.

Professor Worthington turned a valve on her hosepipe and from the nozzle came a thick, soapy substance. She adjusted the aperture and all at once a bubble was growing. She folded the bubble over Sanchez and repaired the ruptured side. Then, like a conjuror, she expanded it over Millie and then Miles. She inflated it more as the three children stared up at her and then she eased them out, into the decompression chamber. Seconds later, the capsule opened and the bubble floated out into the water.

Sam and Ruskin were next, and then Flavio and Routon. Doonan went with Asilah and Sanjay. Henry had to be alone because of his size. Tomaz went with Oli and Caspar and the rest of the orphans broke into small groups at random. Within minutes, nine giant bubbles were rolling out into the depths of the lake, the children standing or sitting with their hands pressed to the soapy walls.

'How long have you been planning this, Clarissa?' said the headmaster, watching them go.

'It was Doonan's idea. It's all about the consistency of the mix – you need elasticity, of course, but you need lightness and strength. Some of the trial runs were disastrous.'

She turned to a row of switches and flicked them one by one. As she did so, floodlights came on all over the lake's bottom. The headmaster stared as the bubbles floated down and bounced upwards. They turned slowly and he could see the children pointing, staring, laughing . . .

'Oh, look. Trust Anjoli . . .'

Anjoli had burst his bubble and he and Israel were swimming. They swam to their friends, waving, and then they both flipped upside down and made for Doonan. Doonan was sitting, his elbows braced against the walls, staring in astonishment. The two diving boys flipped the bubble over and watched with delight as the young man rolled. Then they torpedoed upwards for air.

'They've got more guts than me!' said the headmaster. 'You wouldn't get me out there. I've always been a dry-bob.'

He had not noticed that Professor Worthington had drawn the final sphere over him and now climbed into it with him. She put all her weight against one side and they were rolling, the headmaster losing his balance so the bubble moved faster. In seconds they were floating too, waving to the children as they sailed by.

'What's that?' said Oli, to Tomaz.

'Where?'

'At the bottom. I wish we could steer this thing!'

Caspar said, 'What if all three of us lean together? Where do you want to go?'

'There! Quick!'

Oli gave directions and they managed to bring their bubble lower and round to a shelf of rock that reared up from the mud. An ugly fish peered at them and flipped away.

'Look,' said Tomaz.

'Oh my,' said Caspar. He pressed his face against the bubble.

'That's what they were looking for,' said Oli. 'There it is!'

Something was shining bright as fire. It was caught in one of the floodlights and, as the boys' bubble moved past, it appeared to glitter. The blade was jammed tight in a fissure of rock. The carbon-casing had been worn by the water and most of it had flaked away. Twelve diamonds shone from the hilt: when the light caught the boys' eyes, they found they blinked and turned away.

369

'We must get it!' cried Caspar.

Tomaz was shaking his head. 'Leave it.'

'Yes, but that could be really valuable. It's worth a fortune!'

Tomaz looked back, for their bubble was rolling slowly past. The sword was deep in the rock and he remembered an old story from somewhere – who had told it to him he could not recall – and he knew it was safe.

They watched it until it disappeared and Oli said, 'Shall we go up?'

'Yes,' said Tomaz.

Caspar nodded.

Some boys said they saw crocodiles. Captain Routon said he saw trout and would run a fishing club next term. Miles saw Lord Vyner, but said nothing, though he waved when he knew Millie and Sanchez wouldn't notice.

The voyages lasted no more than five minutes, for the bubbles started to dissolve, getting lighter and lighter. They broke the surface at roughly the same time and Anjoli and Israel were waiting, ready to burst them.

The children and their teachers made for the shore and soon found firm ground under them. They walked up out of the lake, the water running from their hair and clothes. They stood together in the warm morning sun, like explorers who'd found land. For a moment they were silenced by the beauty around them – the beauty of spring and the beauty of their school – and they simply listened to the birdsong.

PRESS-CUTTING BUREAU

from

THE WESTERN MORNING NEWS

'Arts Round-up', Thursday April 4th

Circulation ('000): 39

Readership ('000): 115

Display Rate (£/sqcm): £3.45

1 8 MAY 20

SOLD OUT AND NOT SURPRISING!

It would appear that tickets have been selling for three-figure sums and the queue for returns is halfway round the tent by noon! What's the attraction? Why are people flocking to a rather worn, homemade-looking tent in the middle of Budleigh Salterton's ornamental gardens?

The answer, of course, is Circus Ribblestrop.

Only astronauts and aliens could be excused for not knowing about the show of the century, already booked for a stint in London, followed by New York. Circus Ribblestrop has raised the bar in traditional family entertainment with a difference.

The show starts traditionally enough, with a dance of uni-cycles. I counted twelve in all, and though it's a bit long for an opening number, it's nice to see old-fashioned skills back in vogue. The clowning is splendid, and my children particularly enjoyed the outrageously fat one running blindly round the arena, narrowly missing what appeared to be razor-sharp knives, spinning just in front of his nose at the hands of jugglers.

Be warned, though: these acts are simply warming you up for some truly death-defying stunts. If you have never seen a child dive fifty metres into a paddling pool, and come up smiling, this is a show you must not miss. But don't let the kids try it at home!

The tigers are real and there are no cages. They turn on a sixpence, and the boys that ride them are not into tricks. These beasts love it and I got the distinct impression they were selecting a snack from the audience.

The giant python is boring – that is, until a parrot emerges from its mouth and tells some of the dirtiest jokes you'll ever hear.

But the climax will take your breath away. I lost count of the acrobats – the programme says there are ten, but I'm sure there were twice that. Some are dressed as angels, and some as devils. On wires and trapezes they re-enact some kind of heavenly war above your head, hurling fireworks that rain sparks down onto your shoulders. My seven-year-old said to me, 'Is this real?' and I was lost for words.

The audience would not let the performers leave: the standing ovation went on for a full twenty minutes.

Circus Ribblestrop is a miracle, and if you don't love it, you might as well be dead.

371

ACKNOWLEDGEMENTS

As usual I am grateful to Venetia Gosling for her sensitive editing, and to my agent Jane Turnbull for her constant support. I'd also like to thank Jane Tait for her keen proof-reading eye. I try never to forget the encouragement of my family, and I'd also like to thank Mike Hemsley, Lucy Greig, Paul Beamish, Rachel Beamish and Canon Bill Anderson. Two close friends – Wes Williams and Ed Gaughan – are also in this book, in spirit, and I thank them for their wise counsel over the years. Finally I must thank the British School Manila's 11AC – to whom the book is dedicated – for being the class I have most enjoyed teaching in fifteen happy years as a teacher. Amanda, Akila, Charu, Shaun, Mustafa, Kristen, Charles, Kristoffer, Mykie, Philippe, Patricia, Regena, Nayantara, Chelsey, Veronica and Paolo: thank you for tolerating my mood-swings, and providing fine therapy.

ABOUT THE AUTHOR

Andy Mulligan was brought up in South London, and educated at Oxford University. He worked as a theatre director for ten years, before travels in Asia prompted him to re-train as a teacher. He has taught English and drama in India, Brazil, the Philippines and the UK. He now divides his time between London and Manila.

Where it all began . . .

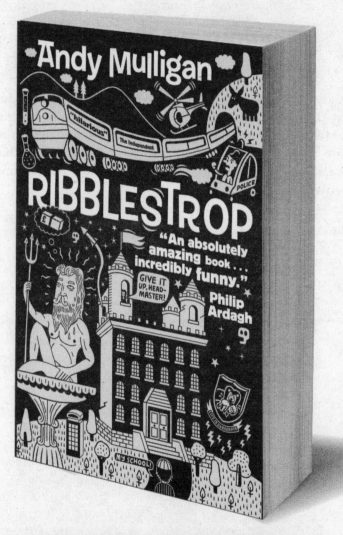

Roofless dormitories, distracted teachers and
a lethally dangerous underground labyrinth -
Ribblestrop's visionary headmaster is out of his
depth even *before* the pupils arrive!